This special signed edition
is limited to
1000 numbered copies.

This is copy 383.

Harry Turtledove
HARRY TURTLEDOVE

OTHER PEOPLE'S PLAYGROUNDS

Other People's Playgrounds

Stories by
Harry Turtledove

Subterranean Press 2024

Other People's Playgrounds
Copyright © 2024 by Harry Turtledove.
All rights reserved.

Dust jacket illustration
Copyright © 2024 by Lee Moyer. All rights reserved.

Interior design
Copyright © 2024 by Desert Isle Design, LLC. All rights reserved.

See pages 305-306 for individual story copyrights.

First Edition

ISBN
978-1-64524-190-4

Subterranean Press
PO Box 190106
Burton, MI 48519

subterraneanpress.com

Manufactured in the United States of America

TABLE OF CONTENTS

Introduction — 7

Trantor Falls — 9

Three Men and a Vampire — 31

Three Men and a Werewolf — 41

Topanga and the Chatsworth Lancers — 51

The Catcher in the Rhine — 91

The Last Word — 109

The Fake Pandemic — 141

The Fillmore Shoggoth — 181

Interlibrary Loan — 195

Nine Drowned Churches — 207

Eyewear — 219

Two Thieves — 249

The Man Who Came Late — 277

Introduction

How do you learn to write? I think my path was a pretty common one: I read a lot, and after a while I started trying to imitate the writers I liked. I was not an overnight success. Few people are. In writing as in any other trade, learning how takes a while. And, for a few years, I paid much more attention to my dissertation than to fiction. So I was in my late twenties before I got my first professional check. (The magazine that bought the story died before it came out. I'm not the only person that's happened to.)

One of the things you notice while you're still just a reader is how much you'd like to write stories set in universes other people have created. This is the urge that sparks fanfic, and I did some of that. When I was eighteen, I wrote a novel that dropped Romans and a cantankerous Celt into Fourth Age Gondor. It was dreadful: unpublishable even if it had been all my own creation. But very little that you write, however bad, isn't useful one way or another. Bits and pieces of that novel's plot show up in *The Videssos Cycle*, which I started a dozen years later.

And, when you become a working professional sf and fantasy writer, sometimes you get to play in other people's playgrounds and get paid for it—you get invited into an anthology where the person who holds the rights to a milieu gives you permission to work in it. There are four main types of these. The first happens when a friend asks you to do a piece in his or her universe. The second is a tribute anthology set in one or another universe a senior author has created. The third, sadly, is an *in memoriam* anthology. I've edited one of those myself, for L. Sprague de Camp. And you can also work with characters who are in the public domain. This collection has stories from all four varieties.

Harry Turtledove

Stories of this kind don't often get collected. People tend to look down their noses at them. After all, they aren't entirely the writer's own work. But, for me, that's part of the fun of doing them in the first place. I enjoy writing pastiche—trying to sound like somebody else. It's a way of stretching myself, of continuing to imitate what I admire. I've done that in several of the stories here. How successfully? You'll have to judge for yourself. As always, I hope these pieces entertain, amuse, and with luck make you think a little. Thanks for looking in.

Trantor Falls

Foundation's Friends, the tribute anthology for Isaac Asimov, was the first one to which I got an invitation. I was delighted to accept; I don't know how often I've been through *The Foundation Trilogy*, and I find something new every time. "Trantor Falls" is set in the period between the two big sections of *Foundation and Empire*, as the Galactic Empire is falling to ruin. It probably tells more than Asimov would have wanted to with *Second Foundation* still ahead of him, but that's an advantage someone writing for an audience familiar with the whole trilogy has.

THE IMPERIAL PALACE stood at the center of a hundred square miles of greenery. In normal times, even in abnormal times, such insulation was plenty to shield the chief occupant of the palace from the hurly-burly of the rest of the metaled world of Trantor.

Times now, though, were not normal, nor even to be described by so mild a word as abnormal. They were disastrous. Along with magnolias and roses, missile-launchers had flowered in the gardens. Even inside the palace, Dagobert VIII could hear the muted snarl. Worse, though, was the fear that came with it.

A soldier burst into the command post where the Emperor of the Galaxy and his officers still groped for ways to beat back Gilmer's latest onslaught. Without so much as a salute, the man gasped out, "Another successful landing, sire, this one in the Nevrask sector."

Dagobert's worried gaze flashed to the map table. "Too close, too close," he muttered. "How does the cursed bandit gain so fast?"

One of the Emperor's marshals speared the messenger with his eyes. "How did they force a landing there? Nevrask is heavily garrisoned." The soldier stood mute. "Answer me!" the marshal barked.

The man gulped, hesitated, at last replied, "Some of the troops fled, Marshal Rodak, sir, when Gilmer's men landed. Others—" He paused again, nervously licking his lips, but had to finish: "Others have gone over to the rebel, sir."

"More treason!" Dagobert groaned. "Will none fight to defend me?"

The only civilian in the room spoke then: "Men will fight, sire, when they have a cause they think worth fighting for. The University has held against Gilmer for four days now. We shall not yield it to him."

"By the space fiend, Dr. Sarns, I'm grateful to your students, yes, and proud of them too," Dagobert said. "They've put up a braver battle than most of my troopers."

Yokim Sarns politely dipped his head. Marshal Rodak, however, grasped what his sovereign had missed. "Majesty, they're fighting for themselves and their buildings, not for you," he said. Even as he spoke, another sector of the map in front of him and Dagobert went from blue to red: red for the blood Gilmer was spilling all over Trantor, Sarns thought bitterly.

"Have we no hope, then?" asked the Emperor of the Galaxy.

"Of victory? None." Rodak's military assessment was quick and definite. "Of escape, perhaps to fight again, yes. Our air- and spacecraft still hold the corridor above the palace. With a landing at Nevrask, though, Gilmer will soon be able to bring missiles to bear on it—and on us."

"Better to flee than to fall into that monster's clutches," Dagobert said, shuddering. He looked at the map again. "I am sure you have an evacuation plan ready. Implement it, and quickly."

"Aye, sire." The marshal spoke into a throat mike.

The Emperor turned to Yokim Sarns. "Will you come with us, Professor? Trantor under Gilmer's boots will be no place for scholars."

Trantor Falls

"Thank you, sire, but no." As Sarns shook his head, strands of mouse-brown hair, worn unfashionably long, swirled around his ears. "My place is at the University, with my faculty and students."

"Well said," Marshal Rodak murmured, too softly for Dagobert to hear.

But the Emperor, it seemed, still had one imperial gesture left in him. Turning to Rodak, he said, "If Dr. Sarns wishes to return to the University, return he shall. Detail an aircar at once, while he has some hope of getting there in safety."

"Aye, sire," the marshal said again. He held out a hand to Yokim Sarns. "And good luck to you. I think you'll need it."

By the time the aircar pilot neared the University grounds, Yokim Sarns was a delicate shade of green. The pilot had flown meters—sometimes centimeters—above Trantor's steel roof, and jinked like a wild thing to confuse the rebels' targeting computers.

The car slammed down on top of the library. Dr. Sarns' teeth met with an audible click. The pilot threw open the exit hatch. Sarns pulled himself together. "Er—thank you very much," he told the pilot, unbuckling his safety harness.

"Just get out, get under cover, and let me lift off," she snapped. Sarns scrambled away from the aircar towards an entrance. The wash of wind as the car sped away nearly knocked him off his feet.

The door opened. Two people in helmets dashed out and dragged Sarns inside. "How do we fare here?" he asked.

"Our next few graduating classes are getting thinned out," Maryan Drabel answered somberly. Till Gilmer's revolt, she had been head librarian. Now, Sarns supposed, chief of staff best summed up her job. "We're still holding, though—we pushed them out of Dormitory Seven again a few minutes ago."

"Good," Sarns said. He was as much an amateur commander as she was an aide, but the raw courage of their student volunteers made up for much of their inexperience. The youngsters fought as if they were defending holy ground—and so in a way they were, Sarns thought. If Gilmer's men wrecked the University, learning all over the Galaxy would take a deadly blow.

"What will Dagobert do?" asked Egril Joons. Once University dietitian, he kept an army fed these days.

Sarns had no way to soften the news. "He's going to run."

Under the transparent flash shield of her helmet, Maryan Drabel's face went grim, or rather grimmer. "Then we're left in the lurch?"

"Along with everyone else who backed the current dynasty." *Two generations, a dynasty!* Sarns thought. The way the history of the Galactic Empire ran these past few sorry centuries, though, two generations *was* a dynasty. And with a usurper like Gilmer seizing Trantor, that history looked to run only downhill from here on out.

Maryan might have picked the thought from his mind. "Gilmer's as much a barbarian as if he came straight from the Periphery," she said.

"I wish he *were* in the Periphery," Egril Joons said. "Then we wouldn't have to deal with him."

"Unfortunately, however, he's here," said Yokim Sarns.

The thick carpets of the Imperial Palace, the carpets that had cushioned the feet of Dagobert VIII, of Cleon II, of Stannell VI—by the space fiend, of Ammenetik the Great!—now softened the booted strides of Gilmer I, self-proclaimed Emperor of the Galaxy and Lord of All. Gilmer kicked at the rug with some dissatisfaction. He was used to clanging as he walked, to having his boots announce his presence half a corridor away. Not even a man made all of bell metal could have clanged on the carpets of the Imperial Palace.

He tipped his head back, brought a bottle to his lips. Liquid fire ran down his throat. After a long pull, he threw the bottle away. It smashed against a wall. Frightened servants scurried to clean up the mess.

"Don't waste it," Vergis Fenn said.

Trantor Falls

Gilmer scowled at his fleet commander. "Why not? Plenty more where that one came from." His scowl stabbed a servant. "Fetch me another of the same, and one for Vergis here, too." The man dashed off to do his bidding.

"There, you see?" Gilmer said to Fenn. "By the Galaxy, we couldn't waste everything Trantor's stored up if we tried for a hundred years."

"I suppose that's so," Fenn said. He was quieter than his chieftain, a better tactician perhaps, but not a leader of men. After a moment, he went on thoughtfully, "Of course, Trantor's spent a lot more than a hundred years gathering all this. More than a thousand, I'd guess."

"Well, what if it has?" Gilmer said. "That's why we wanted it, yes? By the balls Dagobert didn't have, nobody's ever sacked Trantor before. Now everything here is mine!"

The servant returned with the bottles. He set them on a table of crystal and silver, then fled. Gilmer drank. With all he'd poured down these last couple of days, he shouldn't have been able to see, let alone walk and talk. But triumph left him drunker than alcohol. Gilmer the Conqueror, that's who he was!

Vergis Fenn drank, too, but not as deep. "Aye, all Trantor's ours, but for the University. Seven days now, and those madmen are still holding out."

"No more of these little firefights with them, then," Gilmer growled. "By the Galaxy, I'll blast them to radioactive dust and have done! See to it, Fenn, at once."

"As you would, sir—sire, but—" Fenn let the last word hang.

"But what?" Gilmer said, scowling. "If they fight for Dagobert, they're traitors to me. And smashing traitors will frighten Trantor." He blinked owlishly, pleased and surprised at his own wordplay.

To his annoyance, Fenn did not notice it. He said, "I don't think they *are* fighting for Dagobert any more, just against us, to hold on to what they have. That might make them easier to deal with. And if we—if you—nuked the University, scholars all over the Galaxy would vilify your name forever."

"Scholars all over the Galaxy can eat space, for all I care," Gilmer said. But, he discovered, that wasn't quite true. Part of being Emperor was acting the way Emperors were supposed to act. With poor grace, he backpedaled a little: "If they acknowledge me and stop fighting, I suppose I'm willing to let them live."

"Shall I attempt a cease-fire, then?" Fenn asked.

"Go ahead, since you seem to think it's a good idea," Gilmer told him. "But not if they don't acknowledge me, understand? If they still claim that unprintable son of a whore Dagobert's Emperor, blow 'em off the face of the planet."

"Yes, sire." This time, Fenn did not stumble over the title. *He's my servant, too*, Gilmer thought.

The new Emperor of the Galaxy took a good swig from the bottle. He made as if to throw it at one of the palace flunkies, then, laughing, set it down gently as the fellow ducked.

GILMER WENT down to the command post in the bowels of the Imperial Palace, the command post from which, until recently, poor stupid Dagobert VIII had battled to keep him off Trantor. Gilmer's boots clanged most satisfactorily there. Whoever had designed the command post, in the lost days of the Galactic Empire's greatness, had understood about commanders and boots.

The televisor screen in front of Vergis Fenn went blank. He swiveled his chair, nodding in surprise to see Gilmer behind him. "Sire, we have a cease-fire between our forces and those of the University," he said. "It was easy to arrange. Our troops and theirs will both hold in place until the final armistice is arranged."

"Good," Gilmer said. "Well done."

"Thank you. The leader of the University has invited you to meet him on his ground to fix the terms of the armistice. He offers hostages to ensure your safety, and says he knows what will happen to everything he's been fighting to keep if he plays you false. Shall I call him back and tell him no anyhow?"

"No, I'll go there," Gilmer said. "What, d'you think I'm afraid of somebody without so much as a single starship to his name? Besides"—he smiled a greedy smile—"like as not I'll get a look at whatever treasures they've been fighting so hard to hang on to. If I can't beat 'em out of him, I'll tax 'em out—that's what being Emperor is all about. So go ahead and set up the meeting with this—what's his name, Vergis?"

"Yokim Sarns."

"Yokim Sarns. What do I call him when I see him? General Sarns? Admiral? Warlord?"

Fenn's expression was faintly bemused. "The only title he claims is Dean, sire."

"Dean?" Gilmer threw back his head and laughed loud and long. "Aye, I'll meet with the fierce Dean Yokim Sarns, the scourge of the lecture halls. Why not? Set it up for me, Vergis. Meanwhile"—he turned away—"I'll check how we're doing with the rest of the planet."

Banks of televisor screens, relaying images from all over Trantor, told him what he wanted to know. Here he saw a platoon of his troopers carrying plastic tubs full of jewels back toward their ships; there more soldiers looting a residential block; somewhere else another squad, most of the men drunk, accompanied by twice their number of Trantorian women, some scared-looking, others smiling and brassy.

Gilmer grinned. *This* was why he'd taken Trantor: to sack a world unsacked for fifty generations, even more than to rule it after the sack. Watching his dream unfold made what came after seem of scant importance by comparison.

Watching... His eyes went back to that third screen. All the women there would have been heart-stopping beauties on a lesser world, but they were just enlisted men's pickings on Trantor. With so many billions of women to choose from, the ones less than spectacular were simply ignored.

Smiling in anticipation, Gilmer took the spiral slidewalk up to the Imperial bedchambers. Not even in his wildest dreams had he imagined anything like them. Thousands of years of the best ingenuity money could buy had been lavished there on nothing but pleasure.

Billye smiled too, when he came in. Her tawny hair spilled over bare shoulders. Disdaining all the elaborations the bedchamber offered, Gilmer took her in his arms and sank to the floor with her. There he soon discovered an advantage of thick carpeting he had not suspected before.

She murmured lazily and lay in his arms through the afterglow. She'd been his woman since he was just an ambitious lieutenant. He'd always thought her splendid, both to look at and to love.

He did still, he told himself. He even felt the truth of the thought. But it was not complete truth, not any more. The televisor screen had shown him that, by Trantorian standards, she was ordinary. And how in reason and justice could the Emperor of the Galaxy and Lord of All possess a consort who was merely ordinary?

He grunted, softly. "A centicredit for your thoughts," Billye said.

"Ahh, nothing much," he said, and squeezed her. Her voice was not perfectly sweet either, he thought.

"Here he comes." Maryan Drabel pointed to the single figure climbing down from the aircar that had descended in the no-man's land between Gilmer's lines and those held by the student-soldiers of the University.

"He's alone," Yokim Sarns said in faint surprise. "I told him we were willing to grant him any reasonable number of bodyguards he wanted. He has more courage than I'd thought."

"What difference does that make, when he can't—or won't—control his troops?" Maryan Drabel said bitterly. "How many raped women do we have in our clinic right now?"

"Thirty-seven," Sarns answered. "And five men."

"And that's just from this one tiny corner of Trantor, and only counts people who got through Gilmer's troops and ours," she said. "How many over the whole planet, where he has forty billion people to terrorize? How many robberies? How many fires, set just for the fun of them? How many murders, Yokim? How do they weigh in the balance against one man's courage?"

"They crush it." Sarns passed a weary hand across his forehead. "I know that as well as you, Maryan. But if he has courage, we can't handle him as we would have before."

"There is that," she admitted. "Quiet, now—he's almost here."

Gilmer, Sarns thought, looked more like a barbarian chief than Emperor, even if a purple cape billowed behind him as he advanced. Beneath it he wore the coverall blotched in shades of green and brown that his soldiers used. Sarns supposed it was a camouflage suit, but in Trantor's gleaming corridors it had more often exposed than protected the troopers. The nondescript gray of Sarns' own coat and trousers was harder to spot here.

The usurper's boots beat out a metallic tattoo. "Majesty," Sarns said, knowing he should speak first and also knowing that, since Gilmer had seized Trantor, the title was true *de facto* if not *de jure*. Sarns did not approve of dealing in untruths.

"You're Dean Sarns, eh?" Gilmer's granite rumble should have come out of that hard, bearded countenance. The Emperor of the Galaxy scratched his nose and went on, "You've got some tough fighters behind you, Sarns. I tell you right now, I wouldn't mind taking the lot of them into my fleet."

"You are welcome to put out a call, sire, but I doubt you'd find many volunteers," Sarns answered. "These young men and women are not soldiers by trade, but rather students. They—and I—care more for abstract knowledge than for the best deployment of a blast-rifle company."

Gilmer nodded. "I'd heard that said. I found it hard to believe. Truth to tell, Sarns, I still do. You spend your whole lives chasing this—what did you call it?—abstract knowledge?"

"We do," Sarns said proudly. "This is the University, after all, the distillation of all the wisdom that has accumulated over the millennia of Imperial history. We codify it, systematize it, and, where we can, add to it."

"It seems a milk-livered way to spend one's time," Gilmer remarked, careless of Sarns' feelings or—more likely—reckoning the dean would agree with him when he pointed out an obvious truth. "What good is knowledge that you can't eat, drink, sleep with, or shoot at your enemies?"

He is a barbarian, Sarns thought, *even if he's lived all his life inside what still calls itself, with less and less reason, the Galactic Empire.* Fortunately Sarns, like any administrator worth his desk, had practice not showing what he felt. He said, "Well, let me give you an example, sire: how did you and your victorious army come to Trantor?"

"By starship, of course." Gilmer stared. "How else, man? Did you expect us to walk?" He laughed at his own wit.

Sarns smiled a polite smile. "Of course not. But what happens if one of your busbars shorts out or a hydrochron needs repair?"

"We fix 'em, as best we can. Seems like nobody in the whole blasted Galaxy understands a hyperatomic motor any more," Gilmer said, scowling. Then he stopped dead. "That's knowledge too, isn't it? By the space fiend, Sarns, are you telling me you've got a University full of technicians who really know what they're doing? If you do, I'll impress 'em into the fleet and make you—and them—so rich they won't ever miss their book-films, I promise you that."

"We do have some people—not many, I fear—studying such things. As I said before, you are welcome to speak with them. Some may even choose to accompany you, for the challenge of working on real equipment." Sarns paused a moment in thought. "We also have skilled doctors, computer specialists, and students of many other disciplines of value to the Empire."

He watched Gilmer nibble the bait. "And they'd do these same kinds of things for me?" the usurper asked.

"Some might," Sarns said. "Others—probably more—would be willing to instruct your technicians and personnel here. Of course," he added smoothly, "they would be less enthusiastic if you shot your way in. You would also likely waste a good many of them that way."

"Hrmmp," Gilmer said. After a moment, he went on, "But any ships with their techs, their medics, their computer people gone—they'd be no more use to us than if they rusted away."

"Not immediately, perhaps, but later they would be of even greater value to you than they could ever be with the inadequately trained crews I gather they have now."

Gilmer lowered his voice. "Sarns, I can't afford to think about later. I'd bet a million credits against a burnt-out blaster cartridge that there's at least three fleets moving on me the same way I moved on Dagobert. Now that Trantor's fallen, all the dogs of space will want to pick her bones—and mine."

Privately, Sarns thought the usurper was right about that. It would only be what Gilmer deserved, too. But the dean-turned-general felt sadness wash over him all the same. No time to bother to learn anything new, no time to think about anything but the moment—that had been the disease of the Galactic Empire for far too long. Gilmer had a worse case of it than the Emperors before him, but the root sickness was the same.

Sarns did not sigh. He said, "Well, in any case this has taken our discussion rather far from the purpose at hand, which is, after all, merely to arrange an armistice between your forces and the students and staff of the University, so both we and you may return to what we consider our proper pursuits."

"Aye, that's so," Gilmer said.

As he had not sighed, Sarns did not smile. *Show a barbarian a short-term objective and he won't look past it*, he thought. "Would you care to examine our facilities here, so you can see how harmless we are under normal circumstances?" he said.

"Why not? Lead on, Dean Sarns, and let's see what you've turned into soldiers. Who knows? Maybe I'll try to recruit *you*." Gilmer laughed. So, without reservation, did Yokim Sarns. He hadn't suspected Gilmer could say anything that funny.

WHAT FIRST struck Gilmer inside the University was the quiet. Almost everyone went around in soft-soled shoes, soundless on the metal flooring. Gilmer's boots clanged resoundingly as ever, even raising echoes that ran down the corridors ahead of him. But both clang and echoes were tiny pebbles dropped into an ocean of stillness.

The people were as strange as the place, Gilmer thought. Those who had fought his men were still in gray like Sarns. The rest wore soft pastels that made them seem to flit like spirits along the hallways. Their low voices added to the impression that they really weren't quite there.

Half-remembered childhood tales of ghosts rose in Gilmer's mind. He shivered and made sure he stayed close to his guides. "What are they doing in there?" he asked, pointing. His voice caused echoes too, echoes that swiftly died.

Sarns glanced into the laboratory. "Something pertaining to neurobiology," he said. "One moment." He ducked inside. "That's right—they're working to improve the efficiency of sleep-inducers."

Somehow the dean pitched his voice so that it was clear but raised no reverberations. Gilmer resolved to imitate him. "And what's going on there?" the Emperor of the Galaxy asked. Then he frowned, for he'd managed only a hoarse whisper that sounded filled with dread.

To his relief, Sarns appeared to take no notice. "That's a psychostatistics research group," the dean answered casually. He walked on, assuming Gilmer knew what psychostatistics was.

Gilmer didn't, but was not about to let on. He pointed to another doorway. Some people in that room were working with computers, others with what looked like chunks of rock. "What are they up to?" he asked. He still could not match Yokim Sarns' easy tone.

"Ahh, that's one of our most fascinating projects. I'm sure you'll appreciate it." Gilmer, who wasn't at all sure, waited for Sarns to go on: "Using ancient inscriptions and voice synthesizers, that team of linguists is attempting to reconstruct the mythical language called *English*, from which our modern Galactic tongue arose thousands of years ago."

"Oh," was all Gilmer said. He'd never heard of English, either. *Well, too bad*, he thought. He knew about a lot of things these soft academics had never heard of, things like field-stripping a blast-pistol, like small-unit actions.

Yokim Sarns might have plucked the thought from his head, and then twisted it in a way he did not like: "Mainly, though, we fought you so we could protect what you're coming to now: the Library."

"Everything humanity has ever learned is preserved here," said Sarns' aide Maryan Drabel.

Gilmer caught the note of pride in her voice. "Are you in charge of it?" he asked.

She nodded and smiled. Gilmer cut ten years off the guess he'd made of her age from her grim face and drab clothing. She said, "This chamber here is the accessing room. Students and researchers come here first, to get a printout of the book-films and journal articles available in our files on the topics that interest them."

"Where are all your book-films?" Gilmer craned his neck. He'd visited libraries on other planets once or twice, and found himself wading in film cases. He didn't see any here. Suspicion grew in him. Was all this some kind of colossal bluff, designed to conceal who knew what? If it was, the whole University would pay.

But Maryan Drabel only laughed. "You're not ready to see book-films yet. Before a student can even begin to view films, he or she needs to have some idea of what's in them: more than a title can provide. What we're coming to now is the Abstracts Section, where people weed through their possible reading-lists with summaries of the documents that seem promising to them."

More people fiddling with more computers. Gilmer almost succeeded in suppressing his yawn. Maryan Drabel went on, "We also have an acquisition and cataloguing division, which integrates new book-films into our collection."

"*New* book-films?" Gilmer said. "You mean people still write them?"

"Not as many as when the University was founded," the librarian said sadly. "And, of course, now that the Periphery and even some of the inner regions have broken away from the Empire, we no longer see a lot of what is written, or only get a copy after many years. But we do still try, and surely no other collection in the Galaxy comes close to ours in scope or completeness."

They came to an elevator. Yokim Sarns pressed the button. After a moment, the door opened. "This way, please," Sarns said as he stepped in.

Maryan Drabel and Gilmer followed, the latter with some misgivings. If these University folk wanted to assassinate him, what better place than the cramped and secret confines of an elevator? But if they wanted to assassinate him, he'd been in their power since this tour started. He had to assume they didn't.

The elevator purred downward, stopped. The door opened again. "These are the reading rooms," Maryan Drabel said.

Gilmer saw row on row of cubicles. Most of them were empty. "Usually they would be much busier," Yokim Sarns remarked. "The people who would be busy using them have been on the fighting lines instead."

As if to confirm his words, one of the closed cubicle doors opened. The young woman who emerged wore the gray of the University's soldiers and had a blast rifle slung on her back. She looked grubby and tired, as a front-line soldier should. Gilmer noted that she also looked as though she'd forgotten all about the fighting and her weapon: her attention focused solely on the calculator pad she was keying as she walked toward the bank of elevators.

"Do you care to look inside a reading room?" Maryan Drabel asked.

Gilmer thought for a moment, then shook his head. He'd been in a few reading rooms; they were alike throughout the Galaxy. The number of them here was impressive, but one by itself would not be.

"Is this everything you have to show me?" he asked.

"One thing more," Maryan Drabel told him. Shrugging, he ducked back into the elevator with her and Sarns.

Down they went again, down and down. "You are specially privileged, to see what we are about to show you," Yokim Sarns said. "Few people ever will, few even from the University. We thought it would help you to understand us better."

The elevator stopped. Gilmer stepped out, stared around. "By the space fiend," he whispered in soft wonder.

The chamber extended for what had to be kilometers. From floor to ceiling, every shelf was packed full of book-films. "The computer can access them and project them to the appropriate reading room on request," Maryan Drabel said.

Gilmer walked toward the nearest case. His boots thumped instead of clanging. He glanced down. "This is a rock floor," he said. "Why isn't it metal like everything else?"

"The book-film depositories are below the built-up part of Trantor," Yokim Sarns explained. "There wouldn't be room for them up there—that space is needed for people. Having them down here also gives them a certain amount of extra protection from catastrophe. Even the blast of a radiation weapon set off overhead probably wouldn't reach down here."

"You also have to understand that this is just one book-film chamber among many," Maryan Drabel added. "We've used both dispersed storage and a lot of redundancy to do our best to ensure the collection's safety."

Gilmer had a sudden vision of the University folk tunneling like moles for years, for centuries, for millennia, honeycombing the very bedrock of Trantor as they dug storehouses for the knowledge they hoarded. Even worse, in his mind's eye he imagined all the weight of rock and metal over his head. He'd grown up on a farming world full of wide open spaces, and had spent most of his life in space itself. To imagine everything above collapsing, crushing him so he would leave not even a red smear, made cold sweat start on his brow.

"Shall we go back up?" he said hoarsely.

"Certainly, sire." Yokim Sarns' voice was bland. "I hope you do see—now—that we are solely dedicated to the pursuit of learning, and will not interfere in the political life of the Empire so long as it does not invade our campus. On those terms, I think, we can arrange an armistice satisfactory to both sides."

All Gilmer wanted to do—now—was get away from this catacomb and return to his own men. He noticed that Sarns hadn't thumbed the elevator button. Maybe Sarns wouldn't, until Gilmer agreed. "Yes, yes, of course." He could hear how quickly he spoke, but couldn't help it. "You have your men put down their arms, and mine will stay away from the University."

"Good enough," Sarns said. As if he had been absent-minded before—and perhaps that was all he had been—he pushed the button that summoned the elevator. Gilmer rode up in relieved silence; every second the elevator climbed seemed to lift a myria-ton from his shoulders.

When he and his guides returned to the level from which they had begun, a man came briskly toward them with two sheets of parchmentoid. "This is Egril Joons," Sarns said. "What do you have for us, Egril?"

"Copies of the armistice agreement, for your signature and the Emperor Gilmer's," Joons replied. He held out a stylus.

Gilmer took it. He skimmed through one copy of the document, signed it, and was reaching for the other from Yokim Sarns when he suddenly thought to wonder how the armistice terms could be ready now when he'd only agreed to them moments before. "You were snooping," he growled to Egril Joons.

"My apologies, but yes," Joons said. "Voice monitoring is part of the security system for the book-films. This time I just made use of it to prepare copies as quickly as possible. I expected that your majesty would have other concerns that would soon need his attention."

Gilmer recalled how badly he'd wanted to get back to his own troops. "Oh, very well, put that way," he said. He signed the second copy of the armistice accord. This Joons fellow was righter than he knew, righter than he could know. Trantor had to be made ready to defend itself from space attack, and quickly, or Gilmer the Emperor of the Galaxy would soon be Gilmer the vaporized usurper.

Gilmer the Emperor of the Galaxy rolled up his copy of the agreement, absent-mindedly stuck Egril Joons' stylus in a tunic pocket, and said, sounding quite imperial indeed, "Now if you will be so good as to escort me back to my lines—"

"Certainly." Yokim Sarns handed the other copy of the armistice to Maryan Drabel. "Come this way, if you please."

Trantor Falls

From behind, Maryan Drabel thought, Gilmer looked much more like an Emperor than from the front. The shining purple cape lent him an air of splendor that did not match the camouflage suit he wore under it. Seen from the front, the cape only seemed a sad bit of stolen booty.

"An Emperor shouldn't look like a thief," she said.

"Why not?" Egril Joons was still feeling pangs over his purloined stylus. "That's what he is."

"Wizards!" Billye shouted. "You went into the wizards' lair, and they enspelled you!"

"There's no such things as wizards!" Gilmer shouted back.

"No? Then why didn't you get anything worth having out of the University, when they were at our mercy?" she said.

"I did. We aren't shooting at them any more, and they aren't shooting at us. They recognize me as Emperor of the Galaxy. What more could I want?"

"To put the fear of cold space and hot death in them, that's what. If you *are* the Emperor of the Galaxy, they should act like subjects, not like equals. Can the Emperor have an equal? And you *let* them." Billye's hair flew around her in a copper cloud as she shook her head in bewilderment. "I can't believe you let them. You have all your men, the whole fleet—why not just crush them for their insolence?"

"Oh, leave me be," Gilmer said sullenly. He didn't need to hear this from Billye; he'd already heard it, more politely but the same tune, from Vergis Fenn. Fenn had asked him why, if the University folk were willing to instruct his personnel, that willingness didn't show up in the armistice document. He'd been sullen with his fleet commander, too, not wanting to admit he hadn't had the nerve to ask for the change in writing. Why hadn't he? All the real power was on his side. But still—he hadn't.

"No, I won't leave you be," Billye said now. "Somebody has to put backbone in you, especially since yours looks like it's fallen out through your—"

"Shut up!" Gilmer roared in a voice that not one of this half-pirate spacemen or troopers dared disobey.

Billye dared. "I won't either shut up. And there are so wizards. Every other tale that floats in from the Periphery talks about them."

"Lies about them, you mean." Gilmer was just as glad to change the subject, even a little. His head ached. If Billye was going to be this abrasive, maybe he *would* find himself some pretty little Trantorian chit who'd only open her mouth to say "yes."

"They aren't lies," Billye said stubbornly.

"Well, what else could they be?" Gilmer said. "There's no such thing as a man-sized force screen. There can't be—the Empire doesn't have 'em, and the Empire has everything there is. There's no way to open a Personal Capsule without having a man's characteristic on file. So stories that talk about things like that have to be lies."

"Or else the magicians do do those things, and do 'em by their magic," Billye said. "And what else but magic could have made you show the University not just mercy but—but—I don't know what. Treat them like the place was theirs by right, when the Emperor has charge of everything there is."

"If he can keep it," Gilmer muttered. He stalked out of the bedchamber—he'd get no solace here, that was plain. A scoutship message had been waiting for him when he returned from the University grounds: a fleet was gathering not ten parsecs away, a fleet that did not belong to him. If he was going to keep Trantor, he'd have to fight for it all over again. Even a pinprick from the University might hurt him at such a time.

Why couldn't Billye see that? Rage suddenly filled Gilmer. If she couldn't, to the space fiend with her! He pointed at the first servant he spotted. "You!"

The man flinched. Unlike Billye, he—all the palace servants—knew Gilmer was no one to trifle with. "Sire?" he asked fearfully.

"Take as many flunkies as you need to, then go toss that big-mouthed wench out of my bedchamber. Find me someone new—I expect you have ways to take care of that. Someone worthy of an Emperor, mind you. But most of all, someone quiet."

Trantor Falls

"Yes, sire." The servant risked a smile. "That, Majesty, I think we can handle."

A ROOM in the Library—*not* a room Gilmer had seen!

Yokim Sarns, Maryan Drabel, Egril Joons...dean, librarian, dietitian... general, chief of staff, quartermaster...and rather more. They stood before a wall of equations, red symbols on a gray background. Yokim Sarns, whose privilege it was to speak first, said, "I didn't think it would be that easy."

"Neither did I," Maryan Drabel agreed. "I expected—the probabilities predicted—we would have to touch Gilmer's mind to make sure he would leave us alone here."

"That courage we saw helped a great deal," Sarns said. "It let him gain respect for our student-soldiers where a more purely pragmatic man would simply have brushed aside their sacrifice because it conflicted with his own interests."

"Mix that with superstitious awe at the accumulation of ancient knowledge we represent, let him see our goals and objectives—our ostensible goals and objectives—are irrelevant to his or slightly to his advantage, and he proved quite capable of deciding on his own to let us be," Maryan Drabel said. "We came out of what could have been a nasty predicament very nicely indeed."

Egril Joons had been studying the numbers and symbols, the possible decision-paths that led from Hari Seldon's day through almost three centuries to the present—and beyond. Now he said, "I do believe this will be the only round."

"The only round of sacks for Trantor?" Yokim Sarns studied the correlation at which Joons pointed; the equations obligingly grew on the Prime Radiant's wall so he could see them better. "Yes, it does seem so, if our data from around the planet are accurate. Gilmer has done such an efficient job of destruction that Trantor won't be worth looting again once this round of civil wars is done."

"That was the lower probability, too," Joons said. "Look—there was a better than seventy per cent chance of two sacks at least forty years apart, and at least a fifteen per cent chance of three or more, perhaps even spaced over a century."

"Our lives and our work will certainly be easier this way," Maryan Drabel said. "I know we're well protected, but a stray missile—" She shivered.

"We still risk those for a little while longer," Sarns said. "Gilmer is so blatantly a usurper that others will try to steal from him what he stole from Dagobert. But the danger of further major damage to Trantor as a whole has declined a great deal, and will grow still smaller as word of the Great Sack spreads." He pointed to the figures that supported his conclusion; Maryan Drabel pondered, and at length nodded.

"And with Trantor henceforward effectively removed from psychohistoric consideration, so is the Galactic Empire," Egril Joons said.

"The *First* Galactic Empire," Yokim Sarns corrected gently.

"Well, of course." Joons accepted the tiny rebuke with good nature. "Now, though, we'll be able to work toward the Second Empire without having to worry about concealing everything we do from prying imperial clerks and agents."

"The Empire was always our greatest danger," Maryan Drabel said. "We needed to be here at its heart to help protect the First Foundation, but at its heart also meant under its eyes, if it ever came to notice us. In the days before we fully developed the mind-touch, one seriously hostile Commissioner of Public Safety could have wrecked us."

"The probability was that we wouldn't get any such, and we didn't," Egril Joons said.

"Probability, yes, but psychohistory can't deal with individuals any more than physics can tell you exactly when any one radium atom will decay," she said stubbornly. The truth there was so self-evident that Joons had to concede it, but not so graciously as he had to Yokim Sarns.

Sarns said, "Never mind, both of you. If you'll look here"—the Prime Radiant, taking its direction from his will, revealed the portion of the

Seldon Plan that lay just ahead—"you'll see that we're entering a period of consolidation. As you and Maryan have both pointed out, Egril, the First Empire is dead, while it will be several centuries yet before the new Empire that will grow from the First Foundation extends its influence to this part of the Galaxy."

"Clear sailing for a while," Joons said. "About time, too."

"Don't get complacent," Maryan Drabel said.

"A warning the Second Foundation should always bear in mind," Yokim Sarns said. "But, looking at the mathematics, I have to agree with Egril. Barring anything unforeseen—say, someone outside our ranks discovering the mind-touch—we should have no great difficulty in steering the proper course. And"—he smiled broadly, even a little smugly—"what are the odds of that?"

Three Men and a Vampire

Like Connie Willis, I first learned of Jerome K. Jerome's *Three Men in a Boat* in the pages of *Have Space Suit—Will Travel*. I was fourteen or fifteen then, and soon discovered we happened to have a copy in the house. I read it, was delighted, and have been an admirer of Jerome's ever since. When the chance came to do a couple of stories involving the Three Men (to say nothing of the dog), I grabbed it with both hands.

It's the most extraordinary thing, it really is. None of this would have happened if I hadn't made a silly mistake.

But life is like that all the time, isn't it? A chap I know married the girl who fell into his lap—yes, literally—when, as was his habit, he stuck out his long legs and big feet in a crowded train compartment and dozed off. Such stories haven't always happy endings. Some years later, I had to trade places with him at a fancy dinner party; they'd seated him next to her, and she was, by then, his former wife.

A happy ending to this particular tale I'm about to tell you? Let us not, as the shilling shockers say, anticipate.

George and Harris and I were coming out of the Oaken Barrel (not the real name of the place, and don't ask it of me, for I shan't tell you) not long before closing time one Friday night: which made it Saturday morning, if you're a stickler for such things. Three or four pints apiece left George and me uncommonly contented with the world. Rather more than three or four pints left Harris wanting to sing a comic song. Take no alarm, dear reader; we did not let him.

But it was the nearest run thing you ever saw in your life, as Wellington, with so much less at risk, said of Waterloo. Thinking of our narrow escape called to mind other times when we were not so lucky. I also recollected another man's "comic" song I once heard, and that is what led me to my mistake.

For, after we'd managed to quieten Harris, looking up I saw walking along the pavement not ten yards ahead of us a man who was, at least from behind, the very spit and image of Herr Slossen Boschen. The fellow was tall and lean, as was the German musician. He dressed in an old-fashioned, almost excessively formal style, as did Herr Slossen Boschen. And the gas-lamps clearly showed an upstanding pouf of white hair like that affected by the man of my acquaintance.

When I sped up and left my companions behind, George called after me, "Here, J., what in tarnation do you think you're about?"

"Making up to an old friend," I answered over my shoulder. *Friend* doubtless stretched the point, but heaven knows I did want to make up to Herr Slossen Boschen. Along with a roomful of other people, I've owed him an apology for lo these many years.

And I owe it to him yet. When I tapped the man on the elbow, he of course turned round to see who it might be. "Yes?" he said.

Like Herr Slossen Boschen's, his accent was indeed Teutonic. I realized at once, though, that I'd never once before set eyes on him. "I beg your pardon, sir," I stammered. "I took you for someone I knew."

"Till now, I agree we have not had the pleasure of each other's acquaintance. Let me remedy that. Abraham Van Helsing, at your service." He bowed stiffly, from the waist, and held out his right hand.

As I shook him by it, I murmured something in what I hoped was German. They made me take the language in my schoolboy days, but I gladly gave it back soon afterwards. George and Harris caught me up then. Reveling in my fragmentary grasp of German, I also used it to present them to Herr Van Helsing.

He smiled thinly. His narrow features had no room for any wider kind of smile. "You are kind, to look to bespeak a foreigner in his own tongue," quoth he, "but, though I know the speech of the Kaiser's Empire, I come from Holland, and it is not mine from birth. English will do more than well enough, I assure you."

Didn't I feel a right fool then! Not only had I thought he was someone he wasn't, I'd thought he hailed from a country he didn't. The disadvantage to paved streets, I find, is that you can't sink down through them no matter how embarrassed you are. My friends weren't about to let me forget it, either. What are friends for but reminding you how big a chucklehead you were while they chanced to be there to see it?

I started to give the professor—that, I soon learned, was his proper title—the best apology I could (in English), but he held up a hand to show he did not want it. "Perhaps we are after all fortunately met," he said. "Providence works in mysterious ways its wonders to perform, and I confess to you all that the services of three bold young men would be of great value to me now."

I nearly wrote that I don't know why he reckoned us bold. I do, however: he must have been looking at George's blazer. You would never dream George works in a bank, not by that blazer. It would make you guess him to be the intimate acquaintance, perhaps even the taskmaster, of young women in the custom of earning the wages of sin.

But I digress. It is a bad habit of mine, digression. I may try to tell a story in the most simple and straightforward fashion, but somehow Uncle Podger and Montmorency will find themselves in the narrative whether they belong there or not. Perhaps it has something to do with the ink with which I prime my pen. Or it may…

Your pardon, pray. I quite forgot. That shall not happen again.

Resplendent in his gaudy blazer, George asked, "What do you think we can do for you?"

"Have you gentlemen"—Professor Van Helsing spread his hands to take in the three of us—"any acquaintance with the supernatural?"

"Ghosts are splendid in tales told after supper, especially on Christmas Eve, when it's almost hallowed to tell them," Harris said.

"That's an acquaintance with stories about ghosts. It isn't an acquaintance with ghosts." George, despite his villainous taste in haberdashery, keeps both feet firmly on the ground. If ever you should see George with his head in the clouds, you may be sure they've risen from his pipe.

"I've told some of those Christmas Eve ghost stories," I said slowly, "and some of the ones I've told are true, or as true as I could make them."

"Fishermen peddle the same nonsense," said George with a snort.

"Never mind, my friends," broke in the professor. "I only wished to assure myself that you would not dismiss the notion out of hand. I see that is true for two of you, at least. Sir"—this to George—"if you do not wish to continue with us, I promise I shall not think the less of you."

"You won't get rid of me so easily, not when you've scratched my bump of curiosity." George struck a phrenological pose. "If there's nothing to it, I'll have a laugh. If there is something to it, you'll need someone who has too much sense to get all hot and bothered. Here, that means me."

"I could get Montmorency," I said. "We're only three blocks from my room."

"He'd give the doubters a bit in the way of brains, anyhow," said Harris. George glowered and growled. He's a large, solid man, George, but his bark is worse than his bite. When Montmorency sinks his teeth into something, he means it.

"This Montmorency is—?" enquired Van Helsing.

"He certainly is," I agreed. "He's my dog."

I looked for him to say we needed a rascally fox terrier even less than did the cat who owned the young lady upstairs from me. I don't suppose he'd met the young lady upstairs—or the cat—but he would have known similar cases. What he did say, however, was, "Excellent! Against the *vrolok*, the *vrkoslak*, all aid is welcome."

I had no idea what he was talking about, which proved just as well. Neither did George. Harris looked thoughtful, as if the strange, barbarous words meant something to him even if he wished they didn't. Or it may be that the bitter he'd downed was having more of its way with him than I imagined.

Three Men and a Vampire

We went upstairs on tiptoe so my landlady would not feel put upon. You would understand why had you ever heard her wax eloquent upon that feeling. You would also wish never to provoke it in her again, in which wish, she being what she is, you would find yourself disappointed.

I opened my door, scraped a lucifer on the sole of my shoe, and lit the gas. Montmorency lay asleep not in his basket but on my favorite chair, where the hair he sheds is more visible and more readily transfers itself to my trousers. He opened his eyes. George and Harris he is used to; he takes them for other pets of mine, which is not so far wrong. He didn't try to bite Professor Van Helsing's ankles, showing himself either impressed by the man or too sleepy to bother.

Before he fully woke, I snapped a leash to his collar. That would, I hoped, keep him from pursuing cats and other distractions. If only people could so easily be kept from haring off in all directions.

"Now," I said brightly, "where are we going?" Montmorency wagged his tail. He was ready to go anywhere.

"Why, to Abney Park Cemetery." Van Helsing clucked. "Excuse me. I thought I already told you, or that you could have pluck the answer from my brain like fruit from a low-hanging tree. It is not far—no more than two or three kilometers."

He used those funny Continental measures, foreigner that he was. Well, I have crossed the Channel often enough to understand that he meant a mile or two. Half an hour's brisk walk, say.

It had been clear when we went in to get the dog. By the time we came out, only ten minutes later, fog was rolling in from the river. The lamps that lit the streets seemed to shrink in upon themselves. They cast little wan puddles of light at the feet of the poles they topped. Between the poles, darkness and mist held sway over all.

"Is the, the *vrkoslak* at the cemetery…in the cemetery?" asked Harris as we walked along. His voice sounded oddly muffled, as if the fog attenuated it like the streetlamps. Or he may have known more than George and I did, and liked what he knew less. By the way he pronounced the odd word Van Helsing had used, he had indeed run across it before.

"Yes, I believe so." The Dutchman sounded grim. "I aim to run it off—to destroy it, if I am able—and to rout as many of its confederates as God may grant me the power to do."

"What *are* we talking about here?" I asked. "In plain English, I mean."

"You will have read *Varney the Vampire*, J., I'm sure," said Harris.

"Mm, parts of it," I allowed. *Varney the Vampire* is not a shilling shocker. It's a penny dreadful, from the days before I was born. Few have gone all the way through it, for it's two or three times as thick as the Bible, Old and New Testaments together. The pair of hacks who perpetrated it also wrote *The String of Pearls*, which loosed Sweeney Todd upon an unready world. They have much to answer for, in other words. I turned to Professor Van Helsing. "You don't mean to say—?"

"Never mind what I mean to say," he told me. "Believe what you see, what you hear, what you feel. Forget all else, and act on that."

"Good advice," said George. His thinking so was not the worst argument to the contrary, but I let it pass.

I had trouble believing Van Helsing could find Kingsland Road, but he did. Kingsland Road became Kingsland High Street, which became Stoke Newington High Street, all without a kink. He, and we, turned off Stoke Newington High Street at Stoke Newington Church Road. Soon we came to the gate of Abney Park Cemetery.

Anyone who knows me knows I am not wild for graves and tombs, except those of my kin. Still, of its kind, Abney Park Cemetery is quite fine. It is one of London's Magnificent Seven. (Curious—as I write that, I feel I ought to hear dramatic music playing, though I can't imagine why.)

"Better to use this entrance than the main one," murmured Professor Van Helsing. "Coming off a road named for a church can only be a good omen." What about forgetting everything save what one saw, heard, and felt? Yes, what about that? Since Van Helsing was already walking into the cemetery, I let it pass, too.

Abney Park is an arboretum as well as a burial ground. It houses all manner of rare and foreign trees and shrubs and flowers, but the flowers were closed for the evening, you might say, and with the fog the shrubs and trees might as well have been. Professor Van Helsing nevertheless bestrode the paths like a colossus who knew where he was going. The rest of us followed as best we could. Montmorency, in fact, tried to follow the professor in front of him a couple of times, till I shortened the lead so he couldn't.

A tawny owl hooted from…well, from somewhere. I believed I could hear it, but I didn't believe I could see it, or much of anything else. The fog seemed thick as meringue, though it tasted of coal-smoke rather than sugar. A properties manager putting on the Scottish play would have set a man who could do bird calls in the rafters to produce that eerie effect.

Little skittering noises came in from amongst the rare and foreign foliage. My frightened imagination wanted to believe wolves and bears were making them, and never mind that England has been centuries free of such savage beasts (but for those that walk on two legs, not four). Reason insisted they came from creatures more on the order of cats and rats, mice and hedgehogs. In the dripping fog, though, reason was an *ignis fatuus*, one that shed little light.

One of us—I don't believe it was me, but I may be wrong—muttered what sounded like a prayer. It was likelier to have been in Latin than English. Even to the sturdiest nonconformist or C. of E. man, Latin feels more powerful than his native tongue. Latin is old. So is God. Therefore… Almost a syllogism, don't you see?

I hadn't worked out whether it was or not when Montmorency yipped, snarled, jerked the leash out of my hand, and charged away. I could just about see him when he was at the end of the lead. He didn't take more than two bounds before disappearing altogether.

Fresh snarls came from off to our left, and then a thin screech that did not burst from a dog's throat. Like any terrier worth his table scraps and tasty bones, Montmorency is a ratter born. The only thing to delight him more than killing a rat is killing one rat after another. That thin screech didn't sound as if it burst from a rat's throat, either, but nothing seemed likelier.

We all hurried over towards where we thought we heard it. How we didn't get separated from one another and lost in the swirling mist I cannot tell you. I merely report the fact.

Then a flame sprang up in our midst. Van Helsing had, not an ordinary paraffin lamp, but something smaller and neater. "What the devil—?" said George. I couldn't have put it better myself.

"It is a Döbereiner's lamp. I light my pipe with it," said the professor. "An ingenious device. A valve releases *waterstof*—ah, hydrogen—over a platinum sponge, which causes it to ignite in the presence of air."

The faintly bluish flame faintly showed Montmorency. Even more faintly, it showed something that made my stomach turn over: the corpse of a naked young man, his throat torn out. I stared at my dog, who was licking from his muzzle I know not what, nor ever want to learn.

"Ah, poor Stivvings. Pity it had to end like this," said Van Helsing sadly. He turned the valve on his lamp so darkness swooped in again. Then he continued, "He was in rat form when Montmorency took him. It is a stage on the road to vampirism; I cannot explain better than that. Only in death did the poor devil return to his birthshape. Christ have mercy on his soul!" He drew a cross in the moist air in front of him. For a moment, it glowed blue like the flame from the Döbereiner's lamp.

I saw that. Did I believe it? I didn't see a rat turn into a man upon death, but I saw the dead man. Did I believe Montmorency could have slain him had he been in human form all that time? Did I believe a naked man would skulk through the undergrowth in Abney Park Cemetery on such a dank and foggy night?

I can tell you what I believed. I believed I'd fallen in deeper than I ever dreamt I might.

"Come, all of you." Professor Van Helsing's voice grew urgent. "If his amanuensis is so near, the fiend will rise at any moment. God bless your dog, sir. He may well have saved us from an attack from behind."

God bless my dog? God bless Montmorency? God bless my soul!

How Van Helsing found the path again is one more thing I cannot tell you. I can only relate that he did. We pattered on, staying together more by the scrape of our feet on the paving stones than by sight. Montmorency, trotting along beside me, seemed content now to stay on the leash. Perhaps one miracle of an evening sufficed even for him.

On we hurried, now left, now right, now straight—it was worse than the maze at Hampton Court, for there was no one to rescue us if we went astray. With the fog and the black night, I have no idea whereabouts in the cemetery we wound up. Van Helsing seemed sure of where he was going. Sure, of course, need not mean right; let anyone who doubts this hang about with George for a bit.

A sudden boom followed by the noise of dirt rolling off something large came to our ears. Many caskets are designed with signaling devices to prevent the horror of premature burial, but I had trouble imagining someone prematurely buried possessing the preternatural strength to throw off the coffin lid and the earth atop it.

Yet I heard what I heard. Did I believe it? I blame the blistering pace of nineteenth-century life in general for how I reply: things were happening too fast for me *not* to believe it.

Professor Van Helsing made the sign of the cross once more. This time, it did not merely shine blue; it blazed like lightning, piercing the fog as if it were a lighthouse lamp warning steamships away from jagged rocks. And what it showed…

When you hear the phrase *a fiend in human shape*, what crosses your mind? Shame on you if it's your least favorite relative. Shame, too, if it's your least favorite politico, though, given the run of politicos these days, your sin there may be more venial.

As for me, I saw the general article that night. Mad eyes glowing like an animal's, fangs longer and sharper than Montmorency's, a pallor as of the grave from which the horrid thing had just emerged… My hair stood on end. It truly did; I could feel it lifting my hat.

"Begone!" cried Professor Van Helsing. "This tomb, this city, this land are not for you!" He sketched the cross yet again. The mystic, purifying sign glowed brighter than ever. That glow hurt the vampire, which flinched away as if from a hot poker.

Yet the foul creature was made of stern stuff. "Damn you!" it cried, its mouth sounding stuffed with dirt. It rushed at its tormentor, and at my friends and me.

Van Helsing coolly pulled a pistol from his pocket. He did not fire it at the fiend, however, for it spat water rather than bullets. The good professor did not seem the sort to annoy his friends with a squirt-gun, but there you are. He did more than annoy the vampire—when the drops touched its skin, it shrieked as if they were vitriol.

"Holy water," said van Helsing. "Quick—fall on it whilst it is weakened!"

We did. Even Montmorency grabbed a trouser leg in his jaws and did his best to impede the monster. Heaven preserve me if ever I meet a vampire at full strength. Weakened as it was, the creature seemed a match for George and Harris and me, to say nothing of the dog.

Along with his squirt-gun, the professor proved to carry a stiletto. He stabbed the vampire again and again. No blood flowed from the wounds. Then the long, thin blade must have pierced its heart. It collapsed in a puff of ashes and dust. In an eyeblink, the opera suit it had worn was empty. Only a faint foul odor lingered in the air.

The cross signs faded away, leaving us again in darkness. "I say," drawled George. "Not the way I planned to spend the small hours, but not the least interesting little while I've passed, either."

"That must be what they call English equanimity," said Van Helsing. "Against such, the *vrolok* might well have struggled in vain even without my trifling intervention. But better, I think, to take no chances."

Montmorency barked agreement. I also thought the professor was right. As a proper Englishman, though, I was of course too modest to say so.

Three Men and a Werewolf

> Here is my other story about the Three Men and the supernatural. The alert reader may also detect the influence of a certain Warren Zevon song. This is, of course, purely a coincidence. Of course. Purely.

Harris and I stood on the corner smoking our pipes for at least twenty minutes before George deigned to honor us with his presence. We would have been more annoyed had we been more surprised. George, I expect, will be late to his own hanging. And, should he somehow evade that fate, the *Times* will surely commence his obituary with the unvarnished truth: "The late George —— passed away yesterday at the age of…"

He did bring it off well. He commonly does, but then custom hath made it in him a property of easiness. Most men who inconvenience their relations or friends by coming late to the ball (or the supper, or the rugby match, or…) will act, and may even feel, flustered and embarrassed. Not George. He assumes you will be glad to see him when at last you *do* see him, and never mind when you should have set eyes on him.

"Hullo, gents!" he said, saluting us with his umbrella. It had rained the night before and was still drizzling when we set out, so we had ours as well. The sun, sliding between clouds, shone off the bright, pointed tip of Harris'. George went on, "Seen any vampires lately?"

"Not this past year, thank heavens," I replied. Harris nodded and looked sober—not the most common look for his face to wear, I know, but I am trying to tell the truth here, however unlikely it may sound. George could have hit upon no better way to make us forget whatever pique we might have felt at his tardiness. Our one brief encounter with the undead was plenty for a lifetime; no, an eternity.

To help ensure I have no more such encounters, I've mounted a small, none too noticeable crucifix above the door to my room. I am not of the Romish persuasion, but why take chances? I keep bulbs of garlic on the window sills, and sometimes even remember to change them. I haven't asked my friends if they take similar precautions, but they would have to be a kind of fool they are not to fail to do so.

"Jolly good," said George. "Let's find this eatery, then. We can tell everyone we know we've tried things most people have never even heard of."

We went down Flamborough Street towards the Thames and into Limehouse. That is a peculiar district, and one less well known than it might be. Though lying just east of the City, it might as well be a different world—several different worlds, in fact. The City runs the Empire; Limehouse is where its dregs wash up. Lascars and Chinese and Lord only knows who all else doss there and drink there and eat there and sometimes even pray there—we passed the Chinese Mission as we walked. It says its name in common English letters and again, lower down, in the peculiar characters the Celestials favor (or at least I think so, being sadly illiterate in Chinese).

Smaller places also showed their names in both the alphabet we use and Chinese, Indian, or Arabic scripts. Some of them—generally the smallest of the small—omitted our letters altogether: you had to belong to the folk they served to know what they were serving.

"Suppose there's a fire," said George. "How do you tell the station which place is burning up?"

"You say which street it's in, and between which two," replied Harris. "If they can't find it after they know that much, it's not very big."

"I wonder how we'll find the place we're looking for if it has no English sign," I said. "It won't be on fire, or it had better not be."

"Leave it to me," declared George.

"You're learning Chinese?" asked Harris.

Three Men and a Werewolf

"Not a bit of it." George tramped up to a ragamuffin hawking newspapers. They were so new, I could smell the ink coming off them. The headline screamed OLD WOMAN MUTILATED LAST NIGHT! Ignoring it, George held a silver shilling a foot in front of the boy's eager eyes. "Here, pal, this for you if you can tell us how to get to Lee Ho Fook's."

"You're almost there. Turn left next time you can. Two doors down, on the left." The newsboy snatched the coin from George and made it disappear. Then he went back to crying up his lurid papers. I wouldn't have given him so much. People lie as naturally as they breathe—I should know—and all the more readily with so much to earn by quick invention.

But the place was where he claimed it would be. It did boast a tiny sign in English, with a bigger one above it in Chinese. I opened the door. A bell rang. I waved George and Harris in ahead of me.

It smelled good in there, meaty and greasy and spicy—not the same smells you'd find in a meat-pie shop, but the same kind of smells. *What you get here will be cheap, but it will taste fine*, they promised.

People shoveling rice and chopped bits into their mouths with chopsticks paused, morsels suspended in midair, to gape at us. They were all Orientals, with golden skins, narrow black eyes, and flat faces. Most of them wore gowns with odd collars; the rest had on cheap Western clothes. Never before had I felt so much a stranger, a foreigner, in my own country.

Harris, now, might become an ambassador if only he could stay sober. He nodded to the pigtailed bloke behind the counter, who was wielding a fat cleaver with might, main, and considerable skill. "May we take a table, sir?" he asked.

"'Elp yourselves, mates." The cook may have looked like a Chinaman, but he talked like any other East Ender. He shoved a badly printed sheet across the counter. "An' 'ere's a menu for yer."

I picked up the menu while George and Harris sat down. Then I joined them. The table held a cruet of the liquor from fermented soya beans (I'd hoped for Worcestershire, but a sniff left me disappointed), a shaker of salt, one of black pepper, and one of red pepper that I eyed with wary respect. We passed the menu back and forth. It was in both Chinese and English, the latter almost as incomprehensible as the former. Chow mein? Egg foo yung? *Egg* I recognized; the rest was gibberish.

"You want forks or chopsticks?" asked the counterman.

As I've mentioned, the Celestials were conveying food to their gobs with those bits of wood. Some Englishmen who go out to the Orient come back with the knack, but none of us possessed it. "Forks," said George with decision, while Harris and I nodded.

They were mismatched and cheap as can be, but they were forks. "What you gonna eat?" enquired the fellow.

Again, George had his mind made up: "We must have some fried shrimp. I don't see how anyone can go wrong with fried shrimp."

"And some fried rice with pork." Harris pointed to the item on the menu. "That sounds exotic."

"Some kung pao chicken, too," I said. "I like the noise of it."

"That's a spicy one," warned the counterman.

I glanced at the red pepper flakes again, but then shrugged. "We'll live dangerously. And may we have some tea while we're waiting for the victuals?"

"Comin' right up." The man set a china pot and three handleless cups on the table. The tea poured out green and thin, not black, and neither milk nor sugar seemed on offer. The Celestials in the place took the style for granted, poor souls. We looked at one another and wordlessly decided to rough it.

A sensible choice: however much I preferred good old English Breakfast or Earl Grey, I could drink this stuff. "It will go well with the food, I hope," said Harris. I held the same hope, though I dare say more gingerly than he did.

The door flew open. The bell clanged. In strode a large, dapper chap, an Englishman, perfectly coifed—not a hair out of place—in a sack suit of such striking pattern and cut that it might have come from a lifetime in the future, not these mundane days of the nineteenth century drawing to a close. I wouldn't have liked to meet his tailor.

"Hullo, Lee Ho, you old crock!" he said cheerily. "How about a big old plate of beef chow mein, and some steamed rice to go with it?"

Three Men and a Werewolf

"You'll have it in a jiffy, Mr. Warren, sir," said the counterman, proving himself to be the eponymous Lee Ho Fook.

"You're famous, you know?" said the newcomer—Mr. Warren. He brandished a menu all wrinkled and teary, probably from the rain the night before. "I found this all the way over in Soho."

Lee Ho Fook's grin showed a gold tooth or two. "The more people 'oo know about us, the more 'oo'll want to eat 'ere."

We got our grub before Mr. Warren, as we should have, standing in front of him in the queue, so to speak. I've had fried prawns at fish-and-chips places now and then, but Lee Ho Fook's outdid them. The rice fried with pork tasted of the fermented soya beans and had bits of egg and scallion and I don't know what all else in it besides. It was strange, but it was good. And the kung pao chicken? I was enjoying the meat and the cashews and the strange spices of the Orient until I made the dreadful mistake of biting down on one of those peppers.

Spicy, the counterman called them. Good heavens, I thought the top of my head would blow off! My mouth might have been full of the hydrogen flame from the Döbereiner's lamp Professor Van Helsing carried. That green tea did go well with the food, but it made a painfully—*le môt juste*—inadequate fire extinguisher.

George started gulping his at almost the same moment I did. Whilst gasping and spluttering and perspiring, I noticed Mr. Warren tucking into his luncheon with chopsticks. He used them as readily as the Chinamen, eating rice and beef and odd vegetables with easy aplomb…and at least as fast as I could feed myself with my ordinary utensil.

George noticed something I failed to. "That's quite curious," he murmured.

"What is?" I asked. Harris' coughing fit said a kung pao pepper had just introduced itself to him.

"He's got hair on the palms of his hands," said George.

And so he did; his palms were almost as hairy as the backs of his hands, which says a great deal. I must confess, I let out a schoolboy snigger and whispered, "Maybe he practices the solitary vice to excess."

George chortled, to use Mr. Lear's lovely coinage. But Harris' bony visage took on a thoughtful—even a sorrowful—aspect. "That may not be the only thing troubling him," he said, also in a low voice.

"How d'you mean?" asked George. But Harris bit down on another of those infernal peppers just then. Smoke might have spurted from his ears. A tear ran down his cheek, but could not douse the flames in his mouth and gullet. George went without an answer.

Mr. Warren set half a crown on the table and went on his way. As none of the meals in the place went for more than one and six, that left a goodly emolument for Lee Ho Fook. I must confess that we, while not niggards, showed the counterman less generosity.

"Well," I said as we also made our exit, "what do you think?"

"Not bad for the money, but I could have eaten more," said George. But then George must carry around inside him a steam boiler in place of a proper stomach. By the way he stokes it, he should tip the scales at twenty-five stone, not his actual twelve, yet somehow he doesn't.

"I'm glad I tried it once, but after those dynamite sticks in the chicken I'm not sure I care to go back," said Harris.

"Oh, come on," I said. "You'll be telling stories about those peppers for the next five years." They wouldn't grow milder in the telling, either. Having braved them myself, I was already sifting phrases that might convey at least a trifle of their inflammatory nature.

"Where now?" asked George as we mooched along. The newsboy had a fresh edition of his paper. The headline on this one compared the old woman slain the night before to the Ripper's slightly less recent victims. Headline writers will compare anything to anything else if it makes readers part with pennies. A scribbler myself, I know whereof I speak.

Harris pointed. "That pub serves up a better than decent bitter. And, should we find ourselves peckish later, the steak-and-kidney pie is first rate." I don't frequent Limehouse; I felt myself slumming when we went there. So far as I can tell you, it's not one of Harris' usual haunts, either. How did he know, then? There is a mystical, even a magnetic, attraction between Harris and pubs: that is as much as I can say.

Three Men and a Werewolf

And the bitter *was* better than decent, and the steak-and-kidney pie everything steak-and-kidney pie should be. Chinese, Lascars, shaggy-bearded Russians, Armenians in peculiar caps, Scotsmen in different peculiar caps—the whole world stopped at that pub. George and Harris and I stopped there for quite a while.

When we came out, it had got dark. Not many gaslamps in Limehouse, I fear. But the sky had cleared, and the full moon, big and bright as a golden sovereign, shone in our faces. Then again, it had looked much the same the night before, until the clouds masked it and the showers started.

No sooner had I remarked on the similarity than George said, "It's the harvest moon, of course," in tones implying that anyone who didn't jolly well know it was the harvest moon had to be too great a ninny to live. Worse, he went on, "It has to do with the autumnal equinox, you see. The moon's eastward path across the heavens looks more nearly parallel to the horizon than at any other time of the year, so it rises only slightly later night by night. Almost the same phenomenon will occur a month from now—hunter's moon, the countryfolk name that one."

Harris and I gaped at each other, astonishment no doubt writ large across both our faces. George so seldom seems to know anything whatsoever, yet now we heard him discoursing learnedly of astronomy? "How on—or rather, above—earth…?" said Harris, beating me to the punch.

George coughed a couple of times and made a small production of lighting his pipe. After he'd got it going and tossed the lucifer to die a hissing death in the wet gutter, he answered, "I've made the acquaintance of a clever young lady who works as a computer at the Greenwich Observatory. I've learned a good deal from her."

"So it would seem," I said in portentous tones. "But what has she learned from you? Or is that a question better left unanswered?"

"Better left unasked, *I* should think," said Harris.

George glared from one of us to the other. He has a temper, George does; the moonlight was plenty to show the flush mounting to his cheeks…and to show his hands folding into large, knobby fists. Then, with what looked to be a deliberate effort of will, he relaxed them. "I nearly forgot what cuckoos the two of you are," he said, as if he were indeed reminding himself.

I was about to tell him that, however far the line of cuckoos should extend, he would always head it. I was about to tell him any number of witty and insulting things. I had them queued up on the tip of my tongue, ready to salvo one after another.

Then we heard the scream, and they all flew straight out of my head.

Anyone who lives in London will hear screams of startlement and rage. Anyone who visits the theatre will have heard screams purporting to be of terror. I have done more than visit the theatre; I have lived there. And I have heard a great many such screams. Never until that evening, though, did the genuine article show how counterfeit they were.

As any proper terrified scream should, it burst from a woman's throat. Queer how the fair sex's fright turns members of the unfair sex to tigers, isn't it? George, Harris, and I dashed towards the horrid noise without a second thought—or, as best I could tell, even a first. Had we thought, we surely would have run away from danger, not into it. Any animal surely would have. Great Scott! Perhaps George is human after all! Perhaps I am myself.

Running, I wondered whether the soiled doves the Ripper slew screamed like that, and yes, I wondered whether this was another one. (This also made me wonder whether a bad paper's headline writer knew what he was talking about, a flight of improbability I should have been incapable of under smaller stress.)

And I wondered what in blazes what we'd do when we got to where the scream came from—this, as we rounded a corner and tore into a dark, smelly alleyway. We still carried our umbrellas: their sails furled, as the night was fine. In my pocket I had a clasp knife with a two-inch blade suitable for despatching almost any infirm cockroach I might come across (oh yes, and with a corkscrew, in case I needed to bleed a wine bottle instead). My friends were similarly armed.

George struck a match. The dim, sputtering light showed—briefly—a huge, dark creature with slavering jaws all full of teeth crouched over a

Three Men and a Werewolf

motionless woman. Wolf? Man? Some unhallowed hybrid of the two? Before I could be sure, the blasted lucifer expired.

George's oaths were frightful things. Harris and I were yelling, too, as loudly as we could, as much to keep up our own courage as to intimidate the monster. It gave forth with a hideous snarl, for the moment balked of ripping the lungs from its defenseless victim.

"I'll teach you!" shouted Harris as George lit another lucifer. Its glow let me see Harris rushing at the great hairy thing (no, not George—the lupine one), his bumbershoot thrust out before him like a knight's lance in days of yore. I rushed after him, not that I felt much hope for either one of us.

This match died just as Harris and the creature came together. They both roared at the same time, Harris in something like triumph and the beast-man (to my amazement) in something like anguish.

Then I scratched my own match against the sole of my shoe, which luckily was not too damp to fire it. In the flickering flame, I saw Harris pulling his umbrella from the chest of a naked man—a man whose nakedness, and whose deceased status, made me need a moment to recognize as the diner who'd chopsticked his way through that plate of beef chow mein at Lee Ho Fook's eatery half a day (or was it half a lifetime?) earlier.

As the match went out, Harris said, "My brolly boasts a silver ferrule. I never looked to use it for a weapon against werewolves, but there you are. And there he is." He sounded almost as excited as he would have after squeezing the last trick from a difficult hand of bid whist.

"What about the lady?" I asked, though even then I suspected I was giving the female in question the benefit of the doubt.

There was a thump and a wriggle in the darkness as the woman pushed the werewolf's corpse—now in human form once more—off herself and scrambled to her feet. She gave forth with a passionate, consonant-clogged paragraph: Russian or Polish or some such tongue. When we could not answer in a language she understood, she darted out of the alley past us and disappeared into the night.

This time, Harris lit a lucifer. Staring down at the body, he murmured, "What on earth do we do now?"

"We take a powder, same as the gal did," answered George without a moment's hesitation. "Bobbies and law judges, all they'll see is a dead man. They'll clap us in straitjackets if we start babbling of werewolves. My own solicitor would have me committed if he heard me going on that way."

He hadn't finished before we were all hurrying to the alley's outlet. A plump man saw us in the moonlight and asked, "Did you hear a screech, like?"

"Not us," we chorused together, and decamped before he could decide to disbelieve us. Looking back over my shoulder, I saw him take one step towards the alleymouth and then visibly think better of venturing in by his lonesome.

Three days later, I discovered a small item on an inside page of the *Times*. *Warren Z. Wolfe, aged thirty-one, was founded stabbed to death in a Limehouse alley*, it read. *Robbery is suspected, as he was despoiled of his valuables down to the skin. The decedent was identified by a cook. He has no known kinfolk.*

I didn't mention the squib to my friends when next we foregathered. While neither George nor Harris spoke of it, something in their eye told me they'd seen it.

Harris raised his glass of cheer on high. "Here's to Three Men well out of the supernatural!" he said.

"Amen!" said George and I together, and the three of us drank the toast.

Topanga and the Chatsworth Lancers

S. M. Stirling and I have been friends for more than thirty-five years. We've bounced ideas off each other. We've put avatars of each other in our fiction; somebody based on me appears in Steve's Nantucket yarns, while somebody based on him is in my Timeline 191. So I jumped at the chance to set a story in his Emberverse universe, where electricity and gunpowder are only memories, and to locate it not far from where I live. Sierra's, the restaurant in this piece, sadly vanished in real life, is still going strong in this otherwise grim alternate world.

Jared Tillman sat in his front room, carefully winding up the phonograph. You had to feel how tight the spring was. It wasn't the original, but it wasn't new, either. One of these days, it *would* break. He just didn't want that day to be today. He felt like listening to music, not messing around inside the mechanism to install the most nearly matching spring he could pull out of his junk drawer.

As things went, the phonograph was modern. It probably dated from the early 1950s, made to be taken to picnics and parties where there was no power. That meant it could play 33-1/3 RPM records, instead of speeding them up to a shrill gabble the way an older player with settings only for 45s and 78s would have.

Where there was no power… Jared's mouth twisted. No power anywhere now, not these past thirty years. He scratched at his mustache and plucked out a hair. It was white. He let it fall to the ever more threadbare wall-to-wall carpeting. He'd been in his mid-twenties when the Change came. He remembered how things had been, and how he'd grown up in a different world.

Carefully, he set the needle on the record's outer grooves. The needle wasn't sharp. The record wasn't new, which was putting things mildly. The speaker was a cheap piece of junk. But Steely Dan—tinny, scratchy Steely Dan, but Steely Dan even so—filled the room in the house off Topanga Canyon Boulevard. Like the ruins that remained from before the Great Southern California Dieoff, it reminded him things hadn't always been this way.

"Shit, I didn't even *like* Steely Dan back then," he muttered. But you took what you could get. Bands he had liked, bands like Nirvana and Green Day, put their music out on CDs. These days, CDs were good for nothing but scaling through the air and for seeing rainbows.

Eucalyptus leaves dappled the sunlight that poured in through the west-facing windows. Eucalyptuses sent roots to the center of the earth to pull up what water they could. Along with olives and scrub oaks and pepper trees and a few hardy pines, they were what could grow in arid Topanga Canyon.

He'd grown up in the canyon. He was a second-generation hippie; his folks had moved here to join a commune, and never left. They'd sold candles and pots from a little shop, and sometimes pot on the side. There'd never been a lot of money, but there'd always been some. Enough, or close enough. They'd always said that, if you didn't sweat it, close to enough *was* enough.

And maybe they were right, and maybe they were wrong, and certainly they were dead. Old Doc Leibowitz gave Jared's mother statins and blood-pressure meds as long as he had them. She had a coronary a couple of years after he ran out, and that was that. A Topangan scavenged more from a Valley house not long afterwards. Someone else got help for a while, but not Mom. Dad… Dad had smoked tobacco as well as weed. Lung cancer would have been a bad way to go even with twentieth-century medicine. Without it… He smoked lots of weed, and as much opium as he could get, and died in less pain than he would have without them. And Jared's wife had hemorrhaged when Connor was born, and the doc and the midwife couldn't stop it.

Topanga and the Chatsworth Lancers

Muttering, Jared pulled a paperback off the shelf. *The Pocket Book of Ogden Nash* had been old even before the Change. Before too long, the cheap paper would crumble, but it hadn't yet. Paper made these days lasted longer, but there wasn't much of it. Ben Franklin would have understood post-Change printing just fine. Books sold across a continent for pocket change were as dead as everything else from the old days.

He found the poem he was looking for, not that he needed to: he'd long since memorized it. No great trick—"The Middle" was only four lines long. But seeing the words made him see the world the words came from. He remembered that world, ached for that world, with a terrible longing that would never go away and that would never do him any good.

Nine and a half million people lived in Los Angeles County when the Change came. They took water and food and electricity for granted—till all of a sudden the power and the internal-combustion engine disappeared. Most of the water came from hundreds of miles away, so it disappeared, too. The food arrived in trucks and ships with engines…till it didn't any more.

Some people tried to get to less crowded, wetter parts of the world on foot—or by bikes if they had bikes. Some hunkered down, trying to ride out what they hoped would be a temporary disaster.

Before the Change, Jared had read that the natural carrying capacity of the area was about a quarter of a million. About ninety-eight percent of the people had died either trying to escape or waiting for help that never came. His nose wrinkled as he remembered the stench that had filled the air for months.

Topanga was lucky, as places around here went when the Change hit. It was isolated and not too crowded. People were more used to doing for themselves than most Angelenos. Streams ran year-round, in good years anyhow. The canyon gave the Topangans an outlet on the sea, and another on the San Fernando Valley: a prime scrounging resource. And, being a canyon, it was defensible.

He read the poem again. It talked about remembering bygone days. The last two lines had the meat. *So many I loved were not yet dead*, Nash wrote. *So many I love were not yet born*. Yes, that was the truth, sure as hell. Any middle-aged person through all the history of mankind had been there. But, for his generation, the Change was The Middle. Reworking the poem, you could say *So much I loved was not yet dead.*

You could, but how much would it help? Steely Dan was singing about the Royal Scam. The song should have had a proper stereo system. *Yeah, and I should have a Mac and a modem*, Jared thought. People in hell were sure they should have mint juleps to drink.

They wouldn't get them. Jared wouldn't get his computer. No one under forty had any idea what the Internet was, or had been. The record would play as well as it played on this windup piece of junk. This was the way the world went on, not with a bang—explosives didn't work any more, either—but a whimper. Tough shit, Eliot.

Shoes scrunched on dead leaves and dry grass outside. Jared's mouth twisted again. Here was Connor, nineteen now and home from patrol. This brave new world was the only one he knew. He had all the answers—he was sure of it. At nineteen, who didn't? Fathers and sons had butted heads since the beginning of time. The Change, the chasm between Before and After, between who remembered and who didn't, only made things worse. And they said it couldn't be done…

OH, FOR Christ's sake! Connor Tillman shaped the words without saying them. His old man was listening to music again. That was always a bad sign. Whenever Dad started playing records, he fell as far back into what his generation called the Good Old Days as you could now.

Get over it, Pop. Connor didn't say that, either. He'd yelled it often enough when he and his father brawled. It was an easy rock to grab and hit with. The world was what it was. You had to roll with it. The Good Old Days were over. Finished. Done with. Done for. Kaput.

Connor was tempted to believe things couldn't have been all that great. He was tempted, yeah, but he couldn't. Too much remained behind that nobody now could or would match: everything from dead cars to the crumbling paved roads they'd run on to the incredible warren of empty houses and shops and who knew what that filled the Valley.

Even Connor's pants were pre-Change Levi's, patched at the knees and butt with leather. His boots and sleeveless leather vest and his broad-brimmed straw hat all belonged to here-and-now. But the zipper and copper rivets on the pants spoke of other times. And no one now made binoculars like the ones on the strap around his neck.

He turned the door knob. The lock had failed; a bar secured the door at night. The locksmith might have fixed it, but putting in the bar had been easier and cheaper. Dad did it himself. He *could* deal with the real world when he decided he wanted to.

"Hey," Connor said. Electric guitars sounded funny to him. No instrument that still worked was anything like them.

"Hey," Dad answered, nodding. His eyes were a million miles and a million years away. They always got like that when he started listening to records. With an obvious effort, he came back to the present. "How'd it go?"

Connor shrugged. "I climbed up to the high ground. Saw some rabbits and some quail and a coyote. Nothing got close enough for the blowgun." He had a green-painted aluminum tube on his back and a pouch of darts by the shortsword on his belt. "Oh, and there were a couple of deer way off in the distance. Nothing much going on on Old Topanga Road."

"Surprise!" Dad said. "There never was." Old Topanga Road ran into Topanga Canyon Boulevard from the west right here, where Topanga village lay. Even back before the Change, Old Topanga Canyon had been sparsely settled compared to Topanga Canyon proper.

"I know, I know," Connor said impatiently. "Gotta keep an eye on it, though. It's our back door, like. The Lancers have come that way before. Don't want 'em doing it again."

"Nope." Dad nodded again. "The Chatsworth goddamn Lancers! Is that funny, or what?"

"Not funny when you've fought them." Connor had a puckered scar on his left arm from a skirmish with the Lancers a couple of years before. That had been his first fight, and came too close to being his last.

"I've done it." Dad had a scar, too, an old pale white one, in almost the same spot as Connor's. "But still… When I was your age—"

"Spare me," Connor said. He'd heard Dad's rap too often. Back before the Change, when everything was wonderful and it was all one country, Chatsworth had been far enough out in the boonies that a lot of people there kept horses. Because they did, now they ruled the west end of the Valley. Petty lords in places as far away as Pacoima and Studio City had a healthy respect for their fighters. So did the Topangans. Chatsworth dreamt of conquering the canyon and reaching the Pacific. For Topanga, that dream was a nightmare.

"Right," Dad said tightly.

"What's to eat?" Connor asked. "I'm starved."

"Still some of the dried, salted grunion left," Dad answered. "Olives. Cheese. Oranges. The porridge is cold, but it still smells okay."

"Cool," Connor said. The porridge was beans and peas from the garden in what Dad still called the back yard, with garlic and onions and wild mushrooms thrown in for flavor. Boil it into mush, and it was…food. Connor'd been eating the same kinds of things his whole life. He took them for granted.

Dad had been eating this stuff even longer—ever since the Change. He let out a sigh, the way he did every once in a while. "What I wouldn't give for a Double Whopper with cheese, onion rings on the side, and a big old chocolate shake," he said, and sighed.

"Yeah, Pop," Connor said patiently. Chocolate was good, but he could count the times he'd tasted it on the fingers of one hand. Onion rings were fried. Who had oil to waste on such luxuries? Nobody in these parts, that was for sure. Olive oil and a little butter—that was about it. What didn't get eaten went into lamps…when there was any that didn't get eaten.

Connor fed his face. He was still a little hungry when he finished. Most people, at least in these parts, were a little hungry most of the time. His father stood just under six feet. His mom had been five-nine. He was barely that himself. Food had been something you took for granted when his folks were kids. There'd been times when the only meat in his stew came from the big green caterpillars that chewed up tomato vines. The scary thing was, they hadn't been too bad. Hunger made you not worry about such things.

The sun set not long after they finished. He and his father went to bed. No need for a blaze in the fireplace. It wouldn't get cold. It hardly ever got really cold, even in the winter. A blanket, maybe two on a bad night, and you were okay. You could easily starve or die of thirst. Millions of people around here had in the years before Connor was born. As far as he knew, though, not a single one of them froze.

SHERMAN'S HOOVES clopped dully on the faded, potholed asphalt as Bruce Delgado rode south down Topanga Canyon Boulevard toward the Ventura Freeway. Just past the freeway lay Ventura Boulevard. A couple of miles south of the Boulevard—a Valley phrase that had connoted money back in the day—his Chatsworth Lancers no longer ran things. The hippie freaks from Topanga took over.

Bruce scowled behind his catcher's mask. His armor wouldn't have made the SCA cream its jeans. Covering the rest of his head wasn't some blacksmith's finest creation. He wore a German helmet his grandfather'd brought back from Europe after World War II. Good luck making manganese steel like that these days! He'd sanded off the swastika decals. They would've given too many people the wrong idea of what the Lancers were all about.

Thick leather gauntlets covered his hands. His pre-Change work boots had steel toes. Greaves and armguards had started life as sheet metal on one dead car or another. His Kevlar flak jacket had steel under it, front and back. The shit had been bulletproof, but that didn't mean it would keep out arrows or sword points. Quite a few people had made their last dumb mistake trusting it too far.

Once upon a time, the aluminum tubing that formed the shaft of his lance would've had a broom on the end so some guy home from work could sweep the bottom of his pool. A blacksmith *had* forged the point topping the lance, and put a little lead in the other end to improve the balance. For now, the lance sat in a boss on the right side of his saddle. He was still well within Chatsworth territory; he didn't expect trouble.

He especially didn't expect trouble with four other Lancers along. Their armor, and that which covered their horses, was of the same catch-as-catch-can style as his own. *Something old, something new, something borrowed, something blue* ran through his mind. The rhyme fit, every bit of it: the nylon fabric covering his Kevlar was cop-uniform blue, somewhat faded now from years of sun.

They ambled past a long-dead 76 station. "You ever gas up here before the Change, Eddie?" he asked one of his comrades.

"Couple times, maybe," Eddie Epstein said. "I hadn't had my license long. How about you?"

"Same deal," Bruce said. He leaned forward and laid a hand on Sherman's neck. The gelding was named for the old tank. These days, a mounted lancer was the nearest equivalent. "Who woulda figured cars would crap out and horses'd be the real thing?"

"Not me, that's for goddamn sure," Eddie said. "I didn't give a rat's ass about 'em till the Change, I'll tell you that. We lived in Chatsworth 'cause my mom and my sis were horse people."

"My dad bred 'em—but he got the dough to buy 'em from his used-car lot," Bruce said. "Just goes to show you, don't it?"

The other three Lancers rolled their eyes. They were young bucks, born since the Change. Listening to old farts yatter on about bygone days bored the crap out of them. But they had the sense not to show it too much when one of the old farts was the ruler of the west end of the Valley and the second was his right-hand man.

West of the defunct gas station, some fig trees had been planted on ground cleared after the power died. They looked peaked. There wasn't enough water to keep them happy. There was barely enough water to keep the people who took care of them happy. Cisterns, catch basins in the concrete-bottomed L.A. River, using pipes and lining canals with old plastic sheeting wherever possible…

In dry years, none of it was quite enough. You got through as best you could. The Lancers and their kin and the warhorses had first call on what there was. The rest of the people took their chances and prayed for rain.

The freeway sat above the usual street level. A watchtower built atop it gave the Lancers a long look to the south. Semaphores—fire signals at night—could relay news north the half-dozen miles to Chatsworth proper in a matter of minutes. *As modern as last week*, Bruce thought sourly. But with radios and phones and even telegraphs dead as Stalin, it was the best system he'd been able to dream up.

He muttered to himself when he rode under the 101. He'd been starting high school when the Northridge quake rocked the Valley in '94. One of these years, a new one would bring down the overpass. If you happened to be below it just then…well, at least everything would be over in a hurry, anyhow.

A wagon pulled by a two-horse team came along Ventura Boulevard. Front and rear axles had been taken from a car. The wheels were wooden, with iron tires, and bigger than the old rubber tires would have been. The teamster on the wagon doffed his straw hat—not quite a sombrero, but close—to the Lancers.

Gravely, Bruce returned the salute. He demanded respect from his subjects. But you had to show you deserved it. He'd learned that playing Pop Warner football a million years ago. A coach who was an asshole might get the outward trappings of respect, but people would tell jokes about him behind his back. Bruce didn't want that happening to him. So when he got, he gave, too.

A couple of blocks south of Ventura lay what had been a shop that sold cameras and telescopes and binoculars. Some of its products extended the range of the signal towers. What had been the parking lot next to it was a field now. Opium poppies, redder and darker than their native cousins—which had been the state flower when California was a state—nodded in the breeze.

Pre-Change painkillers were hard to come by these days, and of uncertain worth. You fought pain any way you could; it was everybody's enemy.

The land to either side of the road rose as you got deeper into the canyon. The Valley's street grid disappeared; the little streets that branched off from Topanga Canyon Boulevard wandered every which way. The land got greener as the Valley floor gave way to the Santa Monica Mountains—not green, but greener.

Then the ground dropped away from the west of the main road, down a slope that had made many a drunk driver in the old days go *Oops!* or *Shit!* just before he hit bottom. Even on horseback—hell, even on foot—getting down there or back up again was a bastard and a half. No wonder the Topangans chose that Glenview stretch to hold as their frontier.

Well before he got there, Bruce held up a hand and reined in. The Lancers with him also stopped. The Topangans had a watchtower there. Somebody with binoculars or a spotting scope would be keeping an eye on them right now. The road was open—trade mattered to Chatsworth as well as to the hippies down the canyon. But the Topangans could close it in a matter of minutes, and have the closed stretch as strong as the rest of their works inside of an hour.

"So what you got in mind, boss?" Eddie asked. He figured Bruce had to have something on the fire.

"We can't go through 'em. It'd cost us too much. We've got to find some way to slide around 'em." Bruce had less in the way of a scheme than he wished he did. But he knew he was right about that. He had more people to draw on than the Topangans, but they would enjoy the defenders' advantage. They had catapults by their walls, too. They wouldn't just throw man-squashing boulders. They'd throw big pots full of pre-Change oil and gasoline: homemade napalm. If that stuff clung to you, you begged somebody to cut your throat. And you thanked him with your dying breath when he did it for you.

"Go down Old Topanga?" one of the younger Lancers suggested.

"We've tried it before, Garth," Bruce said. "It wouldn't be a surprise even if we hadn't. They're ready for it—and they hold the high ground."

Topanga and the Chatsworth Lancers

"You wouldn't have come all this way if you were just gonna do the peaceful coexistence thing," Garth Hoskins said.

All this way. They'd ridden maybe eight miles, and they'd ride back before the end of the day. With the horses walking, an hour and a half or so in each direction. Probably two hours on the way home—take it easy on the beasts in the heat of the afternoon. By modern standards, it *was* a long way. No hopping in the car now. Too bad.

But Garth wasn't wrong. He was only about five-seven, but he was built like a brick. When he wasn't practicing with sword and lance and axe and mace, he was pumping iron. He got off on exercise the way stoners got off on pot. He wasn't stupid, either. Not subtle, maybe, but not stupid.

He sure did have the post-Change view of distance, though. In Bruce, it still warred with what he'd known as a kid. He'd flown in an airliner. He'd seen the ground from six miles up. Garth never had. He never would.

"We've got to have the right approach," Bruce said. He might have been channeling his old man. Nacho Delgado had got rich unloading clunkers on suckers with bad credit. His son cared little about money. Power was a much headier drug as far as Bruce was concerned. He wanted that outlet on the Pacific so bad he could taste it. It would put the Valley back into direct touch with the rest of the world, make it a force to be reckoned with.

It would…if only the Topangans weren't in the way. They didn't want to follow his orders. They didn't want to follow anybody's orders. Rotten hippies! What were you supposed to do with people like that?

"We'll smash 'em for you, boss," Garth said confidently. "Just tell us what to do, and we'll take care of it."

Listening to him made Bruce feel good. Garth was a human pit bull. Point him at something and he'd bite chunks out of it for you. With enough guys like him at your back, you could really accomplish something. And if the hippies stood in your way, hey, that was just their bad luck.

Jared and Connor trudged north up Topanga Canyon Boulevard toward the Theatricum Botanicum, where the Topangans' assemblies had met since not long after the Change. The little outdoor theater held maybe three hundred people. Most of the time, that was plenty.

A redtail lazily circled overhead, peering down at the grassy hillsides in hopes of spotting a rabbit or a ground squirrel. A neighbor rode by on a bicycle. He lifted a hand from the handlebars to wave. "Hey, guys!" he called.

"Hey, Stu," Jared answered. Connor nodded. Stu pedaled on.

"Lucky bastard," Connor muttered once Stu was out of earshot. Jared nodded. Bicycle tires were something for which the Topangans had found no good replacement. Time and bad roads had done in most of the ones from before the Change. Jared and Connor had bikes that sat under tarps for lack of rubber. Connor went on, "Ought to go into the Valley and scavenge."

"The Happy Hunting Ground—if you're lucky," Jared said. The Valley was square mile upon square mile of houses and shops, almost all abandoned, almost all crumbling. Even this long after the Change, you could find almost anything there. Fancy booze, medicine, clothes from fabrics bugs wouldn't touch, bicycle tires, tools, books, spectacle lenses… You could, yeah. But— "The Lancers don't exactly love foreigners on their turf."

"Fuck 'em. In the neck," Connor said.

"That's what they want to do to us," Jared said. "That's what the assembly's about. Bruce is cooking something up."

"We ought to have spies up there so we'd know what's going on," Connor said.

"My guess is, we do," Jared answered. The Valley was a big place. You could be inconspicuous there. In Topanga, strangers stood out more.

"Yeah, but they'd have to do, like, what Bruce's stooges told 'em to most of the time, wouldn't they?" Connor might have been describing the ultimate perversion. Chances were, he thought he was.

"If we aren't careful, we'll all have to do what Bruce's stooges tell us all the time," Jared said dryly.

Topanga and the Chatsworth Lancers

"In his dreams!" Connor exclaimed. He didn't really grok that some people *did* dream that way, and that some of the dreamers made others dream along with them. Bruce Delgado was one of those. He wasn't a monster like that guy up in the Northwest sailors had talked about in the early post-Change years. He was only—only!—a hard-nosed, power-hungry SOB. Whether that made him less dangerous or more was an interesting question, but not one today's assembly would debate.

At the grounds to the Theatricum Botanicum, juncos hopped under the shade of small-leaved pepper trees, pecking for seeds and bugs. They were winter birds in most of Southern California, but lived here year-round. Jays screeched in the branches above them. More trees gave some shade to the theater itself. The bench space under the shadows went first; Jared and Connor had to sit in the sun. Jared had long since quit worrying about melanoma. His son might never have heard of it. They were both tan as leather. Something else—quite possibly, one of Bruce's stooges—would kill them before skin cancer mattered.

The five men in folding chairs on the stage were called the Brains when they were called anything at all. Topangans distrusted every kind of authority. That was a big part of what made them Topangans. They sometimes saw the need for it, though. Somebody had to keep a handle on dealing with the Chatsworth Lancers.

Pete Reilly looked at his watch. It was, of course, a rude mechanical, adjusted every so often by gauging noon from the shortest shadow. "Well, let's get this show on the road," he said. He was the Brainiest Brain of all. He'd landed an engineering slot at UCLA the year before the Change came. That he could think in numbers made him unusual, and unusually useful, in what had been one of the touchy-feely capitals of the world till the Change forced a certain pragmatism on everyone who managed to live through it.

He nodded to Kwame Curtis, who sat to his right. As a very young Marine lieutenant, Curtis had lost three fingers from his left hand in Iraq. He wasn't young any more. He was the Brain who worried about military matters.

"They're going to try something," he said flatly. "We've got to find out what. We don't know yet. But something. Our boys at the wall spotted Bruce looking us over. He doesn't do that shit for the fun of it."

His deep voice held an odd mix of scorn and worry. Once upon a time, he'd been a professional soldier. Bruce Delgado was very much an amateur. But Bruce was a shrewd amateur, and he had a lot more men and resources at his disposal than Curtis did.

"What would you do if you were trying to get rid of us?" Reilly asked.

Curtis' medium-brown face twisted into a scowl. "Drop a match in the woods when the wind was right and hope he could come by three days later and stick apples in our mouths after we roasted."

"Christ!" Jared muttered. Beside him, his son nodded. Jared had feared fires long before the Change. No more chemical-dropping airplanes. No more fire engines. Hell, no more fire departments. No more water mains. Nothing but hand pumps and picks and shovels and prayer.

Reilly nodded as if the answer were no surprise. No doubt it wasn't. The Brains would have worked this out ahead of time. "How are the firebreaks?" he asked Connie Wong.

The only female Brain brushed graying bangs back from her eyes. "Bad," she answered. "We have so many things to do just to stay alive from day to day, we don't put enough work into the stuff we need maybe once every twenty years."

People were supposed to spend a couple of hours a week in the woods, cutting brush and knocking down saplings to keep fire from getting a running start. Jared knew he and Connor hadn't gone out there anywhere near so often as they should have.

"We'll have to start taking better care of that," Reilly said. Heads in the Theatricum Botanicum bobbed up and down. Whether that would translate into work… They were Topangans. Organization and discipline didn't come naturally to them.

"We have to do something else, too," Kwame Curtis said.

"What's that?" Reilly asked, as he was no doubt meant to do.

Topanga and the Chatsworth Lancers

"We have to let him know that we understand about mutually assured destruction. If he plays with fire, we'll play with fire, too," Curtis said savagely. "The Santa Anas blow things down onto Chatsworth, same as they do with us. If he wants to fight a war, we'll fight a war. If he wants to burn us out, does he think we can't get around him and light up the Santa Susana foothills? He better not!"

Pete Reilly nodded. "I could say I don't want to give him ideas, but that one's too obvious. He's bound to have it already. He needs to know he's not the only one who can play that game. If the Lancers lose their horses, they won't be able to boss the Valley around any more, and all the ranches are up at the north end, near the Santa Susanas." He looked out at the assembly. "Any volunteers to go bell the cat?"

Jared's hand rose, almost of its own accord. "I'll do it," he said. "The message is pretty simple. And it'll be interesting to see what the Valley looks like these days. I haven't been up there for a long, long time."

"This is better," Reilly said.

"Sure it is." Jared nodded without even thinking. He'd grown up an American. He was a Topangan patriot now, though. "But I'll see what they're selling, too. They've got a lot more stuff to scrounge through than we do."

"Have any money?" Reilly asked, his voice dry. Topanga was small enough that it mostly ran on barter. The Valley wasn't.

But Jared nodded. "Yeah, some." Gold and silver were always good. So were pre-Change metal-sandwich coins. No one now could make anything like them. The metal might not be precious, but the package was.

"Okay, go for it," the big Brain told him. "And check out how things are. If we can stir up trouble for Bruce from his own people, he'll stay too busy to give us grief."

"I'll do it," Jared said.

That seemed to settle the meeting. As the crowd filed out of the Theatricum Botanicum, Connor said, "I want to come, too." He sounded like a small-town kid who longed to see the big city. The way things were these days, that was about what he was.

"Let's see what Pete says," Jared answered. The idea of having his headstrong son along didn't thrill him. Neither did the idea of quarreling with Connor. If he could say no and blame it on someone else, he had the best of both worlds.

Because they were ambassadors, Jared and Connor rode horses out of Topanga and into the lands the Chatsworth Lancers called their own. Pete Reilly, blast him, hadn't minded Connor coming along. Jared hadn't learned to ride till he was an adult. He could do it, but feared his clumsiness showed. Connor took horses for granted. He wasn't betwixt and between in the post-Change world the way his old man was.

They hadn't gone far north of the fortified frontier before a couple of men with strung bows came out of what had been a State Farm office back in the days when there were such things as State Farm offices. They had quivers on their backs, but didn't bother nocking arrows. "What's happening, dudes?" one of them called.

"We've got a message for your boss from Topanga," Jared answered.

"Oh, yeah? What kind of message?"

"One for your boss," Jared repeated—pointedly enough, he hoped, to get the point across but not to piss off the archer.

He must have gauged it about right. The man frowned, but said, "Well, go on up to Chatsworth Boulevard and turn right for a couple blocks. He's, like, at home, far as I know. You know where Chatsworth Boulevard's at?"

"Past Devonshire. Yeah." Jared had studied a Thomas Brothers road atlas before setting out. His memory of Valley streets was old, old, old.

"You got it. Awright, go ahead."

Ahead they went. The farther up Topanga Canyon Boulevard they rode, the wider Connor's eyes got. "Buildings fucking everywhere," he said in a low voice. He stared east, toward the mountains. "Do they go all the way there?" He pointed to show what he meant.

Topanga and the Chatsworth Lancers

"They sure do," Jared said. "More than a million people used to live in the Valley. Most of them are just bones now, but still…"

"People throw those big numbers around. They don't mean squat. Then you see—this." Connor shook his head in wonder. "Where do the ones who are left get their food?"

"Here and there, around the edges and in what used to be parks and torn-up parking lots like the ones we've seen," Jared answered. "Not a million people now. Say, twenty or thirty thousand. That's a lot next to Topanga, but it would've been a small town before the Change."

"So what are we?" Connor asked. "Ghosts rattling around inside all that stuff they built?"

Now that you mention it, Jared thought, *yes.* Topanga didn't prompt such gloomy reflections. Topanga had always been way the hell out in the boonies. Being out in the boonies and built to human scale was the whole point to Topanga. Long before the Change, someone had written of Los Angeles, *The future is here—and it's coming to get you.* That future might be past now, but it sure left a big corpse.

Men with picks broke up the asphalt on what had been a parking lot in front of a Ralphs supermarket. Men with wheelbarrows hauled away the rubble. No one moved very fast, not on a hot day like this. Deadlines were, well, dead. Sooner or later, the work would get done. If not today, tomorrow. If not tomorrow, the day after. *Mañana.*

As Jared and Connor came to the north end of the Valley, things began opening out again. There were empty lots that looked as if they'd been empty since before the Change. The vineyards and half-grown olive trees came from after the Change. Wine from these parts would probably be crappy, but even the nastiest plonk, as Jared had reason to know, beat hell out of no wine at all.

A little naked blond boy with a stick watched chickens pecking under the olives. Jared smiled; he could have seen the same kind of thing in Topanga. "This looks more like home," he remarked.

"It's too wide," Connor answered. The Valley was a valley, yeah, but a big valley. Topanga Canyon was, and looked like, a canyon. Jared's son went on, "I feel like a bug on a plate."

Jared had the same feeling. There were mountains on the horizon, but you could tell that horizon lay a long way away. He wondered how he would do somewhere like Kansas or Nebraska, where all you could see was miles and miles of miles and miles. Not too well, was his best guess. But, while he was more likely to end up in the Midwest than in, say, Tibet, he wasn't much more likely, so he didn't waste time worrying about it.

"This has to be Chatsworth Boulevard," he said after a while. They swung the horses down the narrower road. Calling it a boulevard didn't make it one. Houses sat on big lots. Horses grazed. Knights—Chatsworth Lancers—practiced with spear and sword. Archers sent arrows whistling toward far-off bales of straw. Men wrestled under the shade of trees. When war was personal again, training was like paying life-insurance premiums.

Just past the first street east of Topanga Canyon Boulevard, they rode up to a house set well back from the road. A tough-looking fellow opened a gate in the rusty chain-link fence fronting Chatsworth Boulevard. "You the Topangans?" he asked. When Jared and Connor nodded, the man went on, "Semaphore said you were on your way. Well, c'mon in. The boss wants to hear what you got to say."

BRUCE DELGADO scowled at the men from Topanga. One was older than he was, the other plainly a chip off the old guy's block. "You're telling me how I can fight a war?" Bruce growled—Eddie and Garth were listening, so he had to sound tough. "You got your nerve."

The older Topangan—Jared Tillman—shook his head. "That's not what I said," he answered. "I'm telling you what we'll do *if* you set fires. If you don't, we won't. We think fires are a nasty way for anybody to fight."

As a matter of fact, Bruce thought the same thing. That didn't necessarily mean he wouldn't do it. Plenty of weapons were nasty but effective. The military-history books filling the shelves of his study showed that all too well.

Topanga and the Chatsworth Lancers

He spread his hands now, and sipped from a glass of brandy. His henchmen had their own, and he'd given the Topangans some, too. The kid had drunk most of his. The older man had sense enough to go easy. Oh, well. It had been worth a try.

Leaning forward, he said, "You think you can sneak firebugs past my patrols? Good luck!"

"You think you can stop us if we try?" Jared Tillman returned. "Good luck to you."

There was a bluff called. Eddie clucked sadly. People in the Valley—in all of Southern California—were too thin on the ground for patrols to do much good. Moving at night, holing up in empty buildings (and how many zillion were there to hole up in?) by day, the Topangans almost surely *could* get up into the hills north of what had been the 118 Freeway. Wait till the winds started blowing, pour the oil, drop the matches… It could work.

"We're not even fighting," Bruce protested, again hoping he could sound as sincere as his father getting a lemon off the lot.

"I hope we don't," Jared Tillman said. "But you people have been scoping us out for a while now. Maybe you think that even though it didn't work the last couple of times, it will now. We're ready—that's the biggest part of what I've got to say, aside from talking about fire."

He made more sense than Bruce wished he did. But the Chatsworth Lancers had to use their army every now and then. Just having it wasn't good enough. An army that sat around or rode herd on peasants all the time started crumbling. It was like a football team that practiced endlessly without ever playing a game.

The other thing, of course, was that when you had an army and didn't use it, somebody else would stab you in the back and take it for a spin himself. Somebody like Garth, say. Bruce didn't think Garth was disloyal—the pup would have had an accident by now if he did. But somebody like him. Somebody who hadn't fought in several wars and didn't know there was no such thing as an ironclad guarantee, double your money back, for victory.

Bruce wondered if Tillman was delivering his warning not least to stir up that kind of trouble among the Lancers. He wouldn't be the only one who kept an eye on the past to guide him through the present. The Topangans were dopers, yeah, but not dopes. They knew what kind of position they held, and they knew how to defend it.

He had to answer the hippie, and in a way that wouldn't turn his own men against him or make them think he'd gone soft. "We'll do what we do," he said, his voice as harsh as he could make it. "You do what you do, and we'll see who comes out on top in the end."

"It doesn't have to be an I-win-you-lose kind of game, you know," Jared Tillman said sadly. "Can't we do better than that? How many million died, just in this county, when the Change came? Do we still have to do all the same stupid shit they did in the old days?"

"Are we not men?" It wasn't philosophy—it was a Devo song you still heard on the radio when Bruce was a kid. Or maybe it was a Devo song and philosophy both. "You think human nature's changed? That would take more than what we went through more than thirty years ago."

"You know what? I'm afraid you're right," the Topangan said. "You know what else? It's a goddamn shame. Okay. Do your worst, and we'll do our best—"

"Your worst, you mean." Bruce knew stolen Churchill when he heard it, and he wouldn't let Jared Tillman get away with that. "Like you wouldn't jump us, start inching into the Valley, if you saw the chance. Yeah, right. Tell me another one."

He didn't look at Jared's face. He looked at Connor's. Sure as shit, the kid dreamt of empty houses and offices and shops to plunder. The Valley wasn't Egypt, dry enough to preserve things for thousands of years. But it hadn't been thousands of years. It had only been thirty. Plenty of stuff from the old days, the great days, was still good, still undiscovered, just waiting for tomb raiders smart enough or lucky enough to grab it.

Like me. Bruce jerked a thumb at the door. "Go on. Beat it. You said what you had to say. Now the time for talking's done. Now it's time for doing."

Topanga and the Chatsworth Lancers

They left. He sat in his fancy office chair, thinking hard. He wondered if he could find enough people to cut a big firebreak through the brush on the other side of the freeway. Not without regret, he decided he probably couldn't, not if he wanted to eat through the winter. Subsistence sucked, when you got right down to it.

He remembered the days when poor people had been fat. If you were fat now, you were either rich, rich, rich or you had something wrong with you. People worked a lot harder than they had when machines did the tough jobs for them. They had less to show for it, too. No wonder they weren't fat. The wonder was that they were here at all.

Too damn bad the Topangans were here. With a little luck, before too long they wouldn't be any more.

Jared and Connor rode south down De Soto, a mile or two east of Topanga Canyon Boulevard. Jared wanted to see more of the Chatsworth Lancers' domain than the chief thoroughfare. A dead McDonald's sat at the corner of De Soto and Devonshire. Actually, it wasn't quite dead: kids played on the slides and crawled through the translucent plastic tubes, squealing the way they had before the Change. Jared had scorned the Golden Arches then. To him, they'd been a big part of what was wrong with America at the end of the twentieth century.

What was wrong with America a good way into the twenty-first century was a lot more obvious. It had nothing to do with French fries and burgers the consistency of hockey pucks. The grease, the salt, the yum…

The salt… "You know," Jared said thoughtfully, "if the Lancers attack us and we win, we ought to stop selling them sea salt for a while, see how they like that."

"What's so special about sea salt?" Connor asked.

"It's got iodine in it," his father answered. Just because electricity and internal combustion and explosives were gone, that didn't mean knowledge was. People couldn't use it all any more—but they still could use some. "Without iodine, people get goiters." He put a hand to the base of his neck to show what he meant. "They get stupid, too—not real, real stupid, but stupid. It used to be a big deal. Then they put iodine in everybody's salt, and it wasn't. Since the Change, it is again, unless you live near the ocean."

"They could probably get it from one of those far-off places—Santa Monica, or even Long Beach," Connor said. "They'd have to pay through the nose, though." He smiled, liking the idea.

Jared also liked it. He wasn't sure Pete Reilly would; he didn't know how much Topanga made from selling its larger neighbor sea salt. Well, if the Lancers attacked—and if they lost—he could bring it up.

One of the street signs at the corner of De Soto and Vanowen still stood. Seeing it made Jared guide his horse north, which he hadn't intended to do till he got to Ventura Boulevard. Just on the off chance… Connor came with him. He could see they were heading back toward Topanga Canyon Boulevard.

Shouting kids played soccer on a vacant lot that likely hadn't been vacant when the Change came. The way the grass grew suggested the shape of a vanished building. Chances were some long-ago fire took it down. It must have been a calm day, or more would have burnt. Soccer was finally conquering the remains of America. All it needed was a ball and a couple of goals, and you could mark those off with rocks if you didn't even have posts and a crossbar. This wasn't the kind of soccer that would take anyone to the World Cup, but there was no World Cup any more, so who cared?

The next good-sized street north of De Soto was Canoga. As the Topangans neared the corner of Vanowen and Canoga, a slow grin spread across Jared's face. "I'll be damned," he said. "It *is* still here! C'mon—we'll stop and get some food."

"Okay by me," Connor said.

Sierra's, the sign announced in script, and, under that and in smaller letters, *Since 1959*. The red-brown paint and the white background were just the way Jared remembered, and just as neat—it had obviously been touched

Topanga and the Chatsworth Lancers

up several times since he last ate here. One or two light bulbs remained in their sockets after all these years, useless nowadays except maybe for swank.

Most of the old parking lot was a vegetable garden now. The people who ran the place had put big windows in the east-, south-, and west-facing walls. Sierra's had been a dark place before, even in the daytime. That didn't work so well now. The hitching rail and trough in front of the door were new. Jared and Connor let their horses drink a little, tied them up, and gave them feedbags before going inside.

"Welcome, strangers," said a gray-haired Hispanic man in a leather apron.

"I'm no stranger," Jared said, "even if I haven't been here since 1997 or so."

"Welcome anyway," the gray-haired man said. "I was here then, too, working for my father. What brings you back after so long?"

"I'm up from Topanga with my son here," Jared answered. "I thought I'd see if the place was still around—and here you are."

"Here we are," his host agreed. "Well, come in, sit down, and get something to eat. First drink is on the house."

The beer wasn't Dos Equis, the way it would have been. It was homebrew, like all beer these days—good homebrew, though. Choice of meat in the tacos and enchiladas was pork or chicken. Jared wasn't sure it all tasted the way he remembered, but it tasted like Mexican food from a place you'd want to come back to. Both meals came to two dollars. Prices weren't what they had been before the Change. Jared set a dozen sandwich quarters on the table.

"You're too kind," the gray-haired man murmured as he scooped up the money.

"Worth it," Jared said. "Eating here makes me feel like I'm my son's age." He clicked his tongue between his teeth. "Been a few changes since then, though."

"*Sí, Señor*, just a few," his host agreed gravely. "In the kitchen, for instance. No gas stove now. No running water, either. But we keep going on. What else can we do?"

"We're lucky if we can do that much." Jared got to his feet. So did Connor, a beat later. "Way too many people didn't."

"*Sí, Señor,*" the other survivor repeated. "Where do you go now?"

"Back to Topanga," Jared said. "But you can bet I'll come again the next time I head north—say, after your country and mine fight another war."

"It will be a shame if they do." The gray-haired man clicked his tongue between his teeth. "Topanga. Another country. Who would have imagined *that* when we were young and one flag flew from sea to shining sea?"

"Not me. Not you, either. We've got it anyway. Stay well, friend." With a nod, Jared walked out. His son followed. They swung up onto their horses and headed for their home in that other country.

THERE WERE trails through the Santa Monica Mountains. Back before the Change, this had been the Santa Monica Mountains Recreational Area. The way Connor's father and the other old farts told it, people who worked in offices in the Valley and the rest of L.A. drove in cars to the edge of the mountains and then hiked for the fun of it.

Those trails were mostly overgrown now. That they were there at all, though, argued that the old farts weren't just blowing smoke. Connor didn't grok it. Why would you hike for the fun of it? Hiking was work, often hot, sweaty work. Few things you had to do seemed like fun. Most of the time, he had to get from hither to yon on foot.

He was patrolling north and east of the village of Topanga, near Eagle Spring. He wanted to fill his canteen at the spring. Most years, water flowed even through the dry season. Here at the end of summer, it wouldn't be a lot, but he didn't need a lot. He didn't have to have any—the canteen wasn't empty—but he wanted to top up when he got the chance.

Faint in the distance, horns bleated. He cocked his head to one side, gauging the direction. Sure as hell, that racket came from Glenview, where Topanga kept its border with the Valley. "Shit," Connor muttered. The Chatsworth Lancers were attacking after all. They wouldn't blow the alarm for anything less important.

Topanga and the Chatsworth Lancers

Or was it a fire? He scanned the horizon, or the limited part of it he could see. No plumes of smoke jumping into the sky. The Lancers, then. He wanted to run back to the village and join up with his father to fight off the invaders. He wanted to, but he didn't. His orders were to stay on patrol even if the fighting started. Compared to the Topangans, Bruce Delgado had men falling out of his ass. He might use some to distract with a big, showy fight while others cornholed the canyon from behind.

Connor got to the spring. After he filled the aluminum bottle, he splashed water on his face and arms. It wasn't savagely hot, the way the weather could get this time of year, but it was warm. The water felt good. He took a few steps down the trial to the east, then froze. Somebody was coming the other way.

Quite a few somebodys were coming, as a matter of fact. They weren't making a lot of noise, not any one of them, but they weren't tiptoeing along, either. You couldn't very well tiptoe in country like this. And they were talking among themselves, the way people will just because they're people.

Connor flopped down behind some bushes near the trail. He put a dart in his blowgun and set several more on the ground beside him so he could reload in a hurry with minimum motion. He wanted to make as much trouble as he could, then bug out. The blowgun was the right weapon for that. It was silent and next to invisible. If only it had more range!

When you're nineteen, though, you don't really believe anything bad can happen to you. Not by accident do very young men fill out armies. Here came the soldiers from the Valley. They were on foot and not especially looking for trouble. The guy at the front had what looked like a page torn from a pre-Change road atlas. Peering down at it, he said, "Looks like we're coming to a spring."

"Good deal," said someone right behind him. "I'm dry."

They were within twenty-five yards. Connor took a deep breath, aimed, and blew. The business end of his dart was a tenpenny nail. It caught the guy in the lead right between the eyes. He went down on his face.

"The fuck?" said the Valley man behind him. Then he fell over, too. Connor got him square in the right eye. That was fool luck, and he knew it.

"What's wrong with those assholes?" another soldier asked, and bent down to see. He had his helmet slung on his belt so his brains wouldn't bake as he tramped along. They got punctured instead. Connor put the dart an inch or two behind his ear. Down he went, grabbing at his head.

Which was pressing things as far as they'd be pressed. Connor did his best snake impression to slither away. He left his blowgun and the other darts he'd set out. He'd already done more damage than he'd expected. As soon as he got in back of a reasonably thick tree, he scrambled to his feet and ran like hell. The Valley soldiers were still milling around by their fallen buddies. Every second they gave him was like a lifeline.

Then one of them yelled, "There goes the hippie freak!" That wasn't how Connor thought of himself, but the Valley guys wouldn't be in any mood to discuss semantics. They'd want to kill him, fast or maybe slowly.

Wheet! That was an arrow whistling by. Arrows could kill you from a lot farther away than darts could, and Connor didn't even have the blowgun any more. He didn't feel so brave any more, either. All of a sudden, this wasn't a game or an adventure. They were playing for keeps. He had to play the same way. If he won, he'd get to keep his life.

Thunk! That was another arrow, this one slamming into a tree. He ran harder than ever. He knew the trail better than they did, and some parts of it took a good deal of knowing. But some of the bastards behind him would be faster than he was, damn them. And if he tripped over a root and landed on his face, it was all over but the shrieking.

Whatever fickle gods there were doled out a little more luck for him. The one who tripped and did a faceplant was the fastest Valley soldier. The two men on his heels fell over him, too. By the way they yelled, they'd busted ankles or dislocated shoulders or maybe even both. *Hope it's nothing trivial*, Connor thought, stealing a phrase from his father.

It was a little more than a mile back to the village. Connor somehow kept ahead of the cursing Valley soldiers chasing him. Because he was literally running for his life, he had an incentive they didn't.

And he caught one more break when he got to Topanga village. The men from the Valley could have torn it up in spite of his arriving ahead of them, only a detachment from Fernwood farther down the canyon was on its way north to the fight at Glenview, the only one it knew about.

"The Lancers are coming! The Lancers are coming!" Connor wheezed, making like Patrick Henry or Paul Revere or whoever that guy back in the old days had been.

"Say what?" demanded the man in charge of the little contingent from Fernwood.

Connor pointed in the direction from which he'd come. The sun glinted off the helmets and shields of the Valley men. If that didn't get the message across, he had no idea what would.

"Holy shit!" said the Fernwood commander, so evidently it did. He pointed in the general direction of Eagle Spring, too. "Come on, boys!" he yelled. "We've got this to take care of before we go on to the other. Fred, you head on up to the mouth of the canyon and let 'em know we'll be late."

"I'll do it," Fred said, and took off up Topanga Canyon Boulevard. The rest of the Fernwood men drew swords and slung bows and ran toward the houses on the east side of the road. If you were going to fight, fighting from cover beat the hell out of doing it any other way.

Connor trotted back to the east, too. Now he drew his shortsword—he hadn't had time to worry about it before. He wondered if he was too tired to fight. Then he realized he had to be fresher than the Valley men.

Arrows whistled by, going in both directions. One of them pierced a fighter from the Valley about halfway between the pit of his stomach and his belly button. He folded up like a concertina, clutching at himself. The screams that burst from his throat had nothing to do with language. They were animal sounds of agony. They made Connor's stomach want to turn over. Anywhere on the trail back from Eagle Spring, he might have made noises like that. Oh, the arrow that got him would have gone in from back to front, but that wouldn't have changed the kind of shrieks he let out.

Brandishing his shortsword, he rushed at a Valley man. The other fellow, similarly armed, traded a few strokes with him. Neither of them got home on the other, though Connor had to leap back at the last instant to keep a thrust from shish-kebabing him.

The Valley man didn't press his advantage. His comrade's anguished howls seemed to unsettle him worse than Connor. He must have decided that fighting somebody, anybody, even a little bit satisfied his honor. Now that he'd done it—and now that he'd discovered he and his friends weren't taking the village by surprise, the way they must have hoped—he seemed content to fall back into the brush and woods again.

Connor wasn't all that thrilled about chasing him. The Valley men could stage some kind of ambush, and they might come out on top with it. The Fernwood detachment didn't go charging into the undergrowth, either. They'd made sure the village was okay and would stay that way, which was plenty for them.

"Look at the gutless wonders skedaddle!" a Topangan whooped. "They won't stop till they get back up to the Valley!" Connor hoped the man was right. He thought he was. This prong of Bruce Delgado's attack hadn't worked. Maybe the men would be able to get to Glenview and help the Lancers. But weren't they more likely just to give it up as a bad job?

Up on the crest above the village to the west, a semaphore tower's arms began to wigwag. With luck, the towers would take news of the attack and its failure to the defenders at Glenview. Maybe somebody up there would be paying attention. Or maybe everybody would be too goddamn busy trying to keep the Lancers from breaking through.

A Topangan came up to the gutshot Valley fighter. He knelt and asked him something, probably *Do you want us to try to patch you up or just to get it over with?* When he drew his belt knife and slit the other man's throat, Connor knew what kind of answer he'd got.

Suddenly, Connor realized he'd killed three men himself. He swallowed bile again, even though the screams were gone. That blowgun was good for something besides bagging rabbits and doves for the pot. He wouldn't have wanted a big old nail driven hard into *his* head.

There was something in the Bible about that, but he couldn't remember what. Maybe he'd look it up when he got the chance. He was glad his father'd taught him to read. It was a good way to kill time when nothing else was going on. It was even useful every now and then, though it wasn't such a big deal as it would have been before the Change.

He hoped Pop was okay. Right this minute, all he could do was hope.

"Let 'er go!" the boss of the trebuchet crew shouted.

Jared sprang away from the windlass, along with all the others who'd been raising the heavy counterweight. Down it thumped. Up flew the long throwing arm. Away went the hundred-pound boulder from the leather pouch at the end of the arm. It flew through the air with the greatest of ease. The Chatsworth Lancers and their friends on foot all did their best not to be under it when it came down a quarter of a mile away.

A quarter of a mile… That was about the best you could do without explosives to help. "Crank it up, boys!" the crew boss yelled. "Shoulder to shoulder, we'll fling another boulder, and fight for the town we adore!"

"Stick a sock in it, Ronnie!" That wasn't Jared, but only because somebody else came out with it first. Ronnie, predictably, went on singing. If he couldn't inspire his men into action, he'd annoy them into it.

Jared didn't know how much the counterweight weighed. A ton or two, anyhow. The men wrestling it up again with the windless sweated and strained and swore. This was the kind of hard physical labor that would give you a coronary if you sat around on your middle-aged duff all day.

But, post-Change, who sat around on his middle-aged duff all day? There was always gardening and chopping wood and hunting rabbits and simply walking anywhere you needed to go. No hopping in the car to visit the store two blocks away. Cars were metal mines, nothing more. There wasn't so much food these days, either, and what there was had less fat. Doc Leibowitz said he saw far fewer heart attacks and strokes than he had just after he got his M.D.

A good thing, because he couldn't do much for the ones he did see. Yes, knowledge survived. Drugs mostly didn't. And no gauging pulses past a stethoscope and a watch and a trained index finger. No EKGs. No X-rays. He had ether, sometimes, and brandy for a disinfectant. You were better off if you didn't get sick or badly hurt. Doc Leibowitz was the first to admit it.

Which meant you were smarter not going to war. Unfortunately, that wasn't an option. Jared's sword banged on his hip as he heaved at the windlass. His helmet and shield lay close by, along with his comrades' gear. If the Chatsworth Lancers broke through, they'd do what artillerymen always did when things went south: fight as hard as they could till they bought a plot.

"Boy, this is fun," Jared grunted, straining to raise the weight a little more with every yank.

"As a matter of fact," said one of the other sweaty, smelly men doing the same thing, "no. How many men do the fucking Lancers have, anyway?"

"Too many," Jared said, which was always the right answer. The Valley would always have a big lead in manpower. Topanga's advantage lay in geography. Fortify the narrow place and hang on tight—that was Topanga's strategy. "Where are the clowns from Fernwood? Shouldn't they be here by now?"

"Didn't you hear?" the other man said in surprise. "They'll be late if they show at all. There's some kind of dustup back at Topanga village."

"Shit," Jared said. "No, I didn't hear that." Connor was out patrolling down there. Jared had to hope his son was okay.

A couple of shoving, swearing men loaded another boulder into the leather sling. "We ready?" Ronnie asked. When nobody denied it, he shouted, "Let 'er go!" Away flew the stone.

It smashed a man to pieces coming down. Crimson sprayed in all directions. There were worse ways to go—he would never have known what hit him. Even so… A lifetime of hope and love and rage, all done before the poor sap knew the bell tolled for him this time.

But armored men on foot were banging away at the wall with a battering ram. Others protected them with heavy shields. It wasn't quite a Roman *testudo*, but it came close. If they broke through… *Houston, we have a problem*. Jared scowled. He hadn't been born the last time men went to the moon. All he'd done was see *Apollo 13* with a cute girl named Gail. They wouldn't

Topanga and the Chatsworth Lancers

fly to the moon again, not unless the laws of nature changed once more. They wouldn't make any more movies, either, dammit.

The Lancers hung back, waiting to see if they could push through a breach. They couldn't force one themselves. But they could exploit one if it came.

Two Topangans ran down the wall toward the men on the ram with a big kettle of hot oil or hot water or something else unfriendly. An arrow from the Chatsworth side hit one of them in the neck. The Topangan let out a bubbling shriek. Blood poured from the wound, and from his mouth and nose. He staggered and clutched at himself, forgetting what he carried. The kettle tilted and spilled. The other guy who was hauling it also shrieked, on a high, pure, thin note. So did fighters on both sides who got splattered by the horrible stuff.

Jared felt like shrieking himself. Burns were the worst thing that could happen to you these days. About the best treatment Doc Leibowitz had for them was tannic acid—tea, in other words. It had been horribly outmoded at the end of the twentieth century. There'd been a state-of-the-art burn center in the Valley then. But the Change set the state of the art back most of a hundred years. The guy who'd got shot was the lucky one. He'd peg out pretty fast. The other burned warriors would hurt and hurt for a long time.

And the hot stuff in the kettle didn't come down on the bastards serving the ram. They kept pounding away at the wall. Each thud of their iron-tipped telephone pole—which was what the ram had been born as—sounded like the crack of doom.

Which, for the wall, was about what it was. The bricks and chunks of asphalt and cement and rubble that made up the works could take only so much. The wall fell down with a tired groan, as if it had been sick of standing there for so long anyhow. Topangans on the wall shouted in fear. Some of the Chatsworth men from the ram crew shouted along with them, because the garbage coming down from the wall didn't care who got in its way.

Valley foot soldiers scrambled into the breach with spears and swords and axes and anything else they could get their hands on. The Topangans did their best to hold them back, but more Valley fighters kept coming. Bruce

Delgado's kingdom might have been little by any standard this side of Greek city-states, but it dwarfed its western neighbor.

"Well, fuck me," Ronnie said, which was just what Jared was thinking. The boss man stepped away from the trebuchet, stuck his helmet on his head, and slid the straps of his shield over his arm. "Looks like we're gonna have to work for a living." He drew his sword and held it for a moment, as if wondering what to do with such an archaic killing tool. Then he trotted up toward the fighting at the breach with a shout of "Topannnnnga!"

Brawling at close quarters wasn't anywhere near so much fun as serving the catapult. The other guys couldn't reach you then. Now... "I'm getting too old for this shit," Jared announced to nobody in particular. But he was putting on his helmet and picking up his shield, too. You always forgot how heavy the damn thing was till you had to use it.

When he drew the sword, the sun glinted off the sharp edges. He made a pretty fair martial display. All the same, he would sooner have been back in Topanga village smoking dope or drinking bad wine.

Along with the other men from the trebuchet, he trotted after Ronnie. You did what you had to do, not what you would sooner do. If they could keep the Valley soldiers from widening the breach and letting the Lancers get through…

If they could do that, they'd be goddamn lucky. He saw as much right away. The Valley had too many men, and too many of those men carried pikes. With a pike, you could skewer a swordsman before he got close to you. You could, and they were. Troops from a Swiss hedgehog or a Greek phalanx would have gone through them like a dose of salts, but they weren't up against pros like that. The Topangans were odds-and-sods, too.

You did the best you could for as long as you could, that was all. Jared scooped up a handful of dirt and grit as he ran forward. Flipping it in a foe's face might not be sporting, but this was no sport. This was the real thing.

He got the chance sooner than he'd thought he would. The Valley fighters had no quit in them, and they could see they might make a lot of progress if they pushed the Topangans back from the wall. One of them drew back his spear to finish off a downed Topangan already bleeding from a leg wound.

Topanga and the Chatsworth Lancers

Jared flung the stuff in his left fist with a backhand scaling motion, as if he were flipping a Frisbee. Kids still played with the plastic disks. Every so often, new ones—well, new old ones—turned up.

The Valley pikeman couldn't fight with his eyes suddenly full of dirt. No one possibly could. He threw up one hand to claw at his face. Jared stabbed him in his unarmored belly, and twisted his wrist to make sure the blade cut guts. Without antibiotics, peritonitis and blood poisoning would kill even if the wound didn't. The Valley man squealed like a shoat and doubled over. Just in case he was still feeling frisky, Jared kicked him in the face. He grabbed the pike, too. The guy from the Valley sure wouldn't need it any more.

Then he hauled the wounded Topangan upright. "Here." He pressed the pike into the fellow's hands. "Can you get away with some help from a stick, Greg?"

"I better try, huh?" his countryman said.

"Well, unless you want the Valley guys to catch you," Jared answered. Murdering POWs wasn't a favorite local sport, which didn't mean it never happened. What held people back was more a fear of revenge than respect for the Geneva Convention. That was just one more relic from a bygone age. You did what you could get away with.

Using the pike as a staff, Greg stumped away. Jared went in the other direction, toward the center of the fighting. The trouble was, the center was coming his way, too. The Chatsworth men were pushing the Topangans back from the breach and widening it.

"We won't be able to hold on," panted a man fighting next to Jared. He had a cut under the brim of his helmet and above his eyebrow. His face was all over blood—head wounds always bled like mad sons of bitches—but he hardly seemed to know he'd been hurt. If he didn't catch anything worse, the gash would probably heal without much of a scar. No need to worry about lockjaw, not with that gore everywhere.

"'Fraid you're right." Jared turned a spear thrust with his shield. He chopped at the staff. He nicked it, but that was all. The goddamn thing was aluminum, which seemed like cheating.

"Let's go, *Val*ley! Let's go, *Val*ley!" Bruce Delgado's fighters sounded like a high-school football crowd whose team was driving. The rival shouts of "Topanga!" were fewer and more ragged. Sure as hell, this didn't look like one of the movies with a happy ending. By post-Change standards, Hollywood was a devil of a long way from here.

Jared cut at an enemy foot soldier. The guy jerked back, so the stroke missed. Bruce Delgado was smart to have his men cheer for the whole Valley (well, the whole west end of the Valley), not just for Chatsworth. The Lancers lived up in the north, but these guys might come from West Hills or Canoga Park or Reseda or Woodland Hills or Northridge. Those had all been district names before the Change. They might harden into towns or even tiny countries, or they might get subsumed into Chatsworth or the Valley. Time would tell, but it hadn't told yet.

Someone behind Jared blared something horrible on a bugle. A moment later, he blew the same call—Jared thought it was the same call—again. The high, shrill notes did pierce the battlefield din. The call rang out once more. This time, Jared actually recognized it. It was *Retreat*.

He didn't want to do that. But, when he looked around, he saw that the attackers had got over or through the wall at a couple of other spots, too. If the outnumbered Topangans didn't fall back and make a stand somewhere farther down Topanga Canyon, they'd get cut off and cut to pieces right here. Then the Lancers could advance at their leisure.

Of course, breaking away from a fight was harder than getting into one. The enemy's tails were up. They wanted to go right on killing people here. A baseball-sized stone clanged off Jared's helmet—luckily, just a glancing blow or it would have left him loopy even if it didn't cave in his skull.

As the Topangans fell back from the wall, they retreated south down the highway toward the village. Topanga Canyon Boulevard had been hacked out of the cliffside. The Valley men could fight on a narrow front. Or they could go down deeper into the canyon and try to get behind the Topangans. Some did the one, some the other. The Valley had the manpower for both. The Topangans…didn't.

Topanga and the Chatsworth Lancers

Horns also brayed from the north. Jared was afraid he knew what that meant: the Lancers were past the wall. If facing too many foot soldiers was bad, facing homemade knights in homemade armor was worse.

Somebody'd set up a breastwork of sorts at one of the many twists in the road. Rocks, boards, old trash cans full of dirt. None of it would hold up a determined foe very long. Here were the Fernwood men at last, though, doing what they could. One of them helped haul Jared over the breastwork. "You're Connor's dad, aren't you?" he said.

"That's right. Why?" Fear twisted Jared's gut as he came out with the last word.

"'Cause he saved Topanga village's bacon, that's why." The guy from Fernwood—Jared thought his name was Lou, but he wasn't sure—filled him in on what had been going on farther south. Jared had just enough time for a little pride. Then the fighting picked up again, and he got too busy trying to stay alive to worry about anything else.

―

Bruce Delgado's lance had blood on the iron head and on the shaft. He wasn't especially proud of the kill—he'd skewered a fleeing man from behind—but it was better than nothing. Every Topangan down was a Topangan he wouldn't have to worry about later on.

This was building up to be the biggest victory Chatsworth had won over the hippies in a hell of a long time. Maybe the biggest ever. Eddie Epstein grinned at him from behind another catcher's mask. "You ready to go surfing in the Pacific, boss?" he asked.

"That'd be something," Bruce said. "I haven't even *seen* the fucking Pacific since the Change."

"Bet it's still cold," Eddie said.

"Ya think?" Bruce said. They both chuckled. Los Angeles, of course, got hot. The Valley, and especially the north end, got blazing hot in the summertime. Bruce had heard the ocean off places like Florida was warm as bathwater. Strangers who'd come to L.A. before the Change often figured the Pacific worked the same way.

And they'd frozen their asses off finding out it didn't. A current from the north or something kept the water cold all the time. As long as Bruce could claim a stretch of beach as his own, he didn't care if polar bears sunbathed on it.

He gulped mixed wine and water from his canteen. He wished that were cold, but it wasn't. One of the things he missed most from the pre-Change days was ice cubes. You didn't see those in Chatsworth any more.

"Come on, man!" Garth Hoskins called to him. "Let's clean these fuckers out once and for all, y'know?"

"Sounds good to me." Bruce waved the Lancers forward. Infantry screened them. Longbows or crossbows gave even the heaviest cavalry grief. So did barricades. You wanted your horsemen out in the open and moving fast. Momentum was a big part of what made a charging knight so formidable. Yes, you had a nice, pointy lance. But you also had a ton or so of horse and man and ironmongery behind the point. Get all that moving at fifteen or twenty miles an hour…

And it's a medium-bad fender-bender in the old days. There were times when Bruce envied people like Garth. They didn't have memories from a dead world rising up all uneasy out of the grave.

Out in the open and moving fast was what the Chatsworth Lancers couldn't manage here. From Glenview down to the Pacific, Topanga Canyon Boulevard had always been only two lanes wide. The people who'd built it must have been proud they'd managed even that. The road wasn't quite so winding as Pacific Coast Highway or the route along the north shore of Maui, but it wasn't wide and it wasn't straight. Well, if this were ideal terrain for knights, Chatsworth would have reached the sea a long time ago.

A Topangan halfway up the hillside shot an arrow that splintered on the beat-up asphalt a few feet in front of Bruce. That it splintered meant it was post-Change work with a wooden shaft. Valley archers went to war with aluminum-shafted hunting arrows made for deer and bear. Aluminum

Topanga and the Chatsworth Lancers

was wonderful stuff. But they had to keep reusing what they already had. Without electricity, they'd never get more.

Some Valley men shot at the Topangan. Nobody hit him. Agile as a monkey, he scrambled out of range up the steep hillside.

A foot soldier came trotting back to the Lancers. "Little trouble up ahead," he reported, sketching a salute to Bruce. "They've got this chickenshit barricade across the road. It's only, like, chest high, but the way through is real narrow."

"Well, let's have a look." Bruce urged Sherman up to a trot. The rest of the Lancers followed. They were content to let him take the lead—partly because he was the leader, partly because anything bad that happened would happen to him first.

He rounded one more kink in Topanga Canyon Boulevard. Sure as the devil, there it was: a chickenshit barricade. It was enough to have stalled his infantry. Knights weren't the ideal answer to barricades. They weren't bad on foot, either, though. The Lancers' protection wasn't too heavy to move in, but it was far better than anything the Topangans had. Force them back and clear the way…and then do it again half a mile deeper into the canyon?

Bruce was still mulling it over when he heard something and spied motion up the slope out of the corner of his eye. "Oh, shit," he muttered—uninspired last words, but what he came up with as the avalanche thundered down on him and the rest of the Lancers packed together on the narrow road.

Not all the rocks and rockpiles up at the top of the canyon had got there by themselves, he realized now, when he couldn't do anything about it. And the Topangans hadn't set their half-assed barricade where they did by accident or happenstance, either. No, they'd known what they were up to, all right. Oh, hadn't they just? Plan A had been defending the works up at Glenview. This was Plan B.

Sherman snorted and reared. He knew those rocks rolling down on him—and, incidentally, on the man who rode him—were the worst news in the world. Knowing it didn't mean he could do thing one about it, though. A stone the size of a table slammed into his side. Another one, smaller but nothing like small, hit Bruce Delgado in the head. The *Wehrmacht*'s finest manganese steel did zip against a blow like that. Bruce was mercifully unconscious as the rockslide swept him and his hopes off the road and down into the depths of the canyon.

―――

JARED AND Connor eyed the mess on Topanga Canyon Boulevard. The Topangans had cleared away their improvised breastwork. The avalanche still blocked the road, though. Under the watchful stares of Topangan guards with blowguns and bows, glum prisoners from the Valley's failed campaign swung picks and sledges and turned big ones into little ones.

When they got done with that, they'd repair the roadbed itself. The landslide had bitten a chunk out of it. Then the Valley men would go home. Turning them loose was cheaper and easier than feeding them. There'd been talk of putting them to work at the seaside salt pans, which wasn't a job many locals wanted. But Topanga had avoided slavery up to now, and the old farts like Jared, who felt especially hinky about it, still had enough clout to hold the beast at bay.

Kwame Curtis came up to study the prisoners at work. "Hey, it's the hippie Marine!" Jared said.

"Up yours, man," the fighting Brain answered without heat. "I managed to get something to work, that's all. We'd've been in deep kimchi if it didn't."

"Kimchi!" Connor grinned. He loved the stinky stuff. Jared didn't know what real Koreans would have thought of Topanga's pickled cabbage spiced with garlic and chilies, but he liked it, too. The strong flavors perked up food that was too often bland.

The breeze swung around to come from the north. Jared wrinkled his nose at a stink nothing like kimchi's. "I hate that smell," he said. Some men and horses still lay under the rockslide.

"Oh, me, too," Kwame Curtis said. "I smelled it in Kuwait and Iraq, and then in the Dieoff after the Change. Brings back bad memories, you know?"

"Yeah," Jared said. "This isn't as bad as the Dieoff. Then you couldn't get it out of your clothes or out of your hair or off your skin no matter how much you washed."

"I remember. I'm not likely to ever forget. Nobody who lived through it is," Curtis said.

Jared nodded. "You know that Lynyrd Skynyrd song?" he asked.

"'That Smell'?" Kwame Curtis asked. Jared nodded once more. Curtis went on, "The smell of death sure as hell surrounded us, didn't it?"

Connor looked from one of them to the other. There they went again, talking about shit from the dead world, the lost world, the world they still remembered and that still turned real for them in dreams. One of these years, the last person with memories and dreams like that would die. Then the post-Change folks, the ones who'd never known anything different from what they had now, would be able to go about their business without having to listen to *Back in my day, we could do this or that or the other impossible thing*.

It hadn't happened yet. Looking at his son, Jared guessed Connor wouldn't be altogether heartbroken when it did. He'd never lived in the United States, after all. His country was Topanga: a beach, a canyon, an uneasy border with the Chatsworth Lancers—who'd be having their own fun and games now that so many of them had suddenly vanished from the scene.

My canyon, 'tis of thee,
Sweet land of the hippie,
Of thee I sing!

Jared snorted. Then he wondered why. It might not make a bad anthem for Connor's grandchildren. And they wouldn't even know what they were missing. *Poor, sorry buggers*, Jared thought. He turned back to watch the Valley men swinging sledgehammers under the warm sun.

The Catcher in the Rhine

Esther Friesner asked me to do a story for one of her *Chicks in Chainmail* anthologies. I always enjoyed writing those; they gave me a chance to get silly, which doesn't happen all the time. My oldest daughter was in middle school, and reading *The Catcher in the Rye*. My middle daughter didn't know about the book yet, and heard the title wrong. "You're reading *The Catcher in the Rhine*?" she said. Once I had a title, I soon had a story to go with it, in my very best genuine ersatz J. D. Salinger style. And my middle daughter got a hundred dollars from the check I got for it.

I DON'T KNOW HOW I got here. Wait. That's not quite right. What I mean to say is, I know how I got to Europe and everything, for Chrissake. They sent me over here to find myself or something after that trouble I had. I'm sure you know about that. I'm certain you know about it. Practically *ev*erybody knows about it. Some of the biggest phonies in the world think they know more about it than I do. They really think so. It's like they read it in English class or something.

So like I say, I know how I got to Europe. I don't know about this finding myself business, though. I swear to God, if you can't find yourself, you've gotta be some kind of psycho. I mean, you're right *there*, for crying out loud. If you weren't right there, where the hell would you be?

And sending somebody to Europe to find himself has got to be the stupidest thing in the world. You have to be a lousy moron to come up with something like that, you really do. You can't find *any*thing in Europe. Honest to God, it's the truth. You really can't. All the streets go every which way, and they change names every other block, or sometimes in the middle of the block.

Besides, the people don't speak English. Try to have an intellectual conversation with somebody who doesn't know what the hell you're talking about. Go ahead and try. It's a goddam waste of time, that's what it is.

Anyway, I went through France, and some of that was pretty neat, it really was, and all of it was historical as hell—not that I was ever any good at history. What I mean is, every single stinking bit of it happened a long time ago—some of it happened a goddam long time ago—so how am I supposed to get all excited when some phony moron of a teacher stands there and goes on and on about it? It's not easy, I tell you.

After I was done with old France, I went over to Germany because it's next door, you know—and I took this boat trip up the Rhine. I don't know what the hell "Rhine" means in German, but it looks like it oughta mean "sewer." The whole river smells like somebody laid a big old fart, too. It really does. I won't ever complain about the Hudson when I get home, and you can walk across the Hudson, practically.

When I get home. *If* I get home. The boat stopped at this place called Isenstein. It's a real dump, I tell you, but back of it there's a kind of a crag thing with a castle on top. I wasn't gonna get off the boat—I'd paid the fare all the way up to Düsseldorf, wherever that is—but the river just smelled so bad I couldn't stand it any more, so I left. Maybe they'd let me back on the next one. And if they didn't, who cares? I had piles of money and traveler's checks and stuff.

Well, let me tell you, the streets in old Isenstein didn't smell so good, either. That was partly because it was still right *next* to the Rhine, and it was partly because the people there had the most disgusting personal habits in the world. I saw this one guy standing in the street taking a leak against the side of a crumby old dirty brick building, and it wasn't even like he was drunk or anything. He was just *doing* it. And then he went on his way happy

The Catcher in the Rhine

as you please. I wouldn't've believed it if I hadn't seen it with my own eyes, and that's the truth.

They had a church there, so I went inside and looked around. I always tried to look at those cultural things, because who knows when I was ever coming back again? Coming back to Europe, I mean—I wouldn't've come back to Isenstein if you *paid* me, you can bet your bottom dollar on that. But the church was pretty dirty and crumby, too. By the time I got done looking at it, I was feeling pretty goddam depressed. I really was. So I got the hell out of there.

I was feeling pretty goddam *hungry*, too. I was feeling hungry as a sonuvabitch, if you want to know the truth. I didn't exactly want to eat in Isenstein—it really was a filthy place. You have no idea how filthy it was. But I was *there*. Where else was I gonna eat, is what I want to know.

Getting something to eat when you don't speak the language is a royal pain in the ass. If you're not careful, they're liable to give you horse manure on a bun. I'm not kidding. I'm really not. When I was in France, I got a plateful of *snails*, for crying out loud. Real snails, like you step on in a garden somewhere and they go crunch under your shoe. With butter. If you think I ate 'em, you're crazy. I sent 'em back pretty toot sweet. That means goddam fast in French. But whatever they gave me instead didn't look much better, so I got the hell out of *that* place toot sweet myself.

Over across the street from the church in old Isenstein was this joint where you could get beer and food. Nobody in Germany cares if you're twenty-one. They don't give a damn, swear to God they don't. They'd give beer to a *nine*-year-old, they really would. If he asked for it, I mean.

So I got a beer, and the guy sitting next to me at the bar was eating a sandwich that didn't look too lousy—it had some kind of sausage and pickles in it—so I pointed to that and told the bartender, "Give me one of those, too." Maybe it was really chopped-up pigs' ears or something, but I didn't *know* it was, so it was all right if I didn't think about it too much. The guy behind the bar figured out what I meant and started making one for me.

I'd just taken a big old bite—it wasn't terrific but I could stand it, pigs' ears or not—when the fellow sitting next to me on the *other* side spoke up and said to me in English, "You are an American, yes?"

If you want to know the truth, it made me kind of angry. Here I was *starv*ing to death, and this guy wanted to strike up a conversation. I didn't want to talk. I wanted to eat, even if it didn't taste so good. So with my mouth full, rude as anything, I said "Yeah" and then I took another bite, even bigger than the first one.

He didn't get mad. I'd hoped he would, I really had, but no such luck. He was a very smooth, very polite guy. He was a little flitty-looking, as a matter of fact—not too, but a little. Enough to make you wonder, anyhow. He said, "We do not often Americans in Isenstein have." He talked that way on account of he was foreign, I guess. I took another bite out of this sandwich— it probably *was* pigs' ears, it sure tasted like what you'd think pigs' ears'd taste like—and he asked me, "What is your name?"

So I told him, and he damn near—I mean *damn* near—fell off his chair. "Hagen Kriemhild?" he said. Boy, he must've had cabbages in his ears or something, even if I was still kind of talking with my mouth full. "Hagen *Kriemhild*?"

"No," I said, and told him again, this time after I'd swallowed and everything, so he couldn't foul it up even if he tried.

"Ah," he said. "*Ach so*," which I guess is like "okay" in German. "Never mind. It is close enough."

"Close enough for what?" I said, but he didn't answer me right away. He just sat there looking at me. He looked very *intense*, if you know what I mean, like he was thinking a mile a minute. I couldn't very well ask him what the hell he was thinking about, either, because people always lie to you when you do that, or else they get mad. So instead I said, "What's *your* name?" You can't go wrong with that, hardly.

He blinked. He really did—his eyes went blink, blink. It was like he'd forgotten I was there, he'd been thinking so goddam hard. He'd been thinking like a madman, I swear to God he had. Blink, blink—he did it again. It

The Catcher in the Rhine

was crumby to watch, honest. I didn't think he was going to tell me his lousy old name, but he did. He said, "I am called Regin Fafnirsbruder."

Well, Jesus Christ, if you think I even *tried* to say that like he said it, you're crazy. I just said "Pleased to meetcha" and I stuck out my hand. I'm too polite for my own good sometimes, I really am.

Old Regin Fafnirsbruder shook hands with me. He didn't shake hands like a flit, I have to admit it. He said, "Come with me. I will you things in Isenstein show that no American has ever seen."

"Can't I finish my sandwich first?" I said—and I didn't even want that crumby old sandwich any more. Isn't that a hell of a thing?

He shook his head like he would drop dead if I took one more bite. So I went bottoms-up with my beer—they make *good* beer in Germany, and I wasn't about to let *that* go to waste—and out of there we went.

"Whaddaya got?" I said. "Is it—a girl?" Could you be a pimp and a flit at the same time? Would you have any fun if you were? I always wonder about crazy stuff like that. If you're gonna wonder about crazy stuff, you might as well wonder about *sexy* crazy stuff, you know what I mean?

"A girl, *ja*. Like none you have ever met." Old Regin Fafnirsbruder's head went up and down like it was on a spring. "And also other things." He looked back over his shoulder at me, to make sure I was still following him, I guess. His eyes were big and round as silver dollars. I'm not making things up, they honest to God were. So help me.

"Listen," I said, "it's been nice knowing you and everything, but I think I ought to get back to my boat now."

He didn't listen to a word I said. He just kept going, out of Isenstein—which wasn't very hard, because it's not a real big town or anything—and toward that tumbledown castle on the crag I already told you about. And I kept walking along after him. To tell you the truth, I didn't *want* to go back to the boat, or to the smelly old Rhine. The farther away from there I got the better, you bet.

All of a sudden, these really thick gray clouds started rolling in, just covering up the whole goddam sky. It hadn't been any too gorgeous out before, but *these* clouds looked like they meant business, no kidding. "Hey," I said, kind of loud so old Regin Fafnirsbruder would be sure to hear me. "You got an umbrella? It looks like it's gonna pour."

"*Ja*," he said over his shoulder. Yeah it was gonna pour or yeah he had an umbrella? It wasn't like he *told* me, for crying out loud, the stupid moron. I'll tell you, *I* didn't have any umbrella. Jesus Christ, I didn't even have a crumby *hat*. And my crew cut is so short, it's like I don't have any hair at all up there, and when it rains the water that hits on top of my head all runs down right into my face, and that's very annoying, it really is. It's annoying as hell.

But old Regin Fafnirsbruder started up this crag toward the tumbledown old crumby ruin of a castle, and I kept on following him. By then I was feeling kind of like a goddam moron myself. I was also panting like anything. I haven't got any wind at all, on account of I smoke like a madman. I smoke like a goddam *chim*ney, if you want to know the truth.

Sure as hell, it started to rain. I knew it would. I *told* old Regin Fafnirsbruder it would, but did he listen to me? Nobody listens to you, I swear to God it's the truth. This big old raindrop hit me right square in the eye, so I couldn't see anything for a second or two, and I almost fell off this lousy little path we were walking on, and I would've broken my damn neck if I had, too, because it was a *crag*, remember, and steeper than hell every which way.

"Hey!" I yelled. "Slow down!"

That's when the biggest goddam lightning bolt you ever imagined smashed into me and everything went black, like they say in the movies.

WHEN I woke up, there was old Regin Fafnirsbruder leaning over me, almost close enough to give me a kiss. "You are all right, Hagen Kriemhild?" he asked, all anxious like I was his son or something. I think I'd kill myself if I was, I really do.

The Catcher in the Rhine

"I told you, that's not my name." I was pretty mad that he'd taken me all this way and he couldn't even bother to remember my crumby old name. It's not like it's Joe Doakes or John Smith so you'd forget it in a hurry. I sat up. I didn't want to keep laying there on account of he might try something flitty if he thought I couldn't do anything about it or anything. "What the hell happened?"

Right then was when I noticed things had started turning crazy. Old Regin Fafnirsbruder had asked me how I was in this language that wasn't English, and I hadn't just understood him, I'd *an*swered him in it, for Chrissake. Isn't that gorgeous? I figured the lightning had fried my brains but good or something.

Then I realized it wasn't raining any more. There wasn't a cloud in the goddam *sky*, as a matter of fact. Not even one. It was about as sunny a day as old Isenstein ever gets, I bet.

I took a deep breath. I was gonna say "What the hell happened?" again—old Regin Fafnirsbruder hadn't told me or anything—but I didn't. And the reason I didn't is that the breath I took didn't stink. With the nasty old Rhine running right by it, the air in Isenstein always smelled like somebody just cut the biggest fart in the world right under your nose.

But it didn't, not any more. It smelled like grass and water—*clean* water—and pine trees, almost like one of those little air freshener things, if you know what I mean. Too good to be true. It wasn't one of those, though, on account of I could smell cows and pigs and horses, too, somewhere way the hell off in the distance. It was like I wasn't by a town any more, like I'd gone off into the country. But I was still sitting right where that old lightning bolt had clobbered me.

Old Regin Fafnirsbruder started dancing around. I'm not kidding, he really did. He had this grin on his face like he was drunk, and he was kind of halfway between doing an Indian war dance and jitterbugging. Watching the old sonuvabitch shake his can like that was pretty damn funny, it really was.

"I did it!" he yelled, not keeping time with his feet or anything. "My magic worked!" He still wasn't speaking English, but I understood him okay.

"Crap," I said. Actually, I didn't say "crap," actually, but what I said meant the same thing as crap, so that was all right. "What do you mean, your magic?"

He still didn't answer me. He was too busy dancing and hollering and having a high old time. He was a very self-centered guy, old Regin Fafnirsbruder was, egocentric as hell. It made him a real pain in the ass to talk to, to tell you the truth.

"What do you *mean*, your crumby magic?" I said again. I hate it when I have to repeat myself, I really do.

Finally, he remembered I was there. "Look!" he said, and he did this wave like he was in the lousiest, corniest movie ever made. I swear to God, this wave was so goddam big that he almost fell off the side of the mountain himself.

So I looked. I didn't want to give him the satisfaction, but I finally went and did. I looked back over my shoulder, and I almost felt like the lightning plowed into me all over again. There was the Rhine, all right, like it was supposed to be, only it was blue, blue as the sky, blu*er* than the goddam sky, not the color the water in a toilet bowl is when somebody gets there *just* in the nick of time. No wonder it didn't stink any more.

And somebody'd taken old Isenstein and stuck it in his back pocket. Instead of a real town, there were these maybe ten houses by the riverside, and they all had roofs made out of straw or something. So maybe old Regin Fafnirsbruder *had* worked magic. If he hadn't, what the hell had he done? I didn't know then and I still don't know now.

When I got done gawking at Isenstein—it took me a while, believe me—I looked up to the crumby old tumbledown castle at the top of the crag. There it was, all right, big as life, but it wasn't crumby or old or tumbledown any more. What it looked like was, it looked like somebody built it day before yesterday. There wasn't a single stone missing—not even a pebble, I swear—and all the edges were so sharp you could've cut yourself on 'em. Maybe not even day before yesterday. Maybe yesterday, and I mean yesterday after*noon*.

Oh, and there was this ring of fire all the way around the castle. I didn't see anything burning up, but I sure as hell saw the flames. I heard 'em, too—they crackled like the ones in your fireplace do, only these were ten or twenty times as big. When I was a little kid, I had this book about Paul Bunyan and Babe the giant Blue Ox. It was a pretty crumby book with really stupid pictures, but I remembered it right then anyway on account of if old Babe had tried to walk through those flames, he'd've been short ribs and steaks in nothing flat, and I mean well-done.

"Now shall you your destiny fulfill." I already told you old Regin Fafnirsbruder talked like that sometimes. He did it even when he wasn't speaking English. He wasn't much of a conversationalist, old Regin Fafnirsbruder wasn't.

"What the hell are you talking about?" I said. "And where the hell did Isenstein go, anyway?"

"That is Isenstein, Isenstein as it is now," he said, and then a whole lot of weird stuff I didn't understand at all, and what language he was talking in didn't matter a goddam bit. Time flows and sorceries and I don't know what. It all sounded pretty much like a bunch of crap to me. It would've sounded even more like a bunch of crap if I hadn't kept looking back at that little handful of houses where old Isenstein used to be. Then he pointed up the hill. "You shall to the castle go. You shall through the flames pass. You shall the shield-maiden Brunhild asleep there find. You shall with a kiss her awaken, and you shall with her happily ever after live."

"Oh, yeah?" I said, and he nodded. Just like before, his head bobbed up and down, up and down, like it was on a spring. If he wasn't the biggest madman in the world, I don't know who was. But he was calling the shots, too. I may not apply myself too much—people always go on and on that I'm not *apply*ing my goddam self till I'm about ready to puke sometimes—but I'm not stupid. I'm really not. Old Regin Fafnirsbruder knew what he was doing here, and I didn't have the faintest idea. So I figured I'd better play along for a while, anyway, till I could figure out what the hell was going on.

"Go up to the castle," he said. "You will it is all as I have said see."

I went on up. Now he followed me. Like I said before, the old castle looked so new, it might've just come out of its box or something. Sure as hell, the fire went all the way around the goddam place. The closer I got, the more it felt like fire, too. I pointed to it. I made damn sure I didn't touch it or anything, though, you bet. "How the hell am I supposed to get through that, huh?"

"Just walk through. You will not harmed be. My magic assures it."

"Oh, yeah?" I said. Old Regin Fafnirsbruder's head bobbed up and down some more. He looked pretty stupid, he really did. "Oh, *yeah*?" I said. He kept right on nodding. "Prove it," I said to him. "You're such a madman of a wizard and everything, let's see *you* go on through there without ending up charbroiled."

All of a sudden, he wasn't nodding so much any more. "The spell is not for me. The spell cannot for me be," he said. "The spell is for you and for you alone."

I laughed at him. "I think you're yellow, is what I think." I figured that'd make him mad. If somebody's a coward, what's he gonna hate more than somebody else coming out and *tell*ing him he's a coward, right?

I guess it worked. I guess it worked a little too goddam well, if you want to know the truth. Because what happened was, old Regin Fafnirsbruder came up and gave me a push, and he *pushed* me right into those old flames.

I screamed. I screamed like hell, as a matter of fact. But I didn't burn up or anything—he was right about that. The fire felt hot, but hot like sunshine, not hot like fire. It hurt a lot more when I fell on my ass from the push, it honestly did.

"What'd you go and do *that* for, you goddam moron?" I yelled, and then I started to go on *out* through the fire. I didn't get very goddam far, though. It wasn't just hot like sunshine any more, let me tell you. It burned the tip of my shoe when I stuck it in there, and it would've burned the rest quick enough, too, if I'd been dumb enough to give it a chance.

Old Regin Fafnirsbruder was laughing his ass off watching me looking at my toasted toe. "You must what I want do," he said. "Then will you what you want get. When you come out with Brunhild, you may through the fire pass. Until then, you must there stay."

"You dirty, filthy, stinking goddam moron," I said. "I hope you drown in the goddam Rhine."

The Catcher in the Rhine

He just ignored me, the lousy sonuvabitch. He had no consideration, old Regin Fafnirsbruder didn't. I started up toward the fire again, but I didn't stick my foot in it this time—you bet I didn't. I sat down on the ground. I felt so depressed, you can't imagine how depressed I felt.

But after a while I stood up again. What can you do when you're just sitting around on your butt and all? I thought I'd get up and look around a little, anyway. So I did that, and I came to this door. I opened it—what the hell? At least old Regin Fafnirsbruder couldn't keep staring at me through the flames any more. And after I went through, I slammed the hell out of that old door. To tell you the truth, I kind of hoped I'd break it right off the hinges, but no such luck.

I thought I'd end up in this big old hall full of guys making pigs of themselves and getting stinking and pinching the serving girls on the butt the way they did back in medieval times, but that isn't what ended up happening. I walked into this little—bedroom, I guess you'd call it, but it wasn't a bed this girl was laying on, it was more like a little sofa or something.

She was kind of cute, as a matter of fact, if you like big husky blondes. But I'd never seen a girl in chainmail before. To tell you the truth, I'd never seen *any*body in chainmail before, and sure as hell not anybody sleeping. It looked uncomfortable, it really did.

She had on a helmet, too, and a sword on a belt around her waist, and this shield was leaning up against the bed or sofa or whatever the hell it was. I stood there for a while like a crumby old moron. In the fairy tales you're supposed to kiss the princess, right, and she'll wake up and you'll both live happily ever after. That was what old Regin Fafnirsbruder had told me would happen, but you'd have to be a real moron not to see he was playing the game for him and nobody else. And if I kissed this girl and she didn't happen to like it or she thought I was trying to get fresh with her or something, she was liable to *mur*der me, for Chrissake.

I wished I could've figured out some other way to get out of there. I hate doing what anybody else tells me to do. I hate it like anything, if you want to know the truth. Even when it's for my own good and everything, I still hate it. It's nobody's goddam business but mine what I do. Not that anybody listens to me. Yeah, fat chance of that. You think old Regin Fafnirsbruder gave a damn about what I thought? Fat chance of that, too.

But I was stuck in this old castle. I was stuck really bad. If Brunhild there couldn't get me the hell out, who could? Nobody. Just nobody. So I leaned down and I gave her this little tiny kiss, just like it *was* a fairy tale or something.

Her eyes opened. I'd expected they would be blue—don't ask me why, except she was a blonde and all—but they were brown. She looked at me like I was dirt and nobody'd invented brooms yet. Then she said, "You are not Siegfried. Where is Siegfried?" She spoke the same language as old Regin Fafnirsbruder, whatever the hell it was.

"I dunno," I said. I bet I sounded really smart. I sounded like a goddam moron, is what I sounded like. "Who's Siegfried?"

Her face went all soft and mushy-like. You wouldn't think anybody who was wearing armor could look so sappy, but old Brunhild did. "He is my love, my husband to be," she said. Then she sort of frowned, like she'd forgotten I was there and was all of a sudden remembering—and she didn't look any too goddam happy about it, either. "Or he was to have been my husband. The man who came through the fire can claim my hand, if he so desires."

I've always been backasswards with girls. Here she was practically saying she'd *let* me give her the time, but did that make me want to do it? Like hell it did. What it did was, it scared the crap out of me. I said, "I don't want to marry *any*body, for crying out loud. I just want to get the hell outa here, if you want to know the truth."

Brunhild thought about that for a couple seconds. Then she sat up. The chainmail made little clink-clank noises when she moved—molding itself to her shape, you know? She had a hell of a shape, too, I have to admit it. A really nice set of knockers.

"What is your name?" she said, so I told her. Just like old Regin Fafnirsbruder's had, her eyes got big. "Hagen Kriemhild?"

The Catcher in the Rhine

If you really want to know, I was getting pretty goddam tired of that. I said it again, the right way, louder this time, like you would to somebody who was pretty dumb.

But it went right by her. I could tell. Old Brunhild wasn't much for intellectual conversation. She said, "How came you here, Hagen Kriemhild?"

"That's a goddam good question." I explained it as well as I could. It sounded crazy as hell even to *me*, and I'd been through it. She was gonna think I'd gone right off the deep end.

Only she didn't. When I finally got through, old Brunhild said, "Regin Fafnirsbruder is an evil man. How not, when Fafnir his brother is an evil worm? But I shall settle with him. You need have no doubt of that."

She stood up. She was almost as tall as I was, which surprised me, because I have a lot of heighth and she was a girl and everything. But she really was, so help me God. She took out her sword. It went wheep when it came out of the old scabbard, and the blade kind of glowed even though the bedroom wasn't what you'd call bright or anything.

"What are you gonna do with that thing?" I said, which has to be one of the stupidest goddam questions of all time. Sometimes I scare myself, I really do. Am I a goddam moron, too, just like everybody else?

But old Brunhild took it just like any other question. "I am going to punish him for what he did to me, for this humiliation. Come with me, Hagen Kriemhild, and guard my back. He has besmirched your honor as well as mine."

I don't know what the hell she thought I was gonna guard her back *with*. I had some German money in my pocket, and my traveler's checks and all, and a little leftover French money I'd forgotten to change, and that was about it. I didn't even have a *pock*et knife, for crying out loud, and I'm not what you'd call the bravest guy in the world anyhow. I'm pretty much of a chicken, if you want to know the truth. But I followed old Brunhild outa there just the same. If she could get out through the fire, maybe I could too. I hoped like hell I could, anyway.

There was old Regin Fafnirsbruder on the other side of the flames. He gave Brunhild the phoniest bow you ever saw in your life. "So good you to see," he said. What he sounded like was, he sounded like the headwaiter at this fancy restaurant where all the rich phonies and all their whory-looking girlfriends go to eat and he has to be nice and suck up to the sonsuvbitches all day long even though he hates their stinking guts. "Does your bridegroom you please?" He laughed this really dirty laugh. Pimps *wish* they could laugh the way old Regin Fafnirsbruder laughed right then, honest to God.

Old Brunhild started yelling and cussing and whooping and hollering like you wouldn't believe. She started waving that goddam sword around, too. She wasn't very *care*ful with it, either—she damn near chopped *me* a couple of times, let me tell you. I had to duck like a madman, or I swear to God she would've punctured me.

All old Regin Fafnirsbruder did was, he kept laughing. He was laughing his ass off, to tell you the truth. He really was.

Well, that just made old Brunhild madder. "You will pay for your insolence!" she said, and so help me if she didn't charge right on out through the fire. I halfway thought she'd cook. But she was hotter than the flames, and they didn't hurt her one bit.

Anyway, I figured I'd better try and get outa there, too. Old Regin Fafnirsbruder had said Brunhild was my only chance of doing that, and *she'd* said I was supposed to guard her back even though I didn't know what the hell I was supposed to do if somebody did go and jump on her. So I ran after her. People always say I never listen to *any*body, practically, but that's a goddam lie. Well, it was this time.

I didn't run all that goddam *hard*, though, on account of I didn't *know* for sure if the fire would let me go the way it did for old Brunhild. But it felt like it did when that goddam sonuvabitch moron bastard Regin Fafnirsbruder pushed me through it going the other way—it was hot but not *hot*, if you know what I mean.

Let me tell you, old Regin Fafnirsbruder didn't look any too happy when Brunhild burst out of the ring of fire with me right behind her—not that he paid all that much attention to *me*, the lousy crumby moron. Actually, when you get down to it, I can't blame him for that, to tell you the truth. Here was this ordinary guy, and here was this goddam *girl* with chainmail and this sword coming after him yelling "Now you shall get what you deserve!" and swinging that old sword like she wanted to chop his head off—and she *did*, honest to God.

But old Regin Fafnirsbruder was a lot sprier than he looked. He ducked and he dodged and she ran right on by him. The sword went wheet! a couple times but it didn't cut anything but air. And old Regin Fafnirsbruder laughed his ass off again and said, "*Your* blade is my life to drink not fated."

Well, old Brunhild was already madder than hell, but that only pissed her off worse. She started swinging that sword like a madman—up, down, sideways, I don't know what all. I swear to God, I don't know how old Regin Fafnirsbruder didn't get himself chopped into dog food, either, I really don't, Hou*di*ni couldn't have gotten out of the way of that sword, but Regin Fafnirsbruder did. He was a bastard, but he was a *slick* bastard, I have to admit it.

Finally, he said, "This grows boring. I shall another surprise for you one day have." Then he was gone. One second he was there, the next second he wasn't. *I* don't know how the hell he did it. I guess maybe he really was a magician, for crying out loud.

Old Brunhild, she needed like half a minute to notice he'd disappeared, she really did. She just kept hacking and slashing away like there was no tomorrow. She'd already hit the ceiling in fourteen different places, and she wasn't anywhere close to ready to calm down. I wanted to keep the hell out of her way, was all I wanted to do right about then, if you want to know the truth.

Only I couldn't. There was this castle with the ring of fire around it, and there was the slope that headed down toward old Isenstein and the Rhine that didn't stink any more, and there were me and old Brunhild. That was it. Talk about no place to hide. If she decided I was in cahoots with old Regin Fafnirsbruder after all, she'd chop me in half. I didn't know how the hell he'd dodged her, but I knew goddam well *I* didn't have a chance.

Anyway, Brunhild *fi*nally figured out old Regin Fafnirsbruder'd flown the coop. She didn't rub her eyes or go "I can't believe it" or anything like that. She just sort of shrugged her shoulders, so the chainmail went clink-clank again, and she said, "Curse his foul sorcery."

Then she remembered I was there. I swear to God, I wouldn't've been sorry if she'd forgotten. She walked over to me, that crazy armor jingling every step she took, and she looked up into my face. Like I said before, she didn't have to look *up* very goddam far, on account of she had almost as much heighth as I did.

"You came through the fire for me," she said. "You did it unwittingly, I think, and aided by Regin Fafnirsbruder's magecraft, but the wherefores matter only so much. What bears greater weight is that you did it."

"Yeah, I guess I did."

Old Brunhild nodded. The sun shone off her helmet like a spotlight off the bell of a trombone in a night club. She took this deep breath. "However it was done, it was done. As I said when first you woke me, if you would claim me for your bride, you may." And she looked at me like if I was crumby enough to do it, she'd spit in my eye, honest to God she did.

Isn't that a bastard? Isn't that a bastard and a half, as a matter of fact? Here's this girl—and she's a *pretty* girl, she really is, especially if you like blondes about the size of football players—and she was saying "Yeah, you can give me the time, all right, and I won't say boo," only I know she'll hate me forever if I do. And when old Brunhild hated somebody, she didn't do it halfway. Ask Regin Fafnirsbruder if you don't believe me, for crying out loud. And she was holding on to that sword so tight, her knuckles were white. They really were.

I said, "When I woke you up back there, in that crazy old castle and all, didn't you tell me you were in there waiting for Sieg—for somebody?" I couldn't even remember what the hell his name was, not to save my life.

"For Siegfried." Old Brunhild's face went all gooey again. I'd kind of like to have a girl look that way when she says *my* name—or else I'd like to puke, one. I'm not sure which, I swear.

"Well," I said, "in that case maybe you'd better go on back in there and wait some more, dontcha think?"

The Catcher in the Rhine

She swung up that old sword again. I got ready to run like a madman, I'm not kidding. But she didn't do any chopping—it was some kind of crazy salute instead. "*Ja*," she said, just like old Regin Fafnirsbruder, and then she put the sword back in the sheath. "I will do that." And then she leaned forward and stood up on tiptoe—just a little, on account of she was pretty goddam tall, like I say—and she kissed me right on the end of the nose.

Girls. They drive you nuts, they really do. I don't even think they *mean* to sometimes, but they do anyway.

I wanted to grab her and give her a real kiss, but I didn't quite have the nerve. I'm always too slow at that kind of stuff. Old Brunhild, she nodded to me once, and then she walked on back through the fire like it wasn't even there. I heard the door close. I bet she laid down on that old sofa again and fell asleep waiting for old Sieg-whatever to get done with whatever he was doing and come around to give her a call.

As soon as that door closed, I decided I wanted to kiss her after all. I ran toward the ring of fire, and I damn near—*damn* near—burned my nose off. I couldn't go through it, not any more.

No Brunhild. Damn. I shoulda laid her, or at least *kissed* her better than that little tiny poke that woke her up. I'm *always* too goddam slow, for crying out loud. I swear to God, it's the story of my life. No Regin Fafnirsbruder, either. I don't know where the hell he went, or when he's coming back, or if he's *ever* coming back.

If he's not, I'm gonna be *awful* goddam late making that Rhine boat connection to old Düsseldorf.

What's left here? A crumby castle I can't get into and that little tiny town down there by the river where Isenstein used to be or will be or whatever the hell it is. That's it. I wish I'd paid more attention in history class, I really do.

Well, what the hell? I started toward old—or I guess I mean new—Isenstein. I wonder if they've invented scotch yet. I swear, I *real*ly wish I'd paid more attention in history class.

Jesus Christ, they're *bound* to have beer at least, right?

The Last Word

This story is set in another of Steve Stirling's universes: the Domination of the Draka, about as nasty a dystopia as anyone has ever created. Some of you may possibly recognize the person on whom the main character is based, though I have him born rather later than his model was in real life. Some of you may also recognize one of the bit players here, though he has a rather different role here from the one he played in our world. I take modest pride in noting that this story was written in 1999, a couple of years before everybody heard about him.

Commodore Anson MacDonald strode into the underground refectory. "What's the latest?" he asked.

Nobody paid any attention to him. All eyes were riveted on the big, wall-mounted televisor. The news reader, her pretty face worn and haggard, her eyes red with tears that hadn't—quite—poured down her face, spoke like a machine: "—San Francisco now definitely known to be vaporized. The government did not escape. Along with the destruction of Manhattan and Washington, this confirms—"

Someone had a remote control. He aimed the little box at the televisor as if it were an assault rifle. And the infrared beam killed the screen, which went black. "That's that," somebody else said. "The Alliance for Democracy is washed up."

Across the room, someone said, "For God's sake, get me a beer."

MacDonald looked from one soldier to another. He was a lean, bald man in his mid-fifties, the graying hair he had left cropped close to the sides and back of his skull, a thin line of mustache—darker than the hair on his head—just above his upper lip. He felt very much a stranger here: he'd been rotated to the Nantahala Redoubt for a familiarization tour…just at the exact moment the Snakes chose to launch the Final War.

Even his uniform was wrong. He was a thirty-year Navy man, and proud of the deep blue, the blue of the tropical ocean at night, but it didn't fit here, not with everyone else in mottled woodland camouflage.

And the Navy-blue uniform wasn't the only thing that didn't fit in. Anson MacDonald felt as devastated as the news reader had sounded. The country he loved, the system he believed in, going down under the Domination of the Draka? What had that Englishman called the Snakes? *A boot in the face of mankind forever*—something like that, anyhow. He had every right to feel as if the world had just ended. For all practical purposes, it had.

But the men in the mottled uniforms seemed grimly content with their fate, with their country's fate. One of them, a fellow with captain's bars on his collar tabs, came up to MacDonald and said, "Take it easy, Commodore. They didn't put us in the Redoubt for when things were going fine. This is what we're here for: to give the Draka as much trouble as we can for as long as we can, even though the Alliance for Democracy has lost the war."

"Madness," MacDonald said. "I've always thought so. Defeatist madness."

"No, sir." The captain—the name tape above the right breast pocket of his uniform said FISCHER—shook his head. "Strategy. The Draka have won the phase of the game that just ended. Now we have to make sure they get as little joy from it as possible. We have to tie them down in endless cleanup operations, make sure they'll need to worry about us ten years from now, twenty years from now, maybe fifty years from now. We've got men and women in here, you know. We can raise up a whole new generation to give the Snakes grief."

"What's the point?" MacDonald asked bitterly. "The Afghans gave them grief after the Great War. The Finns gave them grief after the Eurasian War.

The Last Word

The Afghans are Draka Janissaries these days; the Finns, poor bastards, are mostly dead. And those sons of bitches are going to turn the free men and women of the United States and the rest of the Alliance into serfs. Do you know what that is, Captain? It's the biggest rape in the history of the world."

"Yes, sir." Fischer had a long, skinny face that seemed stupid till you studied it for a little while. MacDonald had known a few men like that; what made them seem not quite in the real world wasn't stupidity but intense concentration. After a few seconds, Fischer returned to the here-and-now. "Sir, like it or not, you're here for the duration. Ever play a game of chess where you threw away your queen like a damn fool?"

Caught off guard, MacDonald let out a couple of syllables' worth of barking laughter. "Unfortunately, yes."

"Okay." When Fischer grinned, he looked years younger, almost like a kid. "You aren't going to win after that. But if you're feeling stubborn and you've got a halfway decent defense, you can go into a shell and make the other fellow work like a son of a bitch to finish you. That's what we're all about."

"But what's the point?" Anson MacDonald demanded. "The point was, we never should have lost our queen in the first place. Now that we have, we're still facing a lost game. We would have done better to put all this energy, all this manpower, all these resources, into first-strike capability. I always said so, to anyone who would listen. Not enough people did."

"And maybe we would have lost all those people, all those resources, on account of the Snakes' stinking virus," Captain Fischer said. "We're *still* dealing with that; the drugs only help so much. But that's not the point. The point is, this isn't chess. The rules are more elastic, when there are rules. And you've forgotten something else."

"What's that?" MacDonald barked—he didn't like getting a lecture from this whippersnapper. Captain Fischer spoke two quiet words. MacDonald stiffened to attention. "I am at your service, sir."

JANISSARY SERGEANT Hans rubbed at the orange slave tattoo behind his left ear. It didn't itch, but he imagined it did. He held up a hand. The squad he led was glad to stop for a blow. They liked the look of the mountainous woods ahead no better than he did. Even if the leaves were off the trees, anything could be hiding in there. It probably was, too.

"Where's the map say we're at, Sarge?" asked a trooper named Usama.

Being a sergeant, Hans had been trained in such mysteries. He didn't even need to consult the map to answer, "That last little town we just went through was called Cheoah." His English was the slurred dialect of the Domination—not so very much different from what the folk here in the U.S. district of North Carolina spoke—with something guttural underneath, a reminder that both his grandfathers had fought for the *Reich* and the *Führer* against the Draka. They'd lost, and now he marched under the dragon that held chains and sword. He didn't worry about it. He just did what his officers told him, and handled the squad with a veteran's lack of fuss.

"Nothing left of that place no more, not after the gunships gave it the once-over." Usama was tall and lean and dark, with a long scimitar of a nose and a neat black beard. He carried a scope-sighted sniper's rifle on his back.

"No more town there, sure enough." Hans spat. He lit a cigarette. "But those bastards nailed Boris and Kemal. Shouldn't never have happened."

Everyone nodded. "Stinking civilians," somebody said. "What're they doin' with so many rifles?"

"It's like they're all Citizens," Hans said.

"My ass." That was Usama again. "*We* can lick these Yankees hand to hand. Real Citizens, they'd have 'em for breakfast."

"No, not Citizens like that." A thoroughly hard man, Hans admired the Draka not least because he knew they were harder. "But they've all got the right to carry weapons. Somethin' in their constitution—the…fifth amendment?" He shrugged. He couldn't precisely remember the briefing. "So we got to deal with more goddamn *francs-tireurs* than you can shake a stick at, on top of whatever real soldiers—holdouts—they've got left."

The Last Word

He scowled at the last sentence. The USA wasn't pacified. Hell, it wasn't even occupied. That was his job. It was a nasty one, too. He wondered what his chances were of getting old enough to retire and buy himself a tavern or something. He shrugged against the weight of body armor. Not so good, probably.

"That one old bastard got Boris right between the eyes." Usama spoke with grudging professional respect. "Had to be five, six hundred meters, too. Good shot."

Corporal Soshangane was a Zulu; his folk had been under the Draka yoke longer than almost any other. From what he'd told Hans, he was a sixth-generation Janissary, and he thought very much like his masters. "Damn fools," he said now, in accents that might almost have belonged to a von Shrakenberg. "Kill a coupla us, cost 'em that whole damn town."

"I don't think they reckon that way," Hans said. "This here's like it was in Europe fifty years ago, only more so. They ain't gonna go down easy."

"Long as they go down." Soshangane grinned, white teeth extra bright in his dark face. "Some o' the girls, they go down mighty nice."

"*Ja*," Hans said, a word that did duty for *yeah* in the English spoken between the Rhine and the Oder. He ground the cigarette out under his bootheel. "Come on—into the woods." He pointed north and south. "We aren't gonna let those bastards go in all by themselves, are we?" Nobody said no. You didn't let your buddies down. The Janissaries fought by few rules, but that was one of them.

Hans' boots scrunched in dead leaves. He cursed under his breath, in English and in the German he'd learned as a child. Nothing to be done about it. The leaves were everywhere, here and there drifted deep like snow. Hans' eyes flicked back and forth, up and down. He wished for eyes in the back of his head. His buddies were the eyes in the back of his head, but that didn't seem enough.

Back and forth, up and down. They didn't have woods like this in Germany—not anywhere in Europe that he knew of. This place looked as if he were the first man who'd ever set foot here. It would probably be glorious in spring, with the trees in full leaf, with the birds singing songs he'd never heard before, and with squirrels peering at him out of beady black eyes.

Everything was quiet now, except for the small sounds he and his men couldn't help making. The hair on the back of his neck kept wanting to prickle up. He couldn't have proved he was being watched, but he had that feeling. He'd learned to pay attention to it. If you didn't pay attention to such feelings, you ended up buying a plot, not a tavern.

Still, he was taken by surprise when automatic-weapons fire ripped into the squad *from behind*. He whirled and dove for cover, his Holbars T-7 already spitting death. Even as he thudded down onto the ground, he knew he was up for a court-martial. How the devil had he walked right past those Yankee bastards without even knowing they were there?

Then a grenade burst half a meter in front of his face, and such questions became academic.

ANSON MACDONALD felt uncomfortable in a uniform of green and brown camouflage splotches, even though the holdouts had supplied him with one with a star on each collar tab—brigadier general was the Army equivalent of commodore. *I'm not betraying Annapolis*, he told himself. *This is the only way to hit back at the enemy I have left. Oh, some of the Alliance submersibles are probably still out there, but I'd have just as easy a time getting to the asteroid belt as going aboard one of them. They're on their own now, same as I am. I hope they do a lot of damage before the Snakes finally sink 'em.*

"Did you spray yourself with insect repellent?" Captain Fischer asked as they emerged from the mouth of a cave.

"Of course I did." MacDonald knew he sounded offended. He couldn't help it. "I grew up in Missouri," he told the younger officer, frost still in his voice. "I knew about chiggers twenty years before you were a gleam in your old man's eye."

"All right, sir." Fischer remained unruffled. "Some people need a head start." *I've just been given the glove*, MacDonald thought, and chuckled under his breath. Fischer went on, "Now—can you see the cave we just came out of?"

After looking back, Commodore MacDonald had to shake his head. "No—and we can't have moved more than three or four meters."

"That's right." Fischer smiled. Again, the grin took years off him. "That rock overhang hides it unless you know exactly where to look—and even then it's not easy to spot. It's even harder in the summertime. The trees have their leaves, and the wild rhododendrons and such grow like madmen underneath 'em. If you can't see it, the Draka won't, either."

"Not until we come out and give 'em a hard time." Anson MacDonald grinned a grin of his own, a savage grin that made his teeth seem extraordinarily sharp. "Those Janissaries never knew what hit 'em." He looked to the east. It was after ten in the morning, but the sun still hadn't climbed over the edge of the valley near whose bottom they stood. "This country's even more rugged than I thought coming into the Redoubt."

"Nantahala's a Cherokee word, they tell me," Fischer answered. "Supposed to mean 'Land of the Noonday Sun.' A lot of the valleys hereabouts are so steep, noon's the only time the sun gets down into 'em at all. Add in all the caves and all the mineshafts—people went after mica and talc and emeralds, but they hardly ever made enough to pay their way—and you've got some nasty terrain to overrun."

"And we've tied a lot of the caves and the shafts together into a nice network," MacDonald said.

"No, sir," Fischer said, quietly but emphatically. "Not *a* network. A lot of different networks, all through this whole area. Sooner or later, we'll lose prisoners. We have to assume they won't all be able to suicide, and that means the Draka will start squeezing things out of them. We don't want the Redoubt unraveling when the first string comes loose, the way a cheap sweater would. If they want us, they'll have to come in and dig us out, and it'll cost 'em."

"I should hope so." Anson MacDonald looked around. "You could turn most of this to radioactive glass without bothering us much."

Fischer nodded. "That's the idea. We come out, give them hell in four different states, and then disappear again." He grimaced. "The only rough spot is, since we're up against the Snakes it's hard as the devil on the civilian population."

But now Commodore MacDonald shook his head. "If the Draka want to kill hostages, that's their mistake. Better for Americans to die as free men than to live as slaves."

"Sir, do me a favor," Fischer said. "Take that to the Propaganda Section. One of our biggest worries is how to get our personnel to carry on with the Snakes holding a gun to the country's head."

MacDonald's face and voice were bleak. "The gun's already gone off. The Alliance is dead. The USA is dead. We're not fighting to win—you said so yourself. We've fighting to hurt the Draka and keep on hurting them. That's a different business. I presume everyone in the Redoubt is a volunteer?" He'd never asked before, but the answer seemed obvious.

And, sure enough, Captain Fischer said, "Yes, sir."

"All right, then." Anson MacDonald had never been a man to brook much nonsense from anyone. "I presume they knew what they were volunteering for, too. We've got no magic way to throw the Snakes back across the Atlantic. We can't very well start a new religion and go crusading against them. All we can do is give them grief."

"That's right," Fischer said. "That's the attitude. If I'm down to my king, I want the other fellow down to a king and a pawn, and I want to make him have to work like hell to promote that pawn."

"There you go, son." Suddenly, crazily, MacDonald felt years younger than he had any business being. Maybe Fischer felt the same, for he grinned again. They both slid down into the cave. Once they'd scrambled a little way back from the entrance, there was room to stand up. The air inside was cool and damp and smelled of dirt. From what Fischer said, it was always like that, winter and summer. Fischer reached up and touched a piece of the cave roof that looked no different from any other piece. A doorway opened. Till it did, MacDonald couldn't have told it from the rest of the back wall. He and Captain Fischer walked into the Redoubt. The door closed behind them.

IN A tent outside Gastonia, North Carolina, two Draka officers studied a map that looked as if it had a bad case of the measles. "Wotan's prick, what're we gonna do about this place?" Moirarch Benedict Arnold asked. These past couple of generations, every male Citizen surnamed Arnold seemed to have that first name, a reminder of just what the Domination thought of the Yankees they'd been hating for two hundred years.

"I know what I'd like to do, Ben," answered his superior, Merarch Piet van Damm. His family had deeper roots in southern Africa than anyone this side of the Bushmen. When Arnold raised a questioning eyebrow, he went on, "I'd like to air-burst enough H-bombs over that country to turn it all to slag."

"Still wouldn't get rid of the holdouts," Arnold said mournfully. "From what the Security Directorate says, they're based underground. They've been gettin' ready for this for a *long* time, the sons of bitches."

Merarch van Damm chuckled. "And we ain't?" But the grin slid off his face. He was all business as he went on, "I don't care if it'd get rid of 'em or not. It'd take away their cover. That's triple-canopy forest there—underbrush up to your chest, then a second layer twice as high as a man, and then the big hardwoods and pines on top o' that. Blast it down to the ground an' we'd be able to spot those bastards when they came topside to do their mischief."

"Sounds good to me," Arnold said. "We've lost too many men already—not just Janissaries, either, but Citizens, more'n we can afford. Damn the Yankees, they stashed some of their best down there. How do we go about gettin' authorization for it?"

"I tried," Piet van Damm answered. "We don't. Won't happen. Forget about it. Wish for the moon. Hell, we've *got* the moon."

"Who's got his head up his ass in the high command?" Arnold asked. The two of them were old friends. Had they been anything else, the moirarch wouldn't have put his career on the line like that.

Before answering, van Damm walked out of the tent into the cold, nasty rain that drummed down outside. Benedict Arnold pulled up his head and followed. "Never can tell who might be listening," van Damm remarked. "Even out here, I won't name names. But the initials are *v.S.*"

Benedict Arnold stared. "The von Shrakenbergs? Jesus Christ, why?" He was horrified enough to swear by something stronger than the neopagan pantheon.

"As best I can make out, two reasons, maybe three," Merarch van Damm said. "Number one, they say both sides have already used too many atomic weapons."

"Something to that," Arnold admitted reluctantly.

"Something," van Damm said. "Not enough, if you ask me. Number two is kind of related to number one. Those Yankee bastards there are enough of a nuisance to keep our soldiers sharp for years to come. They won't get soft from lack of anything to do. Our grandfathers used the Finns the same way fifty years ago."

"Something to that, too," Moirarch Arnold said. This time, he raised the objection himself: "But not enough, like you said before. We needed to stay sharp after we licked the Nazis and the Reds—we still had the Alliance to worry about. But now it's whipped. The world is *ours*, sir."

"I know." His superior walked a little farther from the tent, as if to put more distance between himself and any possible listening devices. Arnold followed once more. After a dozen squelching steps, van Damm deigned to continue: "And there's a third reason, or I've heard there's a third reason." He moved on again.

So, perforce, did Benedict Arnold. "Well?" he asked at last.

"You didn't hear this from me," Merarch van Damm told him. "I don't care if the Security Directorate shoves burning pine slivers up under your fingernails, but you didn't hear this from me."

The Last Word

"I got you," Arnold said. If the SD boys ever started grilling him, burning pine slivers were the least he had to worry about in this electronic age, but van Damm had made his point.

"All right." The senior officer nodded heavily. "The third reason, from what I hear—and you don't need to know where I heard it—is that the von Shrakenbergs want that whole region kept as a game preserve for the days after we whip this continent into our kind of shape. It's one of the last stretches of this kind of forest left in eastern North America."

"A game preserve?" Benedict Arnold didn't say the words out loud. He couldn't. He just mouthed them. After a few seconds, he found his voice again: "The von Shrakenbergs are going to let us bleed for the sake of a *game preserve?*"

Piet van Damm chuckled. "Sounds like them, doesn't it? And it fits together with number two. After all, what are the Yankees these days but game? You ever read the story that Englishman wrote back before we were born?"

"Who hasn't?" Arnold said. "But a proper Draka wouldn't have let that bastard bushwhack him. You hunt the way you do everything else: to win. You don't win, there's no point to it."

"Of course not." Van Damm nodded. "But he wrote it for Englishmen and Americans, so naturally the Draka had to lose." One hand folded briefly into a fist. "Well, we didn't lose, and we're not going to lose. The world is ours, and we'll do whatever we damn well please with it."

Benedict Arnold started to say something, then checked himself. When he did speak, it was after some little thought: "You're right, sir. And on that scale of things, what's one game preserve more or less?" He came to attention, ignoring the rain with the ease of a man who'd known worse. "Service to the State!"

"Glory to the Race!" Piet van Damm finished the secular—the nearly secular—invocation. He peered west toward the Great Smoky Mountains, not that visibility was even a kilometer right this minute. "All the same, the sooner we stop hunting holdouts and start hunting boar, the happier I'll be."

Anson MacDonald sat down at a table and opened an MFR. The initials stood for Meal, Fully Ready. The troops, predictably, had come up with a rather different meaning for the acronym, one that Oedipus would have approved of. The MFRs were supposed to be able to sustain life indefinitely. *Maybe it only seems like forever*, MacDonald thought as he opened the foil-wrapped serving of what was alleged to be beef stew.

Captain Fischer sat down beside him. His MFR held chicken à la king—*chicken à la thing*, in the parlance of the soldiers of the Redoubt. He spooned up a mouthful, then grimaced. "Eating these bastards is about the only thing that tempts me to surrender to the Snakes," he said.

He meant it for a joke, but MacDonald frowned. "Do you suppose that might prove enough of a problem to lead to desertions?" he asked.

"I doubt it, sir." Fischer waved to the televisor screen, which was showing Draka programming these days: at the moment, instructions on the proper behavior for serfs in the presence of Janissaries or Draka Citizens themselves. That was fairly innocuous. But Fischer went on, "Remember last night?"

MacDonald grunted. "I'm not likely to forget it." The Snakes had broadcast what they called an object lesson: the execution of several men who'd presumed to shoot at one of their vehicles. It had taken a long time, and it hadn't been pretty.

"I hope that's not going to be a problem with the troops here," Fischer said in worried tones. "They've been briefed that they have to think of the civilian population of the USA as if it were already taken off the board."

"And so it is," Commodore MacDonald replied. "Say what you will about the Draka, they're the most efficient slavemakers this poor sorry world has ever seen." He dug into his MFR, then wished he hadn't.

"I know," Fischer said. "But some of those new slaves are family or sweethearts or friends to our men here. Watching what happens to them as they go under the yoke can't be good for morale."

"Not for ours, and not for that of the other bands of free men still running around loose," MacDonald agreed. "But it's a military reality, Captain. We have to deal with it as best we can."

"I know that, sir." Was Fischer showing exaggerated patience? MacDonald studied him. He probably was. He went on, "And it's one more problem the goddamn Snakes don't have to worry about and we do."

Anson MacDonald frowned, partly because of the alleged meal in front of him, partly because he saved profanity and obscenity for special occasions, and disapproved of those who didn't. He said, "You know, Captain, in a way this is a judgment on us. Worse than we deserved, maybe, but a judgment all the same."

Fischer frowned. "I'm not sure I follow that, sir," he said stiffly.

"By which you mean you think I ought to go soak my head," MacDonald said.

The younger officer chuckled. "Now that you mention it, yes, sir."

"You don't tell a man to go soak his head when you don't understand him. You ask him what he means." MacDonald forced his deep voice, raspy from too many years of too many cigarettes, up the scale to imitate Fischer's: "'What *do* you mean, sir?'"

Fischer snorted, then tried to pretend he hadn't. "Go on ahead without me. You seem to be doing that anyhow."

"It's not hard, Captain." MacDonald went over to a tap to pour hot water on the instant coffee from the MFR. It was lousy, but better than no coffee at all. "We were soft, and we've paid the price for being soft. Draka Citizens are A-Number-One bastards, but they've always known what's on the line for them. If they ever let up, even for a second, they were doomed. They had responsibility and discipline forced on them. We didn't. And so…we're in the Redoubt, and they're out there."

That got under Captain Fischer's skin. MacDonald had thought it would—he'd hoped it would, anyhow. Voice wooden with disapproval, Fischer said, "I don't think it's anywhere near so simple as that, sir."

"Probably not," Commodore MacDonald said cheerfully. "But are you going to tell me it's not one of the reasons they won and we lost?"

Fischer's lips skinned back from his teeth in what was anything but a grin. He hid from the Draka down here in the Redoubt, but he hesitated to admit the USA and the Alliance for Democracy had failed all over the Earth, all over the Solar System. He said, "We did the best we could, sir. We hurt the Snakes bad, and we're going to hurt 'em worse."

"And can you imagine anything more useless and more expensive than the second best military in the world?" Anson MacDonald asked. Fischer turned a dull red. MacDonald jabbed a thumb at his own chest. "That includes me just as much as it does you, son. Remember Lenin saying that the capitalists would sell him the rope he'd use to hang them?"

"I've heard of Lenin," Fischer said, at which MacDonald rolled his eyes. But it had been a crowded century, and Lenin and Communism both lay on the ashheap of history long before the younger officer came on the scene. As if to point that out, Fischer went on, "Anyway, it was the Draka who hanged the Russians."

"That's true, but the principle still holds," MacDonald said. "Right up till the end, we kept dealing with the enemy, selling him things he couldn't make for himself, treating him as if he were just another neighbor. You don't trade steaks to the lion next door; it just makes him hungry."

"Nobody wanted this war," Fischer said. "You don't win a chess game by kicking over the board."

"You do if you see the other fellow's about to promote a pawn," MacDonald said. "Nobody *here* wanted this war. The Draka? That's liable to be another story. We might have beaten them economically. Some of our most effective propaganda went into letting their serfs know what we had and they didn't and couldn't. So they kicked over the board—and we helped. By rights, they should have been stretched too thin to charge full speed ahead into electronics and space engineering and genetic engineering all at the same time. But we sold them half of what they needed. Even after they gobbled up India, we kept on selling to them. I can't think of anything in the universe that will kill you deader faster than stupidity."

"You...have strong views on these things," Fischer said after a brief pause for thought.

"So I do, and much good it's done me," Commodore MacDonald replied with lighthearted bitterness. "People kept telling me I'd have two stars, maybe three, by now if I could learn to keep my mouth shut. They were probably right, but…" He shrugged. "I've always been a loose cannon."

Captain Fischer's eyes said something like, *I never would have guessed*. But all he said aloud was, "Well, they're not going to court-martial you for it now."

"No, indeed." MacDonald laughed. "They can't even discharge me. They're stuck with me, is what they are."

By Fischer's expression, he felt stuck with Commodore MacDonald, too. Again, though, he kept his speech circumspect—more circumspect than MacDonald thought he would have been able to manage himself: "Yes, sir." Hard to go wrong with that.

"And speaking of which," MacDonald persisted, "as things stand right now, I'm just eating up food—to use the term loosely—that would do better going to a genuine fighting man. We can't really afford to keep noncombatants down here. When do I get my rifle and my Snake-hunting license?"

"You're, ah, not so young as you might be, sir," Fischer said.

"I know that. I get reminded every time I look in the mirror," MacDonald said. "One good reason for not looking in the mirror very often." That jerked a chuckle from Captain Fischer, even if it was the heartless chuckle of a man who didn't yet have to worry about such things—and who wasn't likely to get that old, anyhow. MacDonald pressed on: "I'm not asking to be a brigadier up there. But I know how to shoot. I've got marksman's medals on my record, even if they are from Annapolis and not West Point."

"There is one thing you have to take care of first, you know," Captain Fischer told him. "You have to go to the dentist."

Anson MacDonald winced. Somehow, going up against the Draka was easier to contemplate in cold blood. But, after a moment, he nodded. "The sacrifices I make for my country," he said. Fischer laughed again, though MacDonald hadn't altogether been joking. And the United States was already a sacrificial victim. That being so, how could he begrudge one more sacrifice? He couldn't, and he knew it.

"Idiots. Fools. Morons. Bureaucrats." Merarch Piet van Damm glowered at the orders the fax had just delivered. "But I repeat myself."

Moirarch Benedict Arnold nodded. "If they were going to send us into the mountains after those holdouts, why did they wait till springtime? Why didn't they do it three months ago?"

"'More urgently prioritized tasks elsewhere,'" van Damm read, as if the words were scatological rather than insipid. He came to stiff attention. *Ave, Imperator! Nos morituri te salutamus!*"

"Maybe it won't be as bad as that," Arnold said.

"You're right. Maybe it'll be worse. Matter of fact, you can bet your balls it'll be worse." Van Damm pointed west, toward the Great Smokies. "Pretty, aren't they—all nice and green?"

"Yes, sir," Moirarch Arnold agreed. "No country like that back in Africa. Hardly any like it anywhere in the Domination. I suppose the Urals come closest, but they aren't really what you'd call a good match, either."

His superior suggested that the powers that be use one of the Urals—or perhaps the whole range; van Damm was more irate than precise—as a suppository. Before Benedict Arnold could do anything more than begin to contemplate that, van Damm went on, "Do you know what all that bloody green means?"

"Spring," Arnold said. "Some of the oddest birds you've ever seen, too," he added, for he was an enthusiastic amateur ornithologist. "I saw my first hummingbird the other day. Astonishing creatures—it's as if vertebrates were evolving to compete with bees and butterflies."

"Hummingbirds!" Piet van Damm clapped a hand to his forehead. "We're all going to get our nuts shot off, and the man's babbling about hummingbirds. Thor's hammer!—and don't I wish I could drop it on those mountains? What the green means is, all the trees and bushes in Wotan only knows how many square klicks are in new leaf. And do you know what *that* means, or are your brains still flitting like those hummingbirds?"

"No, sir." Moirarch Arnold, like any Citizen officer, quickly returned to the business at hand. "It means our airborne infrared and satellite reconnaissance views aren't going to be worth much."

The Last Word

"Give the man a cigar!" van Damm said sourly. "That's just what it means, and they want to commit more Citizen troops along with the Janissaries: have to set the proper example, you know."

"Oh, yes." Benedict Arnold nodded. Of necessity, the Domination fielded far more slave troops than Citizen formations. Never letting the Janissaries believe even for a moment that the tail might wag the dog was a cornerstone of Draka administration. Suppressing mutinies was feasible, but expensive. Making sure they didn't happen in the first place sometimes cost Citizen lives, but paid dividends in the long run.

"We *will* have some ghouloons," van Damm said, brightening for the first time. "They'll help in the tracking—but not enough, dammit, not enough."

"When do we go in?" Moirarch Arnold asked.

"Orders are to commence the operation at 0600 hours tomorrow and to continue until there are no more Yankee holdouts in the area," his superior answered. "We're allotted three weeks to root 'em all out."

"Three…weeks?" Arnold burst out laughing: it was either that or burst into tears, and he hadn't cried since he was a little boy. "What's the High Command been smoking? Whatever it is, I want some, too."

"Oh, yeah." Piet van Damm nodded. "But we've got our orders. And ours is but to do—or die." He turned soldierly again. "I'll see you at 0600. Let the games begin. Service to the State!"

"Glory to the Race!" Benedict Arnold finished the formula. Moirarch and merarch exchanged somber salutes.

COMMODORE ANSON MacDonald didn't like the feel of the automatic rifle he held. He hadn't been lying about his marksman's medals. But he'd won them a long time ago, at a Naval Academy far, far away. Since then, he hadn't worried much about firearms light enough for one man to carry. The Navy was the gentlemanly service, the one that did its killing at ranges too far for the human eye to note the details of what it had done. Close-in fighting, the sort that involved assault rifles and entrenching tools with sharpened blades? That was why God made Marines.

He hefted the Colt-Enfield again. It wasn't the weapon with which he'd trained, either. No long wooden stock here. No elegance. No beauty. No class. Just steel and plastic, as functional as a hacksaw and about as lovely. He shrugged. As a tool for killing people, it was first-rate.

Captain Fischer watched him with some amusement. "Well, sir, you wanted the chance. Now you've got it. The Snakes are coming in—and they're loaded for bear."

"Good!" MacDonald's doubts about the weapon he held vanished, swept away in a hot wind of fury and blood lust. "Now we make them pay."

"We've already started." Fischer's grin had a certain blithe ferocity to it, too. "You know about their ghouloons?"

"Oh, yes. Horrible things. A bad sign, too. If it hadn't been for their biotech, we *would* have licked them. Damned time-bomb virus." How were you supposed to fight a war while half your key personnel were having psychotic breakdowns?

"Dangerous things, too," Fischer said. "They started sending 'em into the woods to sniff out our doorways." The grin got wider. "But they missed a trick—no such thing as a gas mask for a ghouloon."

"That *is* a missed trick," agreed MacDonald, an avid, and highly skilled, bridge player. "Back in the Great War, they had masks for horses and even for runner dogs. I've seen the old photos. Well, too bad for the Snakes." He paused. "I presume they can't use the gas to find any of our tunnel entrances."

"Oh, no, sir." Fischer still wore that grin. "Canisters, carefully set out while none of our little friends was looking. Some of them are close to the cave mouths, some a long ways off: the Draka won't be able to draw any conclusions by where we turned the gas loose and where we didn't."

"Sounds like good tactics." Commodore MacDonald set a pot helmet on his head. It was of some fancy synthetic, lighter and stronger than steel. Unlike the steel helmets U.S. soldiers had worn in the Eurasian War, this one offered proper protection for the back of the neck, as Draka headgear always had. As a result, the soldiers universally called it a Snake hat. They sneered at it, but they wore it.

"You ready, sir?" Captain Fischer asked.

"Ready as I'll ever be," Anson MacDonald answered. His heart thuttered—part eagerness, part buck fever. The stars he wore for rank badges were a joke. He was just an overage grunt, ready to do or die—ready, in the end, to do *and* die—for the United States and against the nastiest tyranny the world had ever seen.

As he followed Fischer through winding corridors towards a cave mouth, he pondered the strangeness of the Draka. A lot of the Snakes he'd met had been perfectly charming, but they all kept that slight…carnivorous undertone, as if descended from hunting dogs rather than social apes.

Or maybe *tribal* was a better word for the undertone. As technology advanced, so had the recognition of who counted as a fellow human being. After a while, it wasn't just your family or your clan or your tribe or the folk who spoke your language or looked like you. For most people, *human* came to mean *walking on two legs and speaking any language at all*. Not among the Snakes, though. To them, anybody not Draka counted as fair game.

And now the whole world was their oyster.

Well, here's to grit, MacDonald thought. Along with Captain Fischer and six or eight other men half his age or less, he came out of the Redoubt and into a natural cave. When Fischer closed the door behind them, it seemed to disappear.

Inside the cave, it was as cool and damp as it had been back in the fall. Once MacDonald and his comrades left that cave and came out into the real world, though, he knew the season had changed. Even under the trees, it was warm and humid. And it would get worse when summer replaced spring. *Of course, by then there may be no trees left standing*, he thought.

Just pushing through the underbrush took work. It also made a frightening amount of noise. "Take it slow and easy," Captain Fischer called from somewhere ahead—he'd vanished into the thick greenery. "No Snakes anywhere close. We've got plenty of time to get where we're going and set the ambush."

"Right, Captain." That wasn't Anson MacDonald. It was one of the youngsters moving along with him. His voice also came from in front of MacDonald, who fought down worry. *Can I keep up? Can I nail some of those bastards? Can I get some tiny bit of revenge for my raped and murdered country?*

Sweat sprang out on his forehead. *I'm an old man. I feel like an old man, by God, trying to get through this brush.* He coughed. His eyes watered. He knew it was just pollen in the air, but it made him worry more, about his lungs this time. As a young officer just out of Annapolis, he'd come down with TB. A few decades earlier, before antibiotics, that would have washed him out of the Navy. He wondered what he would have done. Politics? He'd always had strong views about everything. Engineering? He made a decent engineer, but no more, and he always wanted to be the best at whatever he did. Writing? He'd been called on the carpet plenty of times for making his reports and evaluations livelier than the wooden official style. Reading that stuff bored him; writing it bored him worse.

But, thanks to wonder drugs, it was moot. Even though he worried about his lungs, they were as good as any of those kids', or they would have been if he hadn't kept on smoking in spite of everything.

Somewhere not far off, a mockingbird trilled—except it wasn't a mockingbird. It was Captain Fischer, whistling to let his men know they'd reached the slope where they would meet the enemy.

MacDonald whistled back, fluttering his tongue against the roof of his mouth. He was pretty good at bird calls, but he didn't need to be note-perfect: how many Draka knew what North American birds really sounded like? You used whatever edge you could get.

He found his foxhole in the middle of a laurel thicket. Settling himself, he peered out towards a game track along which enemy soldiers were likely to come. They couldn't possibly see him, not when the undergrowth shadowed his position. His countrymen had had plenty of time to fortify these mountain valleys. They'd had to do most of it at night, of course, but they'd got it done.

He wondered how many soldiers had come up out of the Redoubt to challenge the Snakes here. He didn't know. Nobody'd told him. That made excellent military sense. If he didn't know, neither pharmaceuticals nor wires clipped to sensitive spots nor the impaling stake could rip the information out of him.

What had that Nazi general called the memoirs he'd written once he got to London? *Without Hope and Without Fear*, that was it. That was how Anson MacDonald felt now. He marveled that people had got so exercised about the Nazis and paid the Draka so little attention before the Eurasian War. Hitler's crowd talked the talk, but the Draka walked the walk.

But the Nazis did what they did to white people, to Europeans, MacDonald thought. *The Draka came down on niggers and ragheads and chinks, so it didn't seem to matter so much. One brutalized blond kid is worth a dozen with black skin and kinky hair.* That was how a lot of people had looked at it, anyhow. MacDonald didn't weep that the Nazis had gone down. But who would have thought they'd go down to something worse?

Somebody somewhere stepped on a dry twig—the oldest cliché in the book, but one of the hardest things to avoid just the same. Anson MacDonald stopped worrying about what had happened long ago and what might have been. None of that mattered any more, not compared to staying alive through the next few minutes.

An American screwing up…or a Snake? He had a round in the chamber of his assault rifle, and he peered along the sights down to the little stretch of path he could see. He had an earpiece to listen for Captain Fischer's orders, but Fischer was maintaining radio silence. The Draka would be listening.

And then he saw the bastards: lean, sun-browned white men in camouflage colors that didn't quite fit this forest. Ice and fire ran through him. *Not Janissaries*, he realized. *Those are Citizen troops. They've sent in the first team.* That only made him want to kill them all the more.

Gas masks gave them snouts, making them look like things rather than people. *They* are *things*, he thought as his finger tightened on the trigger. *And they'll make things out of us. But some of them will burn in hell before they do.*

He wanted to kill them all. If that meant gas, he didn't mind. If he'd had a nuclear bomb, he would have used it on Citizens—no point wasting it on Janissaries. He wondered why the Draka hadn't cratered these mountains with atomic weapons. *Their aristocrats probably want to keep them for a hunting park*, he thought. *Come on, you murdering slavemasters. I'll give you something to hunt.*

His finger twitched on the trigger again. He didn't open up. Someone else, someone who had a better notion of when the time was just right, would take care of that. But when the time came—and it could only be moments away—he would take a good many Snakes with him before he went.

Moirarch Benedict Arnold's head kept whipping back and forth, back and forth. In these woods, it didn't do him a hell of a lot of good. It wouldn't have done him much good even if he hadn't been peering out through the lenses of his gas mask. The Yankees could have stashed a couple of armored divisions within a klick of him, and he never would have known it till they started their engines.

The mask was bad enough. Full protective clothing… In this heat and humidity, he didn't even want to think about that. One big reason neither side used gas all that much was that the countermeasures you needed against it made any sort of fighting almost impossible.

But the Americans had been smart to take out the ghouloons that way. Right now, probably, someone was designing a mask they could wear. And somebody else was probably busy figuring out how to persuade them to wear it. In the long run, that would make them more useful to the Race. In the short run, somebody's career had probably just gone down in flames because he hadn't realized they would need masks.

All through the woods, birds chirped and sang. Sweet sounds, but not sounds he was used to. He wouldn't have been surprised if some of those calls didn't spring from feathered throats. Easy to hide information there.

And he wouldn't have been surprised if some of those calls weren't the sound of a goose walking over his grave. The Yankees had shown they didn't want the Domination sending semianimal reconnaissance patrols into these woods. They wouldn't take kindly to soldiers marching through.

If somebody opened up on him right now, he'd dive behind...that rock. *Unless there's a Yankee behind it already*, he thought. The mask hid his chuckle. *If there is, I'll kill the bastard.* Hand to hand, the odds were with him; even American soldiers were soft and slow by Draka standards. But nobody dodged the bullet with his name on it.

Those folk who took their neopaganism seriously—a tiny minority, a century after the old Germanic gods were reborn and then seen to be no real answer—would have called him fey. He didn't look at it that way. He wanted to live. It was just that his superiors had set things up in such a way that his chances were less than they would have been had those superiors had any real idea what the devil they were doing.

No sooner had that thought crossed his mind than small-arms fire started barking. A second later, after two or three bullets cracked past his head, he was behind that rock, with no company but a little lizard with a blue belly that scurried off into the leaves when he thudded down.

"Base, we are under attack!" he shouted into his radio. "Map square Green 2. I say again, we are under attack at Green 2. Do you copy?"

The only noise that came from the set was the one bacon might have made frying in a pan. Benedict Arnold cursed. The Yankees had always been too stinking good with electronics. They were jamming for all they were worth. No instant air support. No friendly helicopter gunships rushing in to hose down the enemy with Gatlings and rockets. No fighter-bombers screaming down out of the sky to plaster the Americans with napalm. If he and his men were going to come out of this in one piece, they'd have to do it themselves, for the time being, anyhow.

He squeezed off a short burst in the direction from which the enemy fire seemed heaviest. A couple of Citizens were down in spite of body armor, one writhing with a leg wound, the other motionless, shot through the head. Moirarch Arnold cursed again. Dammit, the Race shouldn't be spending men like this in a country it had already conquered.

One thing—everybody who heard the fighting would move towards it. The Draka took care of their own. They had to—nobody else would. He just hoped the other units in these stinking woods weren't pinned down like his men.

Well, if they had to fight the old-fashioned way for a while till they could beat the jamming, they bloody well would. "Forward by squads!" he yelled, hoping his voice would carry. "Leapfrog!"

What would the Yankees least expect? A movement straight toward them, unless he missed his guess. He didn't think so. He wanted to get at close quarters with them. At close quarters, he and his men had the edge.

He scrambled out from behind the rock and dashed towards a tree up the slope. The men from the squads not moving fired to make the enemy keep his head down. Bullets stitched the ground by his feet. Grenades burst not far away. Mortar bombs started raining down on the Draka. And one of his men stepped on a mine that tore him to red rags.

Arnold dove down behind the tree. Somewhere behind him, more Yankees opened up on his beleaguered men. He cursed every von Shrakenberg ever born. *Hunting preserve, my left ballock,* he thought. *The Americans couldn't have set a better ambush if they'd planned it for years.*

Of course, they *had* planned it for years. And now the Draka would pay the price. Arnold's grin behind the mask was savage. The Alliance for Democracy had already paid the price. In the long run, this was just small change. But a man who got killed in a fight that didn't mean much was every bit as dead as one who got killed any other way. Benedict Arnold didn't want to die. That, after all, was what enemies and serfs were for.

Ground combat was even more chaotic, even more frightening and frightful, than Anson MacDonald had thought it would be. On a ship, he was part of a smoothly functioning team. He didn't have that feeling here. On the contrary: he'd never felt more alone in his life. And every Draka in the world seemed to be trying to kill him and nobody else.

The Last Word

He'd hit a couple of Snakes. He was sure of it. He wasn't sure he'd killed them. Their body armor was at least as good as his, and they could carry more than he and his countrymen did. The sons of bitches were just out-and-out strong.

They were quick, too. As Captain Fischer had predicted, the Draka came straight at the men who opened up on them. "Don't try to duke it out with a Snake," Fischer had warned. "You'll lose. We can't afford that. Shoot him or run away."

Fischer had told that to the twenty-year-olds who were supposed to be fast and strong. *What about me?* MacDonald wondered. But the answer seemed pretty obvious. *If you're dumb enough to volunteer for the Poor Bloody Infantry, you deserve whatever happens to you. And it will.*

I'm putting my body between my home and war's desolation. That sounded very fine and noble…till the bullets started flying. And war's desolation had already visited his home, and all the other homes in the Alliance for Democracy—and a good many homes in the Domination of the Draka, too.

So what am *I doing here?* The answer there wasn't subtle, either. No room for subtlety, not any more. *I'm going to kill a few Snakes before they kill me. All right—fair enough.*

A few tiny holes were left in the jamming that scrambled radio reception through the area above the Redoubt. "Fall back!" Captain Fischer called through the speaker in MacDonald's left ear. "They're putting a little more pressure on us than we thought they'd be able to."

That would do for an understatement till a bigger one came along. Enemy firing came from both sides of MacDonald now, not just from in front of him. In spite of everything, the Draka had got in among the Americans. Guessing what they'd do didn't necessarily mean you could stop them. Who was outflanking whom was now very much a matter of opinion. *They're good, damn them*, MacDonald thought as he scuttled back towards another foxhole. If the Snakes hadn't been so good, he would have been fighting on their home turf, not his.

His heart thudded in his chest as he scrambled through the thick undergrowth. He panted when he threw himself into the new hole in the ground and looked around for targets. *That'd be an embarrassing way to check out—dying of a coronary on the battlefield. You won't do it—you won't, you hear me?* He tried to give his body orders as if it were an able seaman. But if it decided to be insubordinate, what could he do about it? Not much.

Above the crackle and thunder of gunfire came another sound, a loud thuttering. It came literally from above: from over the forest canopy. MacDonald couldn't see the machines making the new racket, but he knew what they were. In spite of the jamming, the Draka had got helicopter gunships over the right part of the field.

They won't use them when their fellows are all mixed up with ours…will they? The Snakes would. They did. They seemed to take the view that getting rid of the holdouts was worth whatever it cost.

Gatlings overhead roared, a sound like giants ripping thick canvas. Snake gunners ripple-fired rocket pods under their helicopters. MacDonald had never imagined such punishment. The ground beneath him shuddered as the rockets slammed home. Blast picked him up and flung him down. He tasted blood in his mouth. Those explosions had tried to tear his lungs right out of his body, and they'd damn near done it.

He knew he was screaming, but he couldn't hear a thing. Maybe the din all around was too loud. Maybe he was partly, or more than partly, deafened. He felt all turned around. Where the devil was the closest cave mouth? He could use his compass to find out, he supposed, doing his best to think straight in the midst of hell. But what were the odds he'd get there? Thin. Very thin.

More rockets rained down. One of them burst close to his new hole—much too close, in fact. It picked him up and slammed him down, harder than he was designed to be slammed. He felt things snap that had no business snapping. Pain flared red, then black, as consciousness fled.

The Last Word

With the Yankees' damned jammers still going flat out, Benedict Arnold had no control over the air strikes flown to help the Domination's troopers. He wasn't at all sure they *were* helping; they were right on top of the Americans, sure enough, but that meant they were also right on top of his own men.

He wasn't ashamed to scream when rockets from the helicopter gunships plowed up the landscape right under his own boots. Anybody who said he'd been in combat without getting scared almost out of his sphincters was either a dangerous liar or an even more dangerous psychopath. It was necessary. That didn't make it fun, except talking about it afterwards over booze or kif.

Not far away, one of his men went down, head neatly severed by a chunk of rocket casing. Even through the gas mask, Arnold smelled blood and shit. *Friendly fire*, they called it, the lying bastards.

Another Citizen fell, this one shot in the face. The pounding hadn't settled the Yanks' hash, then. Moirarch Arnold cursed. He'd known it wouldn't, though it did help some.

And then, from a few hundred meters behind him, came a roar louder than any of the mortar rounds or rockets bursting. He cursed again: that couldn't be anything but a gunship going down in flames. Bad luck? Or did the Yankees have some of those nasty little shoulder-mounted AA missiles of theirs? He wouldn't have been a bit surprised. In their shoes, he would have made sure he stocked some.

Another gunship crashed, even more noisily than the first. "Missiles," he muttered. Even without the din all around, the mask would have muffled the word. Not all the helicopters were out of action, though. Gatling fire and rockets flagellated the forest.

Some of that came in much too close to him. He dove into the nearest hole he could find—and then started to dive right out again, because an American soldier, his camouflage uniform a medley of shades different from the Domination's, already occupied it. But the Yankee didn't go for the assault rifle by him—he was either dead or unconscious, Arnold realized. One of his legs bent at an unnatural angle.

An old man, Arnold thought. Then he saw the single stars the American wore; they were almost invisible against his uniform. Excitement coursed through him. *I've caught a big fish, if he's still breathing.*

He felt for a pulse, and felt like whooping. The Yankee had one. And he was coming to; he stirred and groaned and reached for the rifle. Benedict Arnold grabbed it before he could. And the moirarch shed his gas mask. If the American wasn't wearing one, he was damned if he would.

The Yankee's eyes came open. They held reason—reason and danger. *He might be an old man, but he's nobody to screw around with*, Arnold thought. If he looked away for even a second, this fellow would make him pay.

Well, don't look away, then. Field interrogation was an art form in its own right. He smiled. It could be fun, too. "Hello, Yank," he said.

"Hello, Yank." The words told Anson MacDonald the worst. So did the greens of the other soldier's combat uniform—they were jungle greens, not those of the forest. And so did the barrel of the Holbars T-7 aimed at his head. That 4.45mm barrel looked wide as a tunnel.

MacDonald took inventory. Everything hurt—ribs and right leg worst. He could, after a fashion, bear it. If the Draka decided to give that leg a boot… Snakes were supposed to enjoy things like that, and they weren't exactly meeting over a tea party.

"My name is Anson MacDonald," he said. "My rank is commodore, U.S. Navy. My pay number…" He rattled it off. For close to forty years, it had been as much a part of him as his name.

How much good would any of this do? The Draka acknowledged the Geneva Convention only when they felt like it, and now there was nobody on the outside to pressure them to behave. The only rules left were the ones they felt like following.

For a moment, he'd succeeded in surprising this Snake. "Commodoah?" the fellow drawled. "You're a hell of a long way from the water, Navy man."

The Last Word

MacDonald started to shrug, then thought better of it. "I don't have to answer that," he said.

The Draka didn't reply, not in words. He just flicked out a booted foot and kicked MacDonald's right leg. MacDonald shrieked, then clamped down on it. "That there's just a taste," the Draka said mildly. "Don't waste my time, serf, not if you want to keep breathin'."

"Not likely," MacDonald said. "You'd never trust the likes of me as a serf, anyhow. You'll squeeze me and then you'll get rid of me. But I'll tell you this: when I go to hell, I'll have a couple of Draka sideboys along for escorts."

He wondered if that would get him killed in the next instant. But the Draka—a moirarch, MacDonald saw, gradually noticing finer details: *my luck to have one of their colonels get the drop on me while I was out*—just nodded. "All right, pal," he said. "We both know what's what, then. You better remember who's top and who's bottom, though."

Sex slang, MacDonald thought scornfully. But he nodded. "I'm not likely to forget."

"Right." The Draka had an easy, engaging smile. MacDonald might have liked him—had he not been one of the slaveowning sons of bitches who'd murdered the United States. "Now, Commodoah, suppose you tell me all about this holdout base of yours."

"Suppose I don't," MacDonald said.

That earned his broken leg another kick. He'd been sure it would. This time, he couldn't clamp down on his scream. Amid battlefield chaos, who noticed one more howl of anguish? Still smiling, the moirarch said, "You're hardly any sport, Yankee—too easy. But we've got all day, or as long as it takes."

Wrong, Anson MacDonald thought when he was capable of coherent thought again—which took some little while. Panting, he said, "I'll tell you something even more important first."

With a shake of the head, the Draka officer said, "No deal, pal. Tell me what I want to know."

"Afterwards."

"Who's top, Yank? You haven't got much in the way of a bargaining position."

Better than you think. MacDonald braced himself for another kick, not that bracing himself would do the slightest bit of good.

But the moirarch looked thoughtful. "Well, why not? Make it short, make it sweet—and then sing. You know how unhappy I'll be if you're lying or wasting my time. You know how unhappy you'll be, too."

"I have some idea," MacDonald said dryly.

And that made the Snake laugh out loud. "I like you, Yank, stick a stake up my ass if I don't. You're wasted on your side, you know that? Now sing."

"Oh, I will," MacDonald said. "How long do you think it'll take the Domination to clean things up here?"

"Fo'ty, fifty years," the Draka answered at once, and surprised MacDonald with his candor. "You Yankee bastards are a tough nut, maybe even tougher'n we reckoned. But so what? You're busted open now. We can do what we want with you—an' we will."

"No." Anson MacDonald shook his head. In spite of everything, this was what triumph felt like. "Because all the resources you spend here aren't going after what really matters."

"Nothin' really matters, not any more. This is mop-up time," the Draka moirarch said. "The Earth is ours. The Solar System is ours."

Baring his teeth in a fierce grin, MacDonald said, "And the *New America* is *ours*, by God." Those two words, *New America*, had kept him going after disaster engulfed the USA, engulfed the Alliance. "Alpha Centauri will be a going concern long before you Snake bastards can even start to try snuffing it out. *It's not over*, damn you. It's only starting. And I live for that, and so does everybody else in the Redoubt."

The Draka leaned forward. "The Redoubt, eh? So that's what you call it? Now you've made your speech, and you're going to tell me *all* about it…one way or another." Anticipation filled his voice.

MacDonald's smile got wider. "Goodbye," he said, and bit down hard. The false tooth the dentist had implanted cracked. The taste of bitter almonds

The Last Word

filled his mouth, overwhelmingly strong, burning, burning—but not for long. The poison worked almost as fast as they'd promised. He nodded once before everything faded. He'd even got the last word.

The Fake Pandemic

L. Sprague de Camp's *Lest Darkness Fall* changed my life forever. I found it in a secondhand store when I was fourteen or fifteen. Because I did, I ended up studying Byzantine history myself. Most of what I've written springs from that choice (I would have written *something* anyway; I already had the bug). Without it, I wouldn't have met my wife, which I did when I was pinch-hitting for the professor under whom I'd studied while he taught in Greece. I wouldn't have the kids I have, or be living where I live. Other than that, it didn't change my life a bit. I got to tell Sprague so, too. I think he was pleased and appalled in about equal measure. And, as you can imagine, when I got the chance to work in his world, I leaped at it.

TWO DOCKSIDE LOUNGERS, one near the bow and the other at the stern, caught lines sailors from the *Halcyon* tossed to them. As they made the lines fast to bollards sticking up from the pier in Ancona harbor, Tribonian murmured a brief prayer of thanksgiving. He'd made longer sea voyages than this one, but he'd never sailed out of sight of land before. And he was past fifty now, an age when you thought more about how much time you had left than you usually did when you were younger.

Another man on the pier was studying him in a way he wasn't sure he liked. But then the fellow said, "Would your Excellency by any chance be Master Tribonian, the distinguished gentleman from Constantinople?"

Tribonian nodded. "*Hoc ille*," he said. "And who might you be, to expect me here?"

"Sir, my name is Quintus Verus," the local replied. That was how he would have written it, at any rate, if he wrote. As anyone who spoke what passed for Latin these days would have, he pronounced it *Quinto Vero*. He went on, "I have the honor to work for King Urias' quaestor, Martinus Paduei." Again, the first name might have been *Martino*. "He sent me here from Florence, to bring you to him."

"How thoughtful," Tribonian said. "How…efficient." A proper Roman from Constantinople expected nothing of the sort from Italians and Ostrogoths. But events of the past few years—events with the mysterious Martinus' stamp on them—showed that such low expectations needed revising. The Emperor Justinian never would have ordered Tribonian to Italy if they hadn't.

"We try, sir. We do try," Quintus Verus said. "If you'll grab your blanket roll or duffel or whatever you've got, I have a carriage for the trip to Florence."

"One moment, and then I'm at your service." Tribonian went back to the stern and pressed a solidus into the callused palm of Appius Pyrrhus, who'd got the *Halcyon* from Dyrrachium to Ancona as smoothly as anyone could have hoped. "Thank you for—" Tribonian paused, embarrassed. He should have had a polite phrase at the ready, but he didn't.

The skipper chuckled and stuck the goldpiece in his belt pouch. "For not sinking you, hey?" he said with a leathery grin, which was indeed what Tribonian had meant. "Well, I would've sunk me, too, and I'm fond of this old skin. It's the only one I've got, after all."

"Er—quite." Tribonian slung an oiled-leather sack over his shoulder and teetered across the gangplank to the pier.

"Here you go, excellent boss." Quintus Verus held out a hand to steady him.

Tribonian took it with a word of thanks. He laughed self-consciously. "Having boards under my feet that aren't shifting on the waves feels strange."

"You can keep your boats, far as I'm concerned," the Italian said. "Come along with me now, if you please."

The Fake Pandemic

The carriage waited on dry land. Quintus Verus tipped the bruiser who'd been keeping an eye on it, the same way Tribonian had tipped Appius Pyrrhus. Verus tossed Tribonian's sack into the carriage, then waved for the man from Constantinople to climb in.

Tribonian wanted to look at the carriage before he boarded. It had a cloth cover to protect people from sun and rain. The front axle seemed odd, although, not being an artisan, he couldn't have said just how. So did the horses' harnesses.

Quintus Verus noticed him eyeing those. "Aren't they clever? Martinus' idea, of course. They let the horses pull without cutting off their wind. Makes 'em better'n oxen for work like this, and for plowing, too."

"Isn't that interesting?" Tribonian got into the carriage. The seat was padded and had a back: uncommon comfort. Quintus Verus took the reins. Off the horses went, at a good clip.

The Via Aemilia ran along the east coast of Italy. Like a lot of things here, it had been neglected the past couple of hundred years. Half an hour north of Ancona, a crew of laborers worked to repair potholes under the eyes of a couple of Goths with spears and swords. Seeing anyone fixing anything always surprised and pleased Tribonian.

A mile or so past the road crew, Quintus Verus stopped at the base of a tall tower built of wood so new, it hadn't yet weathered to grayness. A man in a little room at the top peered out to see what was going on down on the ground.

"Message for Florence," Verus called up to him. "I have Tribonian and I'm bringing him in."

"Florence," repeated the man at the top of the tower. "You have Tribonian and you're bringing him in." Quintus Verus waved to show he'd got it right.

A moment later, two red-painted wooden arms (which had been hanging against the sides of the structure) began wagging out what were obviously signals, though Tribonian had no idea what they meant. A long way up the Via Aemilia stood another tower. As soon as this one's arms stopped moving, that one's started.

"What are they doing?" Tribonian asked.

"Sending my message," Quintus Verus answered matter-of-factly. "Inside an hour or two, Florence will know we're on our way. They'll have time to get ready for us long before we get there. Martinus calls it the telegraph."

"Telegraph." Tribonian tasted the word. It meant *far-writing* in Greek. The Roman hadn't known Martinus Paduei knew the Empire's other language. His messages to Justinian were all in Latin, grammatically accurate but too clipped and concise to show much style.

"Martinus comes up with all kinds of things," the Italian said.

"I know," Tribonian replied on a falling note. Belisarius was Justinian's best general. He'd held his own against the ferocious and cunning Persians. He'd easily retaken North Africa from the Vandals. Everyone in Constantinople had been sure he'd make short work of the Ostrogoths and reclaim Italy, too. And he might have, if not for Martinus' machinations.

Now he served King Urias, not Justinian. In a fit of pique, the Emperor had released him from his oath after he refused to accept a parole Justinian assumed he would break. Tribonian sighed softly. He'd tried to talk the Emperor out of that. He'd failed. Justinian didn't understand honor. He never had. He never would.

The road curved. The carriage smoothly followed the curve. It had been smoothly following curves ever since Tribonian got into it, so smoothly that he only just now noticed it. "How does it do that?" he exclaimed. "Why isn't the front axle squealing and almost tipping us over whenever we change direction?"

Quintus Verus grinned at him. "That front axle's mounted on what mysterious Martinus calls a pivot. It can go with the motion, you might say. Makes the ride a lot nicer, doesn't it?"

"I should say so!" Tribonian answered. In one of his letters, Martinus had bragged that he could see the future. Tribonian hadn't cared to believe him. Now… Now he began to wonder. Whatever you could say about Italy, mired in Gothic barbarism it wasn't.

And the hostel where he and Quintus Verus spent the night only reinforced that impression. It was an inn out in the middle of nowhere, but ran as smoothly as a top-end guesthouse in the metropolis on the Bosphorus.

The Fake Pandemic

You could eat the food without being sorry you had. The beds were soft and comfortable and didn't seem buggy.

In spite of himself, Tribonian fell asleep impressed.

He was on the road from Ancona to Florence for four days. He'd never had a land journey go so well, not even near Constantinople. His driver stayed on the Via Aemilia as it jogged inland to Bologna, then dropped south on the Via Cassia to the new capital of Italy. On the way, the carriage passed several work gangs repairing and improving both roads.

"This isn't the most direct route," Quintus Verus said apologetically. "But the little side tracks…" He shook his head. "Lord only knows what they're like. Martinus may get around to fixing them up one of these days, but he sure hasn't yet."

"This is fine," Tribonian said. Gothic soldiers on horseback patrolled the main highways. For all Tribonian knew, the telegraph towers warned them where trouble was. And country tracks were bound to have country robbers prowling them, looking for foolish travelers trying shortcuts.

Like a lot of places in the Roman west, Florence had been a legionary camp before it became a city. The central square still marked where the camp's main north-south and east-west paths had met. Tribonian sniffed at the basilica in the square. Next to Justinian's splendid new Hagia Sophia, it looked dumpy and outdated.

The palace next to the basilica was also square and plain, but couldn't have been any older than the Constantinopolitan cathedral dedicated to Holy Wisdom. And the servitors who took charge of Tribonian handled getting him settled in a guest room as capably as Justinian's staff would have dealt with someone who needed to stay at the imperial palace. Everything and everyone seemed unusually clean.

Tribonian was still putting things on shelves when someone tapped at the door. He lifted the latch and swung the door wide. In the hallway stood a medium-sized man in his early forties. He had skin nearly as pale as a Goth's, red-brown hair pulling back at the temples, and rather a large nose. He wore a thigh-length wool tunic over a pair of trousers, a style that struck Tribonian as odd even for Italy.

"Good day, your Excellency," the stranger said in fluent if accented Latin. "We've been expecting you—nice that you're finally here. I'm Martinus Paduei." He held out his hand.

Automatically, Tribonian clasped it. "A privilege to make your acquaintance, your Excellency," he replied. "Forgive me, but I expected more, ah, formality."

"We don't go in for much of that in the country I come from—America, it's called," Paduei said. "But I think we can get along together anyway. I sure hope so."

"So do I," Tribonian said. "I should tell you, though, that about two days out of every week my master, the Emperor Justinian, is of the opinion that you are a demon in human shape, sent hither to afflict the world." He paused. "I speak the literal truth here. I do not mean to offend."

He was relieved when the man from—America?—grinned crookedly. "Don't worry," Paduei said. "I know people who think the same thing about Justinian. You may even know some of them, too."

Tribonian started to shake his head. He arrested the motion before it began, remembering a night when Belisarius' secretary had drunk much more wine than he should have. Luckily for Procopius, Tribonian had taken it as the wine talking, not the man. Justinian wouldn't have thought it was funny. Neither would Theodora, whose wrath might have been more frightening still.

"Well, never mind that," Paduei went on. "Do you want food? A bath? Sleep? Or can we get down to brass tacks now?"

"To what?" Tribonian frowned.

"To business, I should have said. Sorry. A figure of speech in my own language, translated literally into Latin. I do that sometimes."

"I see. We can talk for a while now, excellent Martinus, if you care to," Tribonian said.

The Fake Pandemic

"Great. Thanks. Let's do that, then." But instead of getting down to brass tacks—an interesting phrase, even if borrowed from whatever barbarous jargon Americans used—Paduei went off on another tangent: "It was generous of Justinian to order you to come to Italy when that interrupted your compiling of the constitutions in the *Corpus Iuris Civilis*."

Generous was not the word that had sprung into Tribonian's mind when the Emperor ordered him to drop everything he'd been working on, travel overland across the Balkans on the Via Egnatia, and sail the Adriatic to Italy. He'd been horrified and furious in about equal measure. You didn't tell Justinian no, though, not more than once you didn't. He'd make you sorry. Sorry? He'd make you wish you'd never been born.

Then something else occurred to Justinian's quaestor. He gaped at King Urias' quaestor. "How would you know about that? Forgive me, sir, but how much interest does the Ostrogothic Kingdom of Italy have in the codification of the Roman law?"

Martinus Paduei grinned. "Between you, me, and the wall, not a whole lot. But I know anyway. I know things. That's how I'm useful to King Urias. Frankly, that's how I stay alive here."

This time, Tribonian figured out the odd idiom without needing an explanation. Slowly, he said, "Things like your odd horse collars and your odder axles? Things like your telegraph? Like being able to make many copies of a book quickly? Like thoughts on the motions of the planets?" That little publication, even if it had come out under the late King Thiudahad's name, surely sprang from Paduei's pen. Bishops and patriarchs from one end of the Mediterranean to the other were pitching fits about it.

"*Hoc ille*, your Excellency. Things like those." For a couple of heartbeats, Paduei's grin got wider and cockier. Then, like an inflated pig's bladder pricked by a pin, it collapsed. The man from America suddenly looked like Hercules trying to uphold the weight of the heavens for a moment in Atlas' place. "Things like those, yes. And some other things, too."

"In a letter of yours to his Majesty, you mentioned a 'slight ability to foresee the future.' Till now, I took that for an exaggeration, but the Emperor

Justinian didn't," Tribonian said. "He is moving to gain more control over the barbarians of the Arabian desert so as to prevent the rise of the man you mentioned, whatever his name was. When I asked him why, he answered, 'Better safe than sorry.'"

"'Better safe than sorry,' yes. We agree on that, even if we don't agree on a whole lot of other things," Paduei said. "But I was stupid in that letter. I warned him about stuff still a long way down the road, but I forgot some bigger stuff that's already almost right on top of us."

"What do you mean, excellent Martinus? If you're trying to frighten me, you're doing a splendid job."

Martinus Paduei's laugh held no mirth whatever. "You know what, excellent Tribonian? I've scared myself, too. Oh, you bet I have! Let's *not* talk about it right this minute, if that's all right with you. Rest up, why don't you? Have dinner with the king and me. We'll get nice and full. We'll have some wine. Then, maybe, then I can tell you what's on my mind."

"I am your servant, of course," Tribonian said.

"Not here. Not now. Not with this." Paduei shook his head. "What's coming is bigger than both of us. That's what I'm afraid of." Before Tribonian could ask him anything more, he abruptly turned and walked out of the guest room. He closed the door behind him. He didn't—quite— slam it.

―

KING URIAS struck Tribonian as pleasant but bland. He also seemed to trust Martinus Paduei without reservation. That made Justinian's quaestor marvel. The Emperor of the Romans, Tribonian often thought, trusted no one even with reservations.

To the man from Constantinople, the dinner also seemed pleasant but bland. There was nothing wrong with the slab of roast mutton an Italian servant set before him. Nothing wrong with it, no, but it was seasoned only with garlic and pepper, not with the fermented fish sauce that would have

The Fake Pandemic

made it so much more interesting. He didn't complain, not when Urias and Paduei both seemed happy with it as it was.

After a sweet course of apricots candied in honey—nothing wrong with that at all—Urias got to his feet. "You clever fellows will have to excuse me," he said. "I'm going to spend some time with my wife and my little boy before I fall into bed. Try not to get into too much trouble without me." Away he went.

"He's a good fellow. He's a jolly good fellow—that, nobody can deny," Paduei said as more servitors cleared the table. He too stood up. "Why don't you come along with me, excellent Tribonian? We'll have something to wet our whistles, and then I promise I'll tell you what's on my mind."

Tribonian also rose. "How can I say no, excellent Martinus?"

Paduei took him to an admirable study. The furniture was comfortable. The shelves held scrolls and codices. The lamps had polished brass reflectors, to make them throw more light. And the drink… "Go easy at first," Paduei warned as he poured. "This isn't wine. It's what my language calls brandy. It's stronger than you're used to. So you know."

"Thank you. That would be why the cups are so small," Tribonian said. As Paduei nodded, the man from the east went on, "We've had a bit of your new drink brought to the city." To someone like him, Constantinople was and always would be *the* city.

He didn't tell Martinus Paduei that Justinian had tried brandy. The Emperor had got horribly drunk and even more horribly hung over. It made a funny story, yes. But funny stories you told at Justinian's expense had a way of coming back and biting you.

"Your health," Paduei said. They clinked cups and drank.

Tribonian sipped cautiously. It was like drinking fire, sure enough, but very pleasant fire. Slyly, Justinian's quaestor said, "You don't pour out a libation to the gods?"

"Only a pagan would do that, most excellent Tribonian, as I'm sure you know. Not a good Christian like me." Paduei smiled a particular kind of smile. Tribonian found himself returning it. Of all the things he hadn't expected to find in Ostrogothic Italy, irony stood high on the list.

Sure enough, he knew he'd been drinking by the time he got to the bottom of his little cup. Paduei poured it full again, and his own with it. They clinked once more. Tribonian said, "And what is it you didn't want to talk about earlier today?"

Martinus Paduei bared his teeth again, but not in a smile this time: more of a trapped animal's grimace. "I really can foresee the future, you know," he said.

"I'm inclined to believe you. Without some such help, the Ostrogoths never could have stood against our armies," Tribonian said. "What do you see that troubles you so much, you have trouble even speaking of it?"

"The end of the world," Paduei said. "Oh, not literally. Not the way it will be in Revelations. But close enough. A plague is coming, a pestilence. An epidemic—no, worse. A pandemic. It will ruin the Roman Empire and the Kingdom of the Ostrogoths alike, and it's only a few years away."

"Have you spoken of this to King Urias?"

"Not yet. Not a word. I don't intend to, either. The plague will come to Constantinople from Egypt, from Pelusium. We have to keep it from getting to Egypt to begin with, or from spreading if we can't do that."

"Plague..." Tribonian shivered, though the room was pleasantly warm. What could any man do against disease? "Like the one in Athens that Thucydides talks about?"

"Bigger. Worse." Martinus Paduei's voice was harsh and flat. "More like the plagues that tore through the whole Roman Empire in Marcus Aurelius' time."

"Those are much closer to our own day than the Athenian pestilence, but I know much less about them." Tribonian chuckled wryly. "Thucydides was a better historian than anyone Marcus Aurelius could call on."

"*Hoc ille.* Thucydides was better than just about anybody." Paduei fingered the tip of his beaky nose. Was it getting numb? The tip of Tribonian's was. That was one way he knew he'd taken a bit on board.

He said, "What can we do about it, though, excellent Martinus, except bow before God's will? Do you know a cure for this disease?"

The Fake Pandemic

"No. I wish to heaven I did. We have to stop it before it gets well begun and starts spreading like autumn leaves on the wind. I don't think it begins in Egypt. I think it gets there by ship, from the east. If we can stop that, if it doesn't take hold there, we can win. Maybe we can win. If it does take hold in Egypt, maybe we can keep it from going any farther. That would be a lot harder, though."

"I'm sure it would. You spoke of leaves on the wind. I would sooner say that plague spreads like heresy. Leave the tiniest gap anywhere, and it gets through."

"They're both good figures of speech. They make us think about what we have to do." Paduei sipped brandy and, by his expression, thought hard. "Now, you said Justinian was already moving to seize control of Mecca, that Arabian town?"

"I did say that. He is doing that." The way Tribonian answered told him the brandy was starting to have its way with him. Earnestly, he continued, "He takes you seriously, you see. It is a rare courtesy from him. The only other barbarian—forgive me—to whom he extends it is King Khusrau of Persia."

Paduei seemed more amused than offended. "Well, good. He's not just marching down through Arabia to Mecca, right? He'll have ships in the Red Sea to carry his soldiers and their supplies?"

"Yes, certainly." Tribonian wondered how many inhabitants of Urias' kingdom even knew the Red Sea existed. Martinus Paduei spoke of it and of its role in warfare in the Arabian peninsula with casual familiarity. If you could see the future, though, wouldn't you also be able to see a good, wide swath of the world at present?

"All right, then." Paduei might be feeling the brandy, too, but not enough to keep him from thinking straight. "That will help. Or I can hope it will, anyway. Patrols in the Red Sea may stop some trading ship from out of the east from delivering disease along with spices and pearls and whatever else it's got on board. They may. They just may, if God doesn't hate us *too* much."

By the way he said that, he didn't think it likely. Tribonian had his doubts about God's love for mankind, too. As long as he didn't throw them in Justinian's face, he was useful enough to be allowed to hold on to them.

He said, "You are foreseeing the future, you tell me. How far in the future does this dreadful pestilence, this pandemic, lie?"

"The plague is reported in Pelusium in 541. It reaches Constantinople in 542," Paduei said. "It spreads wildly after that. It would. Constantinople is a trade center. People go there from all over the world, and go all over the world from there. Naturally, they take rats and fleas with them."

"What do rats and fleas have to do with anything?" Tribonian asked, honestly perplexed.

Paduei breathed out noisily through his nose, though he might have been resigned, not exasperated. "Excellent Tribonian, I would have to talk for three days straight to give you any chance of getting that. Even then, it's at least even money you wouldn't believe me. So forget I said it, all right?"

"As you wish, of course," Tribonian replied. "Let me ask a different question, then: how many years from now is your 541? Different scholars reckon different years for the birth of our Lord and Savior, Jesus Christ. In which indiction will your 541 fall?"

"Hang on a bit. Now I've got to work that out," Paduei said. The Roman Empire had used the fifteen-year indiction cycle at least since the reign of Constantine the Great. If Martinus Paduei didn't know it well, his America had to lie very far away indeed. At last, after some mumbling and some counting on his fingers, he went on, "If I've done this right, the fifth indiction will start on September first of my 541."

"The *fifth* indiction? Very good! We still have some time, then," Tribonian said. The second indiction would begin in about six weeks. "I was afraid you'd tell me I had to rush right home to the imperial city and start making frantic preparations as soon as I got there."

"What you have to do may be harder yet," Paduei said. "You have to start doing the things that need doing as soon as you get home. Excuse me, first you have to convince your Emperor that you need to do them and you need to spend the money that goes with doing them. Then you have to do them, and you have to keep doing them till quite a while after my date, just to be safe. You have to keep doing them while everybody thinks you're crazy, too."

Tribonian stared at him in unbridled admiration. "In Italy, I never dreamt I'd find a man who understood how bureaucracy worked!"

"Life's full of surprises, isn't it?" Paduei chuckled sourly. "And you know what else? You know what your big reward is for doing every single thing just exactly right and making sure the plague doesn't get a foothold?"

"You have something in mind, I'm sure. Tell me what it is."

"Think for a heartbeat and you'll see it yourself. If you do it all just exactly right, *nothing happens*. Things go on the same way they always have. That's your reward: nothing. Except for the rest of your life people will laugh at you behind your back and call you Tribonian the worrywart who made everybody run in circles even though there really wasn't anything to get excited about. Can you live with that?"

"If my other choice is dying from your pandemic, I can." Tribonian held his cup out to Martinus. "For now, though, if you'd be so kind, load this up again, and keep on doing it. Tomorrow morning, I'll remember what you've told me. Right now, I want to forget."

"You and me both, excellent Tribonian. You and me both." Paduei poured his guest's cup full, and his own. It got very drunk out.

———

TRIBONIAN WOKE the next morning feeling like death. Now he understood the torments of the damned Justinian had gone through after swilling too much brandy. He did the things people did when they'd hurt themselves drinking. He ate raw cabbage. He drank a little olive oil to coat his stomach. He warily sipped watered wine. Nothing helped much.

Martinus Paduei also looked the worse for wear. King Urias snickered at their sorry state. "You boys had fun last night, didn't you?" he said.

"Your Majesty," Paduei said, "shut up."

The sky didn't fall. Urias just laughed. Tribonian was astounded. Anyone who told Justinian anything like that would find out how slowly a man could die, and how much he could hurt while he was doing it. Maybe there were some advantages to living in a barbarian kingdom after all.

Nothing much got done that day. Neither quaestor was in any kind of shape to dicker over the diplomatic and trade issues that had brought Tribonian from Constantinople to Florence. And both of them, no doubt, felt the black, hovering shadow of the thing Paduei had spoken of the night before. Next to that, how much did anything else matter?

On the following morning, Paduei said, "Look, tell me what you want. Whatever it is, I'll give you as much of it as I can without hurting my own kingdom too much. I want you to look good when you go home to Justinian. If he's happy with you, maybe he'll take the important stuff seriously, too."

"*Theou thelontos!*" Tribonian exclaimed. The expression didn't faze Paduei. In Greek, Tribonian said, "You do understand this tongue, then?"

"Not well," Paduei replied in the same language. "I read better than I speak, and I speak better than I understand." His grammar was good, his phrasing old-fashioned, and his accent thicker than it was in Latin.

Tribonian returned to the speech Paduei knew better. "All right. It doesn't matter. I'm at home in both. To work in the law in the Empire, one has to be. I grew up with Greek, but I've used so much Latin for so long, it often feels more familiar to me." Not quite out of the blue, he added, "And, of course, Latin is his Majesty's birthspeech."

"Yes, that would matter, wouldn't it?" Paduei said…sympathetically?

Tribonian wanted no man's sympathy. If someone felt sympathy for you, you'd made yourself vulnerable to him. Many years at the imperial court had taught the quaestor as much. He made a point of changing the subject: "Can you tell me the symptoms of this new pestilence, so I can inform the Emperor and instruct the men who will be trying to keep it out of Egypt?"

Martinus Paduei could, and did. It sounded horrible: swellings of the glands in the armpits and the groin, sometimes their bursting and spewing foul-smelling pus, what looked like bruising under the skin, high fever, death within a few days. "Not everyone who catches it dies, but an awful lot of people do," Paduei said. "If your patrols find somebody on a ship who's got it, they shouldn't board that ship or let him onto theirs. It spreads very easily from one person to another. *Very* easily."

"What should they do, then?" Tribonian asked. "You can order a ship to turn back, but you can't be sure the skipper will obey once he's out of sight. Should they set a ship on fire to make sure it won't bring the plague to land?"

Paduei gnawed at his lower lip. "I hate to say yes, but they'd better. They might be wrong, and harm a few men who don't deserve it. But this disease is so bad, anything they can do that might stop it from getting to Egypt, they have to do it." He muttered to himself in a language Tribonian had never heard before. "In a perfect world, your Excellency, I wouldn't give you an answer like that. In this one, the one we live in…"

"Believe me, excellent Martinus, I understand." Tribonian inclined his head in respect. "You concern yourself with ethics. One finds such men too seldom, and must admire them when one does."

"Thank you, sir. That's one of the kinder things anybody's told me since I got here," Paduei said. "Now, I want to ask you something else, if I may." He waited.

"Go ahead," Tribonian said, as he was obviously supposed to.

"What will you do if Justinian tells you this is all a load of nonsense, and that you need to forget about it and go back to the *Corpus Iuris Civilis*?"

"Ow!" Tribonian flinched. "You don't know any easy questions, do you?" This one might not be easy, but it was good. Justinian might do precisely that. If he didn't believe Tribonian, or if he just didn't care, who could make him? No one in the world. That was what being Emperor of the Romans meant. What you wanted, happened. What you didn't, didn't.

Quod principi placuit legis habet vigorem. What pleases the Emperor has the force of law. That was in the *Corpus Iuris*, in the *Institutes*. Only Justinian's will constrained him. When it constrained him. If it constrained him. None of the law would.

Which didn't answer Paduei's question. "I will do my best to be persuasive," Tribonian said after a longish pause. "If I'm not persuasive enough—" He wanted to say, *Then no one can do anything.* But Martinus Paduei had been persuasive himself. Tribonian believed in the enormity of the coming pandemic, if it came. Sighing, he continued, "Not even the Emperor knows everything that's done in his name. Not for a while. Maybe not for long enough."

Paduei set a hand on his shoulder. "God bless you," said the strange man with the gift of prophecy, the man who'd done far more to check the Roman reconquest of barbarous Italy than any Ostrogoth could have. Tribonian should have hated him for that. He couldn't. He was too impressed. The American, whatever an American was, went on, "Men the Church calls saints and martyrs have done less and dared less."

Tribonian only shrugged. "Let's hope I don't have to worry about it. Because if I do—"

"—everything's gone to hell," King Urias' quaestor finished for him. The Emperor Justinian's quaestor solemnly nodded.

THE TRIP from Florence to Ancona went as smoothly as the one from the port to the capital had. Tribonian traveled in another clever carriage pulled by horses with clever collars. He stayed in hostels different from the ones he'd used coming the other way, but these were equally good. He had no trouble finding a ship bound for Dyrrachium. The voyage was as pleasant as a sea voyage was ever likely to be.

Traveling east along the Via Egnatia… Everything seemed shabby, old-fashioned, and a little slovenly in ways it hadn't when he was bound for Italy. He reminded himself that the Balkans were poor and backward compared to Anatolia, much less to Syria. That helped some, but not enough.

Even returning to Constantinople wasn't the relief and the thrill he'd thought it would be, and not only because of what he had on his mind. All cities smelled bad. How could it be otherwise, when they held many people

The Fake Pandemic

packed tightly together? But the imperial city, though larger than any other, smelled better than most. People bathed more there, and disposed of their waste in civilized fashion rather than chucking it into the street.

Next to Florence, Constantinople stank and seemed filthy. Tribonian hadn't noticed so much while in foreign parts, but coming home rubbed his nose in it, so to speak. Even after visiting the baths, he found himself wanting to scratch all the time.

His majordomo noticed but drew the wrong conclusion. "So sorry, sir, you had to travel to the barbarians' country," he clucked. "I can't imagine why his Majesty, God protect him, wanted a place like that to begin with. Dirty, backward, hardly civilized at all!"

"Ah, Eugenius, you don't know the half of it," Tribonian said. Eugenius clucked again, sure Italy had to be even worse than he'd imagined. Tribonian let him keep his illusions. That was easier than trying to talk him out of them.

He sent to the palace to let Justinian know he'd returned. In his note, he assured his sovereign that he'd settled the differences between the Empire and the Kingdom of the Ostrogoths in a fashion that would please him. Then he added, *King Urias' quaestor, the man known as Martinus Paduei, raised certain other matters whose consideration may be of advantage to us.* He didn't go into detail, not in a letter Justinian's secretaries would read before the Emperor saw it himself.

The following day, a palace servitor came to Tribonian's door. When Eugenius ushered him into Tribonian's presence, the man said, "His Majesty wishes to speak with you, your Excellency. You will please accompany me back to the imperial domicile." The *please* was there purely for politeness' sake.

"I am his Majesty's servant in all things, of course," Tribonian said, which was true of every subject of Justinian's. *Quod principi placuit...*

Tribonian's home was less than half a mile from the palace, which lay just east of the Hippodrome. The palace official's practiced toploftiness kept most of the peddlers and beggars and hucksters and grifters who filled the city's streets from approaching him and Tribonian. Most, but not all. When someone did presume to bother them, the official cursed fluently and vilely in both Latin and Greek.

Emperors had as much space as they wanted. The palace complex sprawled. Gardeners tended flowers and shrubs between buildings. Tribonian admired the hunting mosaics that ornamented courtyard floors. He could hear the crowd roaring at the chariot races, but he hardly noticed it.

The servitor led him to a small, plain building he visited but seldom: the Emperor's private residence. He had worked closely with Justinian for years. All the same, guards at the door gave him a brutally intimate patdown before letting him through. They did the same for the palace official.

Justinian and Theodora both waited in the little reception room. Tribonian prostrated himself, praising the Emperor and Empress as he knocked his forehead on the floor. He normally took that for granted. Now, for some reason, he thought of Urias' easygoing court.

"You may rise," Justinian told him. As Tribonian did, the Emperor continued, "First give us the details of the agreements between our state and the barbarians holding Italy." Tribonian did; if ever a man was made for details, he was the one. Justinian's dark eyes slid to his wife. Ever so slightly, Theodora nodded. Justinian turned back to Tribonian. "Your work satisfies us. There will be documents confirming your statements?"

"Your Majesty, there will." Like Tribonian himself, Justinian had trouble believing anything was real till he saw it written down.

Justinian gestured. The palace official bowed and backed away till he reached the door. Then he turned and left. Tribonian was alone with the Emperor and his powerful consort. Theodora spoke: "Your little letter mentioned some things it did not explain." Her voice was perfectly controlled. She'd been an actress in her younger days, and in her case that wasn't just another name for whore.

"It did, your Majesty," Tribonian agreed. "Discretion seemed advisable."

Theodora's face, pale both by nature and by art, showed as little as her voice. "No need for that now, excellent Tribonian."

The Fake Pandemic

"No, indeed." Tribonian took a deep breath. He'd been rehearsing this moment—both with and without the Empress present—since before he left Florence. As always, rehearsal helped, but it wasn't the real thing. Doing his best to capture not only Martinus Paduei's exact words but also his fearful tone, Tribonian told his sovereigns of the coming pestilence.

They were both silent for some little while after he finished. At length, Justinian said, "You believe this man?"

"Yes, your Majesty. I do." Tribonian didn't hesitate.

"Why?" Justinian demanded. "This Paduei has shown himself to be no friend to our Empire. He may seek to distract us while plotting some new wickedness."

"That is possible, of course, your Majesty, but I think perhaps not altogether likely." Tribonian spoke with great care, as one had to when contradicting an absolute monarch. Justinian didn't need to listen to anyone but himself and perhaps his wife. "For one thing, patrolling to hold the pestilence at bay would take only a relatively small effort on our part. For another, he speaks in his own interest as well as ours. A pandemic that ravages the Empire will hardly spare Italy. And I do not believe anyone could act the terror and dread he showed without truly feeling them."

"People can always act," Theodora declared.

"Not most people, I believe, your Majesty, and not so well. What Martinus Paduei told me, he believed. Barristers also have a feel for this." Contradicting Justinian was dangerous. Contradicting Theodora could be fatal.

"Barristers." Theodora's gesture said what she thought of the whole legal profession. Given some of the things she was supposed to have done before meeting Justinian, that was no surprise.

And the Emperor nodded. "We are with you, my dear. This is a fraud and a deception. It is fakery. We haven't had a plague for centuries. How can this Paduei know another one is coming? He is a fake, and so is his pandemic."

"You did not feel so, your Majesty, when you moved men and ships against the barbarous Arabs," Tribonian said. That had to do with religion, though, and anything having to do with religion hit Justinian where he lived. Something afflicting mere bodies? Much less so.

Justinian scowled at Tribonian. He liked being reminded he was contradicting himself no more than any other man. He had ways of making his displeasure known that any other man didn't, though. "Very well, excellent Tribonian. You say you think Paduei speaks the truth? We will offer you a choice, then. Which would you rather do over the next few years, finish the *Corpus Iuris Civilis* or go down to Pelusium—Pelusium, of all godforsaken places!—and take charge of the patrols that will stop the pestilence that isn't coming from coming?"

Tribonian tried not to show what he was thinking. His sovereign had a nasty way of cutting to the heart of things. Constantinople and the work Tribonian was made for or a miserable fortress between the Delta and the dusty desert? But, no matter how much Tribonian wished he didn't believe Martinus Paduei, he did. The law was important. The plague lay two or three steps above that.

He sighed anyway. Then he said, "I will go to Pelusium, your Majesty, as long as you furnish me with the authority, the men, the ships, and the money to do a proper job."

Justinian rocked back in his chair. He hadn't expected that. He didn't like it, either. Theodora said, "Give them to him. Let him have no excuse for blaming you. If he wants to play sea captain off at the end of the world, good riddance to him."

"Good riddance to him anyhow," Justinian snapped. But then, grudgingly, he nodded. "Yes. Let it be as you say." He turned his fearsome attention back to Tribonian. "By the Father, the Son, and the Holy Spirit, I pledge that I will give you what you require."

If any oath would bind him, that one would. But would any oath? With Justinian, you never knew. All the same, Tribonian answered, "Thank you, your Majesty. I will send you full reports on our efforts."

"Of course you will," Justinian said with scorn that flayed like a lash of scorpions. "Now get out of our sight." As the palace official had before him,

The Fake Pandemic

Tribonian bowed and backed out of the small audience chamber. He was off to save the world if he could—even if the Emperor didn't want him to and didn't think it needed saving.

―

The commandant at Pelusium was a bitter-looking man named Matthew. He addressed Tribonian in Greek: "Well, your Excellency, what the devil did *you* do to get sent here? It must have been *something* juicy, for sure."

Tribonian wondered what Matthew had done, too. No, a place like Pelusium didn't draw up-and-comers. He hoped the officer still remembered what he was supposed to do. If he didn't, Tribonian would replace him…if Justinian allowed it, of course.

He made his answer in easy stages: "You know how his Majesty, God bless him, decided to seize western Arabia not long ago at the urging of a man able to see the future before it happens?"

"I heard about that, yeah." The corners of Matthew's mouth pulled down even more. "Foolishness, if anybody cares what I think. All the Arabs in the world aren't worth a single pinch of owl dung, far as I'm concerned. Not one single pinch of owl dung." He almost smiled for a moment—he must have thought it a happy phrase.

"If the Emperor thinks they are, they are. And he does," Tribonian said. Matthew relapsed into sourness; he couldn't very well argue with that. Tribonian went on, "This same man has warned that a plague will enter Egypt in the fifth indiction unless we stop it. It will afflict the whole Empire." He didn't say anything about the whole world; Matthew would have enough trouble thinking about anything outside Pelusium.

"The Emperor *believes* this?" Matthew sounded as if he couldn't believe his ears.

"I am his quaestor. I am a man not without prominence in the city. I volunteered to come here to try to stop it. I was not condemned to come here, if that's what you're wondering. I came because I could give the Empire no greater service." The really odd thing, Tribonian reflected, was that he was telling the truth.

"You must be out of your fornicating mind. Nobody comes to Pelusium if he doesn't have to. I mean nobody."

There, Tribonian was inclined to believe him. He asked, "Can you tell me what the smell is that lingers in the air?"

"Salt marshes," Matthew said with sardonic relish. "Mud. Rotting plants. Stagnant seawater. Delicious, huh? I thought I'd get used to it, but for my sins I've been here five years and it still stinks."

"I see. Here's a different question for you: how do I command ships on the Red Sea from here? We aren't on the Red Sea. We aren't even on the Mediterranean." Tribonian had thought Pelusium would be a port, but it wasn't, not any more, though it had been once. The harbor had silted up, and the town lay more than two miles from the sea.

"You need to command ships on the Red Sea? Well, by God and all the saints, your Excellency, you're out of *my* hair, because you *can't* do that from here." Matthew sounded delighted, though he looked as dour as ever.

"Where can I do it from, then?" Tribonian hoped he didn't sound *too* plaintive.

"People from Constantinople," the commandant muttered, though he wanted Tribonian to overhear.

Tribonian understood what he meant. The quaestor knew about Alexandria and the Nile. He'd even heard of Pelusium once or twice before beginning this adventure. Past that... With such dignity as he could muster, he said, "This matter is urgent. I left the city without doing all the research I might have." That was also true. The contempt on Matthew's face said it didn't matter.

"You've got to go south from here, past the Bitter Lakes, to Clysma," the commandant of Pelusium explained, as if to a halfwitted child. "Clysma sits on a narrow bay that opens out into the Red Sea, not that the Red Sea's any too wide, either."

The Fake Pandemic

"Cheerful geography you have around here," Tribonian remarked. "All right, give me a mule and a little escort, and I'll try to stop the cataclysm from getting to Clysma."

His pun fell flat. Matthew just shook his head. "You'd do better waiting for a caravan. They have enough guards to give you a decent chance of getting there alive. Not many people in the desert, but all the ones there are, are bandits."

Tribonian started to insist that the commandant give him a large escort, so he could head for Clysma right away. He thought better of it before he opened his mouth. The pandemic was still years away. "We'll do it like that, then," he said. "How long till the next one leaves?"

"I don't know. A couple of weeks, maybe," Matthew answered.

Three weeks later, Tribonian rode a mule south with a caravan of camels and donkeys carrying wine and oil to Clysma. The guards—a lot of them—rode camels or horses. One of them lent Tribonian his spare sword. "You aren't be worth much in a fight," he said in bad Greek, "but maybe you worth something." Tribonian belted it on without argument.

The desert and the Bitter Lakes were desolate, even unearthly. Tribonian bought a broad-brimmed hat from a merchant to hold the fierce sun at bay. "You think this is bad, you should try it in high summer," the man told him. "We're into autumn now."

"*Kyrie eleison!*" Tribonian exclaimed.

"Heh." The merchant gave the ghost of a chuckle. "Long time ago, people say, there used to be a canal from the Red Sea to the Nile. It silted up, like everything does here. They ought to dig one across the Bitter Lakes, to connect the Red Sea and the Mediterranean."

"Maybe. But wouldn't it silt up, too? You'd never get enough trade to make keeping it open worthwhile."

"I bet you're right, curse it." The trader spat in disgust. "I just get tired of plodding back and forth between Pelusium and Clysma, waiting for some fleabitten desert rat to sneak past the sentries and cut my throat while I'm sleeping."

Harry Turtledove

One more thing to look forward to, Tribonian thought. His hand closed on the hilt of that guard's second-best sword. It felt oddly comforting.

Compared to Clysma, Pelusium might have been Alexandria or Antioch or some other great city. It did boast a bishop, an energetic young man named Stephen. The naval commander, an officer called Peter whose red-tracked eyes said he drank too much, reminded Tribonian of Matthew in Pelusium: he'd probably done something bad enough to deserve a posting like this.

Tribonian displayed his orders, which were appallingly official. He explained what he required to Peter, and why. The naval officer stared at him with the blend of misery and cynicism so many losers displayed. "You're telling me you want me to help you shut down our sea trade in the fourth indiction, and the fifth, and maybe even the sixth?"

"That's right." The quaestor nodded. "We can save the whole inhabited world from the coming pandemic of pestilence."

"Bugger the whole inhabited world, uh, your Excellency," Peter said. "Do you know what happens if sea trade here shuts down for two or three years? Half the people in this miserable pisspot of a town starve, and the other half move away. You'll have cheetahs chasing antelopes through the streets."

"Are you telling me you refuse to obey me? Are you telling me you refuse to obey the Emperor of the Romans, who sent me here to do this?" Tribonian's voice went silky with menace. He seldom needed that tone, but, like any accomplished courtier, he had it in his quiver.

It made the naval officer flinch. "No, no, no," Peter whined. "But my sailors, they're mostly from these parts. They won't want to make their kinsfolk go hungry. I can give the orders. Making 'em follow them won't be so easy."

He had a point, of sorts. A good commander would have given the orders and had them obeyed as a matter of course. But good commanders, again, didn't wind up in places like Clysma.

The Fake Pandemic

"We will have more ships. We will have more sailors," Tribonian said. "In the last part of the reign of Justinian's uncle Justin, of blessed memory, our ships carried soldiers from the Kingdom of Axum across the Red Sea to fight the pagan Arabs. It can be done. It shall be done."

"Those ships aren't here now. There are some farther down the Red Sea, helping his Majesty with whatever he's doing in Arabia." Peter's phrasing and tone said he didn't know, or want to know, much about that.

"Splendid. We'll use them, too. I shall send orders to their captains. One of your vessels will deliver those orders. If anything goes wrong with the delivery, excellent Peter"—Tribonian used the title of respect as a threat—"you will regret the failure. I promise you that, and I keep my promises. Do you understand me?"

"Yes, your Excellency," Peter said. *Much too well*, his manner added.

The next day, Tribonian paid Bishop Stephen his respects. By his looks, the bishop was as much an Arab as any desert raider. Tribonian cared nothing about that. In the things that mattered, Stephen was a Roman: he was a pious Christian, and he spoke good Greek. He could get on anywhere in the Empire.

Tribonian told him the truth, too, or most of it. He warned of the plague that might come, and went into gruesome detail about its symptoms. But, instead of mentioning Martinus Paduei, he said that God had vouchsafed the forewarning of the pandemic to a holy, ascetic monk in Italy.

Stephen crossed himself. "We must not let this divine warning come in vain!"

"Exactly my thought, most reverend sir," Tribonian replied. "Some of the people I've talked with here—I name no names, mind you—seem to have trouble grasping this. I was hoping you might offer a sermon or two on the subject…"

"I might." Stephen cocked his head to one side and waited. Had he not chosen the Church, he would have made a formidable trader.

Having played those games himself, Tribonian recognized them right away. "I understand, most reverend sir, that you hope to set up a monastery in the hills back of Clysma. You would have an easier time reaching your goal if the Emperor heard of your eagerness to protect his realm and his folk."

"He would hear of it?"

"I assure you, he would."

"I hope to see you in church Sunday, your Excellency."

"I'll be there," Tribonian said. The bargain didn't even require a handclasp.

Clysma's church, built of the same red-brown stone as the rest of the town, was much the largest building there. It even dwarfed the warehouses that served the fitful trade coming up the Red Sea. Everyone came to Mass. It was as much a social as a religious gathering. Tribonian smiled to see Peter there. Peter did not smile on seeing him.

Stephen went through the familiar, comforting ritual. Then he mounted to the pulpit. "People of Clysma, we who go down to the sea in ships have the God-given chance to preserve our brethren in Egypt, in Palestine, and in all the Roman realm from a sending of Satan! God has chosen *us* to protect our world from this coming scourge." As Tribonian had with him, he elaborated on the horrors of the plague. Then he went on, "We must not be lukewarm, or God will spit us out of His mouth, and we will deserve it. We can stop this danger before it torments us. We can, we must, and we shall!"

People burst into cheers. That likely wouldn't have happened in Constantinople, but people there had all kinds of things to get excited about. Not here in Clysma. Tribonian stole a glance at Peter. The naval officer looked as if he'd taken a fist to the chin in a tavern brawl. Tribonian didn't smile. Back in the room he'd rented, he wrote a letter.

> *Tribonian the quaestor to his Radiant Clemency, Flavius Anicius Justinian, Emperor of the Romans, Greetings.*
>
> *I am established in Clysma, carrying out your orders to the best of my ability. Reminding your Serene Highness of your generous promise of full support, I require here at least half a dozen swift-sailing ships for patrol work, with full crews. The required expense, when measured against the Empire's safety, is minimal.*

The Fake Pandemic

> *Furthermore, I call to your attention the pious Bishop of Clysma, one Stephen, who is likewise concerned to ward off the feared pandemic. He is a true servant of God who seeks to establish a monastery where other like-minded men can assemble in prayer and holiness. A token of imperial favor would be most welcome in furthering this plan.*
>
> *I await the gracious favor of your early reply, and name myself the least and least worthy of your servants, Tribonian.*

He folded the papyrus and sealed the letter with cord and a lead *bulla*. A few days later, a northbound caravan left Clysma. The letter went with it.

IN DUE course, Bishop Stephen received a hundred solidi and a letter from the imperial chancery praising his eagerness to promote the hope of heaven among sinful men. He kissed Tribonian on both cheeks and then on the mouth, a gesture of appreciation the quaestor could have done without.

No letter came from Justinian to Tribonian. He began to think no ships or sailors would come, either. But then caravans from Pelusium began bringing down timbers already cut and shaped for assembly by local shipwrights. Since the canal through the Bitter Lakes didn't exist and probably never would, that was the only way ships from the rest of the Empire could get here. Sailors started coming down, too.

Not all of them seemed thrilled about having Clysma as their new home port, which was putting it mildly. The same was even more true of their officers. Tribonian would have worried harder if the new arrivals had anywhere else to go. Chances were, desertion meant death. They'd crossed the desert from Pelusium in large, well-organized caravans. Could they get back alone, on foot or on the back of a stolen mule? The quaestor wouldn't have wanted to try it himself.

When all the new captains had arrived, Tribonian took them and the skippers who'd been serving under Peter to the hostel that catered to caravaneers. The cook there made a spicy fish stew that was surprisingly tasty, though some of the fish that went into it were of no breed that a man who'd lived beside the Mediterranean could recognize.

The wine that went with the stew and the flatbread that sopped it up came from Syria and Palestine. It wasn't Chian or Falernian, but you could drink it. Tribonian let the naval officers drink a fair bit before he stood up and waited for them to notice him. Before too long, they did.

"Gentlemen, I know you don't want to be here," he said. "No one wants to spend time in Clysma. I don't want to be here, either. But what you're doing here will be the most important service you ever give the Empire. The same is true for me, and I'm the man who's spent the past good many years putting the Roman law in order."

He told them about the coming pandemic, and about the part they had to play in holding it away from Egypt. He'd done that so often by now, he felt himself an actor playing a part he knew well—and, feeling that, he understood Theodora a little better.

"I'll make it worth your while to serve here, yours and your men's," he said. "Tell them so. You'll be doing something difficult and dangerous, and you'll be rewarded. And do you know what else will happen if you do it right, if the pandemic never comes?"

"We'll be heroes!" one of them burst out. He looked more like a pirate chief than a naval man: he had a scarred hawk's face, a wolf's eyes, and a swordblade for a nose. His name was Arethas. At the moment, he looked like a half-drunk pirate chief.

Tribonian shook his head. "No one will remember you at all. People get remembered mostly for what they do wrong. But you will always know what you've done. You will have kept yourselves safe, and your kinsfolk and friends, and countless people you've never set eyes on and never will. You'll have that to be proud of. And, if you care about your hope of heaven, God will know what you've done, too."

Martinus Paduei hadn't talked about God with Tribonian, even if he claimed to be a good Christian. *He's as pious as I am*, Tribonian thought now.

The Fake Pandemic

The difference is, I'm a better hypocrite, or maybe just a better lute-player. I know which strings to pluck to get the effects I need.

He sent Justinian another letter, this one asking for bonus pay for the men who would patrol the approaches to Clysma. *They are doing dangerous work, in a place remote from any vestiges of civilization*, he wrote. *Surely they deserve a reward for their important service. For myself, of course, having come here of my own free will and desire, I request nothing of your Serene Highness.*

It took a while—anything that connected Clysma to the real world took a while—but the Emperor approved the extra pay for the sailors. He also sent Tribonian a note held closed with his *bulla* and golden cord: an imperial prerogative. When Tribonian opened it, he found it short and to the point. *It is well that you ask nothing for yourself of us, excellent Tribonian*, Justinian wrote: the quaestor knew the Emperor's hand as well as he knew his own. *No favors from us would be forthcoming.*

That Tribonian got a letter from Justinian impressed the naval officers he dealt with and reminded them he remained a man to be reckoned with. That he didn't brag about it impressed them more, and might even have frightened them a little. He kept the broken seal and the golden cords attached to it where people who visited his room could see them. The note itself he quietly burned.

The second indiction had passed into the third when his patrols started going out to check incoming ships and boats. "You all have fire arrows aboard your vessels," he told the skippers. "Make sure you keep a brazier going at all times. If you find a ship with sickness aboard, do what you have to do. The Emperor will approve. God will understand."

By then, Tribonian had spent upwards of a year in Clysma. Though self-imposed, it felt like exile. There wasn't much to do. There was next to nothing to read. Besides the Bible, Bishop Stephen had a couple of theological tomes and an ecclesiastical history that ended more than a hundred years before. Sozomen, the historian, came from Gaza, a town not far east of Pelusium and thus not far north of Tribonian's current abode. He even mentioned Clysma once or twice, so the wider world did vaguely know it existed.

Little by little, Tribonian took up regular Sunday churchgoing. It gave him something to do, something to look forward to. If he took it less seriously than most of the congregants, no help for that. He suspected the bishop understood his reasons perfectly well, but Stephen never called him on them. He was a more sophisticated, more discreet man than Tribonian would have looked to find in a town like this.

And every port had places that catered to sailors. Tribonian visited one or two of the better brothels every now and again. He thought no more about it than he thought about scratching any other itch.

Other itches… He tried to be a cleanly man, but he sometimes got fleabites. When he did, he thought of Paduei's talk about the coming plague, about rats, and about fleas. All he could do when that crossed his mind was scratch his head. Either the man from America was daft or he knew more than he could ever hope to explain even to an educated man from the Roman Empire's beating heart.

Tribonian couldn't say for sure which choice was true. He did know which way he would have bet. That worried him.

Day followed day. In winter, they were warm and sticky. In summer, they were blazing and sticky. People moved as little as they could and as slowly as they could. The heat could make lizards fall down dead from walls. Men and sometimes even women would walk naked into the sea to try to cool off. Tribonian didn't blame them; he joined them. It helped less than he wished it would. The sun heated the sea, too.

The ships from his little fleet went out. They came back. None of the captains reported finding anything out of the ordinary. For all Tribonian could prove, as soon as they got out of sight of Clysma they laid up somewhere shady till it got to be time to sail home again.

He consoled himself by noting that no uncommon pestilence swept through the little town. As summer imposed its will on Clysma yet again and as the fourth indiction neared the fifth, such consolation came harder. Not today, maybe, but what about tomorrow? Or the day after? Or the day after that? He'd done everything he knew how to do, but had he done enough?

The Fake Pandemic

Then, just before the new indiction came, Arethas' ship tied up at one side of the piers poking out from the shore. The piratical-looking skipper had always seemed to take the business of patrolling more seriously than most of his fellows. And he'd named his ship the *Cosmas and Damian*, which Tribonian liked. The healer saints were called the Silverless Ones: they worked their cures without care for payment.

When Arethas knocked on Tribonian's door, the quaestor was dozing in the heat. He woke with a start, ran a hand through his hair in lieu of combing it, and opened up. "Hail, Arethas!" he said, fighting the urge to rub his eyes, which still felt gummy from sleep. "I didn't expect you back for another three or four days."

"Excellent boss, I didn't expect to come in so soon, either, but here I am," Arethas replied. "I'd pretty much given up expecting anything interesting'd ever happen out there, too. Only goes to show you never can tell, don't it?"

"I think you'd better come in." Excitement tingling through him, Tribonian stood aside so Arethas could. He'd also started wondering whether anything interesting would ever happen out on the sea. *Maybe it has. Dear God in Whom I too fitfully believe, maybe it has.* He poured Arethas wine. As an afterthought, he poured some for himself.

"Obliged, sir." The *Cosmas and Damian*'s skipper raised his cup. "Your health!"

"And yours," Tribonian said. *And everyone's?* "Tell me what you've come to tell me."

Arethas drained the cup first. "Ah, that goes down nice! Well, there we were out in the bay, and we spotted a ship coming north. We steered toward her, and curse me if they weren't holding a burial at sea. They had themselves somebody wrapped in a shroud, and they were just about to drop him in the drink." He stopped.

Tribonian could take a hint. He poured from the wine jug into the cup. "In God's name, man, go on!"

Arethas grinned at him. "That's what *she* said. I will, though. I hailed them—asked who they were and what they were up to. They shouted back at me in Arabic, made out that they couldn't follow my Greek." He laughed. "Excellent boss, I grew up talking Arabic. I called 'em dogs and sons of filthy dogs and said I'd sooner sink 'em than look at 'em if they felt like joking around with me."

"Good for you!" Tribonian exclaimed.

"They figured I wasn't kidding, for sure. They said they had sickness aboard, the one man dead, another two or three down with it. They were bound for Clysma, to see if our doctors could do anything for 'em. I asked 'em what the sickness was like. To the crows with me if it wasn't what you talked about when I first got here. How did you do that?"

"In the name of the Father, the Son, and the Holy Spirit!" Tribonian crossed himself with more sincerity than he ever remembered using before. Had he been wearing his sun hat, he would have taken it off in salute to Martinus Paduei. Bit by bit, he pulled himself together again. "What happened then?"

"Sir, I remembered my orders. I hadn't figured I'd need 'em, but I remembered 'em and I followed 'em. The brazier was lit. We got our fire arrows going and we started shooting. Oh, how they cursed us! We set so many fires, they couldn't douse 'em all. That ship burned to the waterline. Not a prayer anybody on her got away alive."

"God bless you!" Tribonian said.

"I hope He does, excellent boss, 'cause it felt like murder." Arethas grimaced. "I've done my share of horrible things, but this was pretty bad. Worse'n I thought it would be. I know the need, and I believe it more now that that fellow talked about the same sickness you knew of beforehand. But I'm not easy about it, and neither are the boys."

"You've saved all the lands around the Mediterranean untold misery and death," Tribonian told him. "Justinian will show you and your crew his thanks. And if by some mischance he doesn't, I will. I am not a poor man, and what the *Cosmas and Damian* did out there on the sea will be remembered."

The Fake Pandemic

Arethas inclined his head with great dignity. "I thank you, sir. We all thank you. And now that we found the sickness and made sure it didn't get here, are we finished? Is it over? Can we go back to what used to be our lives?"

Tribonian had been thinking about just that. He missed his old life, too: missed it all the more now that he could start imagining taking it up again. He hadn't cared to remind himself how much wider the world was than Clysma and the bay that lapped against the shore here. Now, all unbidden, memory flooded back.

Even so, though, he regretfully shook his head. "Not yet, I fear, excellent Arethas. We don't know yet if that's the only ship with the pestilence aboard heading for our piers. I plan to stay here myself and keep the patrols going through the end of the sixth indiction. If nothing happens by then… God may not wish to punish us after all."

"Another two years!" Arethas sighed and shook his head. "You're the fellow who can give the orders. I'll follow 'em. I've been following 'em all along. Some of the other skippers, though—I think it was lucky we came upon that ship, not one of those chuckleheads."

"I feared as much. People *do* start going through the motions when nothing important happens for a long time," Tribonian said with a sigh of his own. "We'll keep on anyway, though. Maybe they'll pick up now that you've shown them it truly matters. Or maybe we'll be lucky twice, and the *Cosmas and Damian* will stop the danger for us. All we can do is try our best."

Arethas sighed again himself, on a different note. "I guess I can manage two more years. I guess the boys can, too. We'll—what was it you said? We'll try our best."

"Thank you. You're a true Roman," Tribonian said from the bottom of his heart.

"Don't think anybody ever called me that before." Arethas considered, then nodded. "I kinda like it."

Tribonian wrote to Justinian, detailing what the *Cosmas and Damian*'s captain and crew had done and asking for appropriate tokens of imperial appreciation. He also detailed how closely the sickness on the doomed ship resembled the one Martinus Paduei had described. He finished, *I aim to continue this work until the end of the sixth indiction to make sure the dreadful disease gains no foothold in the Empire.* When the next caravan headed north toward Pelusium, the letter went with it.

Naturally, what happened to the plague-carrying ship didn't stay a secret. Word spread through Clysma as fast as sailors started drowning their sorrow and remorse in the harborside wineshops.

Bishop Stephen preached a fiery sermon of thanksgiving the following Sunday. He praised God for letting warning of the pestilence reach Clysma before the disease itself did. He praised Arethas and his sailors for shielding the town and the Empire from it. And he praised Tribonian for bringing the warning and starting the patrols.

More surprised and touched than he'd dreamt he would be, Tribonian went up to Stephen after most of the congregants had filed out of the church. "Very generous of you, most reverend sir," he said. "As you pointed out, though, the naval men are the ones who deserve the real credit. And God, of course."

"Of course," Stephen said. The way he said it reminded Tribonian a properly pious man would have put God first. He went on, "You came here from Constantinople when you did not have to. You've stayed here, overseeing work you thought important. Now we've seen how important it was. Don't hide your light under a bushel."

"Kind of you to see it that way," Tribonian said. He knew Justinian never would.

The Emperor did remember his promise, though. He sent two solidi to each of Arethas' sailors. To the skipper himself Justinian gave a gold medallion worth considerably more than two solidi. It showed Justinian in helmet and armor and brandishing a spear.

Arethas showed it off to Tribonian. "This here is something all right, isn't it?"

The Fake Pandemic

"It certainly is." The quaestor remembered that those medallions had been struck to celebrate the Roman victory over the Vandals. Only a few years ago now, but it seemed like another century—indeed, another world.

He had to work to sound impressed. With the money for the captain and crew of the *Cosmas and Damian* Justinian had sent him a letter sealed with an imperial *bulla* and golden cords. *You may stay in Clysma as long as you like*, the Emperor wrote. *It is not as if anyone in this God-guarded imperial city misses you in the least. If you care more for imaginary illnesses than for civilization, please yourself.*

Another letter that will worship fire soon, as the Persians do in their temples, Tribonian thought. What was the phrase Arethas had used? He would burn it to the waterline.

Patrols kept sailing out of Clysma. Tribonian hoped the other captains would show more zeal now that Arethas had proved the sickness was out there and stopping it won not just praise but gold. If those skippers felt more zeal, though, they hid it very well.

He prayed in church, where people could see him do it. He wasn't used to praying alone in his room, where only God could see him. *Lord, if You choose to send Clysma another ship carrying plague, please let Arethas be the man who finds it. Grant Your suffering people so much mercy. Please.*

The fifth indiction ended quickly, or so he thought. The sixth seemed to crawl on hands and knees. Rain fell during what passed for that winter, which didn't happen every year. Then the sun swung north in the heavens once more, and beat down on the little town from a molten sky. Tribonian hated it and took it for granted at the same time. He'd stayed there a long while now, but he would never make a native.

On the Tuesday when the sixth indiction became the seventh, Tribonian assembled all the naval officers at the hostel that catered to caravans for a feast and as much wine as they could hold.

"God bless you all," he told them before more than a couple had slid under the table. Peter was one of the ones who had, but that cheered the quaestor instead of dismaying him: he wasn't so sure he wanted God blessing Peter. "Your labors have stopped the plague from entering Clysma.

No pandemic will sweep across the Empire. You can all take pride in that for the rest of your lives. May they be long and happy and—most of all—healthy!"

He paused to drink more wine himself. Some skippers clapped their hands, but not all. Some of them still resented him for dragging them down to this hot, barren imperial outpost. *Let them*, he thought. Aloud, he went on, "Before too long, I go back to Constantinople. I promise you, I'll do everything in my power—which is not small—to make sure every one of you who wants a different posting gets it."

All of them cheered that. They cared more about themselves than about the Roman Empire. They were people, in other words.

"You know something, excellent boss?" Arethas said. "You've done your best to keep your promises as long as I've known you. Not every important fella's like that—bet your backside they aren't. But you, you could've been a devil of a lot worse."

You could've been a devil of a lot worse. Tribonian cherished that, not least because he was sure it was as much praise as he'd get for doing what he'd done. He was even surer it was far more than he'd ever hear from Justinian.

Pelusium. A voyage across the Mediterranean. A storm at sea, because it was getting late in the sailing season. His ship came through it. She was named *Tyche*. Any ship named for luck had to carry some. Or maybe she didn't have to, but she did.

Tribonian had thought Pelusium seemed large and crowded. Constantinople hit him like a slap in the face. So huge! So many people! So chilly! He did remember where he lived, and how to get there from the pier on the Golden Horn where the *Tyche* had tied up.

When he knocked on his own door, a serving woman opened it. "Yes?" she said, not recognizing him at all.

The Fake Pandemic

"Hello, Irene," he said. "It's good to be home!"

Her eyes widened. Her jaw dropped. "Master Tribonian?" she said, as if she couldn't believe it. "You're so skinny! And so *brown*!"

He looked down at his hand. He was several shades darker than she was. He didn't think he had been before. Clysma'd left its mark on him after all. "It doesn't matter. I'm still me."

"Yes, sir! Of course, sir! Come in, sir!" She almost fled back into the house to let everyone else know he'd come back after all.

Eugenius received him with well-concealed alarm. Tribonian had a good notion why: chances were the majordomo had spent the past few years stealing from him. He took that bull by the horns: "Don't worry about anything too much, Eugenius. As long as you've left me enough to get along, I won't hand you to the torturers."

"I don't know what you mean, sir," Eugenius said. Tribonian just looked at him…and watched him crumble. "Oh, sir, God bless you, sir! I always knew you were a merciful man!"

Tribonian hadn't thought of himself that way before he went to Clysma. He'd tried to be just instead. Another mark the place had left on him? Maybe it was.

Everything seemed familiar and very strange at the same time. At least Eugenius wasn't sleeping in his bedroom and didn't seem to have done much to his study. He'd drawn on his own funds often enough to remind the majordomo he was still alive, anyhow.

He wrote to the Emperor the next day, letting him know he'd returned, urging him to allow the officers and sailors who wanted to come back to the Mediterranean to do so, and finishing, *I shall compose a full report on my time in Pelusium and Clysma as quickly as I may, your Majesty. I am ready for any service to which you wish to put me. May you enjoy many more years of health and vigor.*

He wondered whether Justinian would answer him at all. In a couple of days, the Emperor did: *Our seamen are ours, to be employed as we please. We await your report, and shall peruse it with all the attention it deserves. At present, we have no requirement for your own further service.*

Tribonian read the note several times. Even after so much, even after expecting nothing different, it stung. Later that afternoon, another imperial communication met the brazier.

The report, Tribonian thought when he finished it, was a small masterpiece of its kind. Justinian had as much as told him he would ignore it. It was a small masterpiece anyhow. One of these years, it would impress the demon out of some functionary who pulled it from the files and blew the dust off it.

Again, Justinian's response was short and to the point. It was, in fact, one word long. *Received*, the Emperor wrote, and nothing more. Tribonian would have been more disappointed had he expected anything better.

He spent most of the winter trying to darn up friendships that had come unraveled through years of separation. He succeeded with a few; more often, he failed. Once more, he found himself less surprised than he wished he might. He'd been away for a long time, and it was hardly a secret that he found himself in bad odor with the Emperor. A man had to be brave to want anything to do with him.

A blizzard from off the steppes north of the Danube reminded him that weather could get much too cold as well as much too hot. Shivering and feeding wood chips into a brazier, he almost wished for an August afternoon in Clysma. Almost, but not quite.

Little by little, the weather did warm again. Trees put on new leaves. Fresh green grass pushed up through the yellow-brown dead stuff from the year before. Tribonian had always taken all that for granted. Now it seemed fresh and new and miraculous to him once more.

He realized it probably wasn't a coincidence that Easter, the festival of the Resurrection, fell in springtime. Joyous shouts filled Constantinople's streets: "Christ is risen!" "Truly, He is risen!" In this season of rebirth, those cries seemed easier to credit than they had in desert Clysma.

Like the trees, like the grass, sea commerce revived in spring. Tribonian found a captain bound for Bari with a cargo of wine and paid him to carry a letter to Italy: paid him enough, in fact, for him to spend some money on someone there to carry it to its final destination. He hadn't wanted to write

The Fake Pandemic

to Martinus Paduei from Clysma. An official letter like that would have traveled through the imperial post, and probably would have been opened and reported on. He hadn't wanted Justinian jealous he remained in touch with the mysterious American or reading his words.

As a private citizen, though, he had some chance at discretion. Letters traveling like his took their chances, of course. Maybe it would get to Florence. Maybe Paduei would answer. If he did, maybe his response would reach Constantinople.

Tribonian didn't worry about any of that. *If I hadn't visited Italy myself, maybe I'd be dead of Paduei's plague myself by now*, he thought. When you looked at it that way, whether a letter arrived didn't seem to matter much.

Spring segued into summer. Everyone complained about how hot it was—everyone but Tribonian. "How do you ignore this, sir?" Irene asked him. "It's horrible! I'm melting like tallow."

"It depends on what you're used to," he answered. She rolled her eyes. A lot of rich men didn't let servitors act up like that. All he did was laugh.

One muggy afternoon that even he admitted was respectably warm, Eugenius tapped on his study door. "A sailor just brought a letter, sir," he said, and held it out to him.

"Thanks." Tribonian took it. "I hope you tipped him above the going rate?"

Eugenius nodded. "Yes, sir." He left so Tribonian could open it without anyone looking over his shoulder.

The address read *Tribonian the barrister, Constantinople, near the palaces.* Tribonian thought he recognized the writing, which was very clear. He broke the seal and undid the cords. Sure enough…

> *Martinus Paduei to his friend Tribonian, Greetings. It did my heart good to get your letter yesterday. I did not want to write to you after I heard you had gone to Egypt. It would have made someone you know suspicious, which would have been the last thing anybody needed.*

Tribonian found himself grinning like a fool. "He gets it!" he exclaimed. Then he went back to the letter. He had to hold it at arm's length to read it; his sight was lengthening, as older men's did.

> *That the pestilence did not come to Italy told me you had succeeded. Your letter tells me how. The world owes you a great debt, most excellent and noble Tribonian, a debt of which you will never collect a copper. From things I have heard here and there, I gather that that someone did less than he might have and thought I was telling tales to make him go chase himself. I wish I had been, and I thank heaven that you, at least, believed I might be speaking the truth.*
>
> *The world goes on, and goes on without the great burden of death and misery it would have borne had you also decided I was lying. Maybe, working together, we can continue to improve it here and there in little ways. Thanks to you, we have the chance. If things there ever grow too warm for you, know that I would be proud to welcome you here. I am indeed your true and grateful friend, Martinus Paduei.*

After reading it through again, Tribonian slowly nodded. Here he hadn't thought he'd get any reward for what he'd done down in Clysma. He'd never been so glad to find himself proved wrong.

The Fillmore Shoggoth

Here is the first of three Lovecraftian stories I've included in this collection. They're fun to do, both because of the many weird and terrible things H. P. Lovecraft created and because I get to shoehorn them into the world that went on after he passed away. I should note here that the band HPL isn't exactly the real world's band called H. P. Lovecraft. Nor is Howard Phillips exactly the real world's writer called H. P. Lovecraft. The scientific name for the penguins from the Mountains of Madness is my own invention, though it's plain that they belong to the same genus as Emperor and King Penguins. Finally, you may recognize a cameo from a song by a band that isn't HPL or even H. P. Lovecraft.

HPL comes down to San Francisco from Marin County. They have a gig at the Fillmore tonight, playing with the Loading Zone and Crome Syrcus. Not all the guys in the band have quite come down, but hey, that's, like, just a sign of the times, man. Pharmaceuticals are your friends. Spring 1968. Signs and portents in the air.

Okay, sure, signs and portents are always in the air, but spring of 1968 is especially bad for them. The Tet Offensive. LBJ saying he won't run again. Gene McCarthy and Bobby Kennedy and Hubert Humphrey fighting for the soul of the Democratic Party (though Hubert wouldn't know what to do with a soul if he tripped over one in the street). Martin Luther King shot down like a dog in Memphis. Ghettos exploding. The Antarctic iceberg off the Northern California coast. All kinds of weird shit going on.

When things get weird, what do you do? George and Dave, Mike and Tony and Jeff, they go to the zoo. They park their two old station wagons and get out and stretch. Between 'em, the Plymouth and the Chevy hold all the guys in the band and all the gear they'll need tonight. They go through gas like pigs through swill. It's only a quarter a gallon, though, so what's the big deal?

"Wow," George goes, and then, "Oh, wow." He plays guitar and sings. If HPL has a leader—always an interesting question—he's the man. He's tall and dark and lean, with long hair and longer sideburns. In San Francisco, in spring of '68, he fits right in.

Mike, the drummer, has long hair, too, but he's short and kind of chunky. What he says is, "Brr!" He buttons up his sweater. It was sunny and warm in Marin. But the San Francisco Zoo is stuck in the southwest corner of the city, right on the ocean. The fog hasn't even started burning off yet. No better than even money that it will.

Somebody across the parking lot yells, "Fuckin' hippies!" Not everyone in San Francisco is cool with long hair and funky clothes. But there are five guys in the band, all of them younger than the loudmouthed square. He flips them the bird, but he doesn't want to meet them up close and personal.

A jet—no, two jets—scream by overhead. The roar almost flattens you to the pavement. It dopplers off toward the west. "Whoa!" Jeff says. He's the new bass player, blond and handsome. He's got hotter licks than Jerry did, and a better voice, too.

"Scouting the iceberg—what do you want to bet?" George says.

His bandmates all nod. People have been scouting the iceberg since it broke off the Ross Ice Shelf and headed north more than a year ago. It's on the other side of the Equator now, but it hasn't shrunk. If anything, it's got bigger. That should be impossible. It isn't, not to the guys in HPL. Once you've dropped acid a few times, nothing is impossible.

These days, it often seems as if the whole world has dropped acid. "The Old Ones, or maybe the Shoggoths," Dave says. He's the keyboard man—everything from a small electric organ to a freakin' harpsichord. He's, like, Deep.

The Fillmore Shoggoth

Which doesn't mean he's wrong. Since the Miskatonic University Expedition, people and the Old Ones have warily tried to live with each other. Shoggoths, on the other hand, don't want to live with anything else, ancient or modern. There have been some unfortunate incidents—the radioactive hole that used to be Sauk City, for instance, and the one near the South Pole—but nothing lately. Except the iceberg, that is.

Those jets will carry bombs and rockets and guns. All the scouts do. They haven't used them yet. LBJ has enough other things to worry about without pissing off the creatures from Antarctica. But, in case of trouble, the planes will use what they carry.

HPL can't do anything about the iceberg. So the guys go on into the zoo. It's a WPA project, from about the same time as the Miskatonic University Expedition. No cages—concrete enclosures instead, with moats to keep the animals on the outside from mingling with the animals on the inside.

Well, almost no cages. Moated enclosures don't work real well for birds. So there's a big old aviary you can wander through and see toucans and cocks-of-the-rock and peafowl and like that. It smells like jungle inside, jungle mixed with chicken coop.

And there's a sign, a sign with an arrow: THIS WAY TO THE PENGUINS. Penguins are cool. The guys drift THIS WAY. They go down some concrete stairs, to a chilly, dimly lit underground chamber. It smells of ocean and chicken coop. The penguins swimming in the water and toddling around on the concrete shore don't wear tuxedos. They're white all over, their eyes mere slits. They're big birds, as tall as a man.

"They're funny-looking!" a little boy exclaims. George can't possibly disagree. A sign in front of the moat says CAVE PENGUINS—*Aptenodytes miskatonensis*. The little boy has a flat red plastic elephant in his hand. It's called a Trunkey. He sticks the trunk—the key part—into a Storybook below the sign and turns it. A scratchy recording blares forth: "These rare, dark-adapted penguins were discovered by the Miskatonic University Expedition deep underground in the Old Ones' city beyond the Antarctic Mountains of Madness. Living specimens were brought back by the later

Starkweather-Moore exploration team. This is the only zoo that has bred them in human captivity."

"Now we know what the iceberg's all about," Dave says. "The Old Ones are coming for the baby penguins."

George looks at him. He says, "I know what you're on, man, 'cause I'm on it, too. But it doesn't mess me up *that* bad." The rest of the guys in the band laugh, nervously, not sure whether he's kidding. Well, George isn't quite sure himself. In the spring of 1968, nobody's quite sure of anything, even when he isn't wasted.

It's warmer once they come out into the fog again, which says a lot about how chilly it is in the penguin enclosure. The zoo has every kind of big cat there is. George admires their deadly elegance. He wonders how the tigers like San Francisco weather. They don't seem to mind it. One of them is tearing chunks off a slab of raw meat. Except for the size of the chunks, it could be the cat back at the place gobbling Friskies kidneys-and-liver. But that makes a pretty good *except*.

After a while, George and his buddies get hungry, too. Across the street from the zoo sits the Doggie Diner. It's topped by a big old dachshund's head. The dachshund's wearing a chef's toque and a bow tie. The head, even the hat, make some kind of sense to George. In California, a donut shop will be crowned by a stucco-and-chicken-wire donut. A fried-chicken place will look like a drumstick, or maybe a whole bird. So why *not* put a dog and something that means cooking on top of a hot-dog stand? No reason at all, not here. Chicago wasn't like this, not even a little bit.

What's happening with the bow tie, though? There are several Doggie Diners in San Francisco. George freaks out about the bow tie every time he drives past one. They do dish out good dogs—he has to give them that.

After lunch, he and the rest of HPL slide into the station wagons and drive to the Fillmore. It's a big square building at the corner of Fillmore— wow! surprise!—and Geary. It's west of downtown, a little north and east of Haight-Ashbury. *Of but not in*, George thinks. He nods to himself, liking the notion. Without the freaks from the Haight, and without the

The Fillmore Shoggoth

people who think like the freaks there, the Fillmore would have no reason for being.

Neither would HPL. Before the band came together, he'd been singing in a hotel lounge in the Windy City. It paid the bills. It put food on the table. This is a hell of a lot more fun.

It is while they're playing, anyhow, and while they're enjoying their almost-fame. Getting ready for a gig is a different story. The Fillmore parking lot is the size of a postage stamp. The dressing rooms are even smaller. They get ventilation strictly by hearsay.

The guys change into their working clothes: embroidered pants, shirts with bell-bottom sleeves, jackets halfway between Nehru and Napoleonic cavalry general. George sports ruffles at his throat, and wears his jacket open to show them off. While they wait for their turn to have a sound check and work with the lighting guys, they smoke some weed. It makes the time goes by, and they play better when they're mellow. They're convinced of it.

When they go up on stage, another odor wars with the sweet smell of pot. It is strange and ancient-seeming: from beyond time and space, you might say. The house isn't quite empty, even without people in the seats. A couple of winged, barrel-shaped Old Ones stand in the aisle to listen to rehearsals.

"Holy smoke," Dave breathes. "I heard they liked the noise and the beat, but I didn't know if I believed it or not."

"Neither did I," George says. "But they're here, so I guess they do." He feels like Sherlock Holmes for figuring that out. Weed may make you play better. It doesn't necessarily make you think better.

Sitting next to the Old Ones is a tall, thin, white-haired man with a lantern jaw. His suit and stiff-collared shirt come straight from the 1920s. "Is that—?" Dave begins.

"It is." Jeff, the new bass man, sounds awed. "It really is. That's Howard Phillips. I've seen photos of him when he was younger. I've been reading his books since I was a kid."

"Who hasn't?" George puts in. Phillips has to be getting up near eighty now. He knows more about the Old Ones than anybody. He wrote the bestselling chronicle of the Miskatonic University Expedition forty years ago, and he's studied and worked with mankind's forerunners ever since. The comfortable-looking old lady with him must be his wife, Sonia.

A lot of the time, rehearsals are half-assed. You just want to get through them and making sure the lighting crew knows what to do when. Not when you're playing for the Old Ones, though. HPL rocks the joint. The Old Ones spread their wings a little. Jeff gives a thumbs-up—that means they're digging it.

Whether Howard Phillips is into psychedelic rock may be a different question. "Very…interesting," he says after they do "At the Mountains of Madness." He polishes his specs with a silk handkerchief. But if the Old Ones get off on the music, he's too polite to show he doesn't.

After the set, the other bands take their turns. HPL goes back to the dressing room. More jet fighters scream by, racing off to the west. There's a radio in the room. George is about to turn it on and see what's happening when the guy people call Kid Charlemagne shows up. He cooks the best acid in the world, bar none. No kerosene in the mix. No crap at all. Just pure, clean lysergic acid diethylamide. Next to that, nobody cares about the iceberg in the Pacific…or anything else.

Things get a little strange. If you've already dropped acid a few times, or more than a few, you start to get a handle on what's real and what comes from the drug. When you've got to play a gig while you're flying, you make the music you need to make and you groove on the sounds the rest of the band is making. Automatic pilot, you might say. And while your hands and your voice do pretty much what they're supposed to do, the rest of you can trip on the things you're seeing, the things that may or may not be there. If you feel as if God is more your assistant than your copilot, or if you think the whole world is coming after you with sharp sticks, that's the drug talking, too. You try not to let it bum you out too much. Sooner or later, you'll come down.

The place fills up. The swelling noise sounds like surf at the coast, or like the tigers roaring at the zoo, or… The more George chases choices, the more

The Fillmore Shoggoth

they skip away. Going after them seems like too much trouble. A lot of things seem like too much trouble.

Somebody sticks his head into the room. "Five minutes, troops," he says. He looks a little like Howard Phillips, a little like an Old One. He does to George, anyhow. George doesn't suppose he really looks that way. Kid Charlemagne's acid is righteously potent.

There probably isn't a yawning pit filled with fire between the dressing room and the stage, either. There wasn't when the band went out for sound and light checks. Nobody but George seems to think there is now. All the same, he's careful where he puts his feet. He doesn't fall. He doesn't burn. Maybe he's snapping his fingers to keep the elephants away. Or maybe not. You never can tell for sure. You never can tell for sure what *for sure* is, either, not right after Kid Charlemagne comes around.

House lights are still up. George cases the front rows for cute ones. There are some, so he hopes he's seeing what he thinks he's seeing. He takes his place. Damned if Howard Phillips and Sonia and the Old Ones aren't still there—unless it's a flashback from this afternoon.

No. Or he doesn't think so. He can smell the Old Ones, along with pot and cigarettes and perfume and people who could use a shower. Acid doesn't usually play tricks with—play tricks on—his sense of smell. But *doesn't usually* is as much as he can say. Acid does what acid does. You're just along for the ride. That's the fun of it. Once in a while—not too often, but once in a while—that's the terror.

Down go the lights. Scattered whoops and cheers from the crowd. The voice of the Lord (well, actually the voice of the house emcee, amped enough to impersonate Him) booms from the sound system: "Folks, give a warm Fillmore welcome to…HPL!"

More whoops and cheers, still pretty scattered. If they were the Airplane, now, or Big Brother or the Dead, people would be screaming their heads off. That's what everybody in all the bands wants. Fame. The rush that goes with it. The cash that goes with it.

HPL is opening for two other bands that want it but don't have it. *Don't have it yet*, they'd say. So would George. Everybody starts out opening for somebody else. If you've got it, pretty soon some other band is opening for you.

HPL goes into "Wayfaring Stranger." It's a good song to jam on, and everybody in the band can play. A lot of groups sound fine in the studio, where they can do as many takes as they need (as many takes as they can afford, anyway) and the recording engineers can fix their flubs. Sounding fine live—doing it right the first time every time—is a whole different ballgame. HPL is in that league, even when everybody's tripping.

The jam goes where it goes. They let it. On the album, "Wayfaring Stranger" is a two-and-a-half-minute track. Here, it runs four times that long. When it finally winds down, the hand they get is bigger. Next on the set list is "The Drifter," which also, well, drifts. "It's About Time" is tighter. Maybe they're coming down a little.

After that comes "The White Ship," which has to be the most talked-about track from the album. Then they'll do "At the Mountains of Madness." George looks forward to that, as much as the acid lets him look forward to anything. He wants to introduce Howard Phillips and the creatures from the real Mountains of Madness to the Fillmore crowd. It's not a chance he ever dreamt he'd get.

He doesn't get it now. HPL is halfway through "The White Ship" when the house lights come on again, all at once. It's like a bomb going off. The band staggers to a ragged stop, everybody squinting and staring at everybody else.

"May I have your attention, please?" the house emcee thunders. "May I have your attention, *please*? The Antarctic iceberg has come ashore near the zoo. There are Shoggoths loose in the city. I repeat—there are Shoggoths loose in the city! All public assemblies have been banned by the San Francisco Civil Defense Command. Please exit and return to your homes in an orderly fashion. Thank you!" He starts to repeat himself.

Faint in the distance, sirens scream. At first, George figures he wouldn't be hearing them without the acid. Then he realizes they're part of the warning system against Russian bombs and rockets, the one that gets loudly tested at

The Fillmore Shoggoth

ten in the morning on the last Friday of every month. But things worse than Russians—older than Russians, anyhow—are loose in San Francisco now.

Down front, Howard Phillips gesticulates at the Old Ones. He looks like a man with ants in his pants, and fire ants at that. The Old Ones, though, created the Shoggoths—created them, and then let them get out of hand. Maybe they know what to do about the ones rampaging here now. Or maybe they have no idea. *Do not call up that which you cannot put down* is a good rule, but it seems to have slipped past them when they got into the Shoggoth business.

Also faint in the distance, and then not so faint, comes automatic-weapons fire. What will a .50-caliber machine gun do to a Shoggoth? Kill it? Or just piss it off?

Up till now, people leaving the Fillmore have been pretty orderly. The gunfire sets them screaming and running and pushing, though. Right up here on stage seems the safest place the band can stay. Howard Phillips and his wife and the Old Ones don't go anywhere, either. One of the weird creatures from the Mountains of Madness gestures back at Phillips. He nods thoughtfully, as if he's learned something interesting he didn't know before.

But then a shrill, eldritch sound comes from outside—or perhaps from Outside. "*Tekeli-li! Tekeli-li!*": the hideous piping makes George's long hair try to stand on end in terror. The Old Ones, understanding more, also fear more. They spread their membranous wings and flap up through the smoky air toward the ceiling.

Too late! With resistless force, a Shoggoth smashes in through the wall. The lights flicker, then go out. Before they do, George sees enough of the black-slime-coated amorphous monstrosity to haunt his nightmares forevermore. A new stench, fouler than the Old Ones' odor, fills the Fillmore.

Crashes and thuds declare that the ceiling is not high enough to let the Old Ones escape the fury of the thing whose kind they created to be their slaves. A shriek of mortal terror bursts from Howard Phillips' throat, and then a shriek of mortal agony. Sonia Phillips also screams, and goes on screaming.

The Shoggoth oozes out through the opening it made, leaving behind only its filthy fetor. More gunfire hammers outside. Muzzle flashes spear the night. As if they were bolts of lightning, George tries to use them to see what has happened inside the Fillmore. They are too stroboscopic, too soon gone, to let him learn all he wants, but what little he can make out prints fresh horror on his shuddering brain.

San Francisco's defenders prove to have more than rifles and machine guns in their arsenal. A good thing, too, for none of those seems to slow the Shoggoth. But a fighter plane dives to no more than rooftop height. It drops its load of jellied death on the monstrosity and thunders away.

Flames outside cast steadier light into the ruined hall. Not even the Shoggoth's unnatural integument is proof against napalm. "Burn, baby, burn!" someone out there yells: whether soldier or passerby, George never learns.

And burn the Shoggoth does. "*Tekeli-li! Tekeli-li!*" it pipes one last time, now in tormented despair. As it falls silent, fierce, triumphant human shouts fill the smoky, stinking air.

Yet the vile thing has wreaked at least a measure of revenge against the creators of its kind. The barrel-shaped bodies of both Old Ones sprawl, ungainly in death, across smashed seats. Greenish ichor pools beneath them. Their starfish-like heads have been torn away.

And poor, scholarly Howard Phillips has suffered a like fate. The blood under his lifeless body is of an honest scarlet hue. Sonia Phillips screams on and on, her hands pressed to the sides of her head, and who can blame her?

"Wow!" George hears someone say, as if from very far away. With drugs and terror chasing each other through his veins, he needs two or three heartbeats to realize the voice is his own. "Oh, wow!"

A soldier with a flashlight trots into the Fillmore through the hole the Shoggoth made. He slips on its vile slime trail, but stays upright. "Anybody in here?" he shouts. Sonia Phillips' anguished cries should give him a hint, but no doubt he is following some higher-up's orders.

"Yes," George calls from the stage, to make it official.

"Well, get the hell out, then," the soldier says. "This dump is on fire."

The Fillmore Shoggoth

Did some napalm splash onto the Fillmore? Did the thrashing, burning Shoggoth brush against it? George wonders if anyone knows. He also wonders why he cares. He and Dave jump down from the stage together. They bring Sonia Phillips with them when they leave.

"Howard was no Old One!" she sobs, over and over again. The Shoggoth either thought otherwise or, animated by some mad viciousness of its own, simply did not care.

Out on Fillmore Street, chaos is compounded. People who escaped from the concert mill in shock and confusion. That most of them are stoned can't help. Soldiers try to push past them. Fire engines pour streams of water on the blazes the air strikes and other combat started. The air smells of pot and wood smoke and diesel exhaust and Shoggoth and charred Shoggoth.

"What do we do now?" George wonders out loud.

"Hope we get paid," Dave answers. "Hope there's anybody left alive to pay us." As the Fillmore burns behind the band, those both seem forlorn hopes. Nothing worse than this has happened to San Francisco since the 1906 earthquake. And that, at least, was a natural disaster, not one precipitated by perverted, malevolent intelligence.

"Youse guys! Uh, youse guys and the old lady—c'mon! Over this way!" A corporal gestures with his rifle. HPL and Sonia Phillips numbly go where he points. It's only too obvious the kid with the stripes on his sleeve will shoot them if they do anything but exactly what he tells them.

More soldiers shepherd them along. A few blocks north of Geary and a couple of blocks east of Fillmore is Lafayette Park. George had no idea it was there. Now he huddles on the grass with his bandmates and the scholar's widow and hundreds—no, thousands—of other people who, like him, will worry about anything but being alive some other time.

An olive-drab, square-shouldered truck pulls up. It's full of military ration packs. People line up to get them. George gulps canned ham and eggs. It's nasty, but he doesn't care. Been a long time since the Doggie Diner.

He wonders what's happened to the Doggie Diner, and to the zoo. That's where the iceberg came ashore. Maybe it beached there by happenstance.

But how much does happenstance apply to anything connected with the Mountains of Madness?

"I wish they would've let us check our cars," Dave says. George hasn't worried about them. Now he does. Probably nothing left of them but Shoggoth-smashed, burnt-out sheet metal. Well, one thing at a time. The band can always thumb a ride up to Marin. After that… After that will be time enough to worry about after that.

George slowly parachutes down from the acid high to the mundane, Aristotelian world. More explosions come from the southwest, the direction of the zoo. They don't seem very far away. They *aren't* very far away; San Francisco is a big city crammed into a small space. They don't come any closer, for which he is more than duly grateful.

He lies back on the grass. It's cool, but not really cold. San Francisco in May—or August, or November. Next thing he knows, the early-morning sun shining in his face wakes him up. He yawns and stretches and slowly sits up. Jeff is already awake. He nods to George. George nods back. He nods to himself, too: he's all the way straight, or thinks he is. The rest of the guys in the band go on sleeping. Dave snores. So does Sonia Phillips.

Somebody nearby has a transistor radio tuned to the local news station. George cranes his head toward the thin, tinny sound. He came too close to the local news last night. Coming too close to the local news meant coming much too close to getting killed.

"Casualties are widespread in the city," a newsman says. "One Shoggoth reached the Fillmore, where a rock concert was in progress. Seventeen are confirmed dead there, and other losses may not be known for some time. Also slain were two Old Ones attending the concert. Now let's go to Ed Rubinstein, in Golden Gate Park."

"This is Ed Rubinstein, in Golden Gate Park," a different voice says. "I'm reporting from the De Young Museum, which was gutted by two Shoggoths. Until its destruction, the De Young boasted the finest collection of art and artifacts from the Old Ones this side of Miskatonic University in Arkham. Sadly, that appears to be a total loss. Fourteen are known dead near the

The Fillmore Shoggoth

museum, a figure that surely would have been much higher if the building had been open. Now I'll pass the broadcast to Karen Holloway, reporting from the zoo."

"Our prized exhibit of cave penguins is no more," Karen Holloway announces, presumably from the zoo. "A Shoggoth—apparently the first monster off the iceberg—tore through the aviary and into the refrigerated underground exhibit area where the penguins were kept. It seemed indifferent to the other birds, but made a point of destroying the rare white penguins, which have a long association with the Old Ones' city in Antarctica. Sadly, no penguins are known to have survived."

Tears fill George's eyes. Somehow, the Shoggoth's rage against the harmless cave penguins seems sadder than the rest of their attack on the city. He realizes he may not be completely down from the acid after all.

Interlibrary Loan

When I was in grad school, I borrowed a lot of books through interlibrary loan, even though UCLA has its own strong research library. Most of them had titles like *The Third Part of the Ecclesiastical History of John Bishop of Ephesus* or *Studien zur Geschichte des byzantinischen Reiches: vohrnehmlich unter den Kaisern Justinus II u. Tiberius Constantinus*. I also used interlibrary loan to get my hands on H. Beam Piper's *Little Fuzzy*, which was in those days long out of print and unobtainable any other way. Yes, the people who worked there gave me odd looks when I handed them that request form. Along with a lot of Lovecraft, those memories go into this story.

Hafez ibn Abd-al-Rahim strode across the campus of Miskatonic University, heading for the library. He'd never been there before, but he'd studied maps and satellite photos on Google Earth. He knew his way around as well as if he were a senior about to graduate. It was a warm spring day, a little muggy but not too bad.

No one paid him any special mind. He might have been a senior about to graduate himself. He was in his early twenties, with a neat black beard and hair razored on the sides of his head and longish on top. Older people said he looked as if he had a cowflop on his head, but when did older people ever do anything but complain? Half the guys at Miskatonic chose styles not too different from his. At least half.

He was neater than most. He tucked a powder-blue polo shirt into new Levi's. His Topsiders were also new. No ratty T-shirts, tattered cutoffs, or flipflops for him. No Red Sox cap, either; he hadn't succumbed to that idolatrous passion. In fact, he'd never heard of the Red Sox.

His biggest problem, as it had been since he flew in to Logan, was not gaping at the women. Sternly, he reminded himself that staring marked him as a foreigner, and a particular kind of foreigner. It would not do.

But they were sluts. They were all sluts, and even sluttier because in their *kafir* ignorance they had no idea how slutty they were. Bare flesh on display, hair uncovered, peach-ripe bottoms shoehorned into jeans far tighter than his… One girl wore a clinging T-shirt with MISKATONIC UNIVERSITY FIGHTING CEPHALOPODS written across the stomach. The octopus or whatever it was above the top word had tentacles brazenly curling up to circle her breasts. Hafez made himself look away. He bit down, hard, on the inside of his lower lip at the effort it took.

By the time he got to the library, he was sweating from more than the humidity. Its gray, stern, forbidding bulk steadied him somewhat. Even the very pretty blonde in running shorts coming down the broad stairs as he was going up distracted him for no longer than a moment. He was here at last. Now, God willing, to do what he had come to do.

The doors automatically opened when he came up to them. They closed behind him the same way. The air inside had the tasteless, bland perfection of air-conditioning. Twenty-one degrees Celsius, a bit of humidity but not much, unchanging regardless of the hour, regardless of the day, regardless of the season—a useful device, but bloody dull. The shadowless light the fluorescents in the ceiling panels cast was just as boring.

He looked around. Signs directed people this way and that: to the terminals that accessed the library catalogue, to the copy room, to the main stacks, to the circulation desk. He saw none directing people to Special Collections, where he needed to go. He muttered under his breath. Nothing ever went as smoothly as you wished it would.

Still muttering, he took his place in the line at the circulation desk. It moved briskly. Clerks scanned barcodes and stamped due dates in books and periodicals. Or they accepted returns and, if asked, gave back receipts.

Interlibrary Loan

All the motion, all the talk, was stylized, ritualized, as at an airport or a mosque.

Hafez realized he would be a bit of grit in the smoothly running machine. No help for it, though. He bit his lip again when he found himself facing, having to deal with, one of those free-haired young women. He thought she was homely, but it helped less than he would have wished.

"Yes?" she said. "What can I do for you?"

"I am looking for Special Collections, please," Hafez said.

She frowned. "You *are*?"

"I am," he agreed. "Please, let me show you…" He pulled out an Egyptian passport. It was, or seemed, genuine enough to satisfy airline and customs personnel. "I am Ahmad Goma." The passport bore his photo and said he was Ahmad Goma, anyhow. "I am a graduate student to Professor Gamal al-Zubi, of Al-Azhar University in Cairo. I have his letter of introduction here." He plucked that from a manila folder in his backpack. Unlike the ones on the passport, its signature was authentic. Professor al-Zubi had been made to understand what would happen to him and to his family if he didn't cooperate with Hafez ibn Abd-al-Rahim and his companions.

Still frowning, the *kafir* girl said, "I don't quite see—"

Hafez overrode her: "He wishes to interlibrary loan a certain book from Miskatonic University. There was reluctance to post the book overseas because of rarity and value. I have come to take it personally to Professor al-Zubi."

She checked something on a computer monitor. A security alert? No—her face cleared. "It's fine. They're expecting you."

"But how do I find them?"

She pointed to a corridor. "Go along there. Turn left, then left, then left again. It's the first door past room 153. Take the stairs up to the fourth floor. If you come to room 155, you've gone too far."

"I thank you." Hafez went down the corridor and turned left, left, and left again. The corridors were long, so long they hardly seemed able to fit into the library, although it was a large building. With each turn, he went further from what the infidels called the twenty-first century, from scanners and flat-screen monitors and smartphones and the Information Age.

By the time he found room 153, even the air-conditioning faltered. The walls were brickwork. Something nasty—lichen?—sprouted on the mortar. The doors here were stained a dark brown, almost the color of dried blood. Verdigris greened the brass numerals. The doorknobs and locks were of antique style.

Another few steps…and there was room 155. Hafez scowled. He was sure he'd passed no other doorways. Starting back, he murmured, "Truly there is no God but God, and Muhammad is the prophet of God."

Maybe the *shahada* revealed the hidden. Maybe Hafez just hadn't paid attention before. At any rate, there it was, the door with TO SPECIAL COLLECTIONS on it in corroded brass letters. Hafez opened it and started up the stairs.

If anything, the AC in the stairwell did its job too well. It was positively arctic in there. Even the chill, though, didn't quite mask the musty, even mephitic reek rising up from the treads and risers. Hafez couldn't name that faint stench, but, had he had any hair at the nape of his neck, it would have stood on end. Being made of stern stuff, he climbed on regardless.

"THANK YOU, Lucinda," Wilbur Armitage said, and returned the telephone handset to its cradle.

The head of the Miskatonic University Library's Special Collections sighed as he straightened. Armitages had served the university and the library for generations. Wilbur was tall and lean and scholarly-looking, with gold-framed bifocals. People said of him that he might have been born in a three-piece suit.

Right now, his hoped his herringbone tweed waistcoat hid the pounding of his heart. Nodding to his assistants, he said, "He's coming."

All three of them exclaimed in dismay. Marlene Yarrow, who was his niece and who would likely succeed him one day, said, "He shouldn't get the book, Uncle Wilbur."

Interlibrary Loan

"That's right!" Jason Griffith looked like a student himself, but had a thoroughly unmodern respect for the antiquities housed here. "The *Necronomicon* is dangerous—and the sun is warm, and the ocean is damp, and Pluto is a little way off from here." Petros Papagos, the third Special Collections junior librarian, dipped his head in vigorous Hellenic agreement.

But Armitage shook his own head. "No," he said, and then repeated it for emphasis: "No. Interlibrary loan is… Mm, I hesitate to use the word *sacred*, but I mean something not far from it. Not all libraries have all books. Not all scholars can come to a library that does have a book they need. Sometimes the mountain must go to Muhammad rather than the reverse."

Marlene made a face. "Did you have to pick that particular phrase, Uncle Wilbur? With all the chaos in the Muslim world these past few years…"

"Al-Azhar University is a member in good standing of the interlibary-loan system," Wilbur Armitage replied. "Faculty members in the Near Eastern Studies Center here have interlibrary-loaned material from its holdings. And Google shows what a distinguished scholar of early Islamic mysticism Professor al-Zubi is."

"If he really asked for the book." Petros Papagos had a loud, nasal, irritating voice. "If this fellow picking it up really is his grad student. Do you want a book like—that—in the hands of some of the gangs of murderers who use Islam as an excuse to do what they want to do anyhow?"

"All my e-mail and snailmail correspondence with Professor al-Zubi has been impeccably correct," Armitage said. "I have no reason to doubt he has both reason to consult this text and the ability to navigate it with as much safety as anyone is likely to. I also have no reason to doubt that Mr. Goma studies with him. And furthermore—"

He broke off. He and his assistants all heard the footsteps in the small antechamber outside the Special Collections unit. Very softly, Marlene Yarrow said, "He's here."

As he had at the circulation desk, Hafez presented his documents to the old man in charge of Special Collections. Wilbur Armitage looked at them more closely than the *kafir* girl out front had, but even the forged passport was proof against any naked-eye scrutiny and most though not all lab tests.

After a few seconds, Armitage handed back the paperwork. "Everything seems to be in order," he said. "Let me take you to the volume you need. There are certain precautions you will need to follow while transporting it to Professor al-Zubi."

"He has told me to obey you as if you are my father," Hafez said. "What you say to me, I will do."

"Come this way, then," Armitage said.

The *Necronomicon* had a small room to itself. A combination lock kept out the uninvited. Armitage interposed his body while he spun the dial this way and that so Hafez couldn't learn the numbers. After a click, the door swung open. It might have a wooden veneer, but it was at least ten centimeters of solid steel. Hafez didn't know the steel was specially hardened, but who would go to so much trouble for second-rate protection?

"I can understand Professor al-Zubi's eagerness to work with the original Arabic text at last," the Special Collections chief said. "We only, ah, acquired this manuscript a little more than twenty years ago ourselves."

"Yes," Hafez said, and not another word. He thought, *You got it after some* kafir *thief stole it when America invaded Iraq*. While he could think that, coming out with it seemed inexpedient.

Inside, the codex sat on a flat-topped wooden lectern. It was bound in pale, thin, soft leather of a kind Hafez did not recognize at once. Not sheepskin, not even the accursed pigskin... He gulped, realizing what that binding had to be. He had seen and done hard things in service to the rising Caliphate, but never any to match the chilling deliberation that went into the making of that volume.

A belt cut from the same leather held the *Necronomicon* closed. The buckle and tongue were of gold. Four stout steel chains secured the codex to the lectern, which was in turn bolted to the floor. Hafez got the odd feeling that they were there less to protect the book from thieves than to keep it from escaping.

"You will keep the belt closed at all times before the volume reaches Professor al-Zubi," Armitage said as he freed the *Necronomicon* from the chains one by one. "At all times—do you understand me? Otherwise, I cannot answer for your safety, or for that of those around you."

"Hearkening and obedience, my master," Hafez said. "But may I not open it for just a moment, here in this warded room, to make sure it is indeed the work I seek?"

Wilbur Armitage plainly wanted to say no. As plainly, he saw he couldn't. "That is a fair request," he said with a sad cluck. "I will take the risk. Don't waste any time when I undo the belt, though."

"Hearkening and obedience," Hafez repeated.

After closing and locking the armored door, the *kafir* undid the belt and quickly lifted the front cover. Hafez leaned forward. Though no graduate student, he knew what he needed to know. The Arabic script was archaic, much like that on the black flag he followed. The text was as appalling as he'd been led to believe it would be. And the way the words began to run and glow and seemingly take on a life of their own…

"Close it!" he gasped. "In God's name, close it!"

Breathing hard, as if from some uncommon physical effort, Armitage did. The fabric of the world might have let out a sigh of relief as he fastened the belt once more. "You see what I mean," he said heavily.

"I see, yes," Hafez replied. "It will not open again until the professor opens it. He has the wisdom and holiness to wrestle with such and prevail."

"He'd better," Wilbur Armitage said.

"May I take it?" Hafez asked. The *kafir* scholar did not tell him no, but set about unsealing the strongroom again. When Hafez lifted the *Necronomicon*, it was heavier than its size would have suggested, then suddenly lighter, as if accepting him and his purposes. *A good omen*, he thought. *God wills this.*

He put the book in his backpack and carried it out of the strongroom and out of the Miskatonic University library. By the time he left the university campus, it felt feather-light. All would go well. He was sure of it. All could hardly help going well.

⁓

JASON GRIFFITH rolled his eyes. "Wilbur, you're the boss, but I wish you hadn't done that," he said, which would do for an understatement till a bigger one came along. "If that Goma guy is what I'm afraid he is, it's like giving North Korea an ICBM."

"Worse," Petros Papagos said. "An ICBM just sits there. You have to do things with it. That damned book"—not wanting to name the *Necronomicon*, he described it instead—"does things on its own."

"Which is what I was about to say when Mr. Goma got here," Wilbur Armitage replied. "In worrying about what his possible friends may do with the volume, you forget or misunderstand one key fact. As it has shown again and again down through the centuries, my friends, the *Necronomicon* is more than capable of taking care of itself."

⁓

THE RENTAL car from Arkham back to Boston. A redeye from Boston to Rome, one made all the more vein-tracked because the three-year-old in the next row back wouldn't stop kicking Hafez's seat and singing. He knew many ways to kill, some quick, some slow and horrible. On an airplane, he couldn't use any of them. He had to endure.

Having endured, he shambled from the Delta gate to one for Turkish Air for the flight to Ankara. He dozed a little then: just enough to leave him even more exhausted than he would have been with no sleep at all. A Turkish customs inspector with a bushy black mustache eyed the *Necronomicon* with more curiosity than he should have. Three discreetly passed engraved portraits of Benjamin Franklin left him incurious once more.

Interlibrary Loan

Hafez claimed a new rental car with no trouble, but by then his body was threatening revolt. You could run on coffee and nerves only so long. He got a fair meal and a soft bed at a hotel by the airport and came close to sleeping the clock around. Another bowl of lamb stew and he was on the road.

The farther south and east he went, the narrower and more potholed the roads he traveled became. He skirted several checkpoints full of hard-faced man with assault rifles. He wasn't always sure whose checkpoints they were. The Turkish government claimed this land. So did the Kurdish savages who actually lived on it. And the Caliphate's wingspan was grown wide enough to make the hot, barren countryside debatable in a whole new way.

Likewise debatable was the border between Turkey and the wreckage of Syria. The Turks wanted neither Kurdish rebels nor fighters for the Caliphate sliding into their country from the south. They cared much less about who and what went the other way. Hafez would have used a real border crossing if he'd had to. He didn't have to. Driving the little VW down a twisty dirt track from one land to the other proved easy as you please. The rental-car company would never see the VW again, but he wasted no sympathy on it.

Only an hour or so south of the border lay the town of ar-Raqqah, which had flown the Caliphate's black banner for some time. Before Syria's multi-cornered civil war engulfed it, ar-Raqqah had held close to a quarter-million people. Its population was a good deal smaller now. To purify the faith, the Caliphate's Sunni warriors had dynamited Shi'a mosques. What else could one do with those nests of heresy and error?

In ar-Raqqah were the men to whom Hafez was charged to deliver the *Necronomicon*. Having grown up in Iraq, he didn't know the town well. He had to ask for directions twice, the second time because the first man sent him the wrong way. *If I ever set eyes on that son of a diseased sow again*, he thought, *I'll kill him*.

Night was falling when he found the house he needed. The men waiting there, the ones who would send the mad Arab scholar's spells against the accursed infidels, gave their names only as Khalid and Ibrahim. Well, to them he was just Hafez. Khalid was no more than a few years older than he; with gray frosting his beard, Ibrahim had to be nearing fifty, poor man.

"You made sure it was what you were sent for?" the older man asked as Hafez carefully extracted the *Necronomicon* from his backpack. It barely fit. And touching that binding made him want to perform a ritual purification every time he had to do it.

He nodded now. "In the name of the Compassionate, the Merciful, there can be no doubt," he said, fighting back a shudder. "God grant you both the strength to use it to our advantage."

"May it be so," Ibrahim replied.

"The American *kafirs* have their atom bombs and missiles," Khalid said exultantly, "but with this book they deliver the instrument of their destruction into our hands. Would you like to watch as we wreak havoc upon the misbelieving dogs and sons of dogs?"

Cry "Havoc!" and let slip the dogs of war, Hafez remembered from one English class or another. He thumped his head with the heel of his hand to get the worthless fluff out of it. "Nothing would please me more, my brother," he said.

Ibrahim carried the *Necronomicon* into the house. A flat lectern like the one at Miskatonic University waited for the codex. This lectern, though, was surrounded by a pentagram scribed inside a circle. Other circles, each one bearing its own particular mystic symbols, surrounded the small inner one.

Hafez's brow furrowed. "Is this not pagan sorcery?" he asked in a troubled voice.

"It is a sensible precaution," Ibrahim said as he set the book on the lectern. "When you fire an RPG, you try not to let the backblast from the motor scorch anyone, don't you? That's what we're doing here—trying to make sure we don't get scorched. By all means watch, but stay outside the circles if you value your hide."

"I will." Nothing could have persuaded Hafez to venture inside them.

"Let's get on with it." Khalid undid the belt that girdled the *Necronomicon* and opened it to a leaf he and Ibrahim must have chosen in advance.

Interlibrary Loan

Standing at a distance, Hafez could not see the way the text blurred and shifted. He'd watched it before, though, in the Special Collections strongroom. The two operators began reading—chanting—a spell in the most ancient and frightful Arabic. But those transmogrifying letters betrayed them, for at a key juncture one used the imperfect tense while the other chose the future.

They stared at each other in horror. "You donkey!" Khalid shouted at Ibrahim.

"You imbecile!" Ibrahim screamed at Khalid.

A hand that was not there—Hafez didn't know how he sensed it, but sense it he did, not that that helped—erased a centimeter of each chalked circle, from the outermost inward. When the last circle was opened, Ibrahim and Khalid both shrieked before slime and tentacles and darkness overwhelmed them.

Hafez remembered those shrieks as long as he lived. That was no more than another few seconds. Too late, he turned to flee. Darkness poured into his eyes and ears. Stinking slime drowned his shrieks, too.

WILBUR ARMITAGE was in the habit of watching BBC World News in his small, neat bachelor apartment in Arkham. The BBC covered foreign affairs better than the American news networks did. In Armitage's biased opinion, it would have had a hard time covering them worse than the American news networks did.

"Devastation is widespread in the northern Syrian city of ar-Raqqah, which for the past three years has been under the control of the so-called Caliphate," the suave newsreader said. "These satellite images show how the heart seems to have been ripped from the town. There are as yet no pictures from the ground. Intelligence experts and photographic interpreters have differing explanations for the cause of the catastrophe, but there can be no doubt as to its severity."

Sure enough, the center of ar-Raqqah just looked…gone. Armitage didn't need to be a photographic interpreter to see that. To his untrained eye, some buildings had been pulled down, while others were vanished so completely, they might have dissolved.

"Adding to the mystery is the fact that the United States, Saudi Arabia, Turkey, and Israel all deny striking ar-Raqqah," the newsreader continued. "Incoherent early reports from survivors, obviously not translated well, speak of great glowing eyes in the night and sucker disks. Perhaps some experiment with disabling psychedelic drugs went horribly wrong for the Caliphate, although ISIS portrays itself as victim rather than perpetrator." He paused. "We also have breaking news on the latest unrest in Greece."

Wilbur Armitage stood up and stretched. Strange how such strict and strident Muslims chose an English acronym straight from Egyptian mythology. Or perhaps not so strange after all, given the headlines coming out of ar-Raqqah. One never knew, did one?

He went to the kitchen, opened the refrigerator, took out a bottle of a nice California chablis, and poured himself a glass. He raised it in salute, though he wasn't sure what he was saluting. He was sure of one thing, though: he'd done right by the interlibrary-loan system. As he'd told his younger colleagues, the *Necronomicon* could take care of itself. He felt confident the manuscript would sooner or later find its way back to Miskatonic.

He sipped, savored, slowly nodded. That *was* a nice chablis.

Nine Drowned Churches

I've admired Al Stewart's music for half a century now, near enough. Alistair, the fictional viewpoint character here, is *not* Al Stewart, any more than the fictional band HPL in "The Fillmore Shoggoth" is the real band H. P. Lovecraft. But "Nine Drowned Churches" does spring from the real Al Stewart's "The Coldest Winter in Memory," and from the coincidence of names between the real town of Dunwich on the North Sea and the fictitious town of Dunwich the writer H. P. Lovecraft put in Massachusetts. Although, when you think about it, that probably isn't a coincidence at all—if anyone would have known about the English Dunwich and appropriated its name for his own purposes, Lovecraft was the man.

ALISTAIR ALWAYS FEELS funny about coming back to the UK. He was born in Scotland and raised in England, but he hasn't actually lived here for quite a while. Like a lot of British musicians who did well enough when being a British musician was the coolest thing in the world, he's put down roots elsewhere.

The Stones went to the south of France. He doesn't have their fame or their cash, even if you do still hear his songs on the radio now and again. He settled in the south of California instead. It suits him. He likes the weather. Any British expat will. It's not far from the wine country. He does have the money and the taste to be a bit of a wine snob.

And he likes the people. They're open and friendly. To them, his accent sounds exotic, intriguing, even classy. They all talk pretty much the same way, with sharp vowels and cookie-cutter consonants, every *h* and *r* in place.

You hear plenty of accents in Los Angeles. You hear English flavored by Spanish, Farsi, Korean, Hindi, Mandarin, Hebrew—anything under the sun. In Los Angeles, anybody white who speaks without one of those accents counts as an Anglo. Ginsberg? Szymanski? Papastegios? Anglos all, so long as they talk like Anglos.

Not like that here. Here you hear English flavored by history, accents far older than the BBC and the American public-school system (accents older, even, than the British public-school system, which is not at all the same thing). Here, people judge you, weigh you, every time you open your mouth. They know where you come from. They know how much money your people had. They know how much education you got. They know where your piece fits in the puzzle, and they insist on sticking you there.

One more reason to like Los Angeles! There, you can shape your piece as it suits you. Hell, you can make a whole new puzzle for yourself if it suits you. That doesn't work on this side of the pond. Here, you're stuck with your history as much as you're stuck with your accent.

Not that history is bunk. Alistair is no Henry Ford. He's written songs about both World Wars, about a French prophet and an Ottoman sultan and a Carthaginian explorer. He loves history. If you don't understand what we were, how can you understand what we are? But he doesn't care to be trapped in history like an ant in amber.

He drives inland from Southwold, where he's staying. He doesn't care for driving on the left any more, either, or for shifting with his left hand. He doesn't care for shifting at all, come to that. His American cars have all had automatic transmission. The hired auto feels like going back to a typewriter after years on a Mac. He can do it, but it's awkward as the devil.

To get from Southwold to Dunwich, you have to drive around three sides of a rectangle. It's less than five miles as the crow flies, but you can't go as the crow flies. Well, you can, but you'll need an ATV and you'll break several laws if you do. There is no seaside road, only a narrow beach, seaside cliffs, and a nature preserve in back of them. In back of them! Alistair laughs. There's an Americanism that never would have crossed his mind when he was growing up over here.

He turns left off the 12 for the 1125, which is half as wide. He turns left off the 1125 for a road too obscure to earn a number. The numberless road isn't much more than a long piss from one side to the other. Alistair doesn't think two cars will have an easy time getting past each other. He also doesn't think anybody's likely to be coming the other way while he's on the road. By the potholes and cracks in the faded asphalt, hardly anyone uses it or cares about it.

It's a warm summer's day. It will be in the seventies—in the twenties, they'd say here, but he's more used to Fahrenheit now—in Southwold. But, half a mile outside of Dunwich, the sunlight…changes. Not a cloud in the sky, but it does. It becomes at the same time duller and more metallic-seeming.

Alistair nods to himself. The odd effect may be his imagination, but he doesn't think so. He was looking for it: hoping for it, in fact. He's seen it once before, in north central Massachusetts, when he took the wrong fork (the right fork, actually) on the Aylesbury Pike just past Dean's Corners.

Many places in the States are named after older places in England. Boston, Plymouth, Portland (Portland, Maine, that is, for which, in turn, Portland, Oregon, is named)… Dunwich. The Puritans who named the haunted New England hamlet for the eldritch town on—and in—the North Sea—surely wrought better than they dreamt even in their wildest, most fearful nightmares.

More than eighty years ago now, horror came to Dunwich, Massachusetts. No one was left alive who'd beaten back the demoniac assault of eight-foot-tall Wilbur Whateley and his yet more monstrous half-brother, if that was what the thing truly was. But sons and daughters and grandsons and granddaughters of those who had beaten it back still survived in and around the New World Dunwich. The tales they told surely had not shrunk with the passage of time. Even though not told by eyewitnesses, they could still freeze the blood. They'd frozen Alistair's.

Yet the original Dunwich knew older and, if anything, worse horror. It got off to a fine start. As Dommocceaster and then as Dunwyk, it housed East Anglian kings. In the seventh century, St. Felix came thither from Burgundy to bring Christianity back to this part of England. In the *Domesday Book*, Robert Malet and the monastery of St. Æthelthryth are mentioned as holding land there. At one time, the town boasted nine churches.

Folklore says three holy silver crowns are buried along the coast of East Anglia to ward England against foreign invasion. One was at Dunwich. It might be the crown St. Felix set on the head of Sigebert son of Raedwald. Or, of course, it might not. But in Southwold even now they remind you that neither Napoleon nor the Nazis ever did come ashore.

These days, not one of those nine churches survives. The sea has taken them all…the sea and, old books whisper, things that came out of the sea under cover of storm and night. The cliffs in these parts have been crumbling for centuries. If you believe the old books, sometimes the crumbling has help.

Alistair doesn't know whether he believes the whispery old books or not. They also talk about the church bells tolling under the waves of the North Sea. By twenty-first-century logic, that's plainly impossible. He's put it in a song anyway. It may be impossible, but it makes a striking image. When you're writing a song, that counts for more.

Debussy wrote a piece about a cathedral engulfed by the sea. If the theme's good enough for a classical musician, it ought to be good enough for an aging rock-n-roller. But when Alistair thinks of Dunwich and its vanished churches, he also thinks of "La Valse." While Ravel was working on that one, some of the shuddery creatures from those old books must have crept out and whispered in his ear and ruffled the hair at the back of his neck with cold, bony fingers.

"La Valse" would make a terrific short film, or Alistair has always thought so. Plump, dignified musicians in white ties and tailcoats playing somewhere outdoors, like the Hollywood Bowl, at night. The full moon going in and out of clouds. Every time darkness falls, a few more musicians disappear, to be replaced by…other things. By the end, a whole demon orchestra—still in white ties and tails, naturally—saws away at its monstrous music.

Nine Drowned Churches

Alistair sighs. He knows it's one more thing he'll never get around to. A man's life has room for only so much. The rest is moonshine and might-have-beens.

A neat sign, enamel on aluminum (on aluminium, actually, in this part of the English-speaking world), warns of the town ahead: DUNWICH. In the States, plinkers would colander a sign like this in the middle of nowhere. Not here. Here, guns aren't as easy to buy as takeout (or even takeaway) Chinese.

Up a little rise. Down the other side. Yes, that's Dunwich ahead, what there is of it, shadowed under the somehow brassy sun. No great city this. A few houses, set well back from the cliffs. A church among them, a sort of replacement for its nine drowned predecessors. All Saints, the last of those, started falling in 1904 and was completely lost by 1919. A few headstones still stand in what was the All Saints churchyard. One of these days, storm—or something worse than storm—will sweep them into the sea, too.

MUSEUM, says a sign in front of one of the Victorian cottages. By what will do for a miracle in these sorry days, it's even open. The little old man at the front door seems astonished to see a visitor so early, but he's not too astonished to take Alistair's three quid. He walks through the place with him; a little slower than he might, Alistair realizes he lives there.

A Roman coin from the reign of Carausius. A silver crucifix clumsy enough to be from the time of St. Felix, as the yellowing typed label claims. Something odd about the arms... Alistair points to the dusty glass case. "What are those marks?" he asks.

"Well, no one quite knows," the old man replies, "but they may be octopus tentacles: to show how the saint came from the sea, the thinking goes. You'll see the motif on other exhibits."

And Alistair does. A small limestone gargoyle from the long-sunk cathedral has a round head, big staring eyes, a parrotlike beak, and more tentacles. Two brass weights from a miller's shop—their labels say one represents a quarter-pound, the other half a pound—are also octopus-shaped.

"Where were these found?" Alistair asks.

"On the strand by the sea," the old man answers. "Such scavenging's not allowed any more, but no one complains if we show what was uncovered aforetimes." He knows his onions, the old man, and seems glad to have someone so interested going through his little museum.

Alistair is likewise glad the place has such a knowledgeable curator. When he finishes the walk-through—it doesn't take long—he says, "Thank you for your kindness, Mister, ah…?"

"Bishop, sir. Silas Bishop, at your service." The old man knuckles his forehead, a gesture Alistair has thought long obsolete even on this side of the Atlantic.

Nor has he looked to find that name here, not when it is also well known in the other Dunwich. Now rather more than idly curious, he asks, "Are there Whateleys here, too?"

Silas Bishop stares at him in surprise. "How would you know that, sir? Benedict Whateley was Bishop of Dunwich, yes he was, when the great storms in the fourteenth century washed so much of the town into the ocean. And Sebastian Whateley—not a direct descendant of Benedict's, you understand, but in the family even so—runs the Cliff House now. If you're looking for a bite to eat here, you can't do better than the Cliff House."

Alistair has been to the Cliff House in San Francisco, eating lunch looking out over a different sea. Here he has some excellent prawns, along with Brussels sprouts and salad greens from local gardens and a chablis better than he would have expected to find in a village literally on the edge of nowhere. All quite reasonable, too.

His host is most kind and attentive. Sebastian Whateley has very pink skin, blond hair almost white, eyes of the palest blue, and a receding chin. He bears a family resemblance to the Whateleys of Dunwich, Massachusetts, in other words: one more thing Alistair has not looked for.

"Yes, you can go down to the beach if you like," Sebastian tells him when he inquires. "There's a stairway behind my establishment. Iron, not wood. Safe as can be, unless the whole cliffside decides to come down. Nothing anyone can do about that." The propitiatory gesture he makes is not the sign of the cross. Alistair has seen it before, though not often. It calls upon Powers other than He Who was crucified outside the walls of Jerusalem.

Down the stairway he goes. He wears running shoes; the soles do not ring on the wrought iron like swallowed churchbells. Whatever sounds he hears beyond the wind's whistle and the skrawk of seabirds, he hears only inside his mind.

On the narrow beach of mud and stones and sand are a few wooden fishermen's huts. Hand-painted signs shout FRESH FISH! A couple of small boats bob in the waves. A couple of others are pulled up on the strand.

A fisherman in a black Greek-style cap and a thick wool sweater nods as Alistair walks up to his shack. He touches the cap's brim in an almost-salute. "Good day to you, friend," he says. "How can I help you?"

Alistair wishes for a cap of his own. The wind off the North Sea plays with his hair, and he's getting thin on top. Well, no help for it now. "Can you take me out over the drowned churches?" he asks.

"For forty pounds, I can," the man answers at once. "I wish it were less, honest to God I do, but fuel keeps going up and up."

For a little while, half a lifetime ago, Alistair was rich. Sometimes these things slip through your hands—but not too badly, not if you're careful. He know plenty of people who were richer…and are poorer, now that fame has passed them by. He takes two twenty-pound notes from his wallet and hands them to the fisherman. They seem big to him; he's used to smaller American bills.

"Obliged," the man says, and makes the notes disappear. Chances are, Inland Revenue will never hear about them. He sticks out his hand. "I'm Ralph Hoadley, by the way."

Alistair shakes it and gives his own name. There was a Hoadley in the other Dunwich, too; perhaps he should give up being surprised at such correspondences.

This Hoadley shows no sign of recognizing his name in turn. Yes, fame has passed him by. The fisherman points toward the boat. "Come along, if that's what you fancy."

The engine chugs and belches acrid exhaust. The North Sea, greenish gray, looks cold. Well, the Pacific looks green-gray and cold off the Southern California coast, too. It looks that way because it damn well is. In Florida, the ocean is warm as a bath. Los Angeles weather is as warm as Florida's, or near enough. But the first time Alistair charged into the waves breaking on the beach at Santa Monica, he charged right back out again a split second later. He was all over gooseflesh, too.

Only a light chop here: nothing to make his stomach unhappy. He leans over the side of the boat all the same. He wants to see as much as he can. The water may be cold, but it is clearer than he expected. He can see down to the bottom, which is part sand, part mud. The fishing boat passes over a piece of carved stone, and then another. An octopus, its body bigger than his fist, scuttles for cover under the second one when the boat's shadow touches it.

"I have heard," Alistair says slowly, "that when the great storms came all those years ago and swept away so much of Dunwich, it wasn't wind and wave alone clawing at the land."

"People hear all kinds of things." Hoadley's voice shows next to nothing. He puffs on a Marlboro. A moment later, after blowing out a stream of smoke, he adds, "What else could it have been?"

"I've heard it might have been…tentacles." Not without trepidation, Alistair decides he needs to show some of his cards: "Is the name of great Cthulhu known in these parts?"

The fisherman studies him while he smokes the cigarette down to a tiny nub and tosses it into the sea. Under the brim of his cap, his wary eyes are the same color as the water. "It's known, yes," he says at last, "but seldom spoken."

"Good," Alistair says. On the other side of the Atlantic, they take that name too lightly. You can buy T-shirts with prancing octopoids in fishnet tights and the legend THE DUNWICH HORROR PICTURE SHOW.

Like so many American things, that's too clever and not clever enough at the same time. Cthulhu had nothing to do with the horror spawned in Dunwich, Massachusetts. No: that horror came from Yog-Sothoth, another of the Old Ones who walk *between* the spaces known to mortal man. But Cthulhu was his cousin, at least if Olaus Wormius' Latin translation of the *Necronomicon* of Abdul Alhazred was reliable. Alistair had to persuade several somber librarians at Miskatonic University that they should turn the iron key to the locked volume to let him examine the relevant passage with his own eyes.

Research at Miskatonic University—and, here in England, in the British Museum reading room, where they also had to unlock a couple of seldom-consulted antique tomes—has convinced Alistair that Cthulhu was most responsible for the downfall of this Dunwich. Whether Cthulhu worked in concert with Yog-Sothoth or for some strange purpose of his own, the singer cannot say even now. Nor is he sure whether, should a mere man find the answer to such a question, it would mean anything to him.

After a minute's thoughtful silence, Ralph Hoadley says, "There were divers here a few years ago, poking through the churches on the seabottom. I didn't take 'em out—Joe Biggles did." He points towards a shack on the beach that isn't his, and presumably is Joe Biggles'. "He says they knew that name, knew it and laughed at it."

"Ah?" Alistair says, and then, seeing something more is called for, "That would have been the crew from the National Trust, wouldn't it?"

"It would indeed." Hoadley tosses the second Marlboro, or what's left of it, into the water and waits.

"I heard one of them…didn't come up again," Alistair says.

"You heard right, I'm sorry to tell you." Hoadley nods. "Did you hear why she didn't come up?"

"I didn't know it was a woman," Alistair says, which is true and which lets him evade a straight answer.

Another nod. "She was. Pretty gal—a redhead, and I quite fancy 'em. But not so pretty after an octopus bigger'n the one we saw a little while ago yanked off her faceplate."

"I daresay not." Alistair has heard that. It gives him pause—but not enough pause, or he wouldn't be out here on the sea, would he? "I hope I know better than to laugh at such things."

"I hope you do, too," Ralph Hoadley says matter-of-factly. "If you don't, you have no need to come out here looking for trouble. Trouble will come looking for you—and it'll find you, no matter how far from the ocean you go."

Alistair's house in Los Angeles isn't far from the ocean at all. But he is sure the Dunwich man has the right of it. That kind of trouble would find him if he lived in the deserts of Turkmenistan, at the heart of the greatest land mass the planet boasts.

Hoadley swings the boat a little, then stops the engine and, grunting, drops the anchor over the side to hold them in place. "We're straight above the old cathedral now," he says, "or near enough as makes no difference. Look all you please."

At first, Alistair sees little of what he wants to see. A school of small, silvery fish obscures the view, as clouds might if he were looking up rather than down. Herrings? Sprats? He knows next to nothing of small, silvery fish and their varieties. Then, all at once, they vanish. So long, so long, so long. A deadly, dark gray shape, as long as he is tall, suddenly has this stretch of the North Sea to itself.

"Damn sharks," Hoadley mutters, at least half to himself. "I'd eat better if they ate worse."

North Sea ecology strikes Alistair as an argument for another day. Now that the shark has cleared away the little fish, he can see down to the bottom. A reddish starfish slowly crawls across the mud. Anemones grow on a piece of worked stone.

He doesn't know what he expects to see down there. No, actually he does know. The picture he carries in his mind is of a Gothic cathedral, perfect and undamaged except for upwards of six hundred years spent underwater. It isn't like that—nor, he realizes, should it be. There are bits here, pieces there, many of them obscured by mud and silt and sea life. He can tell these are ruins of manmade things. If he hadn't known ahead of time that this was a church, he does not think what he sees would be enough to tell him.

With the engine off, it's eerily quiet out here. Wavelets softly slap the sides of the boat. The breeze mutters under its breath. Other than that, nothing.

Alistair hears his own heart beating. If he listens hard enough, he wonders if he'll hear Hoadley's as well.

Then the silence breaks. Not from above: no airliner heading in to Heathrow from Oslo or Stockholm. Not from the boat itself: Hoadley's mobile phone doesn't go off, nor does Alistair's hired one. No, this sound comes from the depths: a great bronze bell, tolling once and again and yet again. Alistair glances down. The watch on his left wrist tell him it's 2:59. He would bet his soul on the watch's being a minute slow.

Beneath his tan, Ralph Hoadley goes chalky white. "By the God in heaven, I have heard of that happening," he says hoarsely. "Who hasn't? But never before this, never in all my days, have I heard the churchbells ring out myself."

Alistair doubts that the God in heaven has anything to do with the churchbells' chimes. Those other Powers he thought of before, yes, but not that One. Which of them is apt to be Eldest? Alistair has no idea. It is not a question for a singer, even for one with a taste for history. If any man could find an answer, it might have been Georg Cantor, with his mathematics of lesser and greater infinities. If.

Then Alistair stops caring about dead professors of mathematics. He cares about what is happening in the boat instead. Ralph Hoadley yawns, shrugs, curls himself up on some netting, and falls asleep in the sun like a cat. Alistair bends down to shake him by the shoulder. The fisherman makes a wordless noise. He stirs. He does not wake.

He will not wake, even when Alistair bawls in his ear. That's when Alistair realizes his is, can be, no natural sleep. It is as unnatural as…as bells sounding from beneath the sea.

Something in the simile makes Alistair stop trying to wake Hoadley and look into the water once more. The anchor keeps the boat from going far, but doesn't stop it from moving at all. Now he finds himself above a bigger, more nearly intact chunk of church than he has seen before. Out through a shadowed doorway, sinuous as a nest of serpents, slithers not just the largest octopus Alistair has ever seen but the largest one he has ever imagined.

As he stares down at it, so it stares up at him. He once read somewhere that an octopus' eyes and a man's are very much alike. Convergent evolution, the book called it. But could convergent evolution account for the glint of sardonic wisdom he sees, or thinks he sees, in the octopus' golden stare?

And he sees, or thinks he sees, something else as well. Why would any octopus, however sardonically wise, wear a crown of silver atop its bulbous head? Alistair only thinks he sees that, for the undersea creature pulls back into the black doorway before he can be sure.

No sooner has it vanished than Ralph Hoadley stretches and climbs to his feet. He does not seem to have the slightest idea that he's been asleep. "Well," he says briskly, "seen what you came to see?"

"Yes," Alistair answers in a small voice. "I believe I have."

"All right, then. I'll take you back." With animal smoothness and animal strength, the fisherman hauls in the anchor. The boat shakes when it thuds down onto the planking. Hoadley starts the motor. They head west, toward the narrow strand and the cliffs behind it. Alistair is very quiet all the way in.

ALISTAIR STAYS very quiet about what he saw out in the North Sea. From that day to this, he has never said a word about it. If the truth be known, he *cannot* say anything about it, even to the handful of folk at Miskatonic and other like-minded places who might take him seriously. He has, with great effort, slipped a hint or two into a song or two, but somehow no one has ever taken him up on them.

Yes. Somehow.

Then who knows enough to tell this story? Who knows enough and is *able* to tell this story? Well may you wonder. I will say that, when seen from the water, things of the air seem even stranger than they truly are, which is saying a great deal indeed. Past that, I say no more.

Eyewear

"Eyewear" first appeared in *Golden Reflections* (edited by Joan Spicci Saberhagen and Robert Vardeman), a memorial anthology for Fred Saberhagen that includes his terrific novel, *The Mask of the Sun*, and stories based upon it. The eyewear in question, once you get your hands on it, lets you see what you should do in any situation…unless it goes missing just when you're likely to need it most. When I sent my story to the editors, they asked for some rewrites. I did them, and, as editors' suggestions have a way of doing, they improved the piece. When the hardcover came out, though, it came out with the unrevised version. These things happen in publishing now and again; I know somebody else this one happened to. But the story you see here is the rewritten version, which appeared in the paperback and is the one I prefer.

THE SUN WAS going down ahead of them. They were…somewhere. Estevánico had no idea where. Neither did his master, Andrés Dorantes. Alonso del Castillo of Salamanca also didn't know. And neither did Álvar Núñez Cabeza de Vaca, who led the four wanderers if anyone did.

Three Spaniards and a Moor, lost in some of the widest country God ever made. Three white men and a dark brown one, seeing things no one of their color had ever seen before. Estevánico didn't *suppose* he would rather have been sent underground to grub out ore with a pick—but it was a mighty near-run thing.

Harry Turtledove

Cabeza de Vaca pointed toward the setting sun. He was thin as a nail—all four of the wanderers were famished all the time. The sun had burned him almost as dark as the natives: he wasn't much lighter than Estevánico, in fact. Neither was del Castillo or Dorantes, come to that. None of the men wore more than ragged scraps of cloth barely covering their privates.

All the same, grim purpose filled Cabeza de Vaca's voice when he said, "The land of the Christians lies in that direction!"

He said the same thing every day at sunset. Estevánico was sick of hearing it—not that Cabeza de Vaca or either of the other two Spaniards cared a copper what he thought. For that matter, Estevánico was a Christian only because the Portuguese raider who'd captured him said he would kill him on the spot if he didn't convert. In his heart, he remained more than half a Muslim. But he'd got used to the outward forms of Christianity by now. Even he didn't often dwell any more on what lay in his heart.

Cabeza de Vaca pointed again, this time toward some flat ground by the edge of a creek. "We'll camp there," he said. "Alonso, you have the firesafe?"

"I've got it," del Castillo answered, and held it up: a hollowed-out branch, the opening almost entirely plugged, with tinder smoldering inside. It was one of their most precious possessions, not that they had many to compete with it.

They gathered fuel. They had to gather a lot; dry brush burned hot but fast, and this wasn't a country for trees. Estevánico caught a couple of fat lizards. Cabeza de Vaca knocked over a rabbit with a rock and then bashed in its head. Split four ways, that wouldn't be much, but it was something.

By now, Estevánico liked lizard meat. Hunger made a better sauce than pepper. A million stars blazed down after twilight faded. No city smokes hid them. No cities here, not for Allah—no, God—knew how many leagues.

Del Castillo woke Estevánico to take the midwatch. He was the slave, so of course he was the one who got his sleep broken up. That didn't especially bother him. Had the party consisted of three Moors and one enslaved Spaniard, the white man would have got stuck with the watch in the middle of the night. How else would things work?

Eyewear

Yawning, del Castillo curled up by the fire. He soon started snoring. Estevánico walked away from the flames to get his night vision back. He could have run off—but what good would that do him? Then he'd be lost and alone instead of lost and in company. Company was better.

Off in the distance, a little wolf began to yip and yowl, and then another and another, till they sounded like a chorus of devils. No matter how they sounded, they were wary of men. They looked like large, sharp-nosed dogs. The Spaniards said they were smaller and yellower than proper wolves. Estevánico had never seen a proper wolf, but he was willing to take their word for it.

He carried an armlong club with a flaked stone bound to the end by rawhide thongs. No one in these parts would have anything better. He didn't want to fight, but too often life wasn't about what you wanted to do.

Little by little, the hellish chorus died away, only to start up again a few minutes later. Estevánico yawned. "Can't do that," he muttered to himself in the Berber-flavored Arabic that was his birthspeech. The Spaniards wouldn't love him for falling asleep on sentry-go. He wouldn't love one of them who nodded off, either.

They'd kept on good terms with the natives most of the time in their journey through his unknown land. Still and all, it didn't do to take chances. Estevánico didn't *think* the red-brown men would try to sneak up and do unto them as Cabeza de Vaca had done unto the rabbit. He didn't want to find out he was wrong the hard way, though.

He looped around the fire to watch upstream for a while. Then he looped again to go downstream. While he was downstream, he pissed in the creek. He always eased himself downstream from a camp. The Spaniards didn't care one way or the other. Estevánico found that disgusting, but it wasn't as if you could tell your master anything.

He turned to start yet another loop, but he'd taken only a couple of steps when the side of his right foot brushed something lying on the dirt. He almost thought it was a branch and kept walking. But it didn't feel quite like a branch. At any rate, Estevánico didn't think so. And, since this was the most interesting thing that had happened to him since del Castillo shook him awake, he squatted to find out if he was right.

As soon as his hands closed on it, he knew it was manmade. And its feel made him grunt in low-voiced surprise. The natives in this Western land were splendid basket weavers. Many of their tribes had skilled potters. But they knew much less of metal than either the Spaniards or his own folk.

He hefted this…thing. It wasn't heavy enough to be gold—nowhere near. There wasn't much of that up here north of New Spain and New Galicia. There wasn't much of *anything* up here, come to that: only endless leagues of ground thinly settled by hunters and gatherers and a few farmers.

Pámfilo de Narváez had thought there would be more. Well, Pámfilo de Narváez, Satan curse him, had thought all kinds of things that turned out not to be so. His expedition from Cuba was nothing but a disaster. The only four left alive from it on the mainland were Cabeza de Vaca, Dorantes, del Castillo, and Estevánico himself. How long they would stay alive lay mostly in God's hands.

Estevánico himself held up what lay in his own hands. By starlight and firelight he made out what looked like a pair of ungainly spectacles. He frowned. Some middle-aged Spaniards wore eyeglasses so they could go on reading after their sight lengthened. Estevánico, who did not have his letters, thought them a silly affectation. He was as sure as need be, though, that no natives wore them or knew how to make them.

Which meant…what, exactly? That some other Spaniards had stumbled through this wilderness? That other foreigners were loose in these parts? Estevánico couldn't see what else it would mean. Officials in Cuba and New Spain wouldn't be thrilled at the news, which was putting it mildly. Estevánico couldn't do anything about that, either.

He'd never held eyeglasses in his hand before. Awkwardly, he set them on his nose. What *did* they do for the people who wore them? For a few heartbeats, he didn't think these did anything at all. The lenses were even darker than the night. Then, gradually, by flecks and sparkles, they cleared, and he saw as well as he had before.

Eyewear

As well? Better. Starlight suddenly seemed bright as the full moon. He could *see* some of the little yellow wolves that howled at the sky. A wildcat slunk along, paying the wolves no mind. Up near the zenith, an owl glided by all ghostly.

He'd never heard spectacle-wearing Spaniards talk about anything like this. He wondered why not, if this was what eyeglasses did. This wasn't just an aid to sight. This seemed more like magic.

That thought rose again in his mind as his time to go off watch neared. The eyeglasses showed him someone who looked like him walking back to the fireside. He followed the moving figure. It took off the spectacles before kneeling beside Cabeza de Vaca and shaking him awake. He wouldn't have thought he could hide them under his rags, but the moving figure did, and he imitated it again.

"*Madre de Dios*," Cabeza de Vaca said softly as consciousness came back to him. "Is it that hour already?"

"*Sí, Señor*," Estevánico whispered back. They tried to keep from waking the other Spaniards. It was probably wasted care; even on bare ground, all four wanderers slept like the dead every night.

Their leader eyed the stars. Any man with eyes in his head could gauge the hour by their slow whirling. Cabeza de Vaca sighed. "Well, so it is," he said. "Get your sleep while you can. The sun will come all too soon to suit you." He sighed once more, got to his feet, and ambled off in the direction from which Estevánico had come.

Estevánico curled up on his side near the fire like a cat stretching out by the hearth. Next thing he knew, he knew nothing at all.

He looped a bit of string around one earpiece of the strange spectacles and managed to keep them hidden under his loincloth all the next day. It was what the spectacles themselves seemed to want. And they seemed to want to stay in place, too. They didn't inconveniently fall out as he tramped along, for instance. Maybe ascribing volition to them was foolishness. Then again, maybe it wasn't.

Buffalo moved across the plain. They drew off when they caught the wanderers' scent. Some of the natives constantly hunted them, so they were leery of men. Farming was a bad gamble in these parts: rain came sparse and erratic, and even rivers ran dry. Thunderheads piled up high in the sky, flat on top like God's anvils. If you were under one when it chanced to let loose, the storm would pound you flat. If not—which was more likely—you stayed parched. Puddles dried fast under the savage sun; mud soon baked hard as cement.

Estevánico could hardly wait for night to come again so he could see what other marvels the spectacles might show him. He didn't even grumble when Andrés Dorantes shook his awake. His master gave him an odd look and asked, "Are you all right?"

"*Sí, Señor,*" Estevánico replied, so mildly that Dorantes' curiosity found nowhere to light. Muttering, the Spaniard lay down and went to sleep.

Estevánico walked out beyond the red glow the fire threw. He hoped he hadn't hurt the strange spectacles by rolling over on them while he slept. The ones the Spaniards used seemed pretty flimsy; the lenses broke easily, while the wire frames were always getting twisted and bent. But these were unchanged, unharmed, when he fished them out of his loincloth.

He put them on. As he had the night before, he saw more with them than he possibly could have without them. Even the stars seemed a little bigger and brighter and closer than they did to the naked eye.

Rather to his relief, he didn't see himself, or imagine he saw himself, doing anything before he actually did it. That was alarming. The natives here ate mushrooms and drinks made from mushrooms that gave them visions, but he didn't think what he'd seen was one of those. It was too precise, too closely connected to the real world.

"Hello there." The words, delivered in matter-of-fact tones, came from just behind Estevánico's left shoulder.

He jumped and whirled in the air like a startled cat. Whatever the eyeglasses had shown him, they hadn't shown anybody sneaking up on him.

And… As his feet hit the ground again, he realized that impossible greeting had, impossibly, come in his own language. Maybe a few other slaves on this side of the ocean spoke it, but surely no one within a hundred leagues of him.

No one, that is, except the fellow standing there smiling. Though at least as swarthy as the sun-burnt Spaniards, he was plainly a white himself: no other race produced men with such a formidable nose. And his white hair was wavier and finer than the natives'.

"Who the devil are you? How did you get there without me seeing you?" Estevánico demanded, clutching his club. Since he was talking to a white man, he asked the question in Spanish. But he was ready to knock the bastard's brains out if he didn't like the answer he got.

"Well, you can call me…" the white-haired man said. Estevánico scowled. He seemed to hear the name deep inside his head, not with his ears at all. And he seemed to hear it twice, as *Esperanza* and *Amal*. He knew you could see double if you got a knock in the head. Could you hear double, too? More to the point, could you hear double if you *hadn't* got a knock in the head?

He needed another couple of heartbeats to realize both names meant *Hope*, the one in Spanish, the other in Arabic. That could mean anything—or nothing. Estevánico gripped the club tighter yet, ready—eager—to swing it in a deadly arc. "You still didn't say how you snuck up on me like that," he growled.

"It's…complicated." Esperanza/Amal looked and sounded faintly embarrassed. "I can't really explain it to you. If I do it just right, maybe I can show you without getting caught in a temporal loop."

Estevánico also heard that phrase in both Spanish and Arabic. The only problem was, it made no sense in either language. "Talk sense, God curse you," he said.

"I told you—I can't talk so that it'll make sense to you. But try this. Now you see me… Now you—" His mouth open for the next word, Esperanza/Amal vanished like a blown-out candle flame. Not even the miraculous spectacles gave the faintest clue of where he'd gone or how he'd gone there.

Andrés Dorantes would have been disappointed that Estevánico didn't cross himself as a good Christian should have. Instead, the Moor made a two-fingered sign against witchcraft that came straight from his native village.

"Now you see me again," Esperanza/Amal said, once more from behind Estevánico. The Moor spun again, not quite in such horrified astonishment as he had the first time. The big-nosed, white-haired man had an engagingly homely grin.

"How did you do that? What kind of *brujo* are you?" Estevánico still didn't make the sign of the cross, now mostly likely because he feared it would do him no good.

Esperanza/Amal sighed. "I'm no he-witch, only a man who knows how to do things you don't, the same way Spaniards know how to do some things the natives here don't. If you're really curious, I traveled into the future, took a few steps, and came back almost to the moment I'd left. If I'd tried to come back to exactly that moment, I would have created a paradox. If I was lucky, both of me would have disappeared. If I wasn't so lucky… Count your blessings, friend, that you don't know *how* complicated life can get."

His words sounded like a madman's. Estevánico would have been happier had he believed Esperanza/Amal was one. Unfortunately, the mysterious stranger had the air of an artisan who knew his own craft as well as anyone could, even if he struggled to explain it to an ignorant outsider.

And he eyed Estevánico the way a smith, say, might eye an iron bar that wasn't red-hot any more but that would still burn the hide right off your palm if you were fool enough to try to pick it up. "Speaking of paradoxes and complications, I don't suppose I ought to be surprised you found your charming eyewear. Considering what the four of you pull off…" He shook his head, annoyed at himself. "I can't say too much, or I generate a different kind of paradox and I really do disappear—disappear so I can't come back for a while, I mean. But then, speaking of paradoxes, unless you found the toy on your nose there, I don't think you could manage what you do at all."

Eyewear

"Wait." Much too much was happening much too fast for Estevánico. "By some kind of magic you…went into the future?" Esperanza/Amal nodded. "How far into the future?" Estevánico asked.

"I can't tell you," the white-haired man replied.

Estevánico nodded. That made sense—a lunatic's kind of sense, perhaps, but sense even so. "However far it was, somebody whenever it is still remembers what the Spaniards and I did, uh, do, uh, will do here." He struggled with verb tenses, but he knew what he wanted to say.

Esperanza/Amal paid him the courtesy of not pretending not to understand. "You said that. I didn't. I couldn't. If I tried—*pffft!*" He made a noise like a man spitting a slippery melon seed out between his teeth. Estevánico imagined him squirting out of this time like a spat seed.

"Tell me one thing, since you seem to know about it. Tell me what I can do with this." The Moor touched the spectacles' frame.

"Every now and then, it will…suggest things. Maybe you've seen that." Esperanza/Amal waited till Estevánico nodded, then went on, "If you're smart—and it sure looks like you are—you'll follow the suggestions. There aren't many sets of, uh, eyewear like that. For all I know, maybe there's only the one, except in different phases. Or maybe—"

All of a sudden, he wasn't there any more. Estevánico hoped he was playing another trick, but he didn't pop back out of nowhere this time. If he'd been on the point of saying too much (on the point of saying something useful to Estevánico, in other words), something or Someone took him away before he could.

Too bad, the Moor thought. The next thing he wanted to find out was how to tell his Spanish companions he had the—what did Esperanza/Amal call it?—the eyewear, that was it.

Since he couldn't ask the man with the white hair and the big nose, he asked the eyewear itself. An image formed, one of him holding the curious spectacles and saying… Saying what? Saying something. Whatever it was, the eyewear wouldn't or couldn't let him hear. It worked with and through sight, not sound. *Too bad*, Estevánico thought once more.

He hid the eyewear again before waking Alonso del Castillo to take the last watch. But that couldn't go on much longer, and he knew it. After a meager breakfast of muddy water and some leaves the natives chewed, the wanderers set off again. With the morning sun at their backs, their shadows stretched long before them, then slowly shrank.

They followed game tracks and the natives' trails whenever they could. As long as those headed west, they offered an easier way forward than untrodden ground. But when they forked, the men who'd already come so far often hesitated, arguing over which path to take.

They hadn't been walking for more than half an hour when the trail forked for the first time today. Cabeza de Vaca pointed to the more southerly track at the same time as del Castillo jerked his thumb at the northern one. The two filthy, skinny, nearly naked Spaniards glowered at each other. Cabeza de Vaca might be their leader, but he wasn't their king. Estevánico saw another quarrel brewing.

To try to head it off, he brought out the eyewear and put it on. Cabeza de Vaca, del Castillo, and Dorantes all stared at him. He chuckled at their expressions, but not for long. The eyewear showed him four scrawny wanderers heading down the southern track: the one Cabeza de Vaca favored. "I think we should go that way, too," Estevánico said.

"*I* think you want to pucker up on Álvar's backside," Alonso del Castillo said pointedly.

"What is that thing, Estevánico?" Dorantes asked. "Where did you find it?"

"Near our fire, night before last," the Moor answered—why not tell the truth here? "It's…kind of a compass, you might say. If you look through it, it shows you which way you should go." He held out the eyewear, as it had shown him doing.

His master crossed himself. Nothing weak about Andrés Dorantes' Christianity. Indeed, Dorantes often prayed over sick natives, trying to persuade God to drive out their infirmities. He'd succeeded so often, the other

Spaniards and even Estevánico tried their hands at it these days. They might not own a faith quite so firm as his, but they'd all had good fortune more than once.

Cabeza de Vaca held out his hand. "Let me see that thing, Estevánico, if you'd be so kind." He phrased things as politely as one *hidalgo* would when asking a favor of another, which made what he said no less an order.

Naturally, Estevánico was reluctant. He put the eyewear back on for a moment. Through its odd lenses, he saw himself handing it to the Spaniard. Esperanza/Amal had told him to do as the thing suggested. By the way the white-haired man spoke, he knew what he was talking about, too. Estevánico thought he would have worked the same thing out on his own in short order. The visions that came through the lenses compelled belief.

And so, suppressing his momentary pang, the Moor handed Cabeza de Vaca the eyewear. "Ask it which way we should go, and you'll see," he said.

"Never thought we'd find eyeglasses here," Cabeza de Vaca remarked as he settled them on the bridge of his own sharp nose. His mouth turned down at the corners. "I don't see anything… Wait. Now I do. By God, you're right. It shows us walking down my path, clear as if we were already doing it."

"Let *me* see, if you please." Alonso del Castillo was courteous, too, but spoke a challenge nonetheless. Cabeza de Vaca frowned again; he didn't want to give up the eyewear, either. But he did. Del Castillo signed himself, which had to mean the vision was also forming for him. He gave a reluctant nod. "Well, you're right. I do see us going that way. Of course, this thing may be a snare of Satan's, made to lure us to ruin."

That also worried Estevánico. But Álvar Núñez Cabeza de Vaca threw back his head and laughed. "If the Devil wants us so badly, *amigo*, he doesn't have to get fancy to take us. He just has to stretch out his hand."

Dorantes nodded. "That seems sensible to me. May I look through the spectacles, too, please, since everyone else already has?"

Del Castillo seemed no happier to give them up than Cabeza de Vaca or Estevánico had. But, as they had, he did. Estevánico's master peered through the eyewear.

"I also see us going down the southern track," Dorantes said. Then he took off the eyewear and handed it back to Estevánico, which amazed the Moor. His master proceeded to unamaze him, continuing, "If the Devil *is* in the spectacles, better the Moor should wear them than one of us, eh? And if not, he can use them to guide us well enough. We have to stick together till we find a land where Christians live."

That last had already occurred to Estevánico. If Cabeza de Vaca and del Castillo hadn't thought of it, they needed only a moment to see it was sensible. "*Bueno*," Cabeza de Vaca said. "Estevánico, you are now our compass."

"As your service, *Señor*," the Moor replied. They all laughed. Alonso del Castillo didn't even grumble when they started down the path he hadn't wanted. The Devil couldn't have arranged that—Estevánico was sure of it. No, it had to be a miracle, come straight from God's hand.

EVEN WITH the eyewear, they didn't go far and they didn't go fast. For one thing, they were too famished to march as quickly or as long as men with full bellies might have. For another, they kept falling in with native tribes. Word that they could heal had gone ahead of them. Whenever they met a group of the coppery-skinned folk who dwelt in these parts, the natives hopefully brought out their sick. The wanderers had to do what they could to cure them.

Just finding out what ailed the natives wasn't always easy. Estevánico had had to learn a new language when the Christians captured and enslaved him. His master, an educated man, spoke several of the tongues common among them. But all the Spaniards groused that each little native band had its own language. As far as Estevánico could see, they were right. They—and he—picked up a handful of words and phrases from each one, and tried to bring them out without mangling them too badly.

Again, the Moor wished the eyewear helped with words and sounds. It didn't—which didn't mean it was useless in the healing game. The natives thought it was an impressive piece of sorcerous apparatus (at least as often as not, so did Estevánico and the Spaniards). Despite failing as a translator, it sometimes led Estevánico to herbs or roots—once to a leaf with mold growing on it—that helped his patients and those of his comrades.

He and the Spaniards got paid three ways. First and most important, the locals refrained from killing them, which they could have done with ease. Second, they fed them as well as they could. The Spaniards—especially Cabeza de Vaca—and Estevánico were all more easily satisfied than they had been before setting out with Pámfilo de Narváez. But they got more to eat from the natives than they did while traveling by themselves.

And the locals rewarded them with women. The Spaniards thought that was sinful, which didn't keep them from sleeping with the women but did make them feel guilty afterwards. Estevánico said he felt guilty, too: a Christian was supposed to, after lying down with a woman not his wife. He was still Muslim enough not to feel *very* guilty.

One tribe made eunuchs, whether from its own folk or from captives Estevánico never learned. Some of the whole men of that tribe lived with them instead of with women. They offered them to the wanderers, too. Estevánico refused with the same horror the Spaniards showed. Laying a woman was good sport. Laying a man, even one without his *cojones*, was a filthy abomination.

Dorantes and the other two white men preached the Christian Gospel to the natives as well as they could. That probably wasn't very well. They didn't speak any of the local languages fluently enough for proper preaching. They thought God would approve of the effort any which way. Since neither God nor the eyewear told Estevánico they were wrong, he sensibly kept his mouth shut about that.

He did wonder if Esperanza/Amal would make another appearance. For several months, there was no sign of the white-haired man. Estevánico wanted to believe that the stranger who could walk through time was only a figment of his imagination. None of the Spaniards had seen him, after all (and the Moor hadn't mentioned him to them, either). Try as he would, though, Estevánico couldn't persuade himself of that.

A good thing, too. One night when the wanderers were by themselves, with no guides from one tribe leading them toward the next, the Moor was, as usual, given a watch in the middle of the night that broke up his sleep. He yawned and rubbed his eyes as Cabeza de Vaca lay down and promptly went back to sleep. When he was sure he was awake himself, he put on the eyewear. However much the Spaniards admired what the mysterious spectacles did, they stayed content to let him wear them.

By now, the Moor almost took the eyewear for granted. Almost. Ordinary arquebuses seemed like miracles to the natives. They'd never seen horses till the Spaniards brought them across the sea. (How Estevánico wished he and his comrades in misfortune had some! They would have traveled much faster and more easily.) When he donned the eyewear, he felt as much in the presence of the awesome and the unknown as the natives did when a gun went off or a horse neighed.

"*Salaam aleikem.*" As before, the words came from behind Estevánico's left shoulder. *Peace be unto you.*

"*Aleikem salaam,*" he answered automatically. *And to you also peace.* This time, recognizing the dry, intelligent voice, he didn't jump into the air. Instead, he turned slowly and carefully, continuing, "I hoped to see you again one day."

Esperanza/Amal smiled at that. "Well, I hoped to see you again one day, too. It took longer than I thought it would, I'm afraid."

"How can anything take long for you?" Estevánico asked. "Don't you just step up into the times to come and then back to where you need to be?"

"It's not that simple. I wish it were." The white-haired man rubbed his formidable nose, a gesture that somehow showed Estevánico how very unsimple it was. Esperanza/Amal went on, "Besides, I've used up big chunks of duration down in Peru, and I can't appear twice in them. I told you before—complications!" He rolled his eyes.

"Down in where? Piro?" Estevánico scratched at a fleabite. He knew he'd mispronounced the name. "Where's that?"

"South of here. South of New Spain, way south. The people there are even richer than the Aztecs were," Esperanza/Amal replied. His mouth twisted in a sour smile. "So of course they draw *conquistadores* the way dead meat draws flies."

Estevánico laughed—softly, so as not to wake the sleeping Spaniards. How Pámfilo de Narváez and the would-be conquerors who'd gone with him would grind their teeth when they found out about that place! If any of them were left alive, they would, anyhow. They'd gone in the wrong direction. The natives up here had nothing worth stealing.

"Do these other natives fight any better than the Aztecs did?" Estevánico inquired. The red-brown men up here couldn't hope to resist Spaniards. Then again, so long as they had nothing worth taking, they didn't need to worry about it.

"They might, if disease weren't hurting them and if they were sure the Spaniards weren't gods," Esperanza/Amal said. Estevánico nodded. Things had gone that way in New Spain, too.

He said, "Thanks for checking up on me, anyway, even if it took you a while."

"*De nada*," the white-haired man answered. "People have always wondered how you and your, ah, friends made it all the way from where you got shipwrecked to where you end up. It's less surprising now that I know you found the eyewear, but even so…"

"Where do we end up? What kind of people wonder? Less surprising than what?" Every time Esperanza/Amal opened his mouth, he made a million questions form in Estevánico's mind. The Moor also wanted to tell him Dorantes, del Castillo, and Cabeza de Vaca were no friends of his, but the little catch in Esperanza/Amal's voice said he already understood that.

He wagged a finger at Estevánico now. "I can't tell you any of that stuff, not without making paradoxes." He paused, considering. "*Maybe* I can tell you—"

He vanished. A puff of breeze stroked Estevánico's face as air rushed in to fill the space where the other man had been. Estevánico waited for Esperanza/Amal to come back, but he didn't, not that night. For all Estevánico knew, he was off drinking wine and shooting dice with his friends. Or he might really have got trapped in one of those paradoxes…whatever they were. Estevánico knew he didn't fully understand them. He wondered whether Esperanza/Amal did.

THE NEXT day, as the wanderers neared the mountains they'd seen in the west for some time, a native gave them a hollow copper rattle with a face on the side. As best they could, they asked where the fellow had got it. He pointed north and a little west. Words tumbled out of him. The Spaniards and Estevánico could follow maybe one of them in ten.

Thoughtfully, Cabeza de Vaca said, "It *sounds* like he says there are cities in that direction. Lots of people living together, anyhow."

"We've also seen maize meal the past few days," Andrés Dorantes said. "The natives say they get that from the north and west, too."

"Where there's copper, chances are there's silver. Where there's silver, chances are there's gold." Alonso del Castillo might be a perambulating bag of bones in a filthy breechclout, but the *conquistador* inside him lived yet.

Cabeza de Vaca looked down at his own scrawny arm and laughed harshly. "Maybe there is, Alonso, but I don't think we're going to bring it back with us. Four miserable starvelings against a city? Even in these parts, that's long odds."

Del Castillo didn't argue, a telling proof of how weak he was.

A couple of days later, Cabeza de Vaca cut an arrowhead out of a wounded native's chest with a flint knife and used a deer-bone needle to suture the wound he'd made. He took the stitches out the next day, and the wounded warrior did fine. That impressed the man's tribe, which ate mostly prickly-pear fruit and pine nuts. They fed the wanderers as well as they could.

That evening, Estevánico decided to experiment with the eyewear. As his comrades lay snoring not far away, he put on the mysterious spectacles and thought, *I want to go to the place where that copper rattle came from.*

Eyewear

He didn't have to wait long before the eyewear showed him what to do—or, at least, what to start doing. If he walked away from the Spaniards, skirted a couple of sleeping natives (he hadn't even known they were there, but the eyewear did, all right), and headed up a trail that led north, he'd be on his way.

How could the spectacles tell him something like that? How did *they* know? He hadn't the faintest idea. Some sort of fancy witchcraft still seemed more likely to him than anything else.

But, in the end, *how* didn't matter. What mattered was that the eyewear *did* know, and could show him. He'd seen as much often enough to need no further proof. A man who paid attention to the eyewear and acted on what he saw through it couldn't go far wrong; Esperanza/Amal had known what he was talking about there.

Here in this impoverished wilderness, the eyewear kept the wanderers on the right track toward finding a civilized settlement. If someone else in more settled country used a pair of these eyeglasses with the aim of getting rich, Estevánico didn't see how he could go far wrong, either. Idly, the Moor wondered whether the *conquistador* leading the Spanish charge into that rich new southern country did have some eyewear of his own.

Estevánico shrugged. He couldn't do anything about that one way or the other. He could, and did, mutter under his breath about luck and breaks. He'd found his magical eyeglasses in a land full of nothing. If some other fellow had eyewear in a country full of gold...

Richer than New Spain, Esperanza/Amal had said. Estevánico hadn't dreamt a land could be richer than New Spain. But the white-haired man with the big nose plainly knew what he was talking about. For that matter, Esperanza/Amal plainly knew more than he *could* talk about.

"Not fair," Estevánico mumbled. He looked toward the north again, toward the place—the city?—from which the copper rattle had come. If the natives there could work copper, they could also work silver and gold. Alonso del Castillo was dead right about that. *And if some of that silver and gold ended up in* my *hands...* Estevánico thought. Making his mind work like a *conquistador*'s was the easiest thing in the world.

He must have gone on mumbling, because the first thing Esperanza/Amal said was, "Thinking like a *conquistador* may be easy, but it's dangerous, too."

By now, Estevánico wasn't even surprised when the white-haired man popped out of nowhere. "Tell it to Cortés," the Moor retorted.

Esperanza/Amal pointed to the eyewear. "Cortés had the same help you do, and he almost died half a dozen times even so. Maybe more." He held up a forefinger, correcting himself. "Almost the same help, I mean. His set was mounted in a solid-gold mask."

"It would be." Estevánico couldn't even find bitterness. "So did he trip over it in the dark, too? That wouldn't be so easy, not with a golden mask."

"Moctezuma handed it to him," Esperanza/Amal said solemnly.

"Go on! Now tell me one I'll believe!" Up till now, Estevánico had thought the white-haired man a truthteller. But that had to be a lie…didn't it?

"He did. By God, he did," Esperanza/Amal said. Estevánico heard the oath in both Spanish and Arabic. "And, if you're thinking of going north to look for gold, you would do well to watch out for more Aztecs." He let out a glad sigh, as if relieved to have said that without getting caught in a paradox and vanishing halfway through his sentence.

"Now I know you're *loco*," Estevánico declared. "The Aztecs live south of here, not north. And Cortés conquered them years ago. I'm not sure of much, but I'm sure of that. Their empire's dead and gone."

The white-haired man sent him a sweet, sad smile. "As a wise man said—er, will say—many years from now, the past isn't dead. Sometimes it isn't even past. And he didn't know the first thing about journeying through time." Esperanza/Amal looked startled. "Or I don't think he did. But when I tell you to look out for Aztecs if you go north, I'm—" He just had time to look startled again, in a different way, before he disappeared.

"You're what?" Estevánico said scornfully. He answered his own question: "You're talking through your farthole, that's what." Esperanza/Amal didn't come back to contradict him, either.

Eyewear

The four wanderers trudged on…and on…and on. Estevánico began to think they'd keep marching forever without returning to civilization. But they couldn't march all the time. Rain swelled a river and forced them to lie up in a native village for some time. One of the men there wore an amulet of a horseshoe nail and the buckle to a sword belt stitched onto a piece of tanned hide. Alonso del Castillo almost jumped out of his own tanned hide when he saw it. He brought—dragged—the native back to his comrades. The fellow said Spaniards on horseback had come up to the river and killed two natives with lances.

"We're getting there!" Cabeza de Vaca exclaimed. "By the holy Virgin Mother of God, we really are!"

After more long, hungry marches, the leader and Estevánico, who had got ahead of the other two Spaniards, finally met more mounted white men. The eyewear helped guide them on, but Estevánico hid it as soon as he spotted strangers. The soldiers they met didn't know what to make of a couple of shambling, nearly naked skeletons. They hesitated even after Cabeza de Vaca hailed them in Spanish.

At last, though, they took him and Estevánico back to their captain, Diego de Alcaraz. The officer sent three horsemen and fifty natives off with Estevánico to get to Dorantes and del Castillo. No one offered to let the Moor ride. He had to retrace ten or twelve leagues on foot. Any thought of showing off the eyewear to the Spaniards flickered and blew out. If they wouldn't do anything for him, he was damned if he'd do anything for them.

And so he looked through the eyewear only in secret, when he went off behind a bush to ease himself or at night. The strange spectacles did help bring him to the men he sought. Neither his master nor del Castillo mentioned the eyewear once he, the new Spaniards, and the natives found them. Both men probably thought they could use the thing to their own advantage—and in law, of course, anything that was Estevánico's belonged to his master.

They came into Culiacán, by the oceanside, in April 1536. They'd needed four years to pass from the Gulf of Mexico to this arm of the Pacific. When

Cabeza de Vaca said it was a miracle none of them had died along the way, Estevánico couldn't very well tell him he was wrong.

Three months later, they rode into Mexico City. Everyone there celebrated them for surviving their dreadful journey. Even Estevánico, dark-skinned slave of uncertain Christianity that he was, came in for his share of praise and his share of the fiery spirit the Spaniards had started brewing from the local plant called *agave*. Islam forbade drinking and drunkenness. Christianity didn't. As far as Estevánico was concerned, that was a fine reason to profess Christianity: that and the fact that the Spaniards would kill him an inch at a time if he slid back into his old faith.

He had clothes that covered all of him. He had sandals. He had a leather belt, and a leather wallet in which he could hide the eyewear. He had enough to eat: nothing fancy, not for a slave, but enough. After four years of, well, nothing, all that seemed riches unimaginable.

His master, though much richer than he was, still had debts to settle, debts from the days before he sailed with Pámfilo de Narváez. One of those debts was to Antonio de Mendoza, the Viceroy of New Spain: not a man on whose bad side anyone with a grain of sense would want to stay. To settle that score, Andrés Dorantes sold Estevánico to the viceroy. Dorantes told Estevánico to leave the eyewear behind, but the Moor took it with him anyhow. He was sure his old master wouldn't tell his new master—or anyone else—about it.

Antonio de Mendoza studied Estevánico with cold, hooded eyes. "I've heard that you and your comrades came close to seven cities filled with gold," he said, steepling his long, thin fingers. "Is this true, or is it not?"

If it wasn't, Estevánico figured he was in for a lifetime of the hardest, shittiest work the viceroy could find for him. He wasn't a cook or a majordomo or a pretty woman. He was just a Moor…unless he was a Moor who knew how to find seven cities full of gold. Picking his words with care, he replied, "Your Excellency, I cannot say for sure, because we did not see them ourselves, but all the natives in those parts seem sure they are there." That stretched things a bit. Unduly? Estevánico didn't think so. It might get him

Eyewear

off the hook if the cities turned out not to be there after all. A slave, especially a slave with a new master, needed as many ways off the hook as he could find.

The Viceroy of New Spain went on studying him. "If these seven cities *are* there, can you lead an expedition to them?"

"Absolutely, your Excellency." Now Estevánico spoke with perfect confidence. And why not? The eyewear would take him wherever he wanted to go.

Antonio de Mendoza must have heard that confidence and known it for what it was. A man didn't get to be viceroy—a man couldn't come close to such a rank—without recognizing such things. "*Bueno*," de Mendoza said. "Such an expedition is fitting out. Francisco Vázquez de Coronado will command it. You—you and Father Marcos of Nice, who has also traveled in those parts—will guide him to another triumph for Christendom and for good King Carlos."

"It would be an honor, your Excellency," Estevánico said, as he had to.

"No doubt." His new master's voice was dry as dust. No doubt he recognized garbage when he heard it, too. He jerked a thumb toward the doorway to his chamber. "Now get out of here."

Estevánico got. He wondered whether Esperanza/Amal would reappear now that he'd got new orders. He even made a point of going off by himself to give the white-haired man the chance to do it. And, sure enough, the man who walked through years did. "So you're chasing the Seven Cities, are you?" he said without preamble.

"That's right. What about it?" Estevánico wasn't so overawed now as he had been when Esperanza/Amal first showed up. You could start taking even miracles for granted. "When I do, I'll be a big man. I bet the viceroy frees me."

"I could tell you…" Esperanza/Amal shook his head like a man bedeviled by mosquitoes. "No, I probably couldn't, not unless I felt like winking out. But you'd better keep your eyes—and your eyewear—peeled for Aztecs. They haven't improved in seven hundred years, believe me."

"What are you going on about now?" Estevánico asked peevishly.

"Just that they're even better at cutting the—" Faster than a castanet click, Esperanza/Amal *did* wink out. He didn't come back, either. But he didn't need to finish *that* sentence. Estevánico knew about the Aztecs' delight in human sacrifice, and about their delight in the fresh meat they got from the sacrifices. The seven hundred years? He could worry about that some other time.

WORRYING AT it—which was not the same thing—made him keep the eyewear on two nights later as he walked through Mexico City's nighttime streets. Only occasional torches lit them. Even so, the eyewear kept him from stepping in anything nasty and let him evade the noisy, half-drunken patrol parties the viceroy used to keep order.

Then the eyewear showed him doing something out of the ordinary: jumping into one of the canals that survived from the days when this had been Aztec Tenochtitlan. He didn't want to. The canal was full of stinking sewage. Remembering all he'd seen, remembering Esperanza/Amal's advice, he jumped anyhow.

The eyewear said he could stick his head up. Gasping and spluttering, he did. But he stifled the splutters, because soft, determined footsteps were coming up the street.

Two men paused, not six feet from him. They wore coveralls of a style he'd never seen before, and carried weapons that looked something like arquebuses.

A Spaniard reeled around the corner coming the other way like a boat tacking against nasty winds. He was pretty windy himself, bawling out a love song in a creaking, potted baritone. How much *agave* spirit had he poured down? More than was good for him, much more, although chances were he would have said no such thing.

He saw the two strangers just before—*just* before—he ran into them. How he stopped, Estevánico never knew, but he did. He gaped at them. "What kind of monkeys are you, in those stupid, ugly clothes?" he demanded.

Estevánico didn't think much of the men's clothes, either. That didn't mean he would have told them about it. Insulting men who carried arquebuses wasn't the smartest thing you could do. The locks could have their matches smoldering, after all, and if they did you might get shot.

The strangers both eyed the Spaniard as if *he* were the monkey. "Whoever started you in your pox-scarred mother's womb wasted the money he gave her," one of them said. His accent was curious, but Estevánico had no trouble understanding him.

Neither did the Spaniard. Even in the gloom, Estevánico watched his eyes bug. "You—!" he spluttered. "You—!" He couldn't think of anything vile enough to say. He was too fuddled for that. But he wasn't too fuddled to know the stranger had called his mother a whore, and an ugly whore at that.

Estevánico would have tried to murder anyone who said such things. He wasn't surprised when the Spaniard's yard-long blade cleared its scabbard with a nasty *wheep!* The fellow might be drunk, but he could still fight. From everything Estevánico had seen of Spaniards, they never got too drunk to fight. This one lunged at the closer stranger.

He almost skewered him, too. The man in the odd coveralls had to leap back to keep from getting spitted like a pork roast. "Coward! Dog!" the Spaniard jeered, laughing. He advanced purposefully, his sozzled stagger gone.

It did him no good whatever. The stranger raised the weapon that looked like an arquebus. He touched something under it: maybe a trigger, maybe not. The weapon didn't roar or belch fire, the way all the arquebuses Estevánico had ever seen would have. Instead, it chirped softly, rather like a night bird settling down. The Moor thought it had misfired, an accident only too common with such arms.

But it hadn't. The Spaniard fell over. Estevánico couldn't see what had hit him—he couldn't see that anything had hit him. But he had no doubt the man was dead. The sword slid from his hand; the iron blade clanked against a stone in the path. And the fellow's guts made horrible gurgling noises. A moment later, even through the stink of the canal where he hid, Estevánico smelled the latrine reek that meant his bowels had let go.

The stranger who hadn't raised his nearly silent weapon strode up to the Spaniard and kicked him in the face as hard as he could. Estevánico didn't think he'd ever seen so much hatred concentrated in a single blow. The stranger didn't search the dead man for a purse or even check to see if he was wearing a golden ring. Whatever the Spaniard had, the man in coveralls cared nothing for it.

His comrade asked, "Is your foot all right?" He spoke not in Spanish but in a clipped, sharp dialect of Nahuatl, the Aztecs' tongue. Estevánico understood just enough to follow.

"It's fine," the other man answered in the same tongue. "He's already dead. Whatever I do to him isn't enough. I want to carve his heart out myself and roast it and eat it."

They're Aztecs, all right, Estevánico thought, and prayed they wouldn't notice his wet shudder. Most of it was underwater, so they didn't. Was their language what Nahuatl might turn into in…seven hundred years? He wouldn't have been surprised. Esperanza/Amal, damn him, had a way of knowing what he was talking about, even when it seemed completely insane.

"He'd be tough. Gamy, too," said the man who'd used his weapon.

"I don't care. It's the principle of the thing," his friend replied. "If only I could, I'd eat the heart out of every *conquistador* ever born."

"You'd have to wait in line for your share," the other Aztec said.

"I know, I know. Now—where'd that black bastard we want get to, anyway?" said the man who'd kicked the Spaniard after he was dead. The water in the canal was no worse than cool. Ice walked up Estevánico's back anyway.

Pointing in the direction from which the drunken Spaniard had come, the other fellow answered, "Has to be that way. If this stinking turd hadn't slowed us down, I bet we would have caught him by now." Off they went, two hunters intent on their prey—and completely unaware they'd just passed it by.

When the eyewear told Estevánico he could, he clambered out of the canal, shivering and dripping. Without the magical eyeglasses, he *would* have gone that way—but not for long. He waited for Esperanza/Amal to reappear and say *I told you so*.

"I told you so," Esperanza/Amal said, as usual from behind Estevánico's left shoulder.

"You did, as sure as there is no God but God." Estevánico said nothing about Muhammad. What he didn't say, no one, not even the white-haired man, could overhear. "In His name, though, how did you know?"

"I've met their kind before. And if I tell you anything more, I'll vanish again." Esperanza/Amal's big nose wrinkled. "Stinks around here. A lot of it's you."

"Not all." Estevánico pointed to the dead Spaniard, and to the canal.

"I said what I meant." Esperanza/Amal, Estevánico realized, almost always did. He went on, "But you've got to keep watching yourself, because if you don't—" He vanished once more.

This time, he didn't come back. For once, the Moor didn't think he needed to. Estevánico could figure out the end of that sentence all by himself. He wondered what *his* heart would taste like, roasted. He didn't want anybody to find out.

Slowly, following the roundabout route the eyewear gave him, he went back to Antonio de Mendoza's residence. A senior servant chewed him out for getting tipsy and falling into the canal. Estevánico didn't deny it—he apologized again and again. The soft answer turned away some wrath, anyhow. The servant gave him water to wash with and a blanket to wrap himself in, then took his clothes to the laundresses.

It could have been worse. Everything could have been worse. All the same, with those bastards looking for him here, Estevánico could hardly wait to get out of Mexico City.

CORONADO SEEMED a capable man, maybe not ready for anything like Cabeza de Vaca but certainly better than Pámfilo de Narváez. But Estevánico quickly discovered he couldn't stand Father Marcos. The man never shut up. He even talked in his sleep. And he had a shrill, grating voice that reminded the Moor of nothing so much as fingernails scraping across a slate.

Going up into the country through which he'd wandered with Cabeza de Vaca, Dorantes, and del Castillo was a relief. Coronado commanded two hundred fifty riders, seventy arquebusiers on foot, and a thousand natives and Negroes in charge of spare horses, wagons, and meat animals. It was a real army, the first ever seen in these parts.

Along with Father Marcos, Estevánico rode ahead to scout the way. And then he took a few servants and started riding ahead of the padre. It was that or kill him, and the eyewear didn't show Estevánico that he could get away with murder. *A pity*, he thought.

Some of the natives remembered him from his earlier trek through these lands. Others had heard about him from people who'd seen him then. He made the most of it. No matter what the Spaniards thought, the locals had next to no gold. Maybe things would be better up at the cities they talked about, maybe not. He'd worry about that when he got there.

In the meantime… In the meantime, they did have turquoise. The eyewear showed they'd give him some if he asked. Ask he did. The eyewear also showed they'd give him women. You couldn't load screwing onto a donkey and haul it back to Mexico City, which didn't make it any less a treasure.

Because Father Marcos and Coronado and the army followed in his wake, Estevánico spoke of the white men and their god. The Spaniards *were* going to convert the natives. The villagers and wandering hunters needed to get used to the idea.

Get used to it? They thought it was funny. "Here you're so dark, and you're telling us about white men? You expect us to believe that?" one of them said.

"You'd better. It's true," Estevánico answered, not for the first time. He'd heard the joke often enough to get sick of it. The natives thought it was new every time.

One evening, as they camped in a little stretch of flat ground next to a narrow trail set into a mountainside, the eyewear showed Estevánico he needed to talk to his cook. "I need a…a pot of lard, José," he said. The eyewear showed him what to ask for, but he had to figure out what to call it.

"What for, *Señor*?" José was a native, but spoke better Spanish than Estevánico did. He couldn't have been more than five when Cortés conquered Moctezuma, and he'd grown up serving Spaniards. Estevánico wondered how much Nahuatl he remembered.

"Never you mind," the Moor said. He didn't know, either. He could guess, and he did, but he didn't know. The eyewear hadn't shown him yet. He saw the intrigued look on José's face as the cook gave him the pot. How widespread were the rumors that he wasn't a proper Christian? Muslims didn't eat pork or have anything to do with stuff that came from pigs. If he wanted lard, he couldn't be a Muslim, could he?

He'd have to work that out for himself later on. Now? Now he had to see what the eyewear told him to do with the lard. It waited till after nightfall before showing images of him smearing the stuff on a couple of rocks right where the trail was narrowest, at the last bend, about fifty yards farther on than the wide spot that made a campground.

He wondered if he should stand watch after that. But the spectacles showed him wrapping himself in his blanket and looking like a man asleep. He found a lawyer's loophole: that didn't have to mean he actually *was* asleep. And so he lay there, yawning, wondering what would happen next.

The moon was getting close to full. Pearly light spilled down from the sky. Even through half-closed eyes, he had no trouble spotting the man sneaking along the trail toward the camp. If that wasn't one of the Aztecs who'd hunted him in Mexico City… Estevánico didn't have to worry about what he'd do then, because it damn well was. He could even see the quiet but deadly almost-arquebus the son of a dog carried. He thought it was the fellow who'd shot the Spaniard.

But the grim stalker's fancy weapon couldn't match the eyewear's foresight. The Aztec's left foot came down on one of the stones Estevánico had greased. The fellow slipped. As he flailed for balance, his right foot landed on the other greased stone. Coincidence? By now, Estevánico doubted there was any such thing.

With a despairing shriek, the Aztec slid off the trail. The shriek went on for some little while. It was a devil of a long way down.

Estevánico rolled over and pulled the blanket tighter around him. Before long, he really did sleep.

A FEW days later, he got his first glimpse of Hawikuh, the so-called city toward which he was advancing (Father Marcos called it Cibola, for reasons Estevánico never fathomed). He'd seen cities in Morocco and Spain and Mexico. He knew how they were supposed to look. These dwellings stacked on a cliffside seemed distinctly unimpressive.

Some of the natives at the last place he'd stopped had sent him resentful looks when he demanded turquoise and a pretty girl from them. They'd given him what he wanted, but they hadn't liked it. He wondered how the people at Hawikuh would like it. *I'll ask the eyewear*, he thought, and then, *I'll ask it tomorrow*. He was sleepy. The air in this high country was so thin, everybody was sleepy all the time.

Once sunrise pried his eyelids apart, he reached for the leather wallet where he put the eyewear when he went to sleep. His hand closed on… nothing. His eyes opened wide. He looked all around. The wallet wasn't there. That meant the eyewear wasn't there, either.

"¡*Madre de Dios!*" he exclaimed. When that didn't come within leagues of venting his spleen, he swore in Arabic. He felt better, but he didn't feel good. Nowhere near.

He didn't need to be brilliant to figure out what had happened to the wallet. One of José's helpers, a native called Manuel, was also missing. The stony ground wouldn't begin to hold his spoor, and he had a long start.

José stated the obvious: "I am very sorry, *Señor*, but we will never catch him. I hope the coyotes"—his name for the little yellow wolves—"and the pumas fight over his bones." Pumas wanted to be lions, but didn't quite have what it took.

"To the Devil with his bones," Estevánico snarled. "I want the eyewear back."

José spread his hands. "I am very sorry, *Señor*," he repeated.

Eyewear

Estevánico was very sorry, too. What would he do if he couldn't use the eyewear? The question answered itself: he'd damned well do *without*, that was what.

On to Hawikuh, then. It was a bigger assemblage of stacked houses than he'd seen before, anyhow. A city full of gold? That seemed most unlikely. The tribe that dwelt there—they called themselves Zuñis—let down a ladder so he could come up to them and tell his story.

Tell it he did. As other natives had, they laughed at him. "You, a dark brown man, talk about white men behind you?" one of them asked. "And you expect us to believe that?" The assembled Zuñis laughed some more. To Estevánico's ear, the laughter had an uncommonly nasty edge. He wished he could see what the eyewear thought he should do. But he had to go ahead without it. "You'd better believe me," he said. "They *are* coming, and they're bringing their god with them. He is a stronger god than any of yours. If you give me turquoise and let me sleep with a pretty girl, I will talk them into going easy on you."

"I do not think any of this is so," the Zuñi leader said. "Even if it is, I am sure we can deal with these white men." He laughed that unpleasant laugh again.

"You are wrong," Estevánico told him. "You have no idea how wrong you are."

The native chieftain gestured. The eyewear would have warned Estevánico what kind of gesture it was, but he didn't have the eyewear any more. As things were, the spear that went into his back came as a complete surprise. He screeched, more in astonishment than in pain. He was still alive when the Zuñis threw him out of Hawikuh, but not once he hit. Oh, no. Not after that.

Po-pé hated the Spaniards and everything they stood for. For two long lifetimes now, they'd oppressed all the tribes of what they called New Mexico.

They'd even forced their own religion on people who'd long been happy with what they believed on their own. Po-pé had been baptized into the Christian faith. He'd secretly used soapweed to wash himself clean of the baptism, but he didn't feel it had done a good enough job.

He wandered through the rugged country west of the Spanish settlement of Santa Fé. Drive the invaders out of that fort and they would lose their grip on New Mexico. But how? They were strong. They had armor. They had guns.

Something white on the ground—a bone. Po-pé left the trail to see what kind of bone it was. He wasn't surprised to find it had come from a man. Disease and hunger made skeletons anything but rare in New Mexico in this year the Spaniards called 1679.

This poor dead fellow might have lost his flesh, but a leather wallet—an old, old leather wallet—still lay by his hipbone. The scavengers that ate him hadn't bothered it. Curious, Po-pé reached inside. He pulled out...what looked like a pair of the eyeglasses some white men wore.

Curious about white men's magic—for what else could eyeglasses be?—Po-pé put them on. *If only I had some way to get rid of all the invaders*, he thought.

And the eyeglasses started to show him how.

WATCHING FROM behind a fat sagebrush, the white-haired man with the big nose sighed. He might have known the eyewear would be tied up with the New Mexico uprising. How else could the Native Americans drive out the Spaniards and keep them away for thirty years?

And what he'd discovered, the Aztecs and the Incas of Tawantinsuyu would also learn—or already know, depending on how you looked at things. Which meant life in these parts would soon get complicated...again.

Two Thieves

Philip José Farmer's *Riverworld* books are marvelous stories, full of invention and set in a milieu vast enough to let any people an author has in mind plausibly meet one another: worldbuilding on a glorious scale. I was delighted to be asked to do a story for an anthology of stories set in this milieu he was putting together. The two thieves of my title are Alexios I Komnenos, perhaps the most byzantine of all Byzantine Emperors, who ruled from 1081 to 1118, and Richard J. Daley, mayor of Chicago from 1955 to 1976. Nobody who knew either one of them would trust him as far as he could throw him. When they try to cheat each other—well, that's the story.

ALEXIOS KOMNENOS FOLDED his arms across his chest. "You have heard my demands," he said in Arabic, the only language he had in common with New Constantinople's neighbors just down the River. "Obey them or face the consequences."

"You are an infidel. We shall never yield to you." Idris Alooma was the Sultan of Bornu's representative in the town of New Constantinople. Tall and lean and black, he towered over Alexios. To show his contempt, he spat at the *Basileus'* feet.

Alexios' soldiers growled and brandished their flint-tipped spears. He held up a hand. "Let the pagan go in peace for now. Soon enough he will wake up naked and bald somewhere along the River far from here." He used the Greek his people spoke among themselves, then translated for Idris Alooma's benefit.

The big black man laughed scornfully. "You may have been plucked from hell to live beside us on the River here, Christian dog, but you are the one whom Allah will uproot when our armies meet." He turned on his heel and marched back toward the stretch of the Riverbank that owed allegiance to Bornu's Sultan, Musa ar-Rahman.

Alexios watched him go, wondering all the while if he should have let his men enjoy their sport. He tossed his head in a Greek no; he'd done the right thing. If Idris Alooma failed to return to Bornu town, Musa would take his revenge by torturing Michael Palaiologos to death and rebirth. Alexios Komnenos had nothing against killing, but killing to no purpose was stupid and wasteful.

He turned to his brother Isaac, who stood as usual at his right hand. The two men were near twins, especially since being restored to life along the River at the same youthful age. Both were a little below average size, but strongly muscled. Both had a narrow, foxy face beneath a broad forehead; both were swarthy and dark, Isaac a little less so than Alexios. But the best way to tell them apart was to note that Isaac's features were a trifle more open and friendly than Alexios'. Alexios had ruled during his remembered life, Isaac merely aided.

"It will be war," Alexios said now.

"So it would seem," Isaac agreed. "It will not be an easy war, either."

"No." Alexios' scowl was black as the beard he could no longer raise. He still sometimes felt like a eunuch without it. "Why were we resurrected alongside these filthy Muslims?" Were he less pious, he would have wondered about God's mercy. The folk upstream from New Constantinople were peaceful red-skinned pagans who wanted only to be left alone. Given Bornu on his other flank, he'd been happy to oblige them.

Isaac said, "They are infidels, but they are brave. If we meet them head-on, we will lose a great many of our best men, men we cannot afford to be without. That means that if anyone along this stretch of the River succeeds in uniting several little realms behind him, we will be vulnerable."

"This I know." Alexios scowled again. *He* aimed to lead this stretch of the River. Along with a majority of Rhomaioi, he currently ruled a minority

Two Thieves

of peasants from the Egypt of Ptolemy III. As soon as they'd accepted Christianity, they made subjects as good as his own folk—maybe better, for their loyalties were less conditional. Some of them had spoken Greek even before their resurrection; they all did now.

"The war will not wait much longer," Isaac warned. "If we do not begin it on our terms, Musa ar-Rahman will start it on his, for he loves us no better than we him."

"This I also know." Alexios' nostrils flared as he took a long, deep breath. He let it out in a sigh. He didn't want to say what he had to say next: "We shall begin it, brother of mine. But before we do, I aim to go to Shytown."

Isaac's bushy eyebrows flew toward his hairline. "You would deal with those—those aftermen?" *Opisthanthropoi* was a word in no Greek lexicon; the folk of New Constantinople had coined it to describe people on the River who came from a time many centuries later than their own.

"God and the saints know I have no love for them," Alexios said. Aftermen were generally weak in faith, which made them unreliable, and strong in arcane gadgetry, which made them dangerous. Alexios sighed once more. "But they are on Bornu's other flank. If they work with us, the pagans will fall like ripe wheat at harvest time."

"Let us make sure that we reap the full benefit thereof, though, not the men of Shytown," Isaac warned.

At last Alexios found something to amuse him. "Brother of mine, I was *Basileus* of the Romans for thirty-seven years. In all that time, did anyone ever outtrick me?"

Isaac did not answer. Alexios knew he had no answer. He'd stood off rebels from among his own people, Turks and Patzinaks and Normans; he'd even funneled through his Empire the western barbarians who called themselves Crusaders, and taken for the Rhomaioi most of the territory they'd won from the Seljuks in Anatolia. Maybe someone along the endless River was more cunning than he, but he had his doubts.

As if picking that boastful thought from his mind, Isaac said, "Do be cautious nonetheless. Shytown's *Basileus* is not a fool."

"Another truth. He does not style himself Emperor, though. While he is no Frank, he uses one of their titles—he calls himself *Mayor*."

"I wonder why?" Isaac mused.

"Who knows why the aftermen do as they do?" Alexios answered. "Their customs are even stranger than the Franks', and you know what it means for me to say that." No Franks lay anywhere close along the River, for which Alexios thanked God. Unwashed, ignorant, stinking, brutal savages—who happened to be inhumanly good at slaughtering anyone who got in their way. The Emperor rubbed his naked chin. "Where was I? Oh, yes, the customs of Shytown's aftermen. Do you know they didn't pick their Mayor by his courage or birth or anything sensible? No, they had all the people who wanted the job make speeches, and then chose by a show of hands from men and women both. 'Democracy,' they call it. It's idiocy, if you ask me."

"*Demokratia*." Isaac spat in the dirt. In the Greek the two Komnenoi spoke, the word meant *mob rule*. As Alexios said, it seemed a daft way to run a state, but Shytown flourished. Isaac added, "Do you really have to go there yourself?"

"Whom do you propose I send?" Alexios retorted. "The only other two men I might trust for the job are you and Michael Palaiologos. If I pull Michael out of Bornu town, Musa will surely divine what I aim to do. And you, brother of mine, make a better soldier than an ambassador. Meaning no disrespect, but in a dicker the Mayor would eat you up and pick his teeth with your bones."

Since that was true, Isaac could only give his brother a reproachful stare. He said, "How do you even propose to get to Shytown? You let Idris Alooma go, so the Muslim blacks will know trouble lies ahead for them. And Musa ar-Rahman is no fool, either. He will be looking for you to try to stab him in the back like that. Were I he, I'd have rafts in the water day and night. Do you want to be fished out and tortured, then given time to heal and tortured again for years on end?"

"Do I want that? Of course not. But I have to get to Shytown, and I don't think I could pass myself off as a proper subject of Musa's to sneak across

Two Thieves

his domain." Alexios laughed. So did Isaac, but he sounded more dutiful than amused. Black men of Musa ar-Rahman's tribe made up about two thirds of the people of Bornu. Most of the rest were short, golden-skinned, flat-featured, and narrow-eyed. Alexios' chance of successfully impersonating a member of either group was effectively none.

"All right. It will have to be the River, then, but I don't like it," Isaac said.

Alexios laughed. "Here you are, *Kaisar* to my *Basileus*: if I fail, you become Emperor. And yet you caution me. What kind of brother are you?" He knew the answer to that: a loyal one. A loyal brother, especially among the treacherous Rhomaioi, was more precious than rubies. Alexios knew that, too. He clapped Isaac on the back with real affection. "Besides, I have an idea—"

THE STORM blew over not long before dawn. The River rode high and choppy in its banks. Debris drifted downstream—treetrunks, bamboo stalks, part of what had been a hut or a raft.

Isaac Komnenos chuckled. "If the Muslims were out watching for you last night, brother of mine, some of them will have drowned—so many the fewer to face when the time comes."

"True enough," Alexios answered. "I—" The morning roar of the grailstones interrupted him. Lambent blue fire shot into the air, to three times the height of a man. When it faded, the people of New Constantinople crowded forward to see what their grails contained today. Alexios took his with as much curiosity as anyone else.

He opened the hinged lid, smiling as savory steam tickled his nose. Black bread, honey, porridge with big bits of tuna and squid, a soft jar of wine, and a packet of the smokesticks his folk mostly traded to those who enjoyed sucking on them. And— "A firestarter!" he said happily. His grail had produced only a handful of them since his resurrection.

"A good omen," Isaac agreed.

"More than that," Alexios said. "A good weapon, too. I'll carry it along with my knife tonight. If a Bornu spots me, I'll burn out his tongue before he can shout the warning." That was bravado, and he knew it. Still, the new tool gave him one more string to his bow; without its appearance, he might not have thought to take one.

He spend the rest of the day going over his plans till he was sick of it and Isaac sicker. Most of what they talked about had to do with things that were unlikely to happen. Alexios had seen enough unlikely things in his life back on Earth to be sure some, at least, would come true: generally the ones that hadn't been planned for. He was a man who left as little as possible to chance.

The sun set in splendor over the mountains to the west. As dusk darkened toward true night, Alexios walked down to the River. A crew bossed by his brother waited for him there. When they started to prostrate themselves, he waved to show the gesture was unnecessary. "We have work to do here tonight, my friends."

He stripped off the reddish-purple kilt whose color was reserved for him alone in New Constantinople (any pieces of that hue which appeared on the grailstone were either saved for his use or traded away outside his little empire). To replace it, he covered himself with several dark blue lengths of cloth, until only his head, hands, and feet remained bare.

Grunting and cursing, the work crew manhandled a yew into the River. They kept one last grassfiber line attached to it so it would not drift away downstream. Isaac Komnenos slapped Alexios on the back. "God go with you and bring you home again safe."

"You just say that because you don't want the work of ruling," Alexios said.

Isaac laughed. "Too right I don't, brother of mine. Do you have your reed?"

"Here." Alexios held up the yard-long piece of plant. It wasn't actually a reed, as it would have been back on Earth; it was a thin length of bamboo, with all the pith hollowed out. But it would serve.

Alexios slipped into the water. It was cool but not cold. The *Basileus* took hold of a root that trailed from the yew. At Isaac's shouted direction, one of the men cut the last rope with a sharp piece of flint. The yew began to drift down the River.

The land slid slowly past. Settlements in New Constantinople centered on the grailstones. Once the one from which he'd left dropped away behind him, darkness prevailed for most of the next mile. Alexios glanced over to the far side of the River. Lights there were even fewer; a broad stretch of that bank was inhabited by hunters and gatherers even more primitive than the nomadic Patzinaks. They weren't even fierce enough to make decent allies against Bornu; had they been so, Alexios would have tried to recruit them.

Something nibbled his leg. He jerked and thrashed in the water. A croaker let out the mournful call that gave the fish its name, then splashed away. The things were cowards and scavengers and not worth eating if anything better was available. Alexios was glad to be rid of this one.

It could have been worse. It could have been a dragonfish. Dragonfish did not usually attack boats or people in the River. When they did, the people they attacked usually reappeared on a new stretch of River.

Another grailstone, another town of Rhomaioi. This one was called Thessaloniki, after the second city in Alexios' empire. The people had lit a bonfire; Alexios saw men and women dancing around it. Faintly, the music of turtlefish lyres and upraised voices reached his ears. He smiled. He would sooner have been dancing around that fire himself than where he was.

In the middle of the next stretch of quiet dark, another croaker swam snuffling up to Alexios, hoping, no doubt, that he was a piece of offal. He hit the fish with his fist. It nipped him on the leg before it fled. He prayed he wasn't bleeding. Blood in the water would draw a dragonfish to him if anything would.

The last town of Rhomaioi before the frontier with Bornu was Nikaia. More fires blazed at the frontier; a detachment of Rhomaioi kept watch against the infidels. Less than a hundred yards farther on, the black men had their own frontier garrison, of similar size to the one Alexios had posted.

The Bornu capered round their watchfires to the beat of bamboo-stalk drums with redfish leather skins. They brandished flint-tipped spears and shouted threats across the border to the Rhomaioi, most of whom, perhaps fortunately, could not understand them.

Alexios looked ahead. Before long, he spied torches on the River. The Bornu, he had learned since resurrection, came from a desert part of Africa; they did not take naturally to the water. But they were not stupid, either—they knew that if New Constantinople wanted to cut a deal with Shytown, the River was the logical avenue for emissaries.

The *Basileus* slid all the way under the water. He tried to get as far under the trunk of the yew as he could. Only the tip of his hollowed-out bamboo stuck up above the surface. The other end was in his mouth. He took deep, slow, steady breaths. A military manual from hundreds of years before his own time which he'd once read told how the Sklavenoi used this very trick to avoid detection by the Rhomaioi. Now, he thought, a *Basileus* of the Rhomaioi was turning it against barbarians.

He kept his eyes open, though the night-dark water all around him might as well have been ink. Then, through the crazily shifting mirror of the surface, he saw a flickering torchflame. He knew the black men were peering down into the River. If they saw his pale skin despite the gloomy kilts he'd draped round himself, if by some disaster they recognized his breathing tube for what it was…if either of those things happened, Isaac would become *Basileus*. Alexios just hoped the Bornu would eventually kill him instead of torturing him almost to death, letting him heal, and starting over again.

The torchlight receded as the uprooted yew tree drifted on. Alexios sighed relief through hollow bamboo. He stayed submerged for some time, lest the noise of his emerging betray him to his foes.

But before too long, he had to put up his head. He needed to watch the land by the River flow past, so he'd know when he'd gone by Bornu and entered the territory of Shytown. He also needed to keep an eye out for more rafts in the River. He would not have contented himself with a single line of

Two Thieves

pickets had he been Musa ar-Rahman, and dared not assume the Sultan was less cautious than he.

Sure enough, he had to go under and breathe through his tube twice more. But the men of Bornu apparently found nothing suspicious about a tree floating downstream after a storm. Though once their torches seemed right overhead, they never probed the water with their spears.

After the third set of rafts, the Muslims had no further River defenses. Alexios drifted along past one of their settlements after another. He grew bored, and also chilly from having been in the water so long, but willingly endured both for the sake of the reward he might gain from this journey.

Bornu, by the look of things, fortified its border with Shytown more intensively than the one with New Constantinople. A palisade of bamboo and timber ran from the River toward the unclimbable mountains that sealed off the back of each domain.

Not long after he passed the palisade, Alexios kicked himself away from the yew and stroked toward the shore. He held on to his bamboo breathing tube: who could say when it might come in handy again?

He splashed up onto the Riverbank. Shytown's sentries were alert; he'd hardly come out of the water before someone hailed him: "Who are you and what the devil are you doing here?"

He followed that, though he understood only a little of Shytown's language. The people of the Mayor's domain called it English, but it hardly resembled the English he'd learned from the Angles and Saxons of the Varangian Guard, men who'd abandoned England after William the Norman overthrew their kind. Having dealt with Robert Guiscard and his son Bohemund, Alexios did not love Normans, either.

He answered in the aftermen's dialect of English, as best he could: "I am Alexios Komnenos, *Basileus* of New Konstantinopolis. I will to see your Mayor."

"Say what?" It was a sudden, sharp exclamation, meaningless to Alexios. The sentry came up and looked him over. "Goddamn! Maybe you are him." He raised his voice: "Hey Fred, Louie, come here! One of you take my slot, okay? This guy says he's Alexios from upstream, and he wants to see Mayor Daley. I'm gonna bring him to Hizzonor."

Fred or Louie came up. Whoever he was, he had a torch. "Yeah, that's Alexios all right—I seen him once. Okay, Pete, you found him; I guess you get to take him. Beats stayin' here, that's for damn sure."

Alexios caught only part of that, but he gathered Pete would conduct him to the Mayor. He fell into step with the Shytown sentry. All the way to Mayor Daley's residence, Pete bombarded him with questions. Why did he want to see the Mayor? Did it have to do with Bornu? If it didn't, what was it about? From one of his own subjects, Alexios would have found such prodding intolerable. But the folk of Shytown had a reputation for being both free of speech with their betters and insatiably inquisitive. Alexios found it politic to make his English poorer than it really was.

The Mayor dwelt in a fair-sized palace. Alexios thought the profusion of windows on the outside extravagant; houses in New Constantinople kept to the courtyard pattern of the lost imperial city. But enough guards ringed the place that theft was unlikely to be a problem.

Pete spoke to a guard by the door, too fast for Alexios to follow. Then he turned back and said, "Do you mind waiting till sunup? They don't want to wake Hizzonor yet."

Alexios considered and decided to throw a tantrum. He cursed in Greek before trying English again at the top of his lungs: "I am the *Basileus*, God dump you to hell. You keep me to wait like man with fish to sell?" If the Mayor hadn't been awake, he ought to be now, *theou thelontos*.

After listening to some more ranting, the guard went inside. Mayor Daley came out a few minutes later, accompanied by a thin man with red hair who wore a bone cross on a leather thong round his neck. Daley rumbled in his brand of English. The thin man spoke Latin, which Alexios also understood: "I am Father Boyle, Hizzonor's interpreter. He asks why whatever business this is couldn't wait until the morning."

"Because I am as much a ruler as he is, and I am here now," Alexios answered. "Tell him that." *Because he is an upstart and I am* Basileus *of the Rhomaioi*, he thought, though he kept that to himself.

Two Thieves

Daley spoke again: "All right; let's get on with it."

Alexios waved aside the priest's translation; he'd understood that himself. He studied Hizzonor. Like everyone else along the River, Mayor Richard J. Daley was physically perfect and in the prime of youth. That failed to make him handsome; he looked like a bruiser. But his eyes— Maybe it was a trick of the torchlight, but Alexios didn't think so. Those cold gray eyes held more than a youth's experience. Alexios would have bet Hizzonor had lived a long life and done a lot of underhanded things in it. Isaac claimed his own eyes had that look, so no wonder he recognized it.

Aloud, he said, "We aim to fight Bornu soon; we want you to come in on our side. Between us, we can crush the black infidels, take control of their grails, and add to the wealth of both Shytown and New Constantinople. Is that interesting enough to get you out of bed early, Mayor?"

Daley didn't speak Latin; he had to wait for Father Boyle to translate. Even after the priest was done, the Mayor did not change expression. *Yes, he's good*, Alexios thought with reluctant admiration. Daley answered, "Maybe. Depends on when you do it and what's in it for us. I don't have men to throw away on the Suicide Express."

Via Suicida made strange Latin, but Alexios understood: Daley didn't want men loyal to him killed and resurrected far, far up or down the River. Alexios didn't want that for his own retainers, either. He said, "That's why I propose alliance. Between us, we trap and outnumber the men of Bornu. Our casualties should be small."

"Yes, that might work," Daley said. "I also wouldn't mind seeing those shiftless blacks next door working for a living instead of sponging off their grails and lying around like they were in welfare heaven. So yeah, I'm interested. Tell me more."

Even after Hizzonor's priest translated that, Alexios didn't get all of it; *welfare heaven* left him especially puzzled. Mayor Daley also seemed to despise the people of Bornu merely for being black. That confused Alexios. They couldn't help being black. But they had chosen false Islam of their own free will, and would (he continued to believe, despite resurrection along the River) one day suffer the pangs of hell for their error.

Reasons, however, didn't matter. He said, "Are we allies, then? Shall we fix the day for setting the fate of the black infidels?" If Hizzonor didn't like the Bornu because of their color, Alexios would remind him of it.

"It isn't quite so simple," Mayor Daley said. "The one thing the blacks are good for is keeping you and me from bumping up against each other. When we're neighbors, we're going to have to watch each other all the time. Musa's a nuisance to me now, what with his bucks coming in and stealing a white woman every so often, but he's only a nuisance, if you know what I mean. Having you next door might be downright dangerous."

Alexios eyes Hizzonor with surprised respect. If he understood the idea of buffer states, he was indeed no one's fool. After some thought, Alexios said, "Let us agree in advance, then, on which of us will control each grailstone in Bornu. Quarrels settled ahead of time do not turn vexing later."

But Mayor Daley shook his head. "That isn't good enough. I heard you were smart, and I see it's so. So sooner or later, Shytown and New Constantinople will likely fight. We're both going to want to take over as much as we can—we're like that. Am I right or wrong?"

"I think you're right," Alexios admitted. He'd seen the same, but had intended to keep quiet about it. Hizzonor's style was different, almost brutally direct. The *Basileus* asked, "What do you propose to do about the problem?"

"Here's what," Daley said: "A big war would wreck your country and mine both, and leave whichever of us won in bad shape against anybody strong who might come up or down the River at him. So let's keep it clean: we'll go together against the Bornu, sure. But at the same time, I'll name you Vice Mayor of Shytown and you'll name me—what do you call your number two guy?"

"*Kaisar*," Alexios answered.

"Okay. That's what you'll name me, then. You see what I'm driving at?"

"I see," Alexios said slowly. If he took Mayor Daley's terms, whichever of them assassinated the other would rule New Constantinople and Shytown both. Life henceforward would be nervous for the two headmen, but their retainers would live. Alexios went on, "But, you see, I already have a *Kaisar*. He—"

Two Thieves

"I got a Vice Mayor, too," Daley interrupted. "It's no big deal. This is important. It needs doing, if Shytown and New Constantinople are going to end up next door to each other. Am I right, or not?"

Alexios had been about to say that his *Kaisar* was his own brother, the only man he'd ever known upon whom he could rely absolutely. The last thing he wanted was to replace Isaac with someone mainly interested in killing him off. But Daley had made it clear that Shytown wouldn't help against Bornu unless he had his way. And if New Constantinople took on Bornu alone, then even if he won he'd be vulnerable to an attack from downstream.

Better the risk to his person than the one to his empire, he decided. "Let it be as you say," he told the Mayor. "Once Bornu is taken, you will name me Vice Mayor and I will appoint you *Kaisar*." *And we shall see what happens after that, too*, he added to himself.

Daley stuck out his hand. Alexios took it. The Mayor's clasp was brief, firm, and as mechanical as the gears and levers that raised the imperial throne in Constantinople high in the air to overawe barbarous envoys. Daley, worse luck, did not act like a barbarian—he did not show on his face what he was thinking. Alexios reminded himself that the aftermen had had hundreds of years past his own time in which to learn deceit. He hoped his own lifetime of practicing such arts would suffice.

Once the Mayor had what he wanted, he turned businesslike in a hurry. "Let's plan this thing out," he said. "If we're going to do it, we ought to do it right. I think we can, but we need to work things out beforehand—"

The sun came up while Daley and Alexios were still plotting. Only the roar from the grailstones made the *Basileus* notice he no longer needed torches to see. One of Daley's henchmen fetched him breakfast: fried eggs and bacon, toasted bread with fruit jam sweeter than honey, and the hot bitter brew called coffee. He didn't care for that, but drank for politeness' sake. After he finished it, he felt more awake and alert than the long night should have permitted.

Mayor Daley's title was anything but martial, but he had a sound grasp of strategy. If everything went as he and Alexios designed (which seldom happened in war), Bornu would be ground between them like grain between upper and lower millstones. And Daley's scheme for returning Alexios to New Constantinople was simplicity itself: "We'll send you as a sailor in one of our boats, and we'll tell the black boys they'll get instant war with us if they try searching anything of ours that floats. Think that'll work?"

"It should, by the Virgin," Alexios said. To his surprise, he found himself liking Hizzonor. Could the afterman have been trusted for a single instant out of Alexios' sight, he would have made a good *Kaisar*. As it was, he would make a bad enemy if he didn't get his way. Alexios smiled. Of course he intended to keep his promise to Daley...

THE ARMY of Rhomaioi swept over the border a little before dawn. A few sentries shot arrows at the soldiers. More fled screeching into the interior of Bornu.

"Had it been my choice instead of Musa's, I would have had the Shytown boat searched and taken me off it were I found," Alexios said to Isaac. "But Mayor Daley was right there: the men of Bornu dared not antagonize him and me at the same time, and so I came home safely."

"I'm glad of it, too," Isaac Komnenos answered. "From all you've said since you got back, the *opisthanthropos* would be too much for a plain old honest soldier like me." He laughed to show he didn't mean to be taken altogether seriously.

Alexios laughed, too. "One thing at a time, brother of mine. The first thing we have to do is settle Musa ar-Rahman. Only after Bornu ceases to be a problem will Shytown become one...unless, of course, Hizzonor means to sit this fight out, let us and the Muslims weaken ourselves, and then pick up the remains." That he hadn't entertained that possibility earlier was a measure of Daley's skill at lulling him. Something new to worry about...

With every pace the Rhomaioi marched, they could see further. The sun rose as they drew near the grailstone closest to the border. Bornu warriors

Two Thieves

boiled out of the town that had grown up around the grailstone. Like Alexios' men, they carried spears and bows, stone axes and sword-clubs with wooden bodies and flint or obsidian blades. Also like the Rhomaioi, they wore several layers of kiltcloth as armor.

There the resemblance ended. Alexios' soldiers marched in an orderly hollow diamond; the men of the outer ranks carried shields of wood and fish-leather to protect themselves and their comrades from missile weapons. The Bornu scorned both order and shields. Screaming *"Allahu akbar!"*—God is great!—they hurled themselves at their Christian foes.

Isaac Komnenos waited till the black men were very close before he shouted, "Loose!" Hundreds of arrows flew as one. The archers reached over their shoulders for more shafts, shot again and again. Their bows, made from dragonfish mouthparts, were better than any they'd had in their previous lives.

Even so, not many Bornu fell. Draped as they were in kiltcloth, they were armored against most archery. But some were hit in the face, others wounded in arms or calves and thus out of the fight. The Rhomaioi suffered almost no casualties.

The black men's woes grew worse when the fighting came to close quarters. They were as brave as their foes, maybe braver—the Rhomaioi seldom showed more courage than an occasion demanded. But the Bornu fought as individuals; they had no notion of battle as anything but a series of single combats.

They paid dearly for their education. To Alexios and Isaac, the success of the army as a whole came first, with individual glory a long way behind. Alexios fought at the fore, true, but more to inspire his own men than out of love for combat. He cared more for the power that came through war than for war itself.

The Bornu flung themselves at him, one after another. He could read their thought: if he fell, the army's aggressive spirit would perish with him. He knew they were wrong; Isaac was no diplomat, but made a perfectly capable soldier. Alexios took the series of attacks to mean Bornu resistance would fall apart if he killed Musa ar-Rahman.

The *Basileus* carried a stout stone-headed club. It was a pragmatist's weapon, one that would break bones even through kiltcloth. A tall, screaming black man thrust a spear at his face. He ducked, stepped close, and swung that club. A man's ribs were a bigger, less elusive target than his head. The black man moaned. Pink foam spurted from his nose and mouth as he crumpled. The advancing Rhomaioi trampled him into the dirt.

Quite suddenly, the Bornu quit fighting and turned to flight. Alexios was tempted to open his tight formation and pursue, but decided against it: let the defeated Muslims spread panic ahead of New Constantinople's army. Nor could he be sure the Bornu weren't trying to lead him into an ambuscade.

As the Rhomaioi approached, shrieking women fled from the village around the grailstone. That convinced Alexios he really had won a victory worth having. When a few of his warriors seemed about to break ranks and run after the women, he called, "We'll have as many of these wenches as we like once the Bornu are beaten. Till then, we risk ourselves if we chase them without discipline."

His lines held steady. Unlike the black men, the Rhomaioi knew what discipline was worth; they could put off immediate pleasure for the sake of a greater gain later. They made him proud.

Ahead in the far distance, smoke rose against the sky. "Is that what we hope for?" Isaac asked.

"It should be," Alexios answered. "Mayor Daley promised the men of Shytown would burn the palisade the Bornu built to keep them out. The aftermen seem clever with incendiaries, and to be acquainted with more of them than our liquid fire." *Yet another thing to worry about*, he thought. But not until later. Worry about Musa ar-Rahman came first.

Alexios detached a company of troops to fill grails on the grailstone of the captured town. Some of those grails belonged to his own soldiers; others were seized from captured blacks. The *Basileus* pushed on with the main body of his force. The supply company had carts to carry the loaded grails (minus liquor, smoking hemp, and dreamgum) up to the rest of the army. The Bornu in the wake of the imperial forces would go hungry, but that was their hard luck.

Two Thieves

"Do you think they'll try to attack us again, this side of their capital?" Isaac asked.

"*I* wouldn't, if I'd got myself into a mess like this," Alexios said. "But who can read Musa's mind with certainty? He might split his forces against us and Shytown, or he might try to beat one foe first and then turn back and quickly smite the other. But if it were me, I'd await attack where the works of the town favor defense. It's not as if we can starve him out in a hurry, worse luck."

Isaac chuckled. "Grails do make this whole business of sieges more complicated than it used to be."

Here and there, Bornu archers sniped from ambush at the advancing Rhomaioi. They did little damage. Alexios' scouts captured and hamstrung a couple of them and confiscated their grails. If the skirmishers were trying to slow up the *Basileus'* army, they failed.

Musa did as Alexios had guessed. After the first repulse, no sizable Bornu force appeared to challenge the men from New Constantinople. The second Bornu grailtown along the Riverbank was all but deserted when the Rhomaioi reached it. The townsfolk had fled downstream with their grails. The same was true of the third town, where Alexios stopped to fill grails for the noon meal.

The fourth grailtown downstream from the border with New Constantinople was the capital of Bornu. Its grailstone was no bigger than any of the rest, so its normal population was like those of the other little cities, but Musa ar-Rahman had lavished far more care on it than on them. Its tall wall was built of stout timber and bamboo, and draped with kiltcloth to ward against torches. The second story of the Sultan's palace overtopped even the wall. That would be Musa's citadel if he lost the rest of the town, Alexios thought.

The wall was packed tight with black men who bellowed defiance at the Rhomaioi. Isaac Komnenos scowled up at them. "This place would be no joy to besiege even if they weren't able to feed themselves with their grails."

"I won't argue, brother of mine. However—" Alexios nodded to the musicians who accompanied the army. Shrill squeals from the flute and deep notes from the drum ordered the warriors to shift position. Alexios missed military trumpets, but not enough copper had been found in New Constantinople to make even one.

The front ranks of the army opened out, allowing the engineering detachment which had traveled in the middle of the hollow diamond to advance. They pushed their carts (quite different from those of the foragers) up toward the wall. Shieldmen moved forward with them, protecting them from the storm of missiles the Bornu loosed.

A man at the rear of each cart worked a kiltcloth bellows. Kiltcloth also lined the interior of the long bamboo tubes other engineers aimed toward the top of the wall. When the men at the bellows cried a warning, the shieldmen, as they'd practiced, skipped nimbly out of the way.

A golden liquid burst from the ends of the bamboo tubes. The aimers ignited it with carefully hoarded firestarters. Half a dozen streams of flowing fire rose to drip from the wall and the Bornu atop it.

Alexios watched in cold satisfaction as shrieking infidels dashed every which way in their agony, spreading the flames as they ran. The liquid fire dripped between lengths of kiltcloth. In moments, the wall itself began to burn.

Some of the black men had the courage and wit to stick to their posts. They poured buckets of water onto the burgeoning flames. The *Basileus* smiled at their cries of dismay, for the fire refused to go out. It was not the precise recipe the Rhomaioi had used in Constantinople; no one on this strange new world had yet found petroleum oozing up from between the rocks. But dragonfish oil made a good enough substitute. Mixed with naphtha, sulfur, and a few other ingredients so secret the engineer who knew them refused to name them even for Alexios, the oil made a hellbrew that burned until it consumed itself or until it was smothered with sand.

The Bornu, though, were ignorant of that trick and had no time to learn it. More and more of them scrambled or jumped off the wall as the flames spread. The Rhomaioi cheered the thick black smoke mounting to the sky.

Alexios gave new orders to the musicians. Their sharp notes pierced the din. The men of New Constantinople obediently formed themselves into a wedge-shaped formation. Here were soldiers you could do something with, Alexios thought—they were brave and obedient at the same time.

A section of the wall fell over with a rending crash. Sparks flew upwards. The flutes screamed. Crying Alexios' name and *Christ with us*, the Rhomaioi surged into the town.

Fighting raged fierce for a few minutes. Then the Bornu began to break and to stream toward the citadel. Alexios caught Isaac's eye. They both grinned. If the town wall, draped with kiltcloth, had burned, what a merry bonfire Musa ar-Rahman's palace would make! The Bornu capital was as good as theirs.

Some of the black men saw that, too. A detachment of perhaps fifty smashed headlong into Alexios' army, struggling desperately to force the men from New Constantinople outside the walls once more. At the head of the detachment was a hooknosed man with full kiltcloth armor and gleaming copper rings in both ears and one nostril. Such a display of wealth could belong only to Musa.

The Sultan spied Alexios at the same instant Alexios recognized him. "To the death between us!" he shouted in Arabic. "Let the winner rule both folk!"

Alexios advanced on him. But when Musa ar-Rahman charged into what he thought was single combat, Isaac Komnenos and three other Rhomaioi also assailed him. Alexios crushed the Sultan's skull with his club, but was never sure afterwards if that was the mortal blow.

The Bornu wailed in horror at the treachery. Alexios remained unfazed. Like the Frankish barbarians whose crusade he'd had to deflect, they were foolish enough to think war was about honor. War was about winning, nothing more.

Their ruler's death took the heart out of the black men. Soon screaming women impeded the army of New Constantinople more than the soldiery of Bornu. Men raised their hands and gave up their grails in token of surrender. "Keep as many alive as you can!" Alexios shouted. "If they die, we lose the food and other good things controlling them would give us."

Musa had been an exception to that rule. He was too cunning, too dangerous to keep around as a grail slave—better that he be reborn somewhere far from New Constantinople and make trouble there. Mutilating him every few months was another alternative, but Alexios didn't care for it. He had his own notions of honor, and cruelty without cause was not part of them.

Before long, only the Sultan's palace still held out against the Rhomaioi. Alexios sent an Arabic-speaking herald forward with a message: "Yield your weapons and your grails and you will not be badly treated. Otherwise, we will use liquid fire against you. You may be born again afterwards, but your deaths will be slow and hideous. Decide quickly, or we will use it anyhow."

He waited. Just as he was about to order the engineers forward, the palace doorway opened. Dejected black men began filing out. They threw their bows and spears and clubs in a pile to the right of the doorway. The pile became mountainously high. The weapons were as good as anything the Rhomaioi used. Alexios decided to store them against future need.

The foraging detail took charge of the black men's grails. The Muslims gave them up even more reluctantly than their arms. Without grails, they were at their conquerors' mercy. If they did not obey henceforward, they would not eat. Oh, a few might slip off and survive on River fish and fruits and tubers from the plants that grew from the Riverbank back into the foothills. But a stretch of land that would support a thousand people with grails might let only a double handful live on it without them.

After the last of the weapons and grails were surrendered, Alexios' record-keepers began taking the names of the Bornu men, women, and adolescents alike. Bamboo pulp replaced the parchment and papyrus the scribes had used at their desks in Constantinople. The Franks, Alexios remembered, had been amazed at the minutiae his officials recorded. But how were you supposed to run a state if you didn't keep track of the people it contained?

The sun began to set over the mountains to the west. As the town's—now *his* town's—grailstone roared and flamed, he let himself feel how tired he was. Then he had to force himself back to abrupt alertness, for one of the

Two Thieves

scouts who had gone downstream from the former Bornu capital came pelting back, shouting, "An army's heading our way!"

One of the black men must have learned some Greek since being reborn along the River—he made a dash for the piled weapons. Rhomaioi sprang after him and speared him down. He lay writhing in agony. "Finish him," Alexios said. One of his warriors smashed in the Bornu's skull. *Let some other king far away deal with a troublemaker*, the *Basileus* thought.

Another scout panted into town. "It's the men of Shytown," he said. The Rhomaioi cheered as if to make their cries echo from the distant mountains. Alexios instantly ordered the news translated into Arabic. The Bornu sank even deeper into despair.

With a well-armed bodyguard around him, Alexios went out to greet his allies. The Shytowners whooped with glee when they recognized him in the failing light. For the moment, all was concord in the two victorious armies. But Mayor Daley also had protectors when he stepped out to meet Alexios between his men and those of the *Basileus*.

Daley spoke. Father Boyle turned his half-intelligible words into Latin for Alexios: "It really did go just the way we planned. How often does that happen in war?"

"Not very," Alexios said, wondering how much the afterman really knew of war. But that didn't matter, not now. As Mayor Daley had said, they'd won. Alexios pushed through his bodyguards and held out his hand to the Mayor. Daley broke through the ranks of his own soldiers to clasp it. For one brief, proud moment, the alliance between them teetered on the edge of true friendship.

Then Daley said, "When do you think you can come to Shytown to be sworn in as Vice Mayor?"

A curious phrase, Alexios thought. But that was by the bye. He focused again on what he would have to do, the gains and the probable costs. He said, "I think we would be wise first to consolidate and garrison what we have won today. Your men are already largely in place, since you are taking five of Bornu's Riverside grailstones to our four. But we still have to push away from the River to seize our extra inland stone to compensate. We may have a bit more fighting to do, though Musa concentrated his men along the River. I will join you—hmm—in one week's time. Then you will visit New Constantinople to be anointed as our *Kaisar*."

Alexios held his voice steady only with effort. A foreigner as *Kaisar* of the Rhomaioi— It had happened once before, when Justinian II rewarded Tervel the Bulgar for backing in a civil war. Alexios still reckoned it disgraceful. But he'd needed Daley as Justinian had needed Tervel. He would pay the price… in his own fashion.

Father Boyle translated his words for the Mayor. Daley said something in the English of the *opisthanthropoi*. The priest dipped his head, then turned back to Alexios: "Hizzonor gives me leave to say a few words of my own to you. In our time and country, the land Constantinople ruled was more often called the Byzantine Empire than the Roman Empire. *Byzantine* became a word in our English, too, meaning subtle, complex, and cunning diplomacy. Having worked with you now, your Majesty, I can see how the word gained that definition."

"You flatter me." Alexios' voice sounded uncommonly like a purr. The thing about flattery, though, was to enjoy it without letting it sway you. "You may tell Hizzonor that he has no mean ability along these lines himself."

Daley rumbled laughter. "One horse thief knows another," he said. That made Alexios laugh, too, and again friendship nearly flowered. But he saw that Daley's smile never quite reached the Mayor's unsettling eyes. They were two of a kind, all right, each trying to manipulate the other.

The *Basileus* nodded to Hizzonor once more, then backed into the company of his own bodyguard. Trouble would come very soon, he thought, if the men of Shytown didn't draw back from this grailtown. The agreed-upon boundary was halfway between it and the next one downstream.

Fatigue smote Alexios again, this time irresistibly. Tomorrow would be time enough to worry about borders.

Two Thieves

Michael Palaiologos and other dignitaries from New Constantinople watched as Alexios Komnenos became Vice Mayor of Shytown: with Bornu gone, Palaiologos would serve as the *Basileus'* envoy to Mayor Daley. Only Isaac Komnenos stayed home for the ceremony, so treachery from Daley could not wipe out all the leaders of the Rhomaioi at once.

Alexios found himself envying his brother. The aftermen might be devious politicians and clever artisans, but they ran boring ceremonies. Hizzonor made a speech that went on and on. Alexios tried for a while to follow the English dialect the *opisthanthropoi* used, but gave up when he concluded Daley wasn't really saying anything.

The *Basileus* expected Father Boyle to administer the vice-mayoral oath to him. That gave him pause: some of his subjects considered followers of the Roman pope like Boyle schismatics. But in fact, a man dressed all in black kiltcloth swore him in; through Boyle, Daley introduced him as Judge Corcoran.

"Judge?" Alexios asked. "A secular title?"

"We separate church and state," Father Boyle answered. Alexios shrugged; that struck him as falling somewhere between incomprehensible and just plain crazy. But how the Shytowners ran their affairs wasn't his business.

"Raise your right hand," Judge Corcoran said. Alexios obeyed. The judge gave him the oath: "Do you solemnly swear to carry out the duties of Vice Mayor of Shytown honestly and to the best of your ability, so help you God?"

The duties of Vice Mayor were, in essence, none. The oath did not refer to any point that had set theologians from Constantinople at odds with those from Rome. In its way, it was admirably simple. Alexios said, "I swear."

Everyone cheered. Like the oath, Mayor Daley's way of celebrating was simple but effective. "Now let's get drunk," Hizzonor boomed. Servants carried in trays with flasks of wine and whisky.

Since being reborn along the River, Alexios had developed a taste for whisky. He liked the way it burned going down but warmed when it got to his middle. He sipped from a flask. "When you come to us," he told Daley, "I'll show you *our* way of doing things." Hizzonor nodded and reached for another whisky himself.

Harry Turtledove

When Mayor Daley descended from his boat to the Riverbank, he advanced into New Constantinople through a double file of torchbearers. A chorus sang his praises. Pretty girls strewed flowers at his feet. He grinned enormously. "Fancy stuff," he said when he met Alexios in front of the imperial palace.

"Why not?" Alexios answered agreeably. "You've met my brother Isaac, I think—the current holder of the title *Kaisar*."

"No hard feelings, I hope," Daley said, perhaps sincerely—his own former Vice Mayor had been a nonentity, not his brother. But Isaac only smiled and shook his head. Hizzonor beamed. "Good, good."

"And here is the ecumenical patriarch of New Constantinople, Evstratios Garidas," Alexios said, pointing to a man in glittering gold kiltcloth. Most priests among the Rhomaioi took the loss of their beards here along the River very hard, but Garidas had always been smooth-chinned—in Constantinople, he'd been a eunuch. Between having his stones for the first time as an adult and the aphrodisiac effects of dreamgum, his chastity took a beating in the days after New Constantinople's folk were resurrected, but he remained a good and pious man.

Daley bowed politely. So did Father Boyle, which, given his probable attitude toward the church of Constantinople, might have required more discipline. The patriarch, his voice more than an octave deeper than Alexios remembered it from the imperial city, said, "Is the Mayor of Shytown prepared to take the oath as *Kaisar* of New Constantinople?" Alexios translated his Greek into Latin for Boyle, who turned it into the aftermen's English.

"I am," Hizzonor said, his voice solemn.

The oath Garidas had Mayor Daley swear was far more ornate and imposing than the one Judge Corcoran had given the *Basileus*. It invoked all three Persons of the Trinity, the Virgin, and a squadron of saints (among them St. Andrew, patron of Constantinople), and called down upon the mayor anathema and damnation if he violated its terms by so much as an iota. "Will you, then, hold to these terms, in the name of the Father, the Son, and the Holy Spirit?" the patriarch finished.

Daley crossed himself. "By the Father, the Son, and the Holy Spirit, I will."

"Bend your head," Garidas said. When Hizzonor obeyed, the patriarch anointed him with fish oil made sweet-smelling with perfume from the grailstones.

Alexios set a circlet of woven grass dyed scarlet round Daley's head. "Hail to our *Kaisar*!" he cried. The people of New Constantinople cheered along with the delegation from Shytown. The chorus sent up a song of praise and thanksgiving.

"Now what?" the newly made *Kaisar* asked.

When do we celebrate? Alexios took him to mean. He said, "We have one thing left to do before the feast begins." Daley folded his arms across his beefy chest and composed himself to wait. The *Basileus* raised his voice: "By elevating Hizzonor to the rank of *Kaisar*, I have left my brother Isaac without a title to suit him. As he is both flesh of my flesh and always at my right hand, by your consent, people of New Constantinople, I propose for him the dignity of *Sebastokrator*, august ruler, said dignity to rank in honor *between* my rank of *Basileus* and that of the *Kaisar*."

"Let it be so!" the people shouted, as they'd been coached. *Sebastokrator*, a rank Alexios had invented back on Earth, was the title Isaac Komnenos had held most of his life there; in New Constantinople, the *Basileus* had resimplified the hierarchy. But the old title stayed around in case it ever seemed useful, as it did today.

Alexios did not translate his proclamation of Isaac as *Sebastokrator* into Latin for Father Boyle; the longer Mayor Daley remained in blissful ignorance of what was going on around him, the happier the *Basileus* would have been. It transpired, however, that Father Boyle understood enough Greek to realize what was happening. That did not surprise Alexios; the Mayor was merely being prudent by having in his retinue someone who could follow the language of New Constantinople. Alexios had had a couple of English-speakers with him at Shytown.

He could gauge almost to the second when Hizzonor realized he'd been tricked. Daley must have had Celtic ancestors, for his skin was as fair as any Frankish Crusader's. All at once, he turned brick red. "What the hell!" he bellowed, a roar of outrage even Alexios had no trouble translating.

Evstratios Garidas had almost finished administering the oath to Isaac. He paused, looked a question to Alexios. "Continue, your holiness," the *Basileus* said calmly. Garidas continued. Only after he had finished anointing the newly named *Sebastokrator*, thus making Isaac's title indissoluble, did Alexios concern himself with his profanely displeased *Kaisar*.

Voice bland as butter, the *Basileus* turned to Mayor Daley. "Why are you unhappy? I named you *Kaisar* of New Constantinople as I promised. Had we gold, I'd have given you a crown rather than that fillet, but it is no less fine than the one Isaac wears."

Daley threw the red-dyed fillet on the ground and stamped on it. "You son of a bitch, you cheated me!"

"Before God, I did not," Alexios answered. "As a condition for our alliance, you required me to name you *Kaisar*. I agreed, and the alliance did all we hoped it would: Bornu is no more, and we have divided its lands fairly between Shytown and New Constantinople. Nowhere did you require me not to appoint a lord of rank intermediate between mine and yours. That I have done, for the security of my own realm. But cheat you? I deny it, and deny it with clear conscience."

The Mayor stared at him. Cool calculation alone should have been enough to calm Hizzonor's wrath; the Rhomaioi had him and his delegation at their mercy, if they chose to attack. But Daley's glance never went to the gathered men of New Constantinople; he watched Alexios alone. And then, to Alexios' amazement, Hizzonor threw back his head and shouted laughter to the sky. "You son of a bitch, you cheated me," he said again. The words were as they had been a minute before, but their tone altogether different.

The Mayor slapped the *Basileus* on the back, hard enough to stagger him. A couple of Alexios' guards growled and took a step toward Daley, but Alexios waved them back. "Now that you know I can, perhaps we'll have a better chance of living next to each other in peace," he told Hizzonor. "One thing I've noticed about you *opisthanthropoi* is that you think anyone from before your own time has to be foolish. Would you have proposed this arrangement of ours to one of your contemporaries? They would have seen through it to your true intentions, and so have I."

"Most of them wouldn't, by God," Daley said. He did not mention that his true intentions were murderous, any more than Alexios had. Sometimes that was part of the game. Hizzonor laughed again, even louder than before. "All right, I'm *Kaisar* and it doesn't matter worth a damn. I know what I do the first thing I get back to Shytown, though."

"What's that?" Alexios asked.

"Appoint myself an Associate Mayor—what else?"

It was the *Basileus'* turn to laugh. "Fair enough. *Now* we feast."

The Man Who Came Late

Most of what I didn't learn about writing from L. Sprague de Camp, I learned from Poul Anderson. He probably taught me more about how to tell a story and about what a story is than anyone else. That, toward the end of his life, we became friends is one of the things in this business I'm proudest of. This story first appeared in his memorial anthology, dammit. It's set in the multiverse that contains the world of *Three Hearts and Three Lions*; the title is a riff on that of a splendid short story of his, "The Man Who Came Early." If you notice a bit more of a style recalling his here than in most of the other pieces in this book, it's not by accident. I wish he could have seen it. I hope he would have approved.

ALIANORA CARRIED A bucket to the well in the tiny green at the heart of the village. She needed the water. She'd used what there was in the house the night before to soak green and yellow peas. She aimed to cook up a big pot of pease porridge, and enliven the flavor with chopped onion and some fennel she'd got from a wandering trader and bits of salt pork.

Her long wool skirt almost stirred up dust as she walked along. Most village women embroidered flowers or bright birds on their linen tunics. She'd ornamented hers with dragons. Maybe—no, surely—they talked about her behind her back. Well, that was all right. They gossiped about one another the same way. And she joined in. In a place where great things never happened, what could you do but go on about small ones?

She knew about great things. She'd lived through a dragon's onslaught, something of which few mortals could boast. (Not that she *did* boast—what point to it?) She'd met elflords and sorceresses and high nobles of the human kind as well…and here she was, wed to the smith who'd forged the iron hoops that bound the bucket's oaken staves.

Sometimes she wondered whether the war against Chaos that had engulfed the whole world thirty years before was meant to bring nothing more splendid than countless villages, all of them places where great things never happened, scattered through plains and forests. But what better result could the war have birthed? If ordinary folk were able to live ordinary lives free from anything worse than ordinary fears, didn't things wag the way they should?

She smiled when she passed the smithy. Theodo waved back through the open door. He was never too busy to look out whenever someone went by. Part of that came from having two strapping sons learning the trade. Part sprang from life in a place like this. Anything that chanced was perforce noticeable and interesting, because not much did.

The smile stayed on Alianora's face as she walked on. Theodo was a good man, a kind man. He'd never struck her in anger, never once. He'd clouted Einhard and Nithard only when they'd really and truly earned it. His hands might be scarred and callused and hard, but they were gentle in the quiet dark. A good man. A kind man. Perhaps not the most exciting man God ever made, but…

"I've had enough excitements, enough and to spare," Alianora whispered fiercely. Her own work-roughened hands tightened on the bucket's handle. Having magic-dashing cold iron in the family, so to speak, wasn't such a bad thing even today.

No, not half. The blue gloaming that warded Faerie folk from the daylight they could not bear had retreated many leagues after Chaos' latest grand assault on the lands of Law went awry. Yet still you could see it on the horizon from here. It had even moved forward again, a little, once or twice, in the years since then. Law's nature, after all, was to forget and to forgive.

The Man Who Came Late

Chaos did neither, it seemed, and found more agents within Law's borders to work its will than would ever be so in reverse.

Not that all wizardry was wicked. Oh, no! Alianora's smile subtly changed. Her daughter Alianna wore the white, feathered swan-may's tunic these days, and wore it wondrous well. Somewhere in the priests' holy Book it said there was a time for everything, and there as elsewhere the Book spoke true.

Alianora knew without—too much—resentment that her own time for the swan-may's tunic lay behind her. Three decades and four children (one tiny body had lain in hallowed ground since before its first saint's day, an unending sadness) had widened the hips to which that tunic once clung. She'd lost two teeth and gained wrinkles; encroaching gray streaked and dulled her red hair.

But when she dreamt of flying, she knew whereof she dreamt! Everyone flew in dreams. Almost everyone had to imagine what it was like. Alianora *knew* the wind beneath her wings, *knew* the joy of soaring on streams of warm air gusting up from the ground, *knew* the wonder of freedom and speed in three dimensions.

She glanced up into the watery sky to see if she might catch a glimpse of Alianna. No; wherever her daughter flew today, it was not near here. Just as well. Who didn't want to fly wide when young, to streak over the fields and the meadows and the dark woods beyond? A village was for settling down, for later. When you were Alianna's age, you thought later never came. You thought all kinds of things when you were Alianna's age.

Here was the green, and the stone-ringed well. Behind Alianora, Theodo's hammer rang against the anvil. The iron he beat into shape there wouldn't be cold, not yet. As always, she hoped he wouldn't come home nursing a burn. He was careful, but once in a while everyone slipped.

Four or five women stood near the well. Berthrada's twin blond boys toddled by her feet. One of them stooped and plucked up some grass or maybe a bug and stuck it in his mouth. She hadn't seemed to be watching, but she grabbed him, thrust a finger in there, and got rid of whatever it was.

Mothers had, and needed, eyes in the back of the head. Berthrada swatted her son on the bottom, not too hard, and set him down again.

Alianora nodded to the women as she came up. They nodded back. It wasn't quite as if she'd been born and raised here, even if her husband had. She'd been places and done things they were just as well pleased not to know too much about. And the brief, form-fitting swan-may's tunic that had been hers and was now mostly Alianna's brought a whiff of scandal with it.

Still and all, she lived here quietly enough, as she had for many years now. She made eyes at no man but her own. Her sons would be catches; no doubt of that. So Ethelind the miller's wife said, "Have you heard the latest about Walacho and his poor sorry family?"

"What now?" Alianora asked sadly, working on the crank to bring up a bucket of well water. Any sensible man drank beer instead when he could; if you drank water all the time, you pretty much begged for a flux of the bowels. Walacho wasn't such a sensible man. He drank to get drunk, and when he got drunk he got mean. He did things he was sorry for later, which helped him as much as it did anyone else.

Before Ethelind could come out with—or embroider upon—the juicy details of his latest rampage, Berthrada pointed out to the edge of the woods and exclaimed, "Look! A stranger's coming!"

Ethelind shot her a dirty look. Walacho's ordinary folly would have to wait for another time. Strangers didn't come to the village every day, or every week, either. This one might give folk here things to talk about till the next one showed up.

He tramped along with determined strides, like a man who has been traveling for a long time and knows he may have to keep going longer yet. He was a big man, tall and broad through the shoulders. He wore a green plaid wool shirt with a stand-and-fall collar; sturdy, snug-fitting trousers dyed a blue not quite that of woad; and ankle-length brown leather boots. A scabbarded sword hung on his left hip, a sheathed knife on his right.

"Well, heaven knows I've seen worse," Berthrada murmured when he was still a little too far away to hear her.

The Man Who Came Late

"He's too old for you, dear," Ethelind said, also softly. She freighted the last word with poisonous sweetness.

No matter how catty that made her, it didn't make her wrong. The stranger's fair hair—so fair, telling how much gray it held was hard—receded at the temples. Harsh grooves scored his forehead and the skin between his nostrils and the corners of his mouth. When you got a good look at it, his nose had a distinct dent.

When Alianora got a good look at that dent, it was as if someone had punched her, hard, on the point of the chin. She sagged. Her hands slipped off the crank. It spun backwards, and almost did clip her in the face. She wondered if she would even have noticed. She'd already been hit harder than that.

"Holger," she said, and groped for the stone wall around the well to help steady herself.

His eyes snapped sharply toward her. They were blue as she remembered, blue as a deep lake seen from the sky when she soared above it in swan's guise. But he had not known her till she spoke his name. Grief flamed within her for that.

"Alianora?" he said. "Is it really you at last?" Blood drained from his weathered face, leaving it lich-pale.

"Aye," she answered. She'd told him she loved him, there in the ruined church of St. Grimmin's. And he'd taken the sword Cortana, which he'd found hidden there, and he'd ridden forth on his great black horse, and he'd broken the forces of Chaos, for they could not stand against him and what he bore.

And that was thirty long years ago now, even if it sometimes seemed like yesterday. It might seem so, but seeming was not reality.

"My dear," he said. "My love." He took a step in her direction. The village women stared avidly, their eyes wide as saucers. Even Berthrada's twins peeped out from behind their mother's skirts.

Alianora straightened. It was like taking a wound. Once the first shock passed, you steadied—if it wasn't mortal, of course. "You never came back to me," she said, as if that were all the explanation she needed. Perhaps it was. No one died of a broken heart, regardless of how many people wished they could.

Holger's hands dropped. He had started to get his color back. Now he whitened again. "I couldn't, dammit," he mumbled, staring down at the grass and dirt between his feet. "The magics that brought me here swept me back to the world where I'd lived before. I was needed there, too, it turned out."

She believed him absolutely. That more than one world might require the services of such a hero… Well, who could doubt it? In the end, though, what difference did it make? Two worlds might need Holger, but so had she—then. "You never came back to me," she repeated, this time adding, "I thought sure I would never see you again."

He cocked his head to one side. A small, tight, crooked smile came and went. "You don't talk the way you used to," he said, sliding away from what she'd told him.

She knew what he meant. When he'd known her before, she'd had a thick back-country burr. It wasn't the way folk in the villages around here spoke. To fit in better, she'd softened the burr as much as she could.

"I've dwelt in these parts a long time now," she said, talking the way she talked.

"I know. I've been trying to get to these parts for a long time now." Holger stared off toward the horizon, and toward the blue Fairie gloaming darkening one stretch of it. "I've been to a lot of places—a lot of worlds. But Something or Somebody kept holding me away from this one. I can make a pretty good guess Who, too."

Alianora could make that same guess. If the Powers Holger had bested here had their way, they would never want to see him again. And, even if they'd lost their war to rule this world wholly, their strength was not to be despised.

"I wonder that you succeeded in their despite," she said, her voice softening a little.

"You'd better believe I did, kiddo. I don't give up, no matter what." He stuck out his chin. He was in good hard shape for a man his age—in extraordinary shape for a man his age—but the flesh under there still sagged. Well, so did the flesh under Alianora's chin. The earth dragged you down towards it, and then it dragged you down into it, and then…you found out for sure what came afterwards.

"Thirty years. I was thinking on that earlier today," Alianora said.

Holger nodded brusquely. "A devil of a long time," he agreed. "I made it, though." He looked at her as if she were the only thing in all the world—no, in all the worlds.

Once upon a time, that look would have melted her the way a mild spring morning melts the last winter frost. To a certain extent, it still did—but only to a certain extent. She was no longer who she had been in those dark and desperate days. Nor was he. She knew as much. She was far from sure he could say the same.

"So much time gone by," she murmured.

"Not too much. We still have a good bit left," he said.

She made herself meet that intent gaze. It wasn't far removed from crossing swords. "Thirty years," she repeated. "Thirty years of faring betwixt—amongst—the worlds for you."

"I was always trying to get here," Holder said. "Always." The word clanged in his mouth.

Alianora nodded. "I believe you." Even with the white tunic, she hadn't flown so far as she used to do. After the war, the sullen, sulking, beaten Middle World was no longer such a welcoming place. Since Alianna took wing in her stead, she didn't think she'd gone farther than a day's walk from the village. As gently as she could, she asked, "In all your wanderings, did you never, ah, meet anyone who made you want to leave off and bide where you found yourself?"

He looked down at the ground once more: dull embarrassment this time. "I won't lie to you. There's been a girl or three. You know how things are." He spread his hands. A swordsman's calluses marked his right palm.

She did know how things were. A knight errant spent his nights erring—that was what they said, anyhow. How the woman he loved—the woman who loved him—felt when he did, he could always worry about later…if he worried about it at all.

Holger raised his big head. Fierce intensity filled his stare. "But there was never anybody else, babe. Never really. Never so it counted here—" He touched himself on the heart. "Only below the belt, if you know what I mean." He chuckled.

Again, Alianora knew. Pity stabbed through her. "Why not, Holger?" she asked. "Why not, in heaven's name? So many long, dry years…"

She didn't think he heard, or noticed, that last. "I'll tell you why not. Because all I ever cared about in this miserable universe is you, that's why. Because I aimed to go on till I found you, no matter what I had to do, no matter how long it took. And here I am." His pride blazed like a forest fire.

Trying to deflect it seemed wisest. "All you ever cared for is me, say you? You know you speak not sooth. What of Morgan le Fay?"

He didn't flinch. She wished he would have. "Well, what about her?" he said roughly. "That was a long time ago, and in another country, and besides, I hadn't met you yet. I never would've busted my hump the way I did, fighting back to this world for the likes of *her*, and you can take that to the bank. But you, you're worth it."

He was convinced she was; she heard as much in his voice. He had to be, lest all he'd done and suffered this past half a lifetime turn to dust and blow away like fairy gold tried on an anvil of cold iron. "Surely life goes on wherever one wanders," Alianora said. "Surely, had you sought, you would have found many, or one at least, not so very different from me."

"No way. Not a chance." Holger had vast reserves of stubbornness. Without them, he never would have won Cortana, never would have had the chance to scatter the host of Chaos before him. Now… Now he said, "You're the one, the only one."

"Oh, Holger." Alianora tried to make him hear what he would not see: "I am no more the lass you wooed."

The Man Who Came Late

He wasn't listening. And he had his reasons: his eyes shifted away from her, and his yellow-callused hand dropped to the hilt of his sword. "Who're these clowns?" he ground out. "They better make tracks, kid. They mess with me, it's the last dumb stunt they ever pull."

Alianora turned to follow his gaze. One of the other women by the well must have hotfooted it back to the smithy. Alianora hadn't noted anyone leaving, but to say she was distracted only proved the weakness of words. Here came Theodo, a heavy hammer clutched in his fist. Behind his strode Einhard and Nithard, one with an axe, the other with a cleaver.

"Hold!" Alianora spoke quickly to her kinsmen. "This is the famous Sir Holger, come to call after all these years."

Einhard and Nithard broke into delighted grins. They knew she'd been friends with the paladin in the great days before they were born. Now at last they got to meet a hero in the flesh! Theodo's face was a study. He knew rather more than they did, and liked what he knew rather less. So long as Holger was gone and stayed gone, it didn't bother him—much. Now that he got to meet the hero in the flesh…

Seeing them lower their weapons, Holger also took his hand away from his sword, though not very far. He asked once more, "Who are these people?" This time, the question sounded cautious and formal rather than ferocious.

With relief, Alianora too chose formality: "Sir Holger, I have the honor to present to you my sons. The tall one is Einhard; the redhead, Nithard. With them stands my husband, Theodo."

Her sons rushed up to clasp the hero's hand. Theodo hung back a little, but only a little. He also set his hard palm against Holger's. He didn't pound the paladin on the back the way Einhard and Nithard did, or help try to lift him off his feet. The gray streaks in his beard excused his lack of youthful enthusiasm. Other things, perhaps, excused his lack of enthusiasm of any sort.

As for Holger... Alianora might have known—hellfire, *had* known—formality wouldn't be enough. While the puppies pounded on him and Theodo gave him more restrained greeting, he looked like a man who'd just taken a boot in the belly out of nowhere.

When the commotion around him eased a little, he stared over at Alianora with that astonished disbelief still all over his face. "Your...sons?" he said. He might never have heard the word before.

"Aye," Alianora answered stolidly.

"Your...husband?" By the way Holger said it, he had heard that word before, and didn't fancy it a barleycorn's worth. Theodo caught the same thing. He unobtrusively shifted the hammer from his left hand back to his right.

Alianora nodded. "Aye," she said again. It was the truth. Why should she not repeat it? Why should she want to weep when she did?

"But how did that happen?" Holger asked, still lost, speaking as if of flood or fire or other natural catastrophe.

"How do you think?" For the first time, irritation rose against sympathy in Alianora. "You were *gone*, Holger. Gone off the battlefield. Gone from human ken. Gone from the ken of other folk, too, as I have reason to know. Even smarting from their loss, the Middle Worlders laughed that I should have looked for aught else. So I came hither one day, and I met Theodo, and this is all these years and three grown children later." She raised her head and looked him full in the face. She'd essayed nothing harder since she last lay down in childbed, but she did it. "I would not change it now even if I could."

Einhard and Nithard blinked at her. They understood that they didn't understand everything that was going on. She sighed within herself. She would have a deal of explaining to do to them, and to Alianna. One of these days. Not today. Today had its own sorrows.

Theodo hung on to the hammer. How not? Alianora sometimes thought he set it down only to make love to her. Well, she never would have wanted a man who was not a willing worker. His grip eased a bit, though. He must have had his own fears about this moment, if it ever came. She'd slain some of them, at any rate.

The Man Who Came Late

"But... But..." Holger gaped like a boated carp. "I never gave up looking for you, looking for a way back here. Never once, never for a minute, never in thirty years. Now I make it, and what do I find?"

"That life went on whilst you were busy with other things?" Alianora suggested. His gape only got wider. She sighed again, out loud this time. "Holger, how could I know what you strove for, there in your other world? Even did I know, how could I guess you'd succeed?"

"You should've." Holger muttered to himself, scowling and shaking his head. He might bring out the words, but he had trouble believing them himself.

"Here. Wait." Alianora began bringing up the bucket of water again. "Your coming fair made me forget why I was at the well. I aim to stew up a great kettle of pease porridge, for supper this even and for as long after that as it may last. Will you come home and eat with us?"

He grinned crookedly—more the expression she remembered him wearing than the loss and rage that had been chasing each other across his features. "Bread and salt, Carahue would say."

"That's the Moor's custom, not mine, but I think it a good one," Alianora answered. After you ate with someone, trying to cut out his liver ought to be bad form.

"He's probably got himself a harem." Holger's grin widened. "Song girls and dancing girls and girls to peel grapes for him and drop them into his mouth. Oh, and about fifty-eleven kids, too. I bet he's fat, but happy."

"It would not surprise me. He always fancied the good things in life," Alianora said.

"Well, so did I." Holger looked straight at her.

More than anything else, that was what made her say, "Theodo, why don't you close the smithy, and you and the boys come home with us? 'Tis a holiday—an unlooked-for holiday, which makes it but the sweeter."

"Aye, I'll do it," Theodo said at once. He didn't want Alianora alone with Holger. She didn't want—she didn't think she wanted—that, either. Her feelings for him might be buried, but they lay restless in the grave. Best give them no chance to see light of day once more. And also best to give no one here the least excuse to think of scandal. Some of the women would regardless; they were made so. But no one else ought to be able to hearken to their vinegar tongues.

"Not a great big place, is this?" Holger remarked as they walked back to the house. He carried the water bucket. Theodo gave him a quizzical look when he lifted it, but at Alianora's quick gesture lowered his eyebrows and kept quiet. Holger had always been full of such small, strange courtesies.

"Grandest village for twenty miles around," Nithard said proudly. Holger nodded, polite as an elflord. If he also smiled for one brief moment, Alianora was pretty sure she was the only one who noticed.

She stirred the peas and strewed in salt. After adding the fennel—its spicy scent made her nostrils twitch—she cut the pork into little cubes. It went into the kettle, too.

"Will you chop some more firewood for me?" she asked Theodo.

"Aye." He went out to do it without a backward glance. Einhard and Nithard chaperoned Alianora better than well enough, even if they didn't realize that was what they were doing. They wanted every cut and thrust of Holger's adventures in this world, in the one where he'd spent some years, and in the others he'd passed through on his long, roundabout journey back here. To help loosen his tongue, they broached a barrel of beer Alianora hadn't planned on opening so soon.

Holger was a good talespinner, of the kind who could laugh at himself and his blunders: one more thing Alianora recalled from bygone days. She'd lived through some of his stories, and heard others before—how they came back! Others still were new to her. The feathered demons—or were they pagan gods?—who ate hearts and drank blood made her shiver in spite of herself.

Theodo had come back in with an armload of wood. Alianora scarcely noticed. Her husband got caught up in Holger's latest tale, too. When the knight paused to wet his whistle, Theodo asked, "This is truth, not just a yarn spun for the sake of yarning?"

"Truth." Holger signed himself to show he meant it. "Oh, sometimes neatened up a bit for the sake of the story, and maybe the way I remember it now isn't exactly the way it happened then, but…close enough for government work, they say in the other world where I lived a long time."

The phrase sounded odd to Alianora, but Theodo grasped it at once. "That is truth," he agreed gravely. "As near as a mortal man's likely to come to it, any road." He took up the beechwood dipper and poured himself a stoup of beer.

Holger refilled his own mug, not for the first time. He sipped appreciatively. "Mighty fine stuff," he said.

"I have a charm against souring I got years ago in the Middle World," Alianora said. "It works as well on this side of the border, so there must be no harm in it."

"Not unless you're the wrong kind of *microorganism*." That last must have been a word from some other world, for it meant nothing to Alianora—nor, plainly, to her kinsmen. Holger took another pull at the beer. "I saw a tavern near the well," he said. "If you can brew like this, I'm surprised you don't run it out of business."

"We would never do that!" Theodo sounded shocked. "Gerold needs must make his living, too."

"Besides, brewing a barrel of beer now and again is one thing. Brewing enough for a thirsty village, that's summat else altogether," Alianora added.

"Mm, I shouldn't wonder if you're right," Holger said after a little thought. "You always did have a good head on your shoulders, and not just for looks."

Alianora's cheeks heated. Theodo scowled. Then Einhard, not noticing anything amiss, said, "Sir Holger, will you speak more of these… Nasties, did you call 'em?"

"Nazis," Holger corrected. His face went hard. "Though Nasties is a good name for them, too. Some ways, I think they were worse than any of the evils that haunt this world, because the only devils that drove them boiled up from the bottom of their own shriveled souls."

He told some of what they had done. Only two things made Alianora believe him: that his voice held unmistakable conviction, and that no one could or would invent such horrors for the sake of making talk spin along. It was as if, for a time, a shadow hovered under the roof thatching.

Alianora got the fire on the hearth built up the way she wanted. She hung the cauldron of porridge above it. Then she said, "Shall we get out into the open air a while, to let it cook?" That made a fair enough reason, but she also wanted to escape the shadow that—she hoped—wasn't really there. She knew she would never eye a fylfot the same way after this.

"It is a trifle smoky in here," Holger said. Theodo laughed under his breath. Einhard and Nithard both smiled. With the forge always blazing in the smithy, they knew more of smoke than Holger would…or did they?

"What became of your pipe, wherein you burned the nickels' smoking-leaf?" Alianora asked him as they went out to the little plot of vegetables and herbs by the side of the house. A hen that was pecking at something clucked at the interruption and scuttled away.

"I gave it up. Didn't much want to, but I did." Sure enough, Holger's voice was plangent with regret. But he went on, "The miserable doctors have shown it steals years off the back end of your life. I still miss it sometimes, I will say."

"Doctors!" Theodo snorted scorn. "Me, I'd sooner go to a priest. He has a better chance of fixing what ails me."

"In this world, a priest would," Holger agreed. "Not in all of them, though. Some places, a sawbones knows as much about the way your body works as you do about shaping iron. He knows what's good for you, and he knows what isn't. And smoking isn't, and there's no way in the world—in any world—to pretend it is."

Theodo hoisted his tankard. "Next thing you know, you'll try and tell me beer is bad, too." He laughed. So did his sons and Alianora.

So did Holger, but he said, "There are people—bluenoses, we call 'em—across the worlds who'll tell you just that. I'm sure not one of 'em, though."

"I should hope not!" Theodo reached for the knight's mug. "Fill you up again?"

"Much obliged." Holger handed it to him.

The Man Who Came Late

Alianora went back inside, too, to stir the porridge. As Theodo dipped out more beer, he spoke in a low voice: "I do see why you cared for him. And if you think I'm sorry to have a long lead now he's back in the race, you're daft."

"Don't sound more foolish than you can help," she answered tartly. "There is no race, nor shall there be." There wouldn't have been a race had Holger ridden back from the battlefield, either. But that was a different story, one that hadn't happened. She'd done the best she could in the one that had.

All the same, she poured herself a fresh mug before following her husband outside once more. Sometimes the world needed a bit of blurring.

Holger had launched into another tale, about a folk he called Reds. Einhard and Nithard listened, entranced. "Now, the measure of the Reds' damnation was that tens of thousands of their men took service with the Nazis against their own liege lord," the knight said. "The measure of the Nazis' damnation, though, was that almost every other realm in the world allied with the Reds' liege lord, wicked though he was, against them."

Einhard frowned. "Even the realms of Law? Did not this wicked Red serve Chaos as much as the Nazis' chief did?"

"He served Chaos, I think, yes, but less than the Nazis did." Holger gnawed on his underlip. "Things aren't always so black-and-white in that world as they are here. They—" He broke off.

A great white shape gyred down out of the sky toward the vegetable plot. Broad wings thuttered as the swan braked against air. Muscles in Alianora's shoulders tensed, remembering those automatic motions. Only a woman's muscles now, but still...

Suddenly the swan was swan no more, but Alianna, her bare toes digging into the soft, black dirt of the plot. She studied Holger with frank curiosity. "God give you good day, sir," she said; she'd always been a mannerly lass. "Who might you be?"

His eyes almost bugged out of his head. He started violently and shaped the sign of the cross on his chest. "*Jesu Kriste!*" he barked out.

FOR FAR from the first time that mad day, tears stung Alianora. Just so had Holger responded when she first transformed from swan shape to her own before him. Then he'd reckoned the very notion of magic all but incredible. He knew better now; else he'd never have found his way back to this world, this village. Too often, though, you forgot what a useless thing mere knowing could be.

Holger stared at Alianna. She'd just turned eighteen. Her hair was red, though darker than Nithard's. The spotless swan-may's tunic covered enough of her for decency's sake, but accented her sweet young curves.

"*Jesu Kriste*," Holger said again, in a hoarse whisper this time, a whisper that struck Alianora as something close to true prayer. "Oh, *Jesu Kriste!*" Slowly, slowly, his gaze swung from Alianna to Alianora and back again.

Alianora knew what he was seeing, or thought he was seeing: her, as she'd been in the days when they were both young and everything stretched ahead of them. He stared down at the backs of his hands. The loose, age-freckled skin and the harsh tendons standing out like tree roots where the soil was washing away told him how lost those days were.

"Alack, the poor bugger!" Theodo murmured in Alianora's ear. He was thinking along with her again. After so long together, scant surprise there.

"Sir?" In the way Alianna repeated the word, she let her patience show. She had no notion what the sight of her was doing to this unexpected guest.

Alianora did what little she could: "Alianna, here before you stands the great Sir Holger, of whom you'll have heard me speak many a time. Holger, Alianna is the youngest chick in my brood."

Her daughter's face lit like sunrise. "Sir Holger? The famous Sir Holger? Come *here*?" She dropped him a curtsy more heartfelt than practiced.

Holger made heavier going of it. "Your chick? You said you had two—" He stopped short, looking absurdly astonished, and thumped himself in the forehead with the heel of his hand. "No. Wait. You did say you had three kids. You said, and either I didn't quite hear it or I didn't think what it might mean." He managed a ragged bow. "Alianna, you're…as pretty as your mother was." A tiny pause as he looked back to Alianora. "Is."

The Man Who Came Late

"Gramercy, sir knight," Alianna said. "She tells such tales of you, and of the days when you twain strove together against Chaos! I never thought to meet a grand paladin in the flesh!" She clapped her hands together.

"Here I am, such as I am." The old, familiar self-mockery sounded in Holger's snort. He held out his mug to Alianora. Almost plaintively, he said, "This got empty some kind of way. Could you fix that, please?"

"Certes." Alianora took it and went inside.

She gave the bubbling cauldron another stir. As she dipped up more beer from the barrel, she heard Alianna say, "Oh, Sir Holger, will you not grant us the boon of some tales of your brave adventures?"

"What do you suppose he's *been* doing?" Einhard sounded as snotty as only an older brother could. "If you'd stuck around instead of flying all over creation or swimming in a pond and sticking your tail up in the air whenever you spied summat tasty at the bottom—"

Theodo's rumbled "That will be enough—more than enough—of that" rose above Alianna's irate squeak.

"Yes, more than enough," Holger agreed as Alianora came out again. He nodded to her as he took back the stoup and drank from it. Then his gaze returned to Alianna. "I don't mind spinning out a few more stories if you folks can put up with listening to 'em." He might have been talking to all of them, but he had eyes for only one—with the occasional bemused glance at her mother.

Alianna couldn't have made a better audience had she rehearsed for the role. She laughed in all the right places. She clapped her hands some more when the story turned exciting. Whenever magic intruded, her eyes—they were green, not blue like Alianora's—widened.

Theodo blew on a fire with a goatskin bellows when he wanted to make it hotter. All unwittingly, Alianna had the same effect on Holger. He paid less and less heed to anybody else. Alianna basked in his attention, probably because, like Alianora at the same age, she wasn't used to getting much.

Alianora wasn't alone in noticing. After a while, Theodo said, "Sir knight, will you walk a little ways with me? Alianora, you may as well come, too."

When their sons and daughter started to follow along, the smith held up a hand. "Nay, bide you here, an't please you. This is for the older heads. We'll be back betimes, I vow."

Einhard, Nithard, and Alianna all looked dissatisfied, each, perhaps, for different reasons. In the face of Theodo's stony stare, though, and Alianora's, they did not try to press their luck.

Holger didn't seem happy to cut short his latest yarn, either. But he did it with such good grace as he could muster. Theodo and Alianora led him along a narrow, muddy path through the fields—and away from the children. Holger did have the wit to wait till they got out of earshot before asking, "Well, what's this all about?"

"Sir knight…" Theodo stopped and scuffed one boot in the dirt. Then he squared his shoulders. Though shorter than Holger, he was nearly as broad through them. "Sir knight, I want you to understand I speak to you without meaning to offend. Can you do that, please?"

"Go on," Holger said grimly. "I'll try my best."

"For which I cry your grace." Theodo sketched a salute. "Now, I am but a simple fellow, and not a traveled man. I can only tell you how things seem to me, and how they'd look to other village folk."

"You can cut out the sandbagging." Holger's voice was desert-dry. When he saw Theodo and Alianora didn't follow the phrase, he explained it: "Say what you mean to say, and never mind all the 'simple fellow' garbage."

A ghost of a smile crossed Theodo's face and was gone before Alianora could be sure she saw it. "Right well said. I will, then: when a man your age, or mine, looks on a lass like Alianna the way you've looked on her this past hour and more, well, here in the village we make goaty jokes about it. Is it the same other places you've seen, or is it otherwise?"

Holger's cheeks flamed the color of heated iron. "I— I— I—" He tried three times, but nothing more came out. Then he tilted his head back and drained the stoup of beer, larynx bobbing as he swallowed. He took a deep breath, and another one. This time, he managed to speak: "I beg your pardon, Theodo. I did not know I was looking at her that way."

"Well, you were," Theodo said. Holger's eyes asked Alianora a silent question. Regretfully, she nodded. He had been.

He winced. He swore in the language Alianora used, and added things that sounded hot in what seemed like several others. "I must be a perfect jackass," he said at last. He met Theodo's eyes with a courage Alianora had to admire. "And to answer your question, they joke about pretty young girls and not-so-young men everywhere I've ever been. I expect God made those jokes about twenty minutes after He finished making the world—uh, worlds. Maybe even sooner."

"Mm, I'd not know about that," Theodo said uncomfortably. Like Alianora, like most of the villagers, he spoke little of God. Such things were more for priests than for the likes of them. She remembered Holger had always had an easier way with the Deity. She'd got used to it in the bygone days. No doubt she could again.

"Shall we go back now, before the children do come after us?" she said.

She looked to Theodo, but her husband only shrugged. It fell on Holger to answer the question. "Yes, let's," he said. "I'll behave myself, honest."

"We do understand the why of it, Sir Holger," Alianora said as they ambled toward the house once more. She almost said *dear Holger*, as she had so often while he was here before. But it would not do now. It most especially would not do right this minute. After a beat, she went on, "You've had yourself a whole great stack o' surprises since you came forth from yon woods."

"Surprises." Holger's chuckle was mirthless. "Oh, you might say so. Yes, you just might."

Alianora heard the pain that lay under the laugh. "I would not hurt you for the world, Sir Holger," she said, and came even closer than before to *dear Holger*. Theodo heard it whether she said it or not. He made a small noise down deep in his chest. She ignored it; she'd square things with him later. Meanwhile… "The world wags as it wags, not always as we wish it would. We move on. We change." She waved at the impatiently waiting Einhard, Nithard, and Alianna. Alianna waved back.

"Yeah. Right." Holger's forced smile likely masked tears. "Only I didn't, did I? I spent all those years wandering from one world to the next, or else in some of the places between them all. I was going to get back here, and nothing was gonna stop me no matter what. And I don't think I ever once stopped to wonder what in blazes you'd be doing. You were—"

"In amber in your mind?" Alianora suggested. She had a bauble from Theodo, a tear of the sun with a tiny ant trapped inside forever.

"Yes!" Agreement exploded out of Holger. "That's it. That's just it! And a whole fat lot of good seeing it now does me."

"Well, I am glad you came again," Alianora said: one more thing she would have to set right with Theodo. But it was so, even if not the way Holger would have wanted. Like anyone else, she had her own measure of vanity.

Nithard aimed a rather predatory grin at them. "Well, what were the lot of you going on about where we couldn't hearken?"

Deadpan, Holger answered, "What a rotten bunch of brats your mother's gone and raised—what else?"

Alianora's second son opened his mouth, then wisely closed it again without saying anything more. Some scraps you not only couldn't win, you only made yourself look sillier when you tried. He at least had the sense to see as much.

Alianna, now... Alianna batted her eyes at Holger and murmured, "Now, good sir knight, you don't mean that of me?" in tones that should have been sinful if anyone but their intended victim heard them—and were bound to be sinful if he alone did.

But Holger just threw back his head and laughed. All right, he'd been besotted for a little while, likely as much for what he remembered as for what he saw. As with any other man of his years, though, it was more his imagination that kindled than aught else.

"You ought to go wash your mouth out with beer, young lady," he said. "And if that doesn't work, somebody needs to turn you over his knee and paddle you."

The Man Who Came Late

Alianna gaped. Then she looked miffed, as any witch might when one of her spells fell to pieces instead of working the magic she had in mind. And then, after a few tense heartbeats, she laughed, too: she was good-natured Alianora's good-natured daughter. If she didn't quite know yet how to keep a man three times her age inflamed, then she didn't, that was all. *Just as well, too*, Alianora thought.

"I hope you'll go on with your tales, Sir Holger," Theodo said. "They do make the time spin by." He said nothing, now, of not aiming them all at Alianna.

"I can do that," Holger said, but not before he held out the stoup once more to Alianora. "Will you give me a refill first?"

"Surely," she replied. "And after another tale or two, I think we shall pause to sup."

He sniffed and nodded. "Sounds like a plan. It's starting to smell mighty good."

He'd always been full of such small bits of praise, thrown out not for the sake of flattery or seduction but simply because that was his way. It was, Alianora thought with a twisted smile of her own, one of the things that marked him as a man from another world.

After she brought Holger the mug, she went back inside and fed the hearthfire a little more wood to keep the pease porridge above it bubbling. She tasted the porridge with a wooden spoon. In went a pinch of salt and a dash more fennel, but only a dash. It *was* getting there.

Outside, her husband and her children broke into guffaws at something Holger said. Theodo wouldn't have laughed unless the big man from another world wasn't leering at Alianna while he talked. Alianora sighed as she picked up a loaf of brown bread. It wasn't of the freshest—not expecting company, she'd baked day before yesterday—but it would serve.

She got out earthenware bowls, spoons shaped from horn, and one, for Holger today, of silver. That was another gift from Theodo, part of the family wealth and, even in these quiet times, a ward against werewolves. Not long ago, Holger had told of the one they'd tracked through Lourville, the town to the east. In those days, with the Middle World waxing strong, anyone even slightly susceptible to shapeshifting was likely to go were. Not so now. Still, silver kept virtues beyond value and beauty.

One more taste. Alianora nodded again. "Yes, we're ready," she said to herself, and walked to the door. "Can we stop the yarns long enough to eat?"

Trying to hold her sons back would have been harder. Stomachs with legs, that was what they were. Who was the king in fable who'd tried to hold back the tide? She couldn't remember if that was Canute or Louis XIV. Whoever he was, he wouldn't have had much luck with Einhard and Nithard, either.

Holger raised an eyebrow when she handed him the silver spoon with his bowl. His forehead corrugated. Yes, the years had scored him, as they'd marked Alianora—as they marked everyone. "You've done well for yourselves," he remarked: of course he'd understand what the precious metal meant.

"Oh, tolerable. Tolerable," Theodo said. He might be a smith, but he had a peasant's dread of admitting success, much less boasting about it. You threw your luck away when you did anything so foolish.

"Heh." Holger's single syllable said he understood that thinking down to the ground. He ladled porridge into the bowl and tore off a chunk of bread. Alianna had set out the honeypot beside the loaf. Holger grinned. "This is a feast!"

"Pretty good, all right," Einhard said. He was trying to eat and talk at the same time, and swallowed wrong.

His father thumped him on the back till he quit coughing. "Greedy like a hog, you are," Theodo said, but he couldn't make himself sound as angry as he might have wanted to.

Alianna said, "Sir Holger, you'll have seen riches beside which a silver spoon will seem as nothing."

"If you own your wealth, that's not so bad," Holger answered with a shrug. "If it owns you, that's not so good. I never had it in me to chase after gold or jewels or any of that nonsense. The treasure I was after—" He stopped short and upended his mug.

The Man Who Came Late

A considerable silence followed. Alianora unhappily considered it. At last, picking his words with obvious care, Theodo said, "For whatever it may be worth to you, you have my sympathy."

"Sympathy? It's worth its weight in gold," Holger said. Theodo started to beam, then frowned a sudden, stormy frown instead. How much would a word weigh? But Holger held up his hand. "Peace, please. Just a smart-mouthed crack. I know your words were kindly meant."

After another, briefer, pause, Theodo dipped his head. "Aye, let it go."

"Thanks." Holger ate a couple of more spoonsful of porridge. Then he said, perhaps as much to himself as to his companions, "It's funny, you know, when you spend so long looking for somebody who's all you ever wanted, and then you go and find her, and you see she's already got everything *she* ever wanted, and it isn't you."

A house, not one of the smallest and meanest in the village but not one of the finest, either? A garden plot? Chickens and ducks and pigs and a cow? Enough to eat, except at the end of the worst winters? *Is this all I ever wanted?* Alianora wondered.

But that wasn't what Holger was talking about, was it? A good, solid man with whom she'd made a life. Three children well on their way to turning into good, solid people themselves. A place where she belonged, where she fit in, if not perfectly, then better than well enough.

When you got right down to it, what more *could* you want?

"'Scuse me." Holger brushed past her to get to the beer barrel. He'd poured down a lot, and showed it very little. Well, there was a lot of him to soak up beer, and he'd always had that knack. Still, when he raised the stoup in salute, Alianora thought tears glittered for a moment in his eyes. "Here's to all of you," he said, and drank.

"To you, Sir Holger…dear Holger." Alianora returned the salute. "Without you, Chaos would have rolled over this land and swept all we have, all we've built, away for aye." She drank to him. Theodo and the children followed her lead.

"Yeah, well…" A sigh gusted from Holger. "I wonder if the Powers here didn't finally let me come back to rub my nose in what a useless thing a hero is a generation after his war ends. The world goes on without him. What was the point to any of it?"

Alianora glanced at the kettle of pease porridge above the fire on the hearth. She took half a step toward Theodo, though she knew the motion would wound Holder. "This was the point," she answered.

"I guess it was." Holger sounded unconvinced, and who could blame him? Hero he might be—hero he was—but he had none of what Alianora enjoyed. He stared out through the doorway. Sunset reddened the light coming in. So too, perhaps, did escaping smoke from the cookfire. More got out through the hole in the roof above the hearth, but enough did linger to sting eyes and throats. Holger said, "I could show you a way to make all your smoke go outside: a *chimney*, it's called."

"Another day, sir knight," Theodo said, his eyebrows coming down and together at the strange word.

Holger looked towards Alianora. She said, "Is it that you came here for?"

"You know bloody well it isn't." He bared his teeth in another humorless smile. "But it seems to be about what I'm good for, doesn't it?"

Since Alianora had no answer to that, she spooned up some more porridge. The hard moment passed. Holder launched into another tale with the air of a man determined to push pain aside. Sunset gave way to twilight, which dwindled toward darkness. Shadows from the dying fire swooped around the walls.

Alianora lit a fine beeswax candle, and then, after a little thought, a second. Hang the cost tonight! The tilt of her chin defied Theodo to say anything. He was a bold man, but—wisely—not so bold as that. Even the candles' mellow glow could not come close to matching daylight, but it did help the red embers on the hearth.

Holger got to the end of his story. He blinked, maybe noticing the darkness for the first time. A cricket chirped outside. "Well," Holger said, as if it were a complete sentence. He blinked again. "We did walk past that tavern, right? You said a guy called…Gerold runs it." He grinned, pleased he'd come up with the name.

The Man Who Came Late

"Have we drunk the barrel dry?" Alianora squeaked in surprise. They'd applied themselves to it, aye, but that was a lot of beer.

"I don't think so," Holger said. "But the tavern'll have wine, won't it? Other stuff folks here don't fix for themselves, too. Gerold wouldn't make his living if it didn't."

"Well, aye. That's so." Theodo sounded grudging, and had his reasons: "Not the best crowd there—men who'd sooner guzzle than work, most of 'em. And always 'tis dearer to pay the taverner's scot than to brew for yourself. Wine may be sweet, but beer does well enough."

"Don't worry about that." Holger slapped one of the cleverly made pockets on his blue trousers. Whatever was inside clinked sweetly. "I'm buying."

"Mrmm." Theodo still hesitated.

"We thank you, Sir Holger." Alianora didn't. "If you're fain to fare to the tavern, thither we shall fare." They all walked out into the night together.

The tavern wasn't far. Nothing in the village was far from anything else. Stars, a nail-paring of moon, and firelight leaking out between shutter slats and through badly chinked walls and spilling from partly open doorways kept darkness from being absolute. All the same, Alianora planted her feet with care, trying not to step in a hole or a puddle or anything nasty.

A cat's eyes glowed green, then vanished. A dog growled a warning that faded into a whine when it decided it didn't want to take on so many humans after all.

"Right over here, y'see?" Theodo said in a low voice that wouldn't bother neighbors already abed. "Not so far from the well. It's—" He grunted in surprise. "The shape of it's wrong."

"Aye, it is," Alianora agreed wonderingly. The tavern shouldn't bulk so tall against the sky. It looked as if it owned two stories. She'd seen such things in her travels with Holger, but there wasn't a building like that in the village...or there hadn't been. The beam-ends of the roof were oddly and ornately carven.

"I know that shape," Holger breathed. "I half wondered if the Old Phoenix would show up tonight. You don't always find it, but sometimes it finds you."

"How do you mean?" Alianora asked.

"It's one of those places between the worlds that I was talking about. It doesn't belong to any of them," Holger answered. "I can't explain it better than that. I don't think anybody else can, either."

The door opened. For a moment, Walacho's swag-bellied shape stood silhouetted against the light spilling out from within. It wasn't what the village drunkard had expected. But if it wasn't *the* tavern, it plainly was *a* tavern. That would do for Walacho. He waddled inside.

Before the door swung shut, Alianora glimpsed a bar, with a plump man—definitely not Gerold, who was on the lean side—standing behind it. In front were a few small tables. Walacho was heading towards one of them. At another sat… Alianora stiffened. Hair blacker than the night sky; a proud, harsh, beautiful face; long satin dress caressing every lush curve…

"That's Morgan le Fay!" she blurted, and knew not why she should sound so furious. Because the great sorceress had aged not a day these past thirty years? That should have been reason enough and more, but somehow her rage ran deeper yet.

The way Holger said "Yeah" made her understand why. He went on, "I'm not surprised to see her there. She's one the Old Phoenix would draw, sure as sure. And we've got a few things to talk about, the two of us. Uh-huh, just a few."

"Talk?" Alianora snarled the word, as if she'd been in the habit of transforming to cat herself rather than to swan.

"Well, that, too." Holger seemed sourly amused. "You don't want me, but you don't want me having fun with anybody else, either?"

"Not with her!" Alianora said. "When did she bring you aught but grief?"

"There were times, back in the day. There sure were." By the way he answered, he might not have thought of them for many a year, but that made the memories no less sweet.

"Perhaps—for her purposes. Never for yours." Alianora knew trouble when she saw it, no matter how seductive its package.

"That could be," Holger allowed, so he wasn't altogether blind. No, not altogether. He made as if to bow to her in the darkness. "If you want to play nursemaid, you can come in with me."

"When I came out, would I come hither and not into one of your other worlds?" she asked. Would Walacho's family have to make do without him, as if he'd gone into Elf Hill and emerged the next morning to find a hundred years gone in the wider world? They might prove better off, but that wasn't the point.

"You probably would. Most people do, most of the time," Holger said.

"That is not warrant enough," Theodo declared. He wasn't in the habit of speaking for Alianora; he'd learned she didn't fancy it when he tried. He did it now, though, and she liked it fine. Her children stirred. The Old Phoenix and the idea of adventure drew them. Well, naturally adventure drew them— they'd never known much. Alianora had, and knew she'd had a bellyful.

"I stay here," she said. If her voice roughened, then it did, that was all. She reached out and took the knight's hand. "Go where you would, dear Holger, and God keep you safe wherever it may be." Anger and jealousy flared once more. "Whatever else you do, mind yon witch!"

"Oh, I will. I'm not always as dumb as I look—just most of the time. And I've got more miles on me now. I'm not likely to be so stupid that way as I might've been a while back. I hope." Holger squeezed her hand hard. Then he leaned forward and brushed his lips across hers. "Good luck to you, kiddo, and to yours. You found what you were after. Me, I guess I've got to go look some more, don't I?"

He stumped toward the Old Phoenix, footfalls softening as he went away. When he opened the door, he stood limned for a moment by the light beyond him. He waved, once, then stepped inside. The door closed again before Alianora had to hear Morgan le Fay's voice.

She burst into tears anyhow. Theodo put his arm round her shoulder— less comfort than she would have liked, but as much as she could get. "If we're not going in," he said, "we'd better get back."

"Aye." She nodded. He would feel the motion even if he couldn't see it. "Let's do that."

Alianora woke early, before anyone else in the house, after a night of confused dreams. For a moment, she wondered if everything that had happened the day before was only a dream. But no. That was real. She knew the difference.

She tiptoed outside without disturbing her kin. It was still gloomy: twilight, with dawn coming but not yet come. She walked toward the well, far enough to discover that the tavern had its usual seeming once more. Someone sprawled asleep in front of the doorway; a tankard lay on its side near his head. Walacho: she knew his snores.

No sign of Holger. Well, she hadn't thought there would be. She turned around and went home.

Alianna was up when she came in. Even in the dim light, her daughter's eyes glowed. Alianora smiled to see her. She'd glowed like that herself, once upon a time. "Quite a day, yesterday," she said.

"It was! I'll remember it forever!" Alianna said.

"As will I." Alianora hesitated. Then, remembering, she asked, "Might I…wear the white tunic once more, for just this morning?"

Alianna set a palm soft with understanding on her arm. "Of course, Mother. Of course."

Copyright Information

"Introduction" Copyright © 2024 by Harry Turtledove. First appears in *Other People's Playgrounds* (Michigan: Subterranean Press, 2024).

"Trantor Falls" Copyright © 1989 by Harry Turtledove. First appeared in *Foundation's Friends: Stories in Honor of Isaac Asimov*, edited by Martin H. Greenberg (New York: Tor Books, 1989).

"Three Men and a Vampire" Copyright © 2017 by Harry Turtledove. First appeared in *Some Time Later: Fantastic Voyages Through Alternate Worlds*, edited by A. J. Sikes, B. J. Sikes (California: Thinking Ink Press, 2017).

"Three Men and a Werewolf" Copyright © 2017 by Harry Turtledove. First appeared in *Some Time Later: Fantastic Voyages Through Alternate Worlds*, edited by A. J. Sikes, B. J. Sikes (California: Thinking Ink Press, 2017).

"Topanga and the Chatsworth Lancers" Copyright © 2015 by Harry Turtledove. First appeared in *The Change: Tales of Downfall and Rebirth*, edited by S. M. Stirling (New York: Roc Books, 2015).

"The Catcher in the Rhine" Copyright © 2000 by Harry Turtledove. First appeared in *The Chick Is in the Mail*, edited by Esther Friesner (New York: Baen Books, 2000).

"The Last Word" Copyright © 2000 by Harry Turtledove. First appeared in *Drakas!*, edited by S. M. Stirling (New York: Baen Books, 2000).

"The Fake Pandemic" Copyright © 2021 by Harry Turtledove. First appeared in *Lest Darkness Fall and Timeless Tales Written in Tribute*, edited by Shahid Mahmud (Maryland: ArcManor Books, 2021).

Harry Turtledove

"The Fillmore Shoggoth" Copyright © 2014 by Harry Turtledove. First appeared in *The Madness of Cthulhu*, edited by S. T. Joshi (London: Titan Books, 2014).

"Interlibrary Loan" Copyright © 2017 by Harry Turtledove. First appeared in *Tales from the Miskatonic University Library*, edited by Darrell Schweitzer, John Ashmead (Hornsea: PS Publishing, 2017).

"Nine Drowned Churches" Copyright © 2015 by Harry Turtledove. First appeared in *That Is Not Dead: Tales of the Cthulhu Mythos Through the Centuries*, edited by Darrell Schweitzer (Hornsea: PS Publishing, 2015).

"Eyewear" Copyright © 2011 by Harry Turtledove. First appeared in *Golden Reflections*, edited by Joan Spicci Saberhagen, Robert E. Vardeman (New York: Baen Books, 2011).

"Two Thieves" Copyright © 1992 by Harry Turtledove. First appeared in *Tales of Riverworld*, edited by Philip José Farmer (New York: Warner Books, 1992).

"The Man Who Came Late" Copyright © 2014 by Harry Turtledove. First appeared in *Multiverse: Exploring Poul Anderson's Worlds*, edited by Greg Bear, Gardner Dozois (Michigan: Subterranean Press, 2014).